Caesar's Avenger

Alex Gough is an author of Roman historical adventures, and has a decades-long interest in Ancient Roman history. His first series *The Carbo Chronicles* (including *Watchmen of Rome*, *Bandits of Rome* and the short story collection, *Carbo and the Thief*) was the culmination of a lot of research into the underclasses of Ancient Rome.

His second series, *The Imperial Assassin*, is set in the reign of the Severan dynasty, an under-examined period of Roman history. His latest series is based on the larger-than-life character of Mark Antony, the warrior, the commander, the politician and the lover.

Alex would love to interact with readers, and you can follow him on twitter @romanfiction, like Alex Gough Author on facebook, or visit his website for reviews of roman fiction and articles about Roman history: www.romanfiction.com

Also by Alex Gough

Carbo and the Thief
Who All Die

Carbo of Rome

Watchmen of Rome
Bandits of Rome
Killer of Rome

The Imperial Assassin

Emperor's Sword
Emperor's Knife
Emperor's Axe
Emperor's Spear
Emperor's Lion
Emperor's Fate

The Mark Antony Series

Caesar's Soldier
Caesar's General
Caesar's Avenger

CAESAR'S AVENGER

ALEX GOUGH

CANELO

 Penguin Random House

First published in the United Kingdom in 2025 by

Canelo, an imprint of
Canelo Digital Publishing Limited,
20 Vauxhall Bridge Road,
London SW1V 2SA
United Kingdom

A Penguin Random House Company
The authorised representative in the EEA is Dorling Kindersley Verlag GmbH. Arnulfstr. 124, 80636 Munich, Germany

Copyright © Alex Gough 2025

The moral right of Alex Gough to be identified as the creator of this work has been asserted in accordance with the Copyright, Designs and Patents Act, 1988.
All rights reserved. No part of this publication may be reproduced or transmitted in any form or by any means, electronic or mechanical, including photocopy, recording, or any information storage and retrieval system, without permission in writing from the publisher. No part of this book may be used or reproduced in any manner for the purpose of training artificial intelligence technologies or systems. In accordance with Article 4(3) of the DSM Directive 2019/790, Canelo expressly reserves this work from the text and data mining exception.

A CIP catalogue record for this book is available from the British Library.

Print ISBN 978 1 80436 211 2
Ebook ISBN 978 1 80436 210 5

This book is a work of fiction. Names, characters, businesses, organizations, places and events are either the product of the author's imagination or are used fictitiously. Any resemblance to actual persons, living or dead, events or locales is entirely coincidental.

Cover design by Blacksheep

Cover images © ArcAngel, Shutterstock

Printed and bound in Great Britain by Clays Ltd, Elcograf S.p.A.

Look for more great books at
www.canelo.co | www.dk.com

To Ivy, my faithful companion, who keeps me company when I'm writing as long as I keep her supplied with biscuits.

Chapter I

Idibus Martiis DCCX AUC (15 March 44 BC), Rome

Antony stumbled out of Pompey's theatre, blinking in the sunlight. Behind him, in a pool of congealing blood, lay the body of Gaius Julius Caesar. Stabbed to death by men he had thought to be his friends, his allies, men he had raised up from nothing or pardoned for previous acts of rebellion and treachery.

It could not be real. Caesar was so solid. Beloved by the gods. Indestructible.

Slowly Antony's eyes adjusted to the brightness, and he looked out from the top of the theatre steps across an eerily quiet city. A crow circled overhead, cawed twice, and flew on. A dog let out a series of frenzied barks, which were cut short with a little whine.

Most of Antony's clients and slaves had fled with the senators. Only one had bravely remained and he approached Antony now, head bowed.

'Master.'

Antony looked down at him, trying to focus his thoughts.

'Vitalis,' he said, putting a hand on the slave's shoulder. Vitalis had been part of Antony's *familia* for many years, and had even accompanied him on some of his military expeditions. He had never held an elevated position in the household, however, and Antony had previously paid him little attention, considering him part of the fixtures and fittings, like most slaves. That would change from now on, Antony resolved.

'Master, you should flee. It's not safe.'

Antony nodded. 'Come.'

'Yes, Master, but please, first, take my clothes.'

Antony considered for a moment. He was tempted to stride through the streets of Rome in his toga, crying out news of the crime at the top of his voice, calling for vengeance on the murderers. But he was quickly recovering his wits. Always at his finest in a crisis, he started to think clearly. It was clear that, even though Brutus had assured him that he was personally not a target of the assassins, others may believe differently. If he wanted to avenge this outrage, he needed to first ensure his own safety.

And the safety of his family.

Fulvia and his infant son, Antyllus, would be sitting anxiously at home, waiting for his return, waiting for news. History showed that the families of the victims of assassination were often murdered along with the main target, whether for revenge, to send a message or to prevent future retribution.

He had to get home.

Hastily, Antony threw off his toga, leaving it in the dust in a crumpled heap, and pulled on the tunic and cloak that Vitalis was proffering. Vitalis was left naked, but he stood, back straight, apparently proud to be of service to his master. Antony clapped him once on the shoulder.

'I won't forget this, faithful servant. Let's be on our way.'

They hurried through deserted streets, past boarded and shuttered shops and dwellings. The citizens of Rome had lived through too much rebellion and civil war in recent years, with all its accompanying destruction of property and death of innocents, to be prepared to hang around and see what happened next. Antony wanted to run, to sprint homewards, until his lungs burst and his legs gave out. Thoughts of intruders invading his home and brutally murdering his precious wife and son crowded his mind. But he knew that he could not afford to draw attention to himself, in case he was dispatched by an assassin's knife before he could get back to protect his family. So he bustled along, the hood of Vitalis' cloak pulled over his head to conceal his face, trying to appear like a slave anxious to be off the street, rather than a fugitive fleeing for his life.

Whenever he passed someone else he tensed, ready for a fight. But those few who were still out and about were all desperate to be elsewhere, and gave him a wide berth. After what seemed a lifetime, all the while with his guts clenched into a solid rock of anxiety, he came into sight of his house in the Carina district that had previously belonged to Pompey, and saw with relief that there was no one trying to gain entry, no smoke pouring from within, no bloody corpses strewn around.

He rushed up to the front doors and hammered on them. A hatch opened, and the porter looked out at him, anxiety turning quickly to relief. The door swung open and Antony rushed into the vestibule, pulling Vitalis with him. He slammed the door shut behind him and hefted the heavy oaken bar into place.

'Vitalis, go and fetch a hammer and nails. Ask anyone you need to assist you. Get this door boarded up, fast as you can.'

He marched into the atrium, throwing off his cloak as he did so. Fulvia was standing there, her face pale, clutching young Antyllus in her arms. Behind her stood Antony's stepchildren, Fulvia's children by her previous husbands. Little Gaius Scribonius Curio, only six years old, peered out from behind his mother's *stola*. Adolescent Publius Claudius Pulcher held his arm protectively around his younger sister, Claudia.

Antony strode forward and threw his arms around Fulvia, beckoning the other children to join the embrace. Without hesitation, they did so, and Antony's family hugged for a long moment of relief and reassurance.

When they broke apart, Fulvia searched Antony's eyes.

'What is happening, Marcus? Is it true?'

'It's true,' he said, solemnly. 'Caesar is dead.'

Every single person in the room – his family and his slaves and servants – made a noise: a shocked gasp; a sob; a cry of despair.

'What does it mean for us, Father?' asked Publius. 'Are we in danger?'

'I don't know,' said Antony. 'But we must assume we are. Go and fetch my sword, and your own. I need to make sure the slaves are armed.'

He made to leave, but Fulvia grabbed his arm.

'Marcus, wait. I don't understand. Who is responsible?'

'There will be time later to explain. But there is much unclear to me, too. First, we must see to our defences.'

He put a hand on Fulvia's cheek, kissed her briefly, then hurried into the house to take inventory of his manpower and weaponry, slipping from politician, to father, to military commander preparing to repel an assault, with the facility of someone who had grown to become totally at ease with all three roles.

–

After the initial frenetic activity in the household – the noises of hammer on nails, of sword on whetstone, of shouted orders – a fragile peace descended. Antony changed into his military uniform, put on his breastplate and strapped his *spatha* around his waist. He answered Fulvia's questioning as best he could, but what could he tell her? He hadn't witnessed the crime himself. All he really knew was that Decimus Brutus and Trebonius had been in on the conspiracy, having deliberately delayed him so he could not aid Caesar, and that Marcus Brutus was also involved. Antony had noted multiple stab wounds on the body. Surely they couldn't have been inflicted by a single person, especially with the whole Senate watching and standing idly by?

A few answers were supplied when his first visitor of import arrived in the middle of the afternoon. The loud knocking at the door put everyone on edge, but when the porter announced Marcus Aemilius Lepidus wished to be admitted, Antony let out a sigh of relief, and indicated he should be brought straight in.

Antony embraced Caesar's Master of Horse with genuine warmth. Though he had resented Lepidus' elevation to deputy to the dictator, and had little regard for the man's talent, Antony had nothing against the man, who had always been an ally and a friend. Although technically, Lepidus was no longer Master of Horse, since the role lapsed with the death of the dictator, at that moment he was the only man with any military power that mattered, commanding as he did a small detachment that had been stationed on the Tiber island, and also the only legion in Italy. Whoever Lepidus decided to support on that day had the greatest chance of success and survival. And he had come first to Antony.

Lepidus explained that, like Antony, he had barricaded himself in his house immediately after the assassination, but once he had summoned his troops, he felt able to go out into the city. He could have marched to the *Campus Martius* to put down the small group of gladiators that the assassins had apparently hired to support them, but he told Antony that he had decided to seek the counsel of the only surviving consul – Antony himself – before taking any action.

Antony nearly kissed him at that point, but like Fulvia, who sat with them, organising food and wine, he was bursting with questions.

'You were in the Senate?' asked Antony. 'When it happened?'

Lepidus looked down for a moment, tight-lipped. He looked to a slave to pass him some wine and he took a long draught before he spoke.

'Almost the moment that Caesar entered the hall, he was surrounded by supplicants. He took his seat in the *curule* chair and a dozen pressed in on him. It was Cimber who set things in motion.'

'Cimber?' repeated Antony, surprised, in as much as anything could surprise him on this astonishing day. Lucius Tillius Cimber was a hard drinker and a hard fighter, a man much after Antony's own heart. He had been a former commander in Caesar's army and had always appeared to be a loyal supporter.

'He came up to Caesar, pleading for the return of his exiled brother, then grabbed Caesar's toga and pulled it down, exposing his neck. Caesar tried to stand, but he held him down, and Caesar cried out, "Why this violence?" Then Casca stepped forward, drew a dagger and plunged it towards Caesar's neck. But Caesar is – I mean, was – a warrior. He was already moving, and the blow pierced his breast. With a mighty roar, he threw Casca away. If there had been but one assassin, that would have been the end of it. But…'

Lepidus' voice broke, and he paused to take another drink before continuing.

'Casca's brother struck next, and then they were all on him, Cassius, Basilus, Rubrius, Marcus Brutus. He fought like a tiger in the arena, but they were too many, and they were all armed.'

Antony shook his head. 'All those men, who had sworn an oath to protect him with their lives. Did no one come to his aid?'

Lepidus glanced sideways and licked his lips before replying. 'It all happened so quickly. Believe me, Antonius, if I could have stopped it I would have. But I was too far away, and there was a ring of conspirators blocking anyone from giving aid. I believe Censorinus and Sabinus were closer, and fought to reach Caesar, but they were overwhelmed by the traitors, and they were forced to flee.'

Antony sighed, keeping his opinion about Lepidus' lack of defence of their friend to himself. 'Did you see the end?'

Lepidus nodded. 'Eventually, he realised resistance was hopeless. When he fell, he pulled his toga over his head. He kept his dignity even in death.'

'He didn't speak?'

'I heard nothing, but there was a lot of noise. Some I was with say that he looked at Brutus and said, "*Kai su, teknon*".'

You too, child, in Greek, thought Antony. But spoken in that language, those words could have expressed disappointment in one he had treated as a son, or a vicious curse. Knowing Caesar, Antony thought the latter more likely.

'And then?' prompted Antony.

'Then I ran.' Lepidus looked directly into Antony's eyes, chest puffed out, waiting for words of disapproval or condemnation. But Antony felt in no position to accuse Lepidus. He was only just starting to come to terms with the fact that he had been duped by his friends. He knew that if he had been by Caesar's side, he could have prevented the assassination. No group of senators could have stood up to Antony and Caesar fighting side by side, even if they were unarmed. They would at least have held the assassins at bay until help arrived. Besides, Antony knew how precarious his position was at that moment, and he wasn't fool enough to alienate the one man in Rome who could ensure his safety and the safety of his family.

'A wise leader knows when retreat is the best option,' he said in what he hoped was a mollifying tone. 'Only a fool continues to fight when the battle is lost.'

Lepidus looked down, and Antony saw tears filling the corners of his eyes.

'Well, what now?' asked Fulvia, who until then had been struggling to hold her tongue. 'This is a crucial moment. Strong men such as you two must take action.'

'She is right,' said Antony. 'I am the sole consul of Rome. You are the commander of the only military force that matters. We should ally, secure our positions, and ensure Rome does not fall into chaos and anarchy.'

Lepidus nodded, but Antony saw his features change. His eyes darted from side to side, and he shifted in his seat.

'You speak wisely, Consul,' said Lepidus, somewhat formally. 'But as you know, with Caesar's death, I am no longer Master of Horse. I am a man with no power. As such, I fear I cannot be of much assistance.'

'Nonsense,' said Antony. 'All Rome knows you are a man of the highest *auctoritas* and *dignitas*. We can sort out formal positions another time—'

'I think it would be better if I leave here knowing where I stand,' interrupted Lepidus. 'The position of consul has sadly fallen vacant...'

Antony glanced at Fulvia, who gave a subtle shake of her head.

'I don't think that is in my power to grant, friend,' said Antony carefully. 'But I could maybe give you a *propraetorian imperium*.'

Lepidus waved a dismissive hand. 'A temporary and insignificant position,' he said, causing Antony to bridle, since this was the power that Caesar had granted Antony himself to rule Italy in his absence. 'I don't believe that would give me sufficient authority to do what is needed.'

'How about *Pontifex Maximus*?' put in Fulvia.

Both men looked at her in surprise. Lepidus stroked his chin. 'Is that really possible?'

'We can make it so,' said Antony. 'If we prevail, who will gainsay us? If we don't, what does it matter?'

Lepidus paused, then smiled and shook Antony's hand firmly.

'I accept. Thank you, Consul.'

'Thank you, Pontifex.'

Antony's steward entered and cleared his throat.

'Master, there are several senators at the door, anxious to be admitted. They declare they are friends of Caesar's and yours, and they are unarmed.'

Lepidus looked nervous, but Antony said, 'Let them enter, though without slaves or bodyguards. It is time to start gathering our allies around us.'

—

A steady trickle of visitors arrived over the course of the afternoon and evening. Some came merely to pay their respects and pledge their loyalty to the consul. Others stayed, to give counsel, or to make sure they were on hand when positions of power and authority were handed out. They all brought news, much of it contradictory, but sufficient for Antony to make some sort of sense of what was happening in the city.

Immediately after the murder, Marcus Brutus had tried to make a speech to the senators, but they all fled. Then the assassins had marched out into the streets, waving their bloody daggers in the air. Gladiatorial games had just finished nearby, and the environs of Pompey's theatre were crowded, but even as Brutus tried to address the crowds there, they too ran, fearful for their lives, and within moments the city was deserted. The conspirators then paraded through the city, calling out Cicero's name, who was still undoubtedly the most respected senator in Rome. Though he was reportedly disappointed not to have been trusted to be part of the conspiracy, Cicero was delighted with the deed itself, to Antony's disgust but complete lack of surprise.

The conspirators then ascended the Capitoline Hill to the Temple of Jupiter Optimus Maximus, a place where they could not only attempt to sanctify their deed, but which was also highly defensible if that became necessary. Many senators who had not been part of the conspiracy now joined them, anxious to be seen to be on the apparently victorious side. Of all the terrible actions that day, the one that angered Antony most was when he discovered that Dolabella had joined the conspirators and donned the robe of a consul, grabbing the role he claimed Caesar had promised him, now that Caesar had vacated it. The man who had made a cuckold out of Antony, who had stirred up trouble when Antony ruled Rome, and who Antony had done everything he could to prevent becoming consul, had just taken the post, halving Antony's power in a stroke.

Brutus had come down to the Forum to make a speech to the people, accompanied by Dolabella, Cassius and an entourage of eminent men. He stood on the *rostra* and those daring enough to have emerged from their homes listened to his words in deathly silence. He talked of his ancestor who had expelled the kings, spoke of Caesar's violence and tyranny, and how his death had been necessary to restore freedom, independence and correct governance to all.

Dolabella spoke next, praising the assassins and condemning Caesar.

Then Lucius Cornelius Cinna, the brother of Caesar's first wife, whom Caesar had made a *praetor*, spoke. He had not been part of the conspiracy, but now he tore off his robe of office dramatically, saying it had been granted by a tyrant, and he harangued the crowd, saying that the assassins were heroes and tyrant-slayers and should have honours heaped upon them. The crowd, who had until that moment listened passively, were outraged by the ingratitude and bad faith of this man who was tied to Caesar by kin and had been generously treated by the dictator. They jeered, yelled, threw rotten dung and stones. Dismayed, the conspirators retreated back up to the top of the Capitoline Hill, where they began to reinforce its defences.

Heartened by this news, Antony suggested Lepidus send his troops to the Forum. It was the most important place in Rome in which to make speeches that might sway the masses, and clearly their opinion was up for grabs to whoever could show their side was both honourable and would ensure peace.

Soon afterwards, a delegation from the conspirators' camp arrived and asked to be granted an audience with Antony. He agreed, and half a dozen of Rome's most senior men were ushered into his presence. All were former consuls, and they bowed respectfully to Antony and Lepidus the moment they saw them.

'Venerable fathers, to what do I owe the pleasure?' asked Antony, opening his arms and greeting each in turn with a kiss on the cheek. Quintus Fufius Calenus, Caesar's loyal general, who had served alongside Antony when they were besieged in Brundisium, seemed to have been elected spokesman.

'Marcus Antonius, I bring a message of peace and a desire for reconciliation to you, the highest authority in Rome this day, from the Liberators.'

Antony raised an eyebrow.

'"The Liberators"? That is what they are calling themselves?'

Calenus gave an apologetic shrug. 'Not my invention, Antonius.'

'Then what would you call them? Assassins? Murderers? Traitors?'

Calenus looked around at the other ex-consuls for support, who all shifted nervously from foot to foot and looked at the floor or inspected their nails for signs of dirt.

'Consul, a deed has been done this day that history will judge for its honour or treachery. But Rome now stands on a precipice. Surely we have all had an enough of civil war, of shedding the blood of our own on our city streets. Rebellion threatens our provinces, enemies prowl our borders, preparing to strike. Surely we should be turning our shields and swords against these threats, not against each other.'

Antony looked around the group of delegates.

'I see some of the most senior and respected men in Rome in your number,' he said. 'But I do not see Cicero. Where is the old sage? Surely at such a time of crisis, he would wish to be at the centre of affairs, generously spreading his wisdom around.'

Calenus hesitated.

'Speak the truth, old friend, or this meeting is a waste of all our time. You know I will find out Cicero's opinion soon enough, in any case.'

Calenus swallowed and, getting no support from his colleagues, said, 'Cicero opposes negotiation. He praises the acts of the Liberators, and says that there should be no reconciliation with yourself, a mere limb of Caesar. He insists that the Liberators declare you an enemy and have you killed.'

Antony nodded. It was no surprise, though it made his position that much less secure, that Cicero was calling for his death so soon and so openly. He had Lepidus and Lepidus' men on his side, but for how long would that last? Lepidus could be easily turned, he suspected. He needed more ammunition in reserve.

'What do you propose?' asked Lepidus now.

'Let us join hands at this hour,' said Calenus. 'Meet with Marcus Brutus and Cassius Longinus, and show all of Rome that even on this terrible day, the most powerful men of Rome are united.'

Antony watched Lepidus carefully for a reaction, but he gave nothing away. The so-called Liberators had offered them nothing, Antony noted, though neither had they requested anything. Perhaps that would follow at a meeting. He needed to take stock of his position, though, to know his full strength before he could begin a negotiation.

'What do you say, Consul?' asked Lepidus, rightly deferring to Rome's senior magistrate.

'I believe the day has been long and tiring. We should take the night to rest and recover. The... Liberators, may have our answer tomorrow.' The word stuck in Antony's throat, but he was playing the role of politician, not soldier, and he had learned as much from Caesar about political matters as military in his time at the great man's side.

'Very well, I shall take your answer back to the Capitoline Hill, and we shall await the new day.' Calenus shook Antony's hand firmly and said to him in a low voice, 'Stay safe, old friend.'

Antony embraced him, shook the hands of the rest of the delegation and sent them on their way.

'Lepidus, perhaps you should join your men. It is important that you show them you are still in command, in case another tries to suborn your authority.'

Lepidus looked alarmed at this suggestion and, gathering his slaves and guards, he hurried off.

Antony was left alone for the moment with Fulvia.

'What now?' he asked.

'It is time to pay a visit to one of the most important people in Rome,' she said, 'who everyone seems to have forgotten.'

'That being?'

'Caesar's widow.'

—

Antony waited for night to fall, during which time he continued to receive visitors and embassies from friends of Caesar and allies of the Liberators. Then he once more donned the guise of a slave, and made his way out into the streets, leaving instructions for his steward to tell any further visitors that he had retired for the night and was not to be disturbed.

The moment Calpurnia set eyes on Antony, she threw her arms around him and burst into tears, her body shaking against him with loud, violent sobs. Antony held her, and shared her pain. For most of the day, he had been distracted by the immediate consequences of Caesar's death, for Rome, for himself and his family. He had had no time to grieve, and even now could only spare a few self-indulgent moments to think about his friend and hero.

When she regained control of herself, Calpurnia welcomed Antony into Caesar's house and arranged for refreshments.

'I warned him, Marcus,' she said. 'If only he had listened.'

'I'm so sorry, Calpurnia. We had our disagreements, but in the final count, Caesar was my closest friend, and I think I was his, too.'

'You were. He always spoke so highly of you, even when you frustrated him.'

Antony chuckled despite his moist eyes. 'I fear I frustrated him rather often.'

'He loved you for you who you are, Marcus. And he was hardly without flaws himself.'

Antony thought for the first time that day of Caesar's lover, Cleopatra, in Caesar's villa across the Tiber with their son Caesarion. He suspected that she had been overlooked by everyone in the chaos. But did she have a role to play in all this? Was she in danger? He resolved to send her messages of goodwill as soon as he got home. With her money and influence she had the potential to be another powerful ally.

'Do you want to see him?' asked Calpurnia abruptly.

'You have him?' asked Antony in surprise.

She nodded. 'I sent slaves to recover his... to recover him, as soon as I heard. He is lying in the *triclinium*.'

Antony let Calpurnia lead him to the body. Caesar was lying as he had fallen, as Antony had seen him at the foot of Pompey's statue, still wearing the rent and bloody toga. His eyes were closed, his face chalk white, his expression mildly irritated. Antony dropped to his knees and held the stiff, cold hand of his friend and commander. His sorrow when he had first found Caesar's body had been driven by shock and fear. Now he cried tears of genuine loss, that he would no longer hear Caesar's peremptory tone and his dry, witty words, witness his brilliance in battle or in the Senate. He was so much poorer for it, and so was Rome.

After a long while, he stood, and wiped his eyes on the sleeve of his tunic.

'I will avenge him, Calpurnia, I swear it. But that opportunity may not come straight away. First, I may need to make some accords with his murderers to shore up my position. You may hear me say some things that sound disloyal to Caesar's memory. But I promise you, the time will come when I will make them pay for what they have done this day.'

Calpurnia grasped his hands in hers.

'I should have his body cleansed and dressed, but I haven't been able to bring myself to let anyone touch it.'

'Don't,' he said. 'Leave it exactly as it is. When the time comes, the people of Rome will see what has been done to him.'

'Thank you, Marcus. You have a good heart. I suppose you will be wanting his money?'

Antony's eyes widened a little. 'I...'

'Come, Marcus. I am grateful for the visit, but I am a person of no consequence in my own right on such a day as this. You said yourself you need to shore up your position. You could, of course, take Caesar's money, but I give it to you freely. I will have my slaves bring it to your house. There is rather a lot of it.'

'I appreciate that, Calpurnia.'

'And of course, his papers will be of use.'

'His papers?'

'Why, yes. Caesar kept extensive private records on everyone of import in Rome. Their finances, their political persuasions, their frauds and embezzlements, their illicit lovers. I would imagine that would be helpful.'

Antony smiled broadly for the first time that day, and kissed Calpurnia on the cheek.

'Very helpful. I must leave you, dear Calpurnia. Please go ahead with the arrangements for the funeral. I will, of course, say a few words, if that sits well with you.'

'He would have liked that.'

Antony bid her goodbye, pulled the hood up on his cloak and hurried home.

ante diem xvi Kalendas Apriles DCCX AUC (17 March 44 BC), Rome

The pre-dawn sky was blank, a haze obscuring any starlight, as Antony left his house to attend the Senate meeting he had ordered. He wore the toga of a consul, but felt the reassuring weight of a mail cuirass beneath. He was accompanied by his lictors – the official guard of the consul – as well as a small bodyguard of veterans and slaves, a large number of clients, and a handful of pro-Caesarian senators who had pledged their loyalty to Antony the previous day. At that meeting, Lepidus and Balbus had demanded immediate vengeance on the Liberators. Lepidus proposed that he bring his legionaries into the city and storm the Capitoline Hill. The tiny band of gladiators that guarded them could not hope to hold out long against the full strength of a legion. But Aulus Hirtius, with an eye on the long term, preferred a legal route, with a special court convened to prosecute the Liberators. Keeping things official would help legitimise Caesar's rule and his laws and appointments, and would obviate the need for sending soldiers against civilians, never a popular move. Antony, wary of using the army inside Rome after the personal disapprobation he had received when he had to put Dolabella's rebellion down by force, was minded to agree with Hirtius. He had therefore sent messengers to Cicero, much as it pained him, and no doubt equally reluctantly, the orator had agreed to aid in negotiations.

Consequently, Rome held its breath as the Senate met for the first time in the Temple of Tellus on the Carinae, near to Antony's house, an hour before sunrise. The temple was ringed by Lepidus' soldiers, and Antony made sure that his cuirass was clearly visible. It was a trick borrowed from Cicero, from when the orator, who had been consul at that time, had been raising support for his campaign against Catilina, and had made sure everyone knew how much danger he considered himself to be in. To enter the temple, one had to walk past a statue of Ceres, goddess of agriculture and fertility, and more incongruously, a statue of Cicero's brother Quintus, once a loyal commander of Caesar's before he switched sides to join Pompey, eventually receiving Caesar's pardon after the civil war ended. It reminded Antony uncomfortably of how easily alliances and allegiances shifted in these treacherous times.

The temple had been furnished as befitted a Senate meeting – benches on either side of a central walkway and two curule chairs for the consuls. It was Antony himself who had decreed that there be two chairs for consuls, despite Caesar being the other incumbent of that office. Caesar had wished for Dolabella to take his place as suffect consul that year, but had not yet managed to force that through the Senate in the face of Antony's dogged opposition.

Now, as Antony entered the temple and walked with deliberate slowness to his seat, he saw that Dolabella, also wearing the robes of a consul, was already seated in one of the curule chairs. Antony approached, and stood before him. After a moment's hesitation, Dolabella stood. He was a short man, and Antony towered over him. Antony looked down at him for a long moment, and was pleased to detect a tremor in the man's knees.

Antony turned to the Senate and said in a loud voice, 'Conscript Fathers, I present to you my co-consul, Publius Cornelius Dolabella. And I hereby declare that whatever differences have existed between us in the past, these extraordinary days have resolved.'

Then he grasped Dolabella by the shoulders and kissed him on each cheek. 'Don't think this makes us friends,' Antony whispered, and Dolabella stiffened.

The Senate broke out in applause at the first gesture of conciliation between the two men. But it was a calculated move on Antony's part, suggested, of course, by Fulvia. Dolabella had been a strong supporter of Caesar, and his consulship was an appointment decreed by the dictator himself. For Dolabella to oppose Caesar now and support the Liberators would mean the voiding of Caesar's appointments, and thus Dolabella's consulship would be illegitimate. Whether or not Dolabella realised it, despite his support for the Liberators on the Ides of March, his acceptance of the consulship positioned him firmly in the Caesarian camp.

Antony now addressed the Senate. The Liberators had not attended, perhaps fearing for their safety or worried about legitimising Antony's consulship, but they were in a minority. Almost all of the Caesarian and neutral senators were present, and many whose sympathies lay with the Senate, including Cicero, also attended.

Antony's speech, mainly his own work but polished by Fulvia, was full of moderation and conciliation. He spoke of peace, the necessity of coming to terms with adversaries for the sake of the greater good, and advised the Senate that they must find a way to work together. He also reminded them that many of them owed their positions in the Senate to Caesar, as well as future appointments, including Decimus Brutus' governorship of Cisalpine Gaul. If the Senate did not ratify all of Caesar's Acts, then the Senate must be dissolved, more than half the Senators must be expelled, the gifts to the people and the promised entitlements to the soldiers must be revoked, and the disastrous consequences must be borne.

The self-interested Senate would not countenance such a thing, and all debate on Caesar's rulings was forestalled. But when the floor was given to others, it was clear that there was considerable support for the Liberators, even among the neutral and previously Caesarian senators. Several, such as Tiberius Claudius Nero, spoke in praise of their actions, and even proposed they were voted honours for ridding the state of a tyrant and would-be king, motions which were quickly defeated, but which gave Antony cause for concern. His horses were hitched firmly to Caesar's chariot, and linked to Caesar's legacy and honour, he would win the race or crash disastrously.

The meeting dragged on, and tempers, already stretched thin by worry and anger, repeatedly flared. Certain decisions had to be taken, however. Everyone knew how important it was to keep the veterans stationed in Italy appeased, so Caesar's grants of land and money to his retired soldiers were explicitly confirmed. But there was still division about the fate of the Liberators, and for a while it was unclear whether the Senate would vote for their glorification or execution. Antony, despite his inner desires, had his sight firmly fixed on a solution that was of ultimate benefit to himself and to Rome, and continued to argue moderation, as did other senators such as Lucius Munatius Plancus.

Eventually, it was Cicero who decided the matter, calling for an amnesty for the Liberators, recalling the Athenian amnesty after the civil war against the Thirty Tyrants. He proposed this as a formal motion, which was carried, along with the confirmation of all Caesar's deeds, though the words 'because this policy is of advantage to the state' were appended to show that the house did not approve of Caesar's methods, but did not want to submit to the chaos that would ensue by undoing Caesar's Acts.

Finally, Caesar's father-in-law, Lucius Calpurnius Piso, got up to speak on the matter of Caesar's funeral and will. Some of the senators most sympathetic to the Liberators jeered him, and cried that Caesar's body should be tossed in the Tiber. Antony watched carefully, ready to intervene. It was vital to his cause that Caesar was buried with full honours, and also that his will was read, which would surely confirm Antony as his major heir, inheritor of his vast fortune and his clients.

But, in fact, he had no need to step in. When Piso spoke, he seemed genuinely affected by the death of his daughter's husband, grieving and angry at the same time.

'You talk of killing a tyrant,' he said. 'But who are you now, but tyrants yourselves? You forbid me to bury the Pontifex Maximus. You threaten me with prosecution if I produce his will. It is not Brutus and Cassius who do this, but those who encouraged them to murder.' He gave Cicero a long stare at this point. Cicero returned the stare, his back straight, but Antony watched with satisfaction as his face turned crimson.

'You have the power to decide on the matter of Caesar's funeral, though I implore you to allow the proper burial of this great man. But I have the sole power over his will, and I will not betray his trust in me. If you wish to prevent me reading out Caesar's last requests, you must strike me down.'

Piso looked around the Senate in challenge, but no one stirred. After a long moment, he proposed a vote that Caesar be given a state funeral and that his will be read to the public in due course. The proposal for the funeral was carried despite some dissension, but the matter of reading the will in public was put aside for further discussion. Antony didn't mind. The funeral was key to gaining the support of the masses. The will would be made public sooner or later, and it would give him the means to gather all of Caesar's riches, power and influence to himself.

Antony was satisfied. Despite the irritating fact that the amnesty would have Cicero's name against it in the official records, it was clear to everyone that it was Antony himself who had been the cool head, the peacemaker. He didn't know exactly what the future held, but he was sure it involved conflict between the Caesarians and the Liberators, and the political capital he had gained that day would stand him in good stead when it came to persuading neutrals to his cause. He rose to adjourn the meeting, and then went out with Lepidus to address the crowds gathered outside the temple.

—

That evening, Antony reclined on a couch in his triclinium opposite Gaius Cassius Longinus. Two days previously, clutching Caesar's bloody corpse, he could not have imagined he would be dining with one of the murderers. But such were the necessities of politics. Lepidus was at the same time entertaining Brutus. Antony had some misgivings about allowing his ally time alone with that man. He was weak and easily swayed. Nevertheless, Lepidus was genuinely furious about Caesar's murder. When they had jointly addressed the crowds from the rostra in the Forum earlier that day, he had knelt and torn his clothes and wept for an age before he was able to bring himself to speak. The crowds had been so moved by the sight, and by Lepidus' and Antony's words, that they demanded immediate vengeance. Lepidus and Antony agreed with their sentiments, but pleaded that the Liberators' lives be spared for the sake of peace.

Cassius and Brutus had been sceptical of the invitations from Lepidus and Antony to dine and talk, fearing a trap. But the two Caesarians had sent their sons, Marcus and Antyllus, as hostages. It had wrenched at Antony's guts to see his little boy, still a toddler, led away in the company of an armed guard and a slave nurse, perhaps never to be seen again if things went badly. But Fulvia had squeezed his hand and whispered to him to be strong. It had, after all, been her idea, and not for the first time he marvelled at the steel inside her.

He had greeted Cassius personally in the grand atrium, but before he embraced him, he asked with a wry smirk if Cassius had a dagger concealed in his armpit. It was a clever dig he had prepared in advance. Brutus' heroic ancestor, Servilius Ahala, had murdered a would-be king with a dagger hidden under his arm. Cassius had no such venerable family tree, and Antony saw in his eyes that the reference was not lost on him.

'I have no dagger upon me,' said Cassius, 'but if you wish to become a tyrant too, I am happy to fetch a big one.'

Now they surveyed each other suspiciously across the dining table.

'What shall we drink to?' asked Antony, holding a silver goblet filled with the most expensive wine from Pompey's cellars.

'Liberty?' suggested Cassius.

'I prefer peace,' said Antony.

'That is not what your reputation suggests,' said Cassius, but he tilted his own cup in Antony's direction. 'Peace.'

They both drank deeply, and Antony savoured both the delicate taste, and the warmth as the strong liquid flooded down his gullet. They were dining alone apart from the serving slaves. Fulvia had wished to be present, but Cassius' wife Tertulla was in the advanced stages of pregnancy and unwell, so would not join them. Antony had judged it impolitic to have Fulvia at the table – given her reputation for behind the scenes political acumen, Cassius might have felt himself outnumbered. Besides, it gave the two men the opportunity to speak their minds frankly. Antony always had a nagging feeling with Fulvia that she was judging his performance in situations such as this, with her notes and comments reserved for the after-show analysis.

'Why did you do it, Cassius?' asked Antony. 'I mean, why, really? I won't repeat it, on my honour.'

Cassius swirled his wine around in his cup.

'You studied Epicurus, I think? Didn't he talk about how atoms moving through the void will suddenly swerve from their predetermined routes and initiate new pathways?'

'Epicurus said that some things happen by necessity, some by chance and some by free will,' replied Antony, 'and that it is only those events caused by our free will to which blame or praise can be attached. Don't try to tell me Caesar's murder was due to chance or necessity. You chose it, you and Brutus above all others. Own the deed, and take the blame or praise as people see fit to give it.'

Cassius nodded. 'When people look at your strength, and think about your bravery in battle, and your drinking and associations with the lowly, they forget that sometimes you can be truly wise.'

'Sometimes?'

'Oh, yes. At other times, you are truly foolish.'

Antony looked at him for a moment, then broke into laughter and slapped his leg.

'But there is no simple answer to your question. It was a mix of duty, honour, self-interest, and if I am being honest, not a little resentment.'

'Resentment?'

'He was going to Parthia without me. Me! Who saved the remnants of Crassus' army after the catastrophe of Carrhae. Who held Antioch against the Parthian invasion. Who ambushed their army and chased them back across the Euphrates. And who knows Syria and the ways of the Parthians better than I? Yet Caesar made me the Praetor Peregrinus, with Marcus Brutus, my junior in age and experience, promoted above me to Urban Praetor.'

'And for this, Caesar had to die?'

'Of course not,' said Cassius angrily. 'He had to die because he wanted to be king, and because he was a tyrant who would never lay down power of his own accord. My personal feelings, and the increased possibility of advancement with him out of the way, just made the deed easier to stomach.'

'And because he had an affair with your wife?'

'That never happened,' snapped Cassius. 'She promised me that.'

Antony raised his eyebrows.

'Don't project your own problems on to me,' said Cassius. 'I don't know how you embraced Dolabella in the Senate today. I would kill the man who made a cuckold of me.'

'Well, if the rumours are true, you did,' retorted Antony, but the barb had struck home. Dolabella's affair with Antony's former wife Antonia had cut his pride through to the core.

'In any case,' Antony went on, keeping his voice even, 'you carefully planned his death. Even though he pardoned you after the civil war. Even though you took an oath to protect his person, along with the rest of the Senate.'

Cassius shrugged, and reached for an oyster, nestling in a dish of crushed ice on the table between them. He slurped it down, then wiped his mouth delicately with a cloth.

'There is much I admire about you, Cassius,' said Antony, making an effort to be conciliatory. 'You are a skilled general. An intelligent man. It saddens me that we find ourselves on opposite sides of this conflict.'

'I admire you, too, Antony. You are strong, brave, powerful. That is why I urged Brutus that you should die at Caesar's side. I fear we will come to regret his honourable attitude towards you.'

'Honourable?' scoffed Antony, but Cassius ignored the interjection.

'Among your other qualities, no one can doubt your loyalty. But I urge you to put aside your allegiance to Caesar, and join with us in restoring the Republic.'

'The Republic never fell, Cassius. I became consul of the Republic at the beginning of this year, and I remain so now.'

'You know as well as I that the Republic had become a sham. We were a monarchy in all but name.'

It was hard to argue this point, so Antony changed the subject.

'What next? What plans have you prepared?'

'We have no plans.'

Antony stared at him in surprise.

'No plans?'

'We plotted nothing beyond Caesar's death. With that stroke, the tyrant is removed, and all returns to how it was.'

Antony shook his head in disbelief at the naivety.

'Nothing is as it was, Cassius. It never will be again.'

Cassius looked glum, and Antony marvelled at his fortune. With proper strategy, the Liberators could have made sure of a secure power base in Rome and reshaped the Republic in whatever form they desired. As it was, they had trusted to the gods, the people, Fortuna, who knew what, in the hope that everything would turn out for the best. For his part, Antony would pay all due respect to fortune and the gods. But from here on, he would be taking matters in his own hands.

Chapter II

ante diem xv Kalendas Apriles DCCX AUC (18 March 44 BC), Rome

Antony was feeling self-satisfied when the Senate reconvened the next day. His physical safety and that of his family seemed to be assured by Lepidus' soldiers, notwithstanding that little Antyllus was still residing as a hostage on the Capitoline with the Liberators. He had, more or less single-handedly, prevented the breakout of anarchy and civil war as tensions peaked in the immediate aftermath of the assassination. He held all Caesar's treasure and his private correspondence and official decrees. He was the dominant legitimate power in Rome.

Brutus and Cassius took their seats among the other senators for the first time since the assassination. There was a mixture of attitudes towards them, some unabashedly congratulatory, some outright aggressive, but the majority, the moderates and neutrals, just avoided them.

The session began by the passing of a decree, proposed by Dolabella in a clearly conciliatory mood, voting commendations for Antony for saving the Republic in its time of peril, honours he accepted humbly and gracefully.

Antony proposed the abolition of the office of Dictator, which was carried with near unanimity. Whatever the senators' allegiances and political leanings, no one wanted to see another of their number take dictatorial powers and turn themselves into another Caesar or Sulla. Two in living memory was plenty.

Next, the Senate agreed that the allocated provincial assignments were to be taken up immediately. This meant Decimus Brutus, one of the key conspirators, taking command of Cisalpine Gaul with all its powerful legions. This made Antony uncomfortable, but he could hardly oppose it – Decimus had benefited from the amnesty given to all the Liberators, and his position had been decreed by Caesar himself, whose Acts the Senate had confirmed.

Then came the matter of Caesar's will. Piso once again addressed the Senate, announcing the will would be read in private that afternoon, but he wished that its bequests and stipulations were read out later in public for all to hear. Cassius spoke angrily against the idea, and Antony stepped in, speaking with what he considered to be passionate eloquence in favour of allowing the people to hear Caesar's last wishes. It would be much to his own advantage if the people also heard at first hand the riches he assumed Caesar had bestowed upon him. The Senate was already swaying towards Antony and Piso when Brutus declared he was personally content for the will to be read publicly, and the decree was thus carried with a large majority.

Antony adjourned the Senate and after mingling with his peers for some time, handing out vague promises of favours, which were eagerly consumed as if he was scattering fodder to sheep, he retired to his house. Fulvia greeted him warmly.

'Brutus sends you his best wishes and news of Antyllus,' Antony told her. 'The little one is quite content, playing with his nursemaid and his toys. He's apparently oblivious that there is anything out of the ordinary, though he does ask where you are from time to time.'

Fulvia nodded and swallowed. Her eyes moistened, but she dashed the tears away with the back of her hand. Antony suspected she was angered by her own weakness, but he loved her all the more for it, and he hugged her firmly.

'When can we expect our guests?' she asked after he released her.

'Piso will be here with the will this afternoon. There will be maybe half a dozen others, plus the Vestals, but let's not drag the whole thing out with entertainment and ceremony. Just make sure there is food and wine enough for all, and let's get the business done.'

Fulvia set about organising the chefs and serving slaves, and Antony took a cup of wine into the huge garden that Pompey had had lovingly created as part of his luxurious house. He looked up into the sky. Now the calendar accorded with the seasons, the Mediterranean spring should be fully underway, but despite the fact that there were no clouds that day, the sun was pale and the blueness of the sky was washed out, like a faded fresco. Antony had heard stories that Mount Aetna in Sicily had erupted the moment Caesar was killed, and the ash it had spewed was darkening skies across Italy. It seemed right that the death of a giant such as Caesar should be marked by such a portentous event.

His thoughts turned to the will. He had only the vaguest notion of how much money Caesar actually possessed – the sum that Calpurnia had sent to him was just a fraction of the whole amount – but the total was sure to be staggering. Before him, his fellow *triumvirs* Crassus and Pompey had both accrued unbelievable fortunes through different methods – Crassus through wily and unscrupulous business practices, and Pompey from his conquests in Spain and the East. But the wealth that Caesar had accrued – from Gaul, from Egypt, from Africa and from his victories over the Pompeians – probably exceeded even what those two hugely rich men had accumulated.

What would he do with all that wealth? he pondered. The broad answer was self-evident. Money was power. It paid for legions, it paid for bribes, it bought influential clients, it funded games and gifts for the masses that purchased their love and their loyalty. With the power of a consul, his personal reputation for bravery and military leadership, his close association with Caesar, who was beloved of the common folk and the legions, with Caesar's documents, and finally with Caesar's money, Antony could cement his position as the First Man in Rome, and mould the Republic as he saw fit, whether that was along the lines that Caesar had envisaged, or in accordance with a plan of his own.

He drank deeply of the fine Falernian and then took a deep breath, letting it out slowly. He was sure the young boy he had been, his world crashing down on the news of the death of his father, would never have believed he would grow into the man sitting in the most lavish house in Rome, drinking the most expensive wine, and preparing to receive the bequest that would make him richer than it was possible to imagine. He closed his eyes, and dozed lightly.

The sun had shifted somewhat in the sky when Fulvia shook him awake to inform him the guests had arrived. His cup had fallen from his hand, spilling the expensive wine over the flagstones. He wiped the sleep from the corner of his eyes. He hadn't realised how tired he had been, his body pushed to its limits the way a horse caught up in the excitement of a chariot race runs to exhaustion. He stretched, rose, and made his way into the commodious atrium that served as the room for formal ceremonies as well as welcoming guests. It was still decorated with the fine mosaics and frescoes that Pompey had commissioned, as well as some of his original colourful marble statues depicting heroes from Greek mythology, but Antony had personalised the room with the ceremonial wax masks of his own ancestors, and with the figurines that represented the household gods, to which daily offerings were made in the recess in the wall that served as the *lararium*.

He smiled and opened his arms wide to greet, embrace and kiss the cheeks of each of his guests in turn.

'Calpurnia. So brave, you have all my admiration. Piso, thank you for agreeing to have the first reading of the will here in my home. Lepidus, Balbus, Hirtius, thank you for coming.'

He noticed his co-consul Dolabella, at the back, mainly hidden because of his diminutive size, and he stepped forward to shake his hand as warmly as he could. He could hardly have failed to invite his junior colleague in office to such an important event, but he was not going to let the presence of the little snake spoil his mood.

The chief Vestal Virgin was a woman in her early thirties called Metella, a distant cousin of the Scipio who had fought for Pompey. She was flanked by two of her sister priestesses, all three in full formal dress – linen *palla* over white woollen stola, a delicate white veil draped loosely over the head and hair tied back in red and white ribbons. She was of an age where she would soon be released from her vows and allowed to marry if she desired. In her hands she bore a carved maple wood box, and Antony's eyes lingered on it for a moment, knowing it contained the final wishes of Caesar.

Fulvia welcomed the guests, and ensured the slaves brought them all wine. Antony proposed toasts to the gods, to Caesar's memory and to Pax, the goddess of peace. Then, impatient to get things moving, he said, 'Shall we turn to the order of the day? Piso?'

Piso inclined his head, and addressed Metella.

'Priestess, would you hand me the will.'

With a deep bow, she handed the box to Piso. 'I hereby declare we have kept our vow. This will was entrusted into our care by Gaius Julius Caesar in September of last year and has remained with us, sealed and unopened, ever since. I give it to you now, Lucius Calpurnius Piso, as his nominated executor, that his wishes might be known.'

Piso took the box with reverence, and looked at Antony. Antony gave him an impatient gesture with his hand to continue. Piso nodded, displayed Caesar's seal to everyone present to show that it was intact, then cracked the wax with his thumb. He opened the box, which contained a vellum scroll, also sealed. Piso drew out the scroll and broke the seal. He cleared his throat and then, holding the scroll at arm's length – he no longer had a young man's eyes – he read out loud.

'I, Gaius Julius Caesar, hereby declare that this is my last will and testament. At the time of writing, I have no legitimate son or grandson. If a legitimate son is born to me posthumously, they shall be the principal inheritor of my estate, and I nominate Decimus Junius Brutus and Marcus Antonius as his guardians until he should come of age.'

It was gratifying that Caesar would nominate Antony to be responsible for his hypothetical son's upbringing and wealth, though ironic that he should also nominate one of his assassins. But this was irrelevant, and though Antony knew that Piso must read every word aloud, he was impatient to get to the meat of the document.

'In the absence of a legitimate heir, I hereby declare an heir who will become my son by legal adoption. This man, who is much loved by me, who has done me great service, and who will in turn serve Rome with diligence and loyalty, will inherit three-quarters of my estate.'

Three-quarters, thought Antony. What a sum!

'That man is my sister's grandson, Gaius Octavius...'

Piso's voice trailed off. All eyes turned to Antony. He stood, back straight as a *pilum*, jaw clenched to remain expressionless. His first thought was that he had misheard, but the look on everyone else's faces – especially Fulvia's – told him that he had heard correctly. Next, his mind groped around to try to remember who Gaius Octavius actually was. After a moment, he recalled Caesar's great-nephew who had accompanied him on his campaign in Spain, and whom Antony had met a handful of times. What was he – barely eighteen years of age? He had had so little impact on the political scene, Antony had no idea what he had been doing since Caesar had ended the civil war. He didn't think he was even in Rome at present.

'Why have you stopped, Piso?' asked Antony, keeping his voice even and forcing a smile. 'Caesar has simply declared a relative as his heir, as is right. Let us hear the rest of his wishes.'

But he barely heard a word as the rest of the will was read out, and Fulvia later had to tell him what other provisions Caesar had made – most of the remaining quarter of his estate going to his other great-nephews, Lucius Pinarius and Quintus Pedius. He left his gardens near the Tiber to the public for common use, and a gift of three hundred *sestertii* to every freeborn citizen resident in Rome. Minor bequests went to Decimus Brutus and Antony. Finally, he reiterated the formal adoption of Gaius Octavius, naming him Gaius Julius Caesar Octavianus.

When Piso was finished, he looked at Antony apologetically. Everyone in the atrium appeared solemn except Dolabella, who could not keep a smirk from his lips.

'So, that is done,' said Antony firmly. 'We have all witnessed Caesar's last wishes, and we commit to ensure they are carried out. Now, my consular duties demand my attention. Thank you, everyone, for your attendance, but I must be about my business now.'

No one wished to remain any longer than they had to and gratefully took their cue to leave, though Dolabella could not resist one last mocking glance over his shoulder as he departed. When they were all gone, Antony slumped onto a bench and put his head in his hands. Fulvia sat beside him and put her arm around his shoulders. They sat in silence for a while as Antony contemplated the disaster. How could Caesar have done this to him? After all they had been through together.

Fulvia gave him an encouraging squeeze.

'Marcus. It doesn't matter.'

'How can you say that?' He didn't attempt to keep the anguish from his voice, here in private with Fulvia. 'I needed that money.'

He felt as if a giant demon made of liabilities and arrears and debtors was looming over his shoulder, preparing to crush him beneath its fists.

'Because it is true,' said Fulvia in a soothing voice. 'Caesar's riches would have been a boon, true, but you are in a strong position even without them. Take stock of what you have. You are senior consul, the most authoritative man in Rome at this moment. You will get proconsular immunity next year, and the chance to earn large sums in whichever province you take on. You have the love of the army and the people.'

'The people sway like reeds in the wind, and the army will follow the money.'

'Well, this Octavius boy—'

'Octavianus now,' Antony corrected her. 'Gaius Julius Caesar Octavianus.'

'Octavianus. Whatever. He isn't even in Rome. And for now his inheritance is in your hands. There is no clear time period for you to hand it over. In fact, it isn't even clear what part of Caesar's fortune truly belongs to him, and what is actually part of the state treasury, which you as consul are entitled to spend. And what will this child do with the money anyway? Handle him wisely, and he will be your puppet.'

Antony swallowed reflexively, and turned to look at Fulvia's concerned but reassuring features. 'Do you believe this?'

'I believe in you, Antony. I was very proud of how you took the news in front of everyone. Now make me even prouder, and accept the roll of the die, and make the best of it.'

'Wine would help me do that,' he said with a half smile, and Fulvia grinned back, then flicked her fingers at a slave. He hurried off and returned promptly with a full cup, and Antony drained it.

'That's better. Fine. Caesar has done what he has done. He has put his family before me, and I can understand the sentiment, even if I think it's foolish. But I am bound to his star, and even though he is gone, I must capitalise on the love of the common people for him. Especially now he has been so generous towards them. I need them to believe in me, and secure my position as Caesar's successor before that boy arrives in Rome.'

'The perfect opportunity for that is just two days away,' said Fulvia.

Antony nodded thoughtfully. Caesar's funeral.

'I'm going to have to give an oration that will be remembered for generations,' he said.

'Yes,' said Fulvia. 'And I believe you can do it.'

ante diem xii Kalendas Apriles DCCX AUC (20 March 44 BC), Rome

Caesar had entrusted the instructions for his funeral to his niece, Atia, who was also Octavian's mother. But Fulvia had a quiet word with her, and she agreed to hand over the planning to Antony. Antony, in turn, spoke to the two great-nephews of Caesar, Pedius and Pinarius, and asked that they agree that he make the funeral oration, given, as he pointed out, that he was a consul, just as Caesar had been a consul, he was a relative of Caesar, and he was his friend. They readily acquiesced, and Antony could understand how daunting it would have been for one of those youngsters to give the eulogy for the greatest ever Roman — who had just been murdered — in front of an angry mob who loved him.

Fulvia and Antony, with help from Lepidus, Calpurnia and Piso, planned the day with precision, and Antony wrote and rewrote his oration, striving for the right words, the right tone. In the end, Fulvia encouraged him to leave room for improvisation, so he had leeway to read the mood of the crowd and adjust accordingly.

When the day came, Lepidus stationed soldiers at important flashpoints around the city — the docks, the temples, the houses of the chief magistrates. The Liberators, too, employed gladiators as bodyguards. All knew the high level of danger to property and life that day.

A pyre was set up for the cremation on the Campus Martius, in front of the tomb of Caesar's mother, but the ceremony was to take place in the Forum. The body was carried on an ivory couch from Caesar's residence, flanked by an honour guard of Caesar's veterans, with Piso leading the procession and Antony and Calpurnia directly behind him. With them were the rest of Caesar's relatives and friends who were in the city, all the senators who dared venture out of their homes, actors and musicians singing and playing flutes and lyres, and a vast crowd pressing in on all sides. Five actors, one for each of Caesar's triumphs, wore wax masks of Caesar, eerily lifelike since they had been cast when he was alive. Dressed in triumphal robes, they paced slowly behind the bier.

The ivory couch was carried up to the rostra and placed on a gilded shrine, and the honour guard turned with their backs to the platform, facing out into the Forum, and began to beat their shields with their swords, while crying out a loud, rhythmic wailing. Many of Caesar's veterans were in the crowd, and they took up the cry, so the whole Forum echoed with the deafening sound of lamentations. Calpurnia, Atia and Piso took seats behind the shrine. Antony felt a momentary pity for Cleopatra, still in Caesar's villa across the Tiber, who was forbidden by law, as a foreign monarch, from attending. But, of course, having Caesar's mistress present would have been unfair on Calpurnia, and since Cleopatra was not particularly popular in Rome, her presence would have been counterproductive to Antony's aims.

Antony stepped forward and held up his hands, and the veterans ceased their wailing and clashing. An expectant hush settled over the

Forum. Antony turned to where Caesar's body lay and gave it a long, mournful stare, drawing the moment out. Then he turned to the onlookers and drew breath to begin his oration. His trained voice and the physical advantage of his barrel chest allowed his voice to carry to all corners of the Forum.

'Conscript Fathers, citizens, brothers in arms, friends. Here lies before you an extraordinary man. An illustrious man. A man of bravery, dignity and strength, of intelligence and wisdom. A man of kindness and clemency.'

There were nods from the crowd, muttered agreements, but in general they were respectfully quiet.

'Caesar was my friend. He supported me throughout my ascension in the ranks of the military and the *cursus honorum*, and it is because of him that I stand before you today as consul. But he was a friend to all Romans. He defeated our ancient enemies in Gaul and removed them as a threat for all time. He brought untold riches to our city. He unified our country after bitter civil war. His clemency was unsurpassed. He pardoned the enemies who begged for his mercy. Enemies such as Marcus Tullius Cicero. Gaius Cassius Longinus. Marcus Junius Brutus.'

He paused after each name, and the crowd jeered and hissed their disapproval of the ingratitude and treachery of these men.

'He loved every citizen in our commonwealth, and he has shown it by giving each and every one of you three hundred sestertii in his will.'

There was a great cheer at this. The fact was already known – Piso had read out Caesar's will publicly the day before – but it was still a reason to celebrate.

'Was he without fault? Of course not – show me a man who is perfect. But I contest that he was the greatest Roman that ever lived, greater than Scipio Africanus or Marius or Sulla or Pompeius. And he was recognised as such.'

Antony reached out his hand, and his attendant slave passed him a scroll.

'Let me read to you some of the decrees with which the Senate quite rightly honoured Caesar. Father of the fatherland. Prefect of the morals. Liberator. Imperator. The first living Roman to have his face put on a coin. The right to sit on a special chair between the consuls at Senate meetings. Statues erected to him in public temples. The month of Quintilis renamed in his honour. And these were only the honours he chose to accept, vastly outnumbered by those the Senate offered him, but he rejected.

'And, of course, the entire Senate swore an oath to protect his personal safety.'

He turned again to Caesar's bloodied corpse, and there were moans and shouts of shame and disgrace from the crowd.

'Look at him, lying there,' he said, raising his voice in anger for the first time. 'Testament to the betrayal, to the oath-breaking, not just of those who plunged their daggers into his flesh, but of all those others present who had vowed to protect him, who fled like cowards. Well did Trebonius and Decimus Brutus detain me outside the Senate, and prevent me from coming to his defence, for they knew that I would have fought like a lion to protect that man.

'Now what is left for me but vengeance?' He turned his face towards the Temple of Jupiter on the Capitoline Hill. 'The king of the gods himself sees that I am ready to strike for Caesar's sake. To make those traitors and villains and those craven mice pay for their crimes.'

The crowd roared its approval, but the senators nearest the front stirred restlessly and shouted out protests. Antony let his voice drop.

'But I cannot. For the sake of Rome, I have agreed an amnesty. We all know the horrors of civil war, when Roman takes up arms against Roman. We have seen too much of it. I cannot, in all conscience, plunge our country into such chaos and destruction again.'

He looked at Caesar once more. 'I would that the assassins had shown so much restraint, before they plunged their treacherous blades into my fellow consul.'

He took a spear off a nearby soldier, and used its tip to lift up Caesar's toga, which had been draped loosely over the body.

'See here, the blood of Caesar, soaked into the wool of his robe. Look at the rent here, where Publius Servilius Casca Longus struck the first blow as Cimber held him down. Here, the second blow in the ribs, struck by Casca's brother Gaius. This tear here is where Gaius Cassius Longinus stuck him. And here where the knife of his beloved Decimus Brutus struck home. How his heart must have torn in two as the man he loved as a son, who he honoured alongside myself in his will, committed the ultimate betrayal. And finally, in the groin, the killing blow, from Marcus Junius Brutus, who Caesar also loved.'

The crowd had groaned with each name, crying out their disbelief at the ingratitude of the two Bruti. Antony made a gesture, and an actor stepped forward, wearing Caesar's mask with a slice to represent the cut to his face, took the toga from the spear point and folded it around his shoulders. He declaimed in a loud voice, mimicking Caesar's intonation, all the men he had elevated to the most senior positions, which included most of his assassins. When he had finished, the actor quoted a line from Greek tragedy, spitting it out with all the venom his profession had taught him.

'Did I save them, just so they could destroy me?'

The crowd roared out 'No!' in a thunderclap of fury, and like the bursting of a dam, their anger and grief poured out. They rushed the rostra and surrounded Caesar's body. Antony ushered the chief mourners back out of the way, protected by a small ring of soldiers, but he did nothing to intervene, happy to let the crowd have their head.

They lowered the ivory couch on which Caesar's body rested from the rostra into the Forum with as much respect and care as angry rioters could muster. Then, with shouts and cries, they tried to carry him to the Capitoline Hill, where some of the assassins were still encamped. This could have been a bloodbath, but fortunately Lepidus had stationed soldiers on the road to the hill, and their interlocked shields and forward-pointing pila were an impenetrable hedge of thorns. Undeterred, the crowd flowed back into the Forum, and an impromptu pyre was created, using any dry wood they could find, including the benches from the nearby law courts. Eight years previously, Fulvia's first husband, the populist Clodius, had been cremated in an outpouring of anger and grief in this very spot, by a crowd manipulated by Fulvia. Now, just as skilfully influenced by Antony, the even greater populist was being given the same treatment.

Before long, the pyre was lit, and the flames leapt up high, enveloping Caesar's body and hiding it from sight. The crowd groaned and tore their hair and their clothes. At Antony's urging, the actors who had played roles in the ceremony walked mournfully to the pyre and threw their robes and their masks into the flames. The veteran legionaries tossed spears and *gladii* in with them, praising Caesar and cursing the assassins as they did so. Then the general public joined in, offering personal possessions of great value or personal wealth as if they were offerings at a shrine. Bracelets, *fibulae*, necklaces, the clothing from their backs, even the *bullae* that hung around their children's necks to protect them from bad luck and evil spirits.

Rome had never seen anything like this in its long history, this exquisite grief, this white-hot fury. The flames were still burning bright and hot, the smoke palling over the Forum, when some members of the crowd, led by Caesar's most loyal veterans, decided that revenge should be taken into their own hands. With cries of 'death to the traitors, death to the murderers', they set off with swords, agricultural implements, kitchen tools and flaming brands in the direction of the houses of the various conspirators to deal out justice.

As sections of the crowd departed, Antony suggested to the chief mourners that it might be prudent to make their own way home. With his *lictors* and personal bodyguards clearing a way, he invited Lepidus, Calpurnia and Piso to join him in the safety of his house until the riot burnt itself out and order was restored.

Dining with his guests and Fulvia later that day, he was brought the news that Decimus Brutus' gladiators had beaten back the rioters from his home and the homes of Marcus Brutus and Cassius Longinus. Antony commented it was a shame that the people had not been able to rid Rome of the traitors, but Fulvia pointed out that it could be useful to have an enemy with whom to contrast Antony's own loyalty and honour, especially such egregious villains as Cassius and the two Bruti.

Later, a breathless messenger arrived to say that the mob had killed Lucius Cornelius Cinna – who had so infuriated the crowd by tearing off his robes of office and condemning Caesar as a tyrant – and were parading his head on a spike through Rome. Later it emerged they had mistakenly killed the unrelated and inoffensive poet, Helvius Cinna. Antony felt a momentary pang of guilt at his death, but at the same time he was realistic enough to know that if the poet was the only casualty of note that day, Rome – and in particular, the Liberators – had got away very lightly.

Idibus Aprilibus DCCX AUC (13 April 44 BC), Rome

One month after Caesar's murder, Antony was still astonished by how much work was involved in running an empire, quite apart from the matters of keeping the peace in a restless city, shoring up his personal authority, improving his finances, and subtly ensuring the conspirators were edged out of positions of power without alienating the Senate. A few days earlier, Marcus Brutus had visited Antony, troubled by the actions of a previously unknown rabble-rouser who claimed to be the grandson of the great Gaius Marius, seven times consul and Julius Caesar's uncle. His name was Gaius Amatius, and Antony's enquiries suggested he was a freedman and an impostor, but that had not stopped him from taking the name Gaius Marius, and a large section of the credulous common folk from taking him at his word.

Amatius had set up an altar to Caesar on the site of his funeral pyre and incited mass demonstrations against the conspirators. Although superficially, this could have suited Antony, he was all too aware of the power a demagogue with a popular cause could wield, and both he and Dolabella had acted to have the altar removed and the demonstrations dispersed, which had earned the consuls praise in the Senate. However, Amatius continued to whip up unrest, and Decimus Brutus, Cassius and Cicero all decided it was prudent to leave the city. Marcus Brutus, too, wished to depart, but his position as Urban Praetor legally prohibited this, hence his visit to Antony.

Antony, with Fulvia present, had enjoyed extracting as much fun from the audience that he could, outwardly concerned for Brutus' well-being, while making digs about how his heroic act was being received by the citizens in a way that was making him flee for his life. Still, it was to Antony's advantage to have him out of the way, and he proposed a bill in the Senate giving leave for Brutus to be absent from Rome, which was swiftly passed. At the same time, he had Gaius Amatius arrested and publicly executed, hoping to crush the disorder and emphasise his own authority.

Antony met with Lepidus and Dolabella frequently, as well as his brothers Gaius and Lucius, powerful allies in their own rights in their roles of praetor and tribune, but his chief adviser was Fulvia. They spent hours every day ensconced in their study, poring through Caesar's private papers, strategising how to compensate for the gaping hole in Antony's financial plans caused by the unexpected disappointment of Caesar's will, and planning for the future after Antony's consulship finished.

The possession of Caesar's records and correspondence was a treasure beyond price. They enabled Antony to bring forth Caesar's planned legislation, utilising the law passed by the Senate that had legitimised all of Caesar's Acts, much of which was simultaneously beneficial to Rome and improved Antony's popularity. In addition, he was able to exaggerate – and even outright fabricate – documents that enabled him to push through legislation and edicts that suited him, claiming they were Caesar's own wishes. The deceit gave him a small twinge of guilt, but Fulvia would brook no weakness in him, and always pointed him towards the treachery of the conspirators if he needed to be reminded what real wrongdoing looked like.

By this method, Antony announced the decision of Caesar in the matter of the trial of King Deiotarus of Galatia, who had been accused by his grandson of plotting against the dictator, but in which matter no judgement had been pronounced. Antony showed documents that Caesar had planned to declare Deiotarus innocent, and what's more, to add a portion of Armenia to his territory. Caesar had in fact written of his intention to make such a declaration, but Fulvia had arranged for Deiotarus to pay a healthy bribe to Antony to ensure the release of the appropriate documents, and rumours of this deal meant much doubt was expressed as to their authenticity. Nevertheless, it was by means such as this that Antony was able to work towards building up sufficient funds to meet his debts and control the legions.

On that particular day, Antony was discussing with Fulvia and his brother Lucius the plans for the forthcoming Parilia festival, nine days hence. Originally dedicated to Pales, the deity of shepherds and livestock, the festival was regarded in later tradition as the birth date of the city itself. Fulvia had suggested that games in Caesar's honour were added to the celebrations, and Antony had had a coin struck in honour of the occasion. One side of the coin was an acrobat holding a palm and a wreath, but on the other, in a move sure to shock many, was a likeness of Antony himself, his beard grown long as a sign of mourning, veiled and holding the *lituus*, the wand that he used in his role of augur when performing his sacred duties. Caesar had been the first living Roman to put his image on a coin; Antony was demonstrating that he was Caesar's true heir by becoming the second.

His mind drifted off to matters of lunch. His feasting and drinking had been quite moderate over the previous month – he had been simply too busy to indulge in his usual pleasures – but that did not mean he would not take wine and a fine meal when time allowed. Fulvia and Lucius were arguing about how much they were prepared to pay for gladiators, Fulvia erring on the side of financial prudence, Lucius stating adamantly that Caesar deserved only the best.

The arrival of a messenger interrupted the heated but tedious discussion, to Antony's relief.

'What is it?'

The messenger, a young Greek slave, spoke in a clear voice.

'To Marcus Antonius, consul, from Publius Cornelius Dolabella, consul. Greetings, brother. I send news of a riot in the Forum provoked by the execution of Gaius Amatius. Men are needed urgently to restore order.'

Antony stood swiftly, calling for his curaiss and sword, and snapping out orders. Relieved to be called to action, he felt a surge of excitement.

With a swiftness and decisiveness that were second nature after his extensive military experience, he summoned a large detachment of legionaries and marched them past the House of the Vestals and into the eastern side of the Forum. He was greeted by the sight of a large crowd, fully out of control, smashing shops, overturning market stalls, tossing firebrands at public and private buildings. Anguished merchants and citizens stood by, desperate to extinguish the nascent fires, which threatened to grow into a conflagration that could threaten the city still built primarily of wood, but cowed by the angry mob calling out praise for Caesar, protesting the execution of Amatius, and vowing death to the assassins and to anyone who stood in the way of justice.

Antony had had enough. He had tried restraint in the previous civil disturbances. But, reluctant though he was to use force against the people, he had a duty as consul to keep order and to protect the city. He gave the order for the men to move in.

It was a swift and uneven fight. Antony did not draw his own sword, much as his hand itched to grasp the hilt, feeling it would be beneath his dignity to be involved in the fighting against lightly armed civilians. The brief battle left half a dozen rioters dead and a score badly wounded.

The damage was done, Antony knew. The Senate and the property-owning citizens of Rome would be grateful for his intervention, but the common poor would resent his violence against their fellows. Well, command decisions were rarely easy or straightforward, he had learned, and that applied as much to the burdens of a consul as a legate. He hoped he was proving as good a political leader as he was a general.

Nonis Maiis DCCX AUC (7 May 44 BC), Campania

At the end of April, Antony was finally able to get some rest and relaxation on his first journey out of Rome since the Ides of March. He had passed a law, again using Caesar's papers, that allocated land and established new colonies for Caesar's veterans in Campania. It was vitally important for Antony's purposes that he kept the legions and the veterans onside, not least because he was beginning to recruit for his own private army of 'bodyguards' from the veterans of the Gallic and civil wars who were lounging restlessly and discontentedly around Italy. Antony therefore travelled to Campania to maximise the publicity and credit for his actions in the veterans' favour, which had the pleasant side effect of removing him from the myriad day-to-day stresses and irritations of rule. He had minor reservations about leaving Dolabella in charge, but with his brothers – Gaius as praetor and Lucius possessing power of veto as Tribune of the Plebs – and Fulvia continuing her work in the shadows, he was confident his interests were being protected.

He was thus able to spend time in the company of his favourite people – on the one hand soldiers and veterans, and on the other the group of actors, mimes and musicians that he had brought with him. One of the benefits of the actions of the assassins was that he no longer felt Caesar's disapproving gaze on him when he indulged in some of the coarser pleasures of life.

He travelled to Samnium and met with the veterans of the Fifth and Eleventh legions, dined with the retired officers and foot soldiers, and informed them of the land grants he had secured for them. At Casilinum he oversaw the foundation of a colony for veterans, and went so far as to plough the sacred furrow that defined the boundary of the territory, bare chest grimy with dirt and sweat. The veterans cheered him to the skies, honoured him with prayers and ribald songs.

That afternoon he attended a sumptuous open-air feast he had organised for veterans of the Eighth Legion that he had commanded at Pharsalus. Seated on a bench between a centurion and a standard-bearer, he drank, ate and swapped stories about the campaigns in Gaul and Greece.

'But, Legate,' said the standard-bearer, boldness fortified by the strong wine, 'when are we to be avenged on the assassins?'

All eyes turned to him, cups pausing on their way to lips as they hung on his reply.

Antony looked mournful. 'I wish that I could have every one of those cowardly dogs thrown from the Tarpeian rock, just as traitors deserve. But the Senate has forbidden it, and like Caesar, I am no tyrant to take the law into my own hands.'

'They should be tried, then,' said the centurion. 'Then justice can be served.'

Cries of agreement rang out around ranks of veterans, all inebriated to a greater or lesser extent.

'You are right, of course,' said Antony, 'and no one desires that more than I. But there are powerful forces at work here. The Senate is divided. The assassins have many supporters. There is no guarantee that a trial would result in their conviction – in fact, the opposite is most likely. But I tell you all to be ready. Keep your swords sharp, your armour polished, your arms strong. Those who support the assassins also work to take away your awards and rights.'

Anger rumbled through the veterans like an approaching thunderstorm, and some cried, 'Let them try!' One or two even leapt to their feet, shouting, 'Vengeance!' and 'For Caesar!'

Antony raised his arms for calm.

'The day will come when I need you, believe me,' he said. 'Until then, enjoy the fruits of your labours on behalf of Rome. And when the call comes, I know you will be there. For Rome. For Antonius. For Caesar!'

The banging of plates and mugs on the table, the stamping of feet and the cheers of approval echoed off the nearby hills.

That evening Antony retired to a country villa that he had purchased cheaply from the family of a deceased supporter of Pompey. The entertainment that evening that his actor friends had organised involved a banquet of local and exotic delicacies, fine wine, dancing, mime and music. He was reclining in the company of a mime actress – comely, but not a patch on Cytheris, whom he still missed terribly – and had all but forgotten that he was the ruler of the entire Roman Empire.

Then a messenger arrived, bearing a letter from Fulvia. Antony broke the seal and read the words neatly inscribed into the wax tablet.

Dearest Marcus,

I hope that your work in Campania is bearing fruit, and that you are not over-indulging in food, wine and the other pleasures to which I know you are partial. I write with three pieces of important news. Firstly, rioting has once more broken out in support of that man you had executed, who was pretending to be Marius' grandson. Dolabella has put it down with his customary brutality – the free men involved were tossed off the Tarpeian rock and the slaves were crucified on the Campus Martius. But whether or not you agree with his methods, Rome seems calmer now.

Secondly, Cleopatra has departed with that son of hers she claims is Caesar's. She sent you a message that she regrets not being able to wait to bid you goodbye, but that she fears for the safety of Caesarion given the current disturbances.

Of more importance, in my opinion, is the third piece of news – that Caesar's grand-nephew, Gaius Octavius, has arrived in Rome. He arrived on the outskirts with a huge entourage of well-wishers and adherents, but came into the city with just a small number of bodyguards, playing the modest supplicant, requesting the Praetor's court formalise his adoption as Caesar's son. But for all his apparent humility, he is going around the city, making appointments with all the important senators, making speeches to the masses that he is Caesar's heir, and even calling himself Gaius Julius Caesar! He is also letting it be known that he is awaiting his inheritance that you are safeguarding for him!

I suggest that you return to Rome forthwith to put this boy in his place.

With all my affection,
Your loving wife Fulvia. Farewell.

Antony was instantly sober. Safeguarding his inheritance? The impudent little nobody! He called for Vitalis, who because of his good service on the Ides of March, Antony had promoted to his head steward.

'Fetch my travel clothes. Ready my horse. Summon my lictors. We are leaving for Rome.'

'Yes, Master,' said Vitalis. 'When are we leaving?'

'Tonight,' snapped Antony. Vitalis hurried away to do his master's bidding.

Antony turned to his guests, who had watched the change in their host with dismay. With an effort he forced a smile.

'Friends, you are free to continue the revels. But I must leave you. There is a little matter I must deal with in Rome.'

A little matter, thought Antony, calling himself Caesar.

Chapter III

ante diem vi Idus Maias DCCX AUC (10 May 44 BC), Rome

Antony entered Rome with a full-strength legion at his back. His initial reaction to Fulvia's letter had been to jump on a horse and ride like a loosed arrow for Rome before this boy calling himself Caesar could do any more harm. But when he had cooled somewhat, he realised that hastening back to the city would seem as if he was worried about the threat to his position. Better to proceed at a more sedate pace consistent with the dignity of a consul, and take the time to gather his strength. He had therefore sent messages out across the region, promising the veterans good pay for joining his bodyguard. Some of that money might technically belong to Octavian, but if Antony spent it before the adoption was ratified, there would be little the lad could do about that. By the time he reached the end of the Via Appia and rode into the Forum on his gilded chariot drawn by two pure white geldings, six thousand fully armed, battle-hardened legionaries marched behind him.

He was greeted on his arrival in the Forum by a welcoming committee of important senators, including his brothers, along with Lepidus and Dolabella. Gaius and Lucius embraced him and kissed both cheeks, then Lepidus and Dolabella followed suit.

'Impressive,' said Lepidus, nodding towards the troops drawn up in ranks and standing stiffly at attention. There was a hint of irritation in his voice. Lepidus was no longer in command of the largest military force in Rome. But Antony suspected it was of no great importance to him. Not only had Antony, with dubious legality, awarded Lepidus the position of Pontifex Maximus vacated by Caesar's death; they had recently agreed the betrothal of Antony's daughter, young Toni, to Lepidus' son. In any case, Lepidus was due to depart for Spain any day, where Pompey's son Sextus had taken advantage of the crisis in Rome to stir up trouble.

'Why have you brought an army to Rome?' asked Dolabella, rather more pointedly.

'I understand there was further unrest while I was away. It seems that even now Rome is not settled. I therefore sent out word I wanted volunteers for a personal bodyguard, and these men answered my call.'

'A bodyguard of six thousand men?' scoffed Dolabella. 'Well, you should be very safe now.'

'Not just me. These men ensure peace and order in Rome.'

Dolabella spread his hands to show he would not argue further.

'So I suppose you will be granting an audience for Caesar's heir,' said Lepidus.

'Of course,' said Antony. And then, with a subtle smile, he added, 'Eventually.'

ante diem iv Idus Maias DCCX AUC (12 May 44 BC), Rome

Antony received several messages from Octavian petitioning him for a meeting, but with calculated rudeness, he did not deign to reply until he had been in Rome for two days. Not that he wasn't busy, of course. He met important politicians, talked to influential figures in the army – the career officers and the senior centurions – promising donatives and generous pensions in return for their support. He made plans for the betterment of Rome, some of which Caesar had documented in his papers, some of which were his own ideas or suggestions from Fulvia and his brothers. And, of course, there was the constant deluge of routine matters that needed his attention – legal matters to adjudicate, personal and public finances to juggle, foreign affairs. So, although it was a deliberate ploy to not overly elevate Octavian's importance in the eyes of the public by prioritising an audience, Antony had genuine reasons for the delay.

The weather was getting warmer as summer neared – although the reddish haze in the sky from Aetna's eruption persisted – and Antony elected to receive Octavian in the gardens of his villa. But he was not prepared to make things easy for the boy, and as a not-so-subtle reminder of their relative importance in the Roman hierarchy, Antony kept Octavian waiting in his atrium for three hours before he summoned him to the meeting.

Octavian gave no indication that he was put out by the wait when Vitalis finally ushered him into Antony's presence. Antony was seated in a canvas chair, reading from a vellum scroll, when Octavian stopped before him. Antony did not look up, continuing to read without acknowledging Octavian's presence. Octavian stood, still and upright, the only indication to Antony that he was there at all a gentle, rather irritating wheeze as he breathed. Eventually, Antony judged he had made his point. He rolled up the scroll, handed it to Vitalis, and then pretended to notice Octavian for the first time.

'Ah, young Octavius,' he said without standing. 'What a pleasure. It's been a long time, hasn't it? Please accept my condolences at the loss of my close friend, your great-uncle Caesar.'

He didn't offer Octavian a seat or a drink, treating him as a supplicant client rather than an honoured guest.

'Thank you, Consul. But I am Octavius no longer. Caesar has gifted me, among the other items of my inheritance, his name. I am now Gaius Julius Caesar Octavianus.'

Antony frowned. 'A bit premature, aren't you? Your posthumous adoption has not been ratified yet.'

'A mere formality, isn't it?'

'Perhaps. It is, of course, my brother's role as praetor to decide on that. I'm sure he will be amenable.' Antony made sure there was just a hint of doubt in his voice. 'But as you must understand, the affairs of state keep me very busy, so let's get to the point. What can I do for you?'

'I am here to ask for the money Caesar promised in his will, so that I may fulfil his legacies to the people.'

Antony put on a sorrowful air. 'I'm sorry, Octavius,' he said, refusing to use the boy's new name. 'When I took possession of the state treasury, it was all but empty.'

'I find that hard to believe,' said Octavian bluntly.

Antony's brow furrowed. 'Did you just accuse me of lying?'

'I'm merely puzzled. It is well known that you took possession of both the state funds and my father's personal fortune.'

'He is not your father,' snapped Antony. 'Not unless your adoption becomes official.'

'Unless?'

Antony smiled. 'Did I say "unless"? I meant until, of course.'

'To be clear, are you telling me that you will not release to me my rightful inheritance?'

'Listen, boy,' said Antony, almost growling. 'Firstly, you are not yet entitled to a copper *as*. Secondly, there is not enough money to fulfil Caesar's bequest. And thirdly, whatever money there is in the state coffers, I need for the proper conduct of the state business. Have you any idea how much it costs to run Rome? Of course you don't. You are just a boy with no experience, political or military. How could you know the sums involved in equipping and paying the legions, maintaining the roads and the aqueducts and sewers, providing the corn dole, funding public projects, not to mention paying for the games and races that keep the people entertained and passive? You have no idea, and I don't have time to teach you.'

'Very well,' said Octavian. 'I will pay for it myself.'

'Pay what?' asked Antony, confused.

'My father's bequest of three hundred sestertii for every citizen in Rome.'

'And how will you afford that?' asked Antony patronisingly. 'You are talking about something in the region of seventy-five million sestertii in total.'

'I was fortunate enough that when I arrived in Brundisium from Greece, I was met by the officers of my father's armies who were readying themselves for the war in Parthia. Not only did they pledge me their loyalty, they kindly made over to me the contents of my father's war chest.'

Antony gaped. He hadn't realised that Caesar had already moved a significant sum out of the city in preparation for his campaign in the East. He cursed his stupidity. Perhaps if he had looked through Caesar's accounts more assiduously, he would have noticed the movement of the cash, and been able to requisition it before it had fallen into this boy's hands.

'Even so,' said Antony, recovering his composure. 'That would not be enough to cover the full amount.'

'This is true,' said Octavian. 'It is around thirty million sestertii short. I can fund more by the sale of family property. And I have not been idle since I arrived in Rome. It turns out that the name of Caesar and the promise to inherit his wealth is sufficient to be extended a good line of credit.'

'Are you mad? You are going to borrow a fortune in order to give it away to the common people?'

Octavian shrugged. 'It was my father's wish. And since you are clearly not prepared to honour them...'

Now Antony stood up and advanced menacingly on Octavian.

'How dare you?' he roared. 'Where were you when Caesar fought for his life at Alesia? Where were you when the fight for the Republic was decided at Pharsalus? Where were you, when the assassins plunged their daggers into my friend?'

Despite the young boy's insubstantial frame, with Antony towering over him like his antecedent Hercules, Octavian did not flinch or avert his gaze from Antony's face. 'Where were you, Antonius?' he retorted. 'I hear you fled dressed as a slave.'

Barely able to control his fury, Antony drew back his arm, fist balled, ready to strike the youngster. Octavian merely regarded him steadily, unblinking.

Antony took a deep breath, dropped his arm, unclenched his fist. 'I am a consul of Rome,' he said. 'I do not need to account for my actions to a boy such as you, with no official position.'

Then he forced a smile, and put a friendly arm around Octavian's shoulders, squeezing hard enough to make the young man let out a rasping cough.

'But listen... We have no need to quarrel. You have been put in an unenviable position by Caesar's will. No doubt he expected to live a long life, and have you inherit when you were a grown man, with experience and wisdom. Instead, Caesar's murder has burdened you with his promises. Take my advice... abandon this foolish quest you have set yourself. Rome has more pressing problems. Put your new-found fame and fortune to use in supporting me, and I will ensure your adoption and inheritance pass without undue difficulty.'

Octavian stared for a long moment at Antony, until he became uncomfortable.

'Well, boy? What do you say?'

'I say, do not call me "boy". My name is Gaius Julius Caesar Octavianus. And I do not need your help. I have the law on my side, and I will not be robbed of my inheritance.'

'No one is robbing you, b— Octavianus,' said Antony, marvelling at Octavian's composure and obstinacy. 'Look, we have got off on the wrong foot. I apologise for my harsh words. The burdens of office can weigh heavily and fray the temper.'

Octavian gave a faint smile. 'Perhaps some wine would take the edge off your nerves,' he said, and Antony knew there was a dig in the gentle suggestion.

'Not a bad idea. Maybe later. I must get back to affairs of state. If you will excuse me...'

'Of course, Consul. I will take my leave. Thank you for your time. And your advice.'

Antony embraced Octavian and kissed him on each cheek. Vitalis led Octavian away and Antony watched him go, with the uneasy feeling he had just lost a battle.

Fulvia came to join him, put an arm around his waist, and kissed him gently on the lips.

'You heard?' asked Antony.

'Everything,' confirmed Fulvia. 'And I tell you, that boy is dangerous. He has built up a strong following among the common people and veterans already.'

Antony shook his head. 'Dangerous? No. Just an irritant. What could someone with his age and experience achieve, even with Caesar's name and money? Believe me, he will come to nothing. We have far more important men to worry about. Decimus Brutus. Marcus Brutus. Cassius.'

'And Cicero,' said Fulvia. 'You could really do with his support.'

'I fear that ship has sailed. Besides, how could I join with him when he is so publicly gleeful about Caesar's death. It would destroy my credibility with the army and the people.'

Fulvia sighed. 'The boy was right about one thing. You do need a drink.'

She led Antony back to his chair, and ordered them each a large cup of wine.

Kalendis Iuniis DCCX AUC (1 June 44 BC), Rome

Antony had announced a meeting of the Senate for the Kalends of June before he left for Campania, so lack of forewarning was no excuse for not attending. After Caesar's expansion of the membership of the

Senate, up to a thousand senators should have been crammed into the Senate house, minus those too ill to attend and those performing duties outside Rome. But only a few score had turned up. Antony strode up and down the central aisle between the benches impatiently.

'Where are they all?' he demanded, to no one in particular.

Dolabella, who was sitting in his curule chair looking glum, shrugged.

He turned to his brothers, the tribune and the praetor. 'Lucius? Gaius?'

'Sorry, Marcus,' said Gaius. 'Do you think news of your proposals has got out?'

Antony considered this. It would make sense. The ostensible reason for the meeting was to vote on a new land law proposed jointly by Antony and Dolabella that would establish a commission of seven senators to oversee the distribution of land to veterans and the poor citizens of Rome. Reform of land laws had been a popular cause for a hundred years; it was generally supported by the masses and opposed by the rich because of its redistribution of wealth. It had to be handled with care to avoid alienating the Senate, while at the same time satisfying the demands of an armed and potentially aggressive mob of veterans, and forming a committee to take responsibility for the problem was a sensible proposition that should be acceptable to all sides.

But that was not the only reason Antony had called the meeting. He had been allocated Macedonia as a province for the following year, but it was becoming clear that with Brutus and Cassius still at large, Cicero crowing delightedly over Caesar's death, and now the arrival of Octavian on the scene, a two year proconsulship in a province that far from Rome would not be sufficient to protect his interests. Antony therefore had Lucius lined up to propose a Tribunician law that would transfer the governorship of Cisalpine Gaul to Antony, for a period of five years, while still allowing him to take command of the six legions in Macedonia and bring them with him to Gaul. Dolabella was supporting the proposal, since his proconsular term in Syria would also be extended to five years, giving him a long period to enrich himself while immune from prosecution.

This second proposal had not been widely publicised, but enough important people had had to be consulted that it was no secret. Antony could only conclude that the majority of the senators had disapproved of his proposal – unsurprisingly – since it was an obvious power grab, and had decided to stay away rather than risk the wrath of Antony's lictors and bodyguard, and all the veterans who crowded Rome's bars and taverns, by opposing the bill. Even the designated consuls for the following year, Pansa and Hirtius, both of whom were moderates and were involved in attempting to keep the peace between the Caesarian and Liberator factions of the Senate, had failed to attend.

'What do we do?' asked Lucius plaintively. 'I had a fantastic speech prepared about the dangers of a Gallic uprising and the unsuitability of Decimus to deal with it.'

'We can't go ahead,' said Dolabella. 'Any law we passed with this few senators present would have no legitimacy.'

'Then we go to the people,' said Antony decisively. 'If the Senate will not step up to make a decision, the public will do it for them.'

Gaius looked doubtful. 'Are you sure we will win a public vote? There has been some discontent about how public disorder has been handled of late.' He gave Dolabella a pointed stare.

Antony stroked his beard, now impressively bushy.

'I think I need to speak to that boy.'

ante diem iii Nonas Iunias DCCX AUC (3 June 44 BC), Rome

Antony stood on the rostra, looking out across the Forum, supervising the vote. As consul, he was president of the *Comitia Centuriata* – the Centuriate Assembly – and the *Comitia Tributa* – the Tribal Assembly. He had let it be widely known that a vote would be taken by the Comitia Centuriata, the more aristocratic of the two assemblies, but had wrong-footed the complacent senators, who possessed a majority in that body, and had in fact called a vote of the Comitia Tributa. His soldiers surrounded the Forum and roped it off into sections, the so-called 'sheep pens', which showed the ancient origins of the ceremony. He opened the procedure at dawn with a prayer, and then passed over to Lucius to give the fiery speech he had rehearsed so hard.

The cloud cover was low, and there were rumbles of thunder in the distance. One of the augurs muttered about bad omens, but Antony silenced him with a glare. A tribune commented that the meeting was unconstitutional, since not enough advance notice had been given, but

Antony had suggested he tell that to the throng of veterans squashed into the Forum, and the tribune shut his mouth. In any case, he and his fellow tribunes had been heavily bribed not to interpose their vetos, and Antony would have been demanding a refund with interest if any had gone back on their promises to him.

Once the case had been made, Antony ordered the citizens to form into their tribes, and the voting commenced. It was a simple method in which a pebble was placed into one of two baskets, yay or nay, the procedure watched with hawk-like vigilance by officers of the assembly.

The vote was not a foregone conclusion. As Gaius had pointed out, Dolabella's brutal actions against the mob, as well as Antony's attempts at compromise with the assassins, had not been well received by portions of the public and the veterans. Which is why Antony had decided he should make use of Octavian. Swallowing his pride, he had visited the young man, and apologised for his previous harsh words. Suggesting they had too much common cause to be antagonists, he promised to push forward the ratification of Octavian's adoption in exchange for his support in the vote that day.

Octavian had taken him at his word, and now stood near the ballot baskets, clutching the ropes, telling everyone that Caesar's son urged them to vote yes for the good of Rome.

The tribes voted in order of seniority, and the results of each tribal vote was announced as soon as it was finished. It quickly became obvious that the bill was going to achieve a substantial majority, and Antony was able to announce the passage of the Act by late morning, an unusually swift decision. Elated, he came down from the rostra and mingled with his supporters, shaking hands and receiving embraces from soldiers and citizens alike. Octavian approached him with a calm smile and proffered his hand.

'Congratulations, Consul,' he said.

'Thank you, Caesar,' Antony said graciously, shaking his hand with a squeeze strong enough to make Octavian wince.

'Don't forget your promise,' said Octavian.

But Antony was already moving along the line of well-wishers, glorying in his victory.

ante diem ii Idus Iulias DCCX AUC (13 July 44 BC), Rome

Antony's initial intention had been to honour his promise to Octavian straight away. Much as the youngster rubbed him up the wrong way with his precocious arrogance, he knew that Octavian's support, and the name of Caesar, could be useful to his ambitions.

But he was a busy man. Having obtained, more or less legitimately, an equivalent strength to that possessed by Caesar at the time he crossed the Rubicon – and for a five-year duration, no less – he was positioning himself to hold on to his power as the undisputed leader of Rome for the foreseeable future. It was not a path he had ever planned to forge, but power led to power. Besides, like Caesar, it was hard to let go of the tiger's tail. Antony had plenty of enemies: the Liberators; Cicero; even some factions in the army who deplored his accommodations with those they considered traitors. Many of these would happily see him prosecuted, exiled or dead. So, like Caesar, he had to continue to build his power to ensure his own safety.

Fulvia, of course, thrust him forward at every opportunity, and shored up his faith in himself whenever he expressed self-doubt. He often wondered if she wouldn't make a better consul than he, if it wasn't for the accident of birth that made her a woman. When he pondered this aloud, she confirmed that, yes, she would be a far superior consul to him, but they had to work with what the gods had given them.

So, after the vote in the Comitia Tributa, Antony pushed onwards with the plans that he, Fulvia and his brothers had formulated. One priority was dealing with the Liberators. It was clear that the public and the legions detested them and hated his light treatment of them. It had been prudent initially to take that route, despite his personal inclinations. It had prevented a bloody civil war on the streets of Rome, and had helped safeguard him personally while he shored up his position. But now that he was unassailable by the Senate, both in terms of legitimate authority and military power to enforce it, he could discard their opinions and concentrate on building popularity with the army and the people.

To this end, and much to his personal pleasure, he brought forward a law that stripped Marcus Brutus and Cassius of their provinces and instead awarded them the demeaning role of purchasing grain for the city, positions well below their dignity and rank. He had hoped that this would persuade them both to take themselves off into voluntary exile, since although they were no longer in Rome, they continued to agitate from elsewhere in Italy, Brutus in particular giving speech after speech and writing a flurry of letters denouncing Caesar and justifying his acts.

But Brutus was still officially Urban Praetor, and as such it was his right to put on the annual games to Apollo. Lavish games were always a way to the hearts of the people, and Fulvia's informants quickly got wind of his plans, not least of which was to put on a play by the playwright Accius called *Brutus*, about his honourable ancestor who had overthrown the monarchy. This was too much for Antony. He informed Brutus that it was too dangerous for him to appear in Rome, and said that though the games would go ahead in Brutus' name, they would be overseen by his brother Gaius in his role of praetor. They immediately changed the planned play to a different one by Accius.

It was actually Octavian's suggestion that really put Brutus in his place, however. A fawning Senate had voted that the month of Quintilis be renamed July in honour of Caesar, but most had forgotten this, or thought it had lapsed with Caesar's death. Now, Antony announced that the Games of Apollo would take place commencing from two days before the Ides of July. Brutus responded by sending a letter that the traditional games would take place on the Ides of Quintilis, but few took notice of this.

Octavian was closely involved with the games, having had his own games in Caesar's honour vetoed by Antony, and by spending large sums on the entertainment, he made it clear that the games would be dedicated to his father. The first day of the games came and was hailed as a great success. Octavian's extravagant spending matched that of Gaius, and he made sure the people knew it. The gladiator fights and beast hunts were lavish, the music and dancing exuberant, and the play by Accius well received.

Night fell, and as the stars began their circle across the sky, a bright smear with a long tail appeared and climbed upwards.

The crowds at the feasts noticed and soon all were pointing at the appearance of the comet, wondering what was the meaning of the ominous sign.

Octavian was in no doubt. He ascended the rostra and spoke to the crowd.

'See, my father is ascending into the heavens, on the day of these games in his honour. Let no one doubt it for a moment longer. My father, Gaius Julius Caesar, has become a god.'

Chapter IV

Iulius DCCX AUC (July 44 BC), Rome

The haze that had dimmed the skies since the death of Caesar was finally starting to clear. Vitalis told Antony that the slaves and common folk thought the gloom was Caesar's ghost hovering over the city, and now they had seen him pass into the heavens, the fog was dissipating. Antony knew that the eruption of Aetna was the main reason for the greyness, but he was superstitious enough that he couldn't completely rule out that the deceased dictator was responsible for the phenomenon. Antony wondered frequently what his old mentor and friend would have made of his actions since the murder. He had stabilised the Republic. He had prevented chaos and anarchy. He had protected Caesar's legacy. But he hadn't avenged him. Nor had he treated his adopted son and heir particularly kindly.

At least that last was about to change. Although he had initially viewed Octavian as a minor rival and irritant, Antony could no longer ignore the young man's growing support and influence. He was going about growing his following with exceptional vigour and cunning, according to Fulvia, planting agents among the veterans and legions to promote his cause, generously bribing anyone he thought could aid him, using his family assets and monies borrowed against the expectation of his inheritance. And particularly since the appearance of the comet at the games, and Octavian's opportunistic exploitation of the sign, it was commonly accepted among the populace and the legions that Caesar had become a god, and that Octavian, his heir, was the son of a god. Moreover, the legions were becoming increasingly insistent that the two men most beloved of Caesar unite, and together mete justice on the Liberators.

That morning, a deputation of junior military tribunes and senior centurions, the career officers of the legions, called at Antony's house at dawn and demanded an audience. These days there were few people who could demand anything of Antony, but if there was one group of people he could not afford to alienate, it was the army. Still, he kept them waiting a short while, while he washed and dressed and had his slaves comb his hair and oil his beard. It would not do to appear too subservient to the soldiers. When he admitted them to his atrium, attired in his military uniform, but unarmed and unarmoured, they told him that they wanted him to meet Octavian on the Capitoline Hill that day for a formal reconciliation. A similar deputation had been sent to Octavian. It amused Antony greatly to discover later that when the soldiers had appeared at Octavian's door, he had believed they had come to kill him, and he had hidden in an attic until the officers had been able to persuade him that they meant him no harm.

Octavian showed no sign of that weakness now as he stood before Antony in front of the magnificent Temple of Jupiter Optimus Maximus atop the Capitoline Hill, the city far below them. He was straight-backed and his legs appeared firm. The two of them stood in the centre of a circle made by the legion officers, with as many legionaries as could be fitted into the space there to witness the meeting of these two close friends and relatives of their beloved Caesar. Antony still wore his fine military uniform, breastplate, belt, helmet and scarlet cloak. Octavian had, of course, never held an official military rank, and so had come dressed in formal toga. They could not look less alike, the bull-like general, every inch a soldier, and the puny youth. And yet it was clear the legionaries loved them both.

Antony made the first move, and spoke the words that their representatives had agreed earlier in the day.

'Gaius Julius Caesar Octavianus, son and heir of Caesar, I, Marcus Antonius, consul, give you my hand. I swear to you here before the Temple of Jupiter himself of the sincerity of my friendship, and I offer you an alliance.'

Octavian replied, his voice surprisingly strong considering his frame and the perennial weakness in his chest. 'Marcus Antonius, consul, I, Gaius Julius Caesar Octavianus, son and heir of the Divine Caesar, accept your hand. I swear before Jupiter Optimus Maximus of the sincerity of my friendship, and I agree to join you in alliance, for the greater good of the Republic and people of Rome and its legions, and in order to let justice prevail against those who have committed murder and treachery.'

Antony suppressed a frown. Octavian had added a few words to the agreed text of their oaths. There had never been a mention of revenge against the Liberators, and Antony had expressly forbidden the use of the word 'divine'. He had not yet decided if it was to his advantage to acquiesce to the deification of Caesar, given the authority it granted Octavian. He had thought he had taken the initiative by asking to be the one to speak first, showing his superiority in their partnership, but Octavian had used the position of speaking second to mould the occasion to suit himself. Antony reminded himself he must stop underestimating the boy.

Still, he gave no outward show of discontent, and he extended his hand. Octavian took it, and they shook. Antony resisted the urge to grind his bones, but Octavian's grip was stronger than previously, and Antony wondered if he had been exercising. He certainly seemed to be in better health: a little less pale, a little less wheezy.

The soldiers let out a throaty roar that would have been audible across the entire city. They stamped and clashed their swords on their shields and praised the names of Antonius and Caesar. Antony smiled broadly and lifted Octavian's arm into the air, turning in a slow circle to show his face to every man present.

Octavian looked as if he was about to say more, but Antony forestalled him, his booming voice cutting through the cheers.

'My comrades in arms, I have fought beside you, I have broken bread with you, I have drunk your wine – or at least that muck you lot call wine.' This drew rueful chuckles and some catcalling. 'I have served my country on the battlefield and the Senate. I have called Caesar my friend, and I have held his broken body, and I have buried him. I stand with you, and I stand with Octavianus, and I pledge my body to you and to the Republic and people of Rome.'

More cheers erupted and Antony pulled Octavian into a strong embrace. Into Octavian's ear, he said quietly, 'We will be stronger together, lad. Just don't mess me around.'

Octavian replied, voice calm and even. 'This alliance suits me. I suggest you ensure that continues to be the case.'

Antony stiffened, but Octavian pulled away and walked off to mingle with the men. Antony did the same, but couldn't help looking back suspiciously at his new ally.

ante diem iii Nonas Septembres DCCX AUC (3 September 44 BC), Tibur

Antony had further meetings with Octavian and his friends and advisors, and they remained superficially allied, but the tensions and divisions between them were pronounced. Octavian demanded his inheritance repeatedly, but each time, Antony simply told him that the issue was going through the courts, and he was powerless to speed up the process. Meanwhile, Fulvia's agents informed Antony that Octavian was continuing to attempt to suborn the soldiers with bribes, something perilously close to treason. Fulvia suggested her husband could use this as an excuse to do away with this irritating rival, but Antony was hesitant – it was clear how much the common man and the legionaries loved Octavian, and overt action against him was dangerous.

Instead, he turned his attention against the Liberators, a move that had the double benefit of improving his standing with the legions and satisfying his own, hitherto repressed, desire for vengeance. Brutus and Cassius had refused to take up the grain commission he had given them, so he instead got the Senate to allocate to them Crete and Cyrene as provinces for the following year – tiny territories with few troops and little opportunity for personal enrichment. The motion had passed easily, although he was surprised and unhappy when Caesar's father-in-law, Piso, personally attacked him in the Senate for his actions.

Brutus and Cassius were gratifyingly outraged at the affront to their dignity and wrote to Antony to express their indignation. But Antony would not be moved, and the edicts had their desired effect. The two most prominent assassins left Italy, though not to take up their allocated provinces, Brutus going into exile in Athens and Cassius heading further east.

With the Liberators out of the way, and Octavian appearing to be on a leash, Antony finally began to relax. Even Fulvia agreed that his position as the most powerful man in Rome – indeed, the world – seemed to be secure, though she was ever alert for new threats to their safety.

Antony called a meeting of the Senate for the Kalends of September, and was pleased to hear that Cicero would be returning to Rome. Not that he had any love for the self-important old man. Antony was aware that Cicero had been in regular correspondence with the assassins, Decimus and Marcus Brutus and Cassius, and had never ceased praising their heroic actions, nor advising them of what their next steps should be. He also knew that the old man had admonished them for sparing Antony's own life, stating that he was too dangerous to be allowed to live. Antony supposed this was something of a compliment, even if it was an unwelcome one.

But Cicero was toothless now. He might still be respected as Rome's most venerable elder statesman, philosopher, politician and the greatest orator of all time. But he had no actual power, with no legions of his own, and no strong anti-Caesarian allies in Rome. So it was useful to Antony to have Cicero back in Rome and attending the Senate, a sign of normal times returning, of stability and reconciliation.

The day before the Kalends, Cicero had been greeted by rapturous crowds on his arrival in Rome, and Antony himself had sent him a greeting on his homecoming and an invitation to dinner, though Cicero had sent a sarcastic reply back and claimed to be too weary from travel to accept social engagements for the time being. The Senate met as planned on the Kalends to discuss a number of Antony's new bills. Now he was more confident in his own power, he felt able to bring forward motions that were contrary to Caesar's wishes – in this case, a desire to change the composition of the courts, and a right of appeal, which the conservative Caesar had opposed. But more importantly, he proposed that all festivals should have an extra day added in honour of the murdered Caesar. It was an important test of the Senate's sentiment, and it would put Cicero in the position of having to publicly support or oppose Caesar's legacy. Antony sent Cicero an official summons for his attendance at the meeting.

Cicero was no fool, though, and having learned of Antony's plans, he sent a message to the consuls just as the Senate was about to begin that he could not attend due to extreme fatigue from his travels. Antony had not been able to restrain his anger at Cicero's blatant snub, and had threatened to have workmen tear down Cicero's house, the ancient, rarely used penalty for failing to turn up to a Senate session. Calmer heads prevailed upon him to simply issue the customary fine for non-attendance. His bills passed with little dissension, but although the Senate was due to meet again the next day, Antony had had enough of politics. Leaving Dolabella to chair the second session, he quit Rome, taking Fulvia and the children to his villa in the luxury resort of Tibur, from where he was able to take walks in the grounds, bathe in the hot springs, and entertain his friends: the elevated ones, such as those of senatorial and equestrian standing; the worthy ones, from the lower ranks of the army; and the more disreputable ones, from the stages and theatres. Fulvia tolerated these latter provided Antony kept them out of public sight, although she was careful to ensure that Cytheris never received an invitation – she knew that Antony still missed the mime actress, and would not allow that affair to reignite.

It was two days after the Kalends of September, in the mid-afternoon, when the official messenger arrived from Rome with the report of the second meeting of the Senate the day before. Antony was reclining in the garden with Fulvia, mildly drunk, snacking on honeyed figs and nuts, which were placed on a small wooden table before them, while Antyllus toddled around wearing a cloth helmet and trying to wield a wooden sword.

Vitalis brought the message to Antony himself, but Antony was overcome by a deep sense of ennui and waved it away. Fulvia beckoned for Vitalis to hand the scroll to her instead, and she broke the seal and began to read.

Antony realised something was wrong when she sat up abruptly. Her jaw set, and her breath through flared nostrils came faster and deeper.

'What is it?' he said, suddenly anxious.

Fulvia didn't reply until she had finished the lengthy document.

'You should read it for yourself,' she said, and handed him the scroll.

Antony took it and began to scan its contents with trepidation.

It was a copy of a speech Cicero had given in the Senate, the day after he had failed to attend Antony's Senate meeting. By Cicero's standards, it was not overly long; Antony judged from the rough number of words that it would have taken Cicero around an hour to deliver it. And it started mildly enough. He protested Antony's anger towards him for failing to turn up to the Senate the previous day, and with his usual irony asked if Hannibal was at the gates, that the meeting was deemed so important. He also praised Antony's actions after Caesar's death fulsomely: his moderation and efforts towards reconciliation between the two sides, as well as his efforts to keep the peace and save Rome from riots and conflagrations in the wake of the Ides of March. Then, after praising Piso's ineffectual attack on Antony in the Senate the previous month, he went on to talk about the Acts of Caesar as revealed by Antony in Caesar's papers, sarcastically noting the irregularities, and wondering whether the entire government of Rome should be based on reminders jotted in a dead man's notebooks.

Antony grimaced at this. Much of his power came from his control of Caesar's papers, and it was disconcerting to have Cicero diminish their validity. He read on. Cicero addressed Dolabella, who was chairing the Senate meeting in Antony's absence, praising him for his actions in tearing down a column erected in memory of Caesar, and admonishing him for not continuing in the same manner, hinting that money was ruling his actions. He came back to Antony, stating that of course greed would not rule Antony, and that he had never seen anything sordid or mean in Antony, despite what everyone else was saying.

Then he said, addressing Antony directly in his absence, 'Sometimes, no doubt, members of his own household corrupt a man, but I know your strength of will. I just wish that, as you avoid this guilt, you could also avoid suspicion of it.'

Antony stopped reading and looked at Fulvia. She was watching him steadily. No doubt, this was the part that had made her sit up. The malign influences in Antony's own household that Cicero mentioned could only be taken to refer to Fulvia herself. Antony could see the hurt in her eyes, the anger, that this highly respected politician should damn her reputation in front of the Senate, and indeed, all Rome.

Antony took a deep breath, then, struggling to keep his voice even, he said, 'I'm going to kill him.'

Fulvia put out a restraining hand, but Antony was on his feet, casting the scroll to one side, then with a roar, he picked up the table by one leg and hurled it across the garden. Figs and nuts scattered, and Antyllus abruptly ceased his play to stare at his father in fright.

'Fetch my sword,' he yelled to the nearest slave. 'Ready my horse. I'm going to Rome.'

'Marcus, no,' said Fulvia, approaching him and grabbing his upper arm. Her nails dug into his flesh, the sting bringing his attention back to her. 'No,' she said again. 'This isn't the way.'

'It is bad enough that he insults me, a consul of Rome. But to attack you, a noble matron of irreproachable character. The woman I love, no less...'

Fulvia smiled gently. 'You cannot attack him with violence. It would diminish you in the eyes of the people. You must use his own weapons against him, and exploit his weaknesses. Words, Marcus. You are a great orator – your speech at Caesar's funeral proved it. And Cicero's pride is his weakness. He wants to be loved by the nobility, his character to be admired by all. That is where you go for him.'

Antony looked doubtful. 'I have some skill in speaking, yes, but I am no Cicero.'

'That isn't important,' said Fulvia. 'What matters is the words you use. Words that will be written down and circulated around Italy and will show everyone the real character of this stuck-up coward. I will help you. Together, we will write a speech that will rock Rome.'

Antony nodded. 'We can do this?'

'I believe in you, Marcus. You must know that by now.'

Antony slid his arms around her and hugged her gently. 'What have I done to deserve you?'

'Better ask the gods that question. Now, sit down with me. Let's finish reading this drivel together, then we can start working on our response.'

Antony took a deep breath and let it out slowly through his nose. Then he called for wine, and reclined next to Fulvia while she read out the rest of Cicero's infuriating invective.

ante diem xiii Kalendas Octobres DCCX AUC (19 September 44 BC), Rome

Antony stood before the Senate, trying to keep a lid on his temper. The little weasel had disappeared, not having shown himself in the Senate since his speech. It was typical of the coward, he reflected, to flee the consequences of his actions. No wonder he had never had any military success worth speaking about.

But Cicero wasn't the only absentee. Caesar's father-in-law, Piso, who had attacked Antony the previous month, had also stayed away. So had the former consul Publius Servilius Vatia Isauricus, appointed by Caesar during the civil war, and who Antony understood had enthusiastically supported Cicero's speech.

Nevertheless, the Senate was packed. There was still a strong split in sentiment between the pro-Caesar and the pro-Liberator factions and Antony had been performing a complicated flirtation between them, trying always to retain the upper hand. But first Octavian, and now Cicero, were forcing him to pick a side, and ultimately, there was only one choice to make. The veterans and legions who were the main source of his power were Caesarian to a man, and also seemed to adore his posthumously adopted son. Antony could not afford to lose their support, and have that boy usurp his authority.

So today was his chance to show Rome his Caesarian credentials, and to rebut Cicero in the most forceful way he could, without actual resort to arms.

'Conscript Fathers,' he said, his booming voice cutting through the chatter and bringing silence. He paused and looked slowly around the chamber, taking a moment to look pointedly at the empty space where Cicero customarily sat.

'I must first express my absolute astonishment at what I have learned was said in this house the day after the Kalends of this month. My good friend, Cicero, with whom I have always had cordial dealings in the past, has launched a completely unprovoked attack on me. Not only unprovoked, but an example of rank ingratitude. Did I not step aside to allow his candidature for the augurship to pass unopposed after the death of Crassus? Did I not defy Caesar and allow Cicero to stay in Brundisium after Pharsalus, when Caesar had expressly forbidden Pompeius' supporters from being allowed to return to Italy?

'This attack was like a bolt of lightning, so unexpected was it. Why, only in April, Cicero wrote to me telling me that he had always had affection for me, and stating that public affairs have so recommended me to him that there is none for whom he has more regard! How can you explain such a change, even in one with so little steadfastness of character?

'Of course, Cicero has a history of behaving rashly. He himself will never let us forget his deeds in the year of the consulship of himself and my uncle Gaius Antonius, and to this day he considers himself a saviour of the country. But let us examine his actions. As a tool of the *optimates*, he killed Roman citizens without trial. The slopes of the Capitoline Hill thronged with armed slaves he had placed there to suppress the people. He betrayed the democratic ideals he had held in his younger days. He even refused to surrender the bodies of his victims to their families. My own mother, Julia, was not permitted the body of my stepfather, so she could bury him as befitted his rank and honour. And he dared to say of this time, "Let arms yield to the toga!"'

Some of the senators shook their heads and a few called out, 'Shame!'

'But these are not the only murders that stain Cicero's soul. It was at his instigation that my friend and Caesar's, Publius Clodius, was murdered by the thug Milo, Cicero's puppet. He even tried to defend Milo in his murder trial, although he was too scared of the righteous anger of the crowds to give a convincing speech. But that didn't stop him praising the deed.

'And what of his role in the conflict between Caesar and Pompeius? Despite all the benefits he had enjoyed, he was the chief instigator of that terrible war.'

There were some louder mutterings from the benches now. Opinions were still strongly divided as to the cause of the civil war, and Antony knew that Cicero had, in fact, belatedly tried to prevent war. But his anti-Caesarian stance had legitimised the opposition to Caesar, and encouraged Pompey and the Senate to make the decisions that had provoked the crossing of the Rubicon. It was something of a stretch of the truth, but Antony genuinely believed that Cicero was far from blameless when it came to that conflict. Although Antony had to admit he had played no small part himself in shoring up Caesar's resolve to commit to war.

'So with this knowledge of the character and actions of the man, it should not surprise us to discover – and this the veterans and soldiers of the legions should know – that it was Cicero himself who planned Caesar's murder!'

Now there was an outcry from all around. Shouts of denial, disbelief, outrage. Senators were on their feet, shaking their fists, while some of their colleagues argued with them and tried to restrain them. Scuffles broke out, and Antony had to wait for a few moments until peace was restored. This was a calculated move by Antony, and had been Fulvia's master stroke when she helping him compose the speech. Until now, Cicero had been content to praise the act in retrospect, taking the glory for the assassination from those who approved it, while denying responsibility and keeping respectability from those who detested the murder. Antony raised his voice to cut through the hubbub.

'You doubt this?' he demanded. 'Did not Marcus Brutus himself raise the dagger dripping with Caesar's blood, cry aloud Cicero's name and congratulate him on restoring the freedom of the Republic. I tell you, it was Cicero who plotted this foul deed.

'This is the character of the man who attacks me before you. We all know his vanity, his capacity for mockery, so boundless that even in Pompeius' camp at Pharsalus he could not restrain his vicious tongue, to the extent that none was prepared to name him in their wills. But he is more than his cowardice, his mockery, his vainglory. He is a murderer, and his hands have dripped with the blood of noble Romans from the dawn of his consulship, up to this very year!'

Antony yielded the floor, taking his seat in the consul's curule chair next to Dolabella, who was regarding him with amused interest. Vociferous arguments broke out once more in the rank and file of the Senate, but there were none who dared to stand up and speak in support of Cicero on that day.

Among Cicero's slurs against Antony in his speech, he had averred that Antony believed it was better to be feared than loved. Maybe he was right, Antony reflected. But surely it was better to be both loved and feared?

'Nice little speech,' commented Dolabella. 'I think you might make my father-in-law cry.'

Antony wondered. Cicero was a coward, certainly, but he also had his pride. He was sure there would be retaliation. A war of words was underway.

ante diem viii Idus Octobres DCCX AUC (8 October 44 BC), Rome

Antony immediately went about accentuating his pro-Caesarian credentials, giving speeches to the legions and veterans praising Caesar, proposing him honours in the Senate, and even having a statue of Caesar erected on the rostra with the inscription, 'To our Father, for his glorious services.' The wording was deliberate, since it branded the Liberators not only as murderers, but – even worse – as parricides. Not everyone was in agreement with his stance. A *contio* was called in the Forum by the tribune Tiberius Canutius, a strong supporter of the Senatorial faction and the Liberators. Antony attended, and after Canutius had given a speech from the rostra praising the Liberators as saviours of the country, Antony had brusquely shouldered him aside. He accused Canutius of being in Cicero's pay, and that Cicero was also bankrolling the so-called Liberators, whom Antony referred to as enemies of the State. He ended the speech by calling for a trial of Caesar's murderers, among whom he numbered Cicero, and his words were received enthusiastically by the gathered audience.

Overall, Antony was pleased with the results of his shift in political position. His support from the masses and the soldiers, always firm, grew to ever greater strength. The Senate was suitably cowed, Cicero withdrew to his country estate, and Marcus Brutus and Cassius left Italy. Even Dolabella, ostensibly his ally, although no great friend, departed Rome for the province of Syria and a campaign against the Parthians, with which Antony had bribed him in return for his support, leaving Antony the sole consul in Rome.

The only irritation, like a pebble in his sandal, was the young Octavian. Caesar's heir kept agitating for his inheritance, and it was becoming increasingly difficult to stall him. At some point Antony knew he would have to make some sort of token reckoning, and as his grip on power was increasing, maybe he would be in a position to make some sort of gesture in the near future. But Octavian's actions gave Antony no reason to do him any favours. Against Antony's wishes, he put Caesar's properties up for auction, claiming to be their owner, in order that he might pay for Caesar's legacies to the soldiers and the people. But many of these properties had been seized from Pompeians who now demanded them back, and the process was grinding its way through the courts. So Octavian spent his days in the Forum and visiting senators and army officers, bemoaning his treatment at Antony's hands, and handing out promises he was in no position to keep.

But worse, he continued to attempt to suborn the troops, sending agents disguised as tradesmen among them with pamphlets suggesting that Antony had once more come to terms with the Senate and was turning his back on the Caesarian cause. Octavian and Antony had so much common ground, and the legions, as they had shown, would have been delighted if their beloved Antony and the son of their revered – and now widely regarded to be divine – general would put aside their differences and unite against Caesar's murderers. Maybe Antony would have come round to their viewpoint, given time.

But then Octavian made a move that threatened to tear the peace apart.

A few days after his altercation with Canutius in the Forum, Antony was blinking the sleep from his eyes. It was well past dawn, and he knew that he had an atrium full of clients, supplicants and well-wishers to see. Even those important enough to remain after his stewards and secretaries had filtered out the time-wasters and undesirables would take him hours to get through, and he needed time for his head to stop thumping after the hangover and lack of sleep caused by an entertaining evening with some of his actor friends, and then a passionate night with Fulvia.

He splashed water on his face and had his personal slave dress him, then wandered into the garden, hoping the autumnal sun might revive him. Fulvia was there already, reclining on a couch by a fountain, eating a light snack of nuts and bread and reading the Epicurean philosopher Lucretius' *On the Nature of Things*. She looked as fragrant and fresh as a spring crocus, despite the fact that she had drunk just as much and slept just as little as Antony himself. She offered her cheek for him to kiss without looking up from her book, and he slumped down on the couch opposite her and called for food and watered wine.

He watched Fulvia eat and read, taking his time to admire her. She had had four children already – and Antony had resolved they should start working on a fifth – but her beauty and figure were untouched by the ravages of time and childbirth. She did not even need elegant dresses or elaborate make-up; Antony loved how she looked, loved everything about her, in fact, more and more so as she became the rock he knew he could anchor himself to when all around was turmoil and turbulence. He reached out to touch her knee. She threw him a brief smile, then returned to her reading.

A slave appeared clutching a goblet of liquid, and coughed hesitantly. Antony looked up. He didn't recognise the young lad, a blond-haired Greek.

'A new purchase, Fulvia? This one took your fancy, hmm?'

Fulvia didn't look up. 'What are you talking about, Marcus?'

Antony reached out to take the beautiful bronze cup, and noticed that the slave's hand was trembling. It wasn't cold, but Antony supposed if this was the boy's first time serving the ruler of the known world, some nerves were understandable. He took the goblet, prepared to take a draught, then paused. He sniffed it suspiciously. The wine was giving off a musty bouquet, a bit like the urinary smell of a disturbed rodents' nest. Given Antony was still making his way through Pompey's extensive collection of exquisitely expensive vintages, it seemed unlikely that there would be any wines in the cellar that smelled of mouse piss. He looked into the cup. Was that some plant matter at the bottom?

He looked up at the slave, realisation dawning. The boy was trembling violently now.

'Did you do this?' he asked, voice calm but full of threat.

The boy opened his mouth and stuttered.

'Guards!' yelled Antony. 'Here. Now!'

One of Antony's personal guards who had been discreetly stationed on the opposite side of the garden approached at a run, drawing his sword. As he arrived, Antony said, 'Seize this slave. He is trying to poison me!'

But the guard did not seize the slave. Barely breaking his stride, the brawny ex-legionary, a man who had served with Antony in Gaul and Greece, a man Antony trusted with his life, thrust his sword into the slave's midriff. Placing a hand behind the poor boy's neck, he thrust upwards, the tip disappearing through liver into lungs and heart. The slave's eyes went wide, blood spurted around the hilt of the buried blade, and he collapsed against the bodyguard.

'What are you doing?' asked Antony in confusion. 'I told you to seize him, not kill him.'

The guard lowered the dying slave to the ground, slid out his sword and turned to Antony.

'I'm sorry, General,' he said.

Then he lunged, sword arm outstretched, for Antony's chest.

Perhaps a Cicero or a Brutus – one of those noble Romans who occasionally played at being a soldier – would have been paralysed, would have just stared in wide-eyed shock as they were skewered.

But Antony was a battle-hardened veteran himself. He had fought hand-to-hand with Rome's enemies across the entire breadth of the Empire. He threw himself off his couch and the sword stabbed harmlessly into the stuffed leather.

Fulvia screamed, and distant shouts of alarm answered. Unless his entire bodyguard had been suborned, help was a few moments away. But the gardens were large, and the nearest aid was a hundred yards distant. Antony, unarmed, had to hold off the assassin for just a bit longer.

He rolled to his feet and grabbed the silver tray that held Fulvia's breakfast. The assassin stabbed again, and Antony, holding the tray with both hands, batted the blade away. But the back-stroke split the flimsy metal in half, leaving Antony holding two shards. He backed off, seeing the nearest guard still fifty yards away. The assassin knew he was running out of time, too, and he took two swift steps forward and lunged. Antony dodged, and the wickedly sharp blade neatly sliced the side of his tunic.

Antony stepped past the outstretched arm and rammed into the assassin with his shoulder. The veteran staggered back, and Antony whipped the broken plate around as if it was a dagger. The jagged edge sliced deep into the side of the assassin's neck and arterial blood shot out.

The assassin dropped his sword and clamped his hand to the side of his neck, trying to stem the flow, though surely knowing it was futile.

'Why?' asked Antony, breathlessly. 'After all we have been through together.'

The assassin was turning white before Antony's eyes as his blood watered the ground.

'Caesar's money... Too good,' he hissed out. 'Forgive me.'

Then his legs gave way, and he folded in on himself, crumpling to the ground in a blood-soaked heap.

Other bodyguards arrived and Antony tensed, but they immediately organised a defensive ring around him and Fulvia, while others began a search of the premises for any other threats. Fulvia stared at Antony in momentary shock, then, quickly recovering her wits, snapped at a guard, 'Bring my children to me. All of them. Now!'

He hurried off to do her bidding.

'Caesar?' she asked Antony. 'He means Octavianus?'

Antony shook his head in wonder. 'I never thought him capable of this. It doesn't make sense. He may not like me, but he still needs me to protect him from the Liberators.'

'I'll find out,' said Fulvia. 'But whatever the truth, the public should know what Octavianus is capable of.'

Antony looked at her quizzically and she returned his gaze steadily.

'Yes,' he said, 'perhaps they should.'

ante diem vii Idus Octobres DCCX AUC (9 October 44 BC), Rome

The hammering came from the front door again, followed by shouts, curses and threats. Antony sat in the vestibule and listened to Octavian's distress with quiet satisfaction.

'Come out and face me,' cried Octavian. 'You are the real plotter, not I. You have spread this false rumour to discredit me. I will see you in the courts for this!'

'Shall I admit him?' asked Vitalis.

'No, let him stew out there,' said Antony. 'It's amusing, and it's no less than he deserves.'

'Let me in, you dogs, you swine,' screamed Octavian, his high-pitched voice breaking in his anguish. Antony knew the guards on his front door would be unmoved by these entreaties unless a signal was given from inside that he might be allowed entry.

'Marcus Antonius, I will be judged by any jury you choose, even one of your friends. I did not do this foul deed of which you accuse me!'

Fulvia entered the vestibule and Antony smiled at her.

'There is no need for a trial,' she said. 'Public opinion will condemn him more effectively.'

'He seems genuinely upset,' said Antony. 'Maybe it wasn't him.'

'It wasn't,' said Fulvia.

'Very well, if you do not have the courage to face me, I will depart,' cried Octavian. 'But let all be my witness, if any harm should befall me, it will be at the hands of Marcus Antonius!'

The commotion ceased and calm returned.

'What do you mean, it wasn't?' asked Antony.

'My men made some enquiries.' By 'my men', Antony knew she meant the thugs who had once adhered to her late husband Clodius, and by 'enquiries' he knew she meant threats, bribes and physical violence.

'And?'

'It was Octavianus' friend, Agrippa.'

'The violent one,' said Antony, nodding. Marcus Vipsanius Agrippa had been a companion of Octavian since childhood and was known to be absolutely devoted to his friend. 'That makes sense. Shame. I quite like him. What shall we do?'

'Nothing. We are safe. We have gone through the staff and the bodyguard, got rid of any who could be bribed or blackmailed, and raised the pay of the rest. Octavianus' position is weakened in the eyes of the masses.'

'Still,' said Antony, 'I don't like the way he is trying to turn the legions against me. When I was awarded the province of Macedonia, it came with six legions. I have sent one to Syria with Dolabella, and one is to remain in the province for security. I have recalled the other four, and three have just arrived in Brundisium, with one to follow. I fear Marcus Brutus' and Cassius' activities in the East, and Decimus Brutus looks like he will refuse to yield Cisalpine Gaul to me. War will break out again, I'm sure of it.

'But I have got word that Octavianus' agents are already among my legions, sowing disquiet and liberally promising bribes. I must go to them, I feel, and bring them back to Rome in person.'

'It is safe to do so?'

'Of course,' said Antony. 'They are loyal to me, despite that boy's best efforts. I just need to turn up, show them my face and liberally sprinkle some cash around.'

'Very well. May I come with you? A journey to the coast might be pleasant.'

'I think we are both due a relaxing break,' said Antony.

ante diem xiii Kalendas Novembres DCCX AUC (20 October 44 BC), Brundisium

The four centurions of the Martian Legion knelt before Antony, hands tied behind their backs, looking up at him with various expressions of anger, resentment and terror. Antony himself simmered with a white fury. He and Fulvia had taken a pleasant and leisurely carriage ride from Rome to the east coast port of Brundisium, looking forward to being received by the army with welcoming arms, especially when he announced their bonus.

Instead, he had been met by unrest, sedition and outright mutiny. When he had addressed the arrayed ranks of the legions, they had listened to his words attentively, but when he announced a donative of four hundred sestertii per man, they had booed and jeered. The centurions in the front ranks had shouted that Octavian had offered them two thousand each, and was going to avenge Caesar, unlike Antony. Disorder had broken out. Some of the centurions led their men off the parade ground in protest, and fights erupted between Antony loyalists and those who were only interested in who would pay the most.

The officers – the junior military tribunes and the senior centurions – remained steadfast, to Antony's relief. Through them, he was able to restore order, and before long the ringleaders of the insubordination were brought before him: a handful of junior centurions and other ranks.

Antony had considered a range of options, from complete clemency to a brutal decimation, in which one soldier in ten, selected by lot, was beaten to death by his comrades. But this had not been a full mutiny, just discontent and unrest, and Fulvia had persuaded him to make an example of a few, and pay the rest. Being feared or being loved, as Cicero had said. Was it really possible to be both?

A grim-faced legionary with drawn gladius stood behind each kneeling centurion. The executioners had been chosen for their unswerving loyalty to Antony, and he had been told they all believed these traitors deserved their fate. Antony agreed. They had broken their oaths of loyalty for pure greed.

Antony was seated on a dais erected for the execution, and Fulvia, who had insisted she also witness the punishment, was seated behind him. Antony said, in a loud voice that carried out across the ranks of legionaries assembled to witness the price of insurrection, 'Let all here understand the price of oath-breaking and mutiny. These men have rebelled against their rightful commander and against Rome, and are sentenced to death. But to the rest of you, my loyal comrades, I award the sum of two thousand sestertii.' It pained him that loyalty needed to be bought, but even Caesar had had to resort to bribing his men on occasion.

As the cheers of joy rang out across the ground, Antony nodded to the executioners. In unison, they thrust their gladii down, through the space behind the collar bone and into the chest, the killing stroke of the gladiator. The four victims gurgled and died. An arc of blood from a severed vessel shot through the air and splashed across Fulvia's face. She didn't flinch, but merely drew a silk cloth from a fold of her dress, and wiped herself clean.

Antony waited until the cheers had died down and the dead men had stopped twitching. Then he stood and cried out, 'Thus die all traitors! Now go and ready yourselves. We march to Rome.'

The legionaries cheered loudly again, and then their officers went about dismissing them. Antony took Fulvia's arm and retreated to his headquarters, feeling his anger dissipate, replaced with some satisfaction, but also a sensation of unease that he couldn't shake.

Chapter V

November DCCX AUC (November 44 BC), Italy

Of course, once it was clear that the loyalty of the legions was for sale, Pandora's box was open. Before Antony had even set off for Rome, Octavian had travelled to Campania, where the Seventh and Eighth legions were based, and where thousands of retired veterans lived in new colonies near the city of Capua. His purpose was ostensibly to view his father's colonies, but in fact his sole intent was to bribe the legionaries and veterans to join him. In an act of rank treason and illegality, he raised a private army of three thousand men and marched on Rome, occupying the Forum on the tenth day of the month of November.

Antony received news of the attempted coup as he was leading his legions from Brundisium to Rome. The journey would only take nine days at a forced march, but he was in no mood to test the limits of the dissatisfied troops unnecessarily, and so had ordered the standard military pace, which meant the journey would take double that time. When the courier arrived by horse relay with the messages about Octavian's actions, Antony was already halfway to Rome, though he wished he had departed Brundisium sooner – he had spent a few days mingling with the troops and assuring them of his love for them, his gratitude and appreciation for their loyalty, and his intentions to avenge Caesar.

His first reaction was outrage and disbelief. Was the boy mad? What did he expect would be the outcome? Further messages clarified the position. In speeches from the rostra facilitated by his pet tribune Canutius, Octavian had claimed to be defending Rome against Antony, and had petitioned the Senate to recognise his position. But the senators had been conspicuous by their absence, and as the days passed and Antony neared Rome, an ever-increasing number of deserters from Octavian's cause indicated that they had believed when they joined Octavian that they would be fighting against the Liberators, not against a lawful consul of Rome — their beloved Mark Antony, no less.

So when Antony arrived in Rome, it was to find that Octavian had already departed for Arretium with what remained of his army. With a delighted smugness, Antony called a meeting of the Senate for two days hence, the twenty-fourth day of November, with the intention of denouncing Octavian as an enemy of the state.

But the day before the Senate meeting, as Antony pored through papers in his study in his Rome residence, a nervous-looking messenger arrived with news from the legionary camps. The Martian Legion had declared for Octavian and removed themselves to the town of Alba Fucens, some fifty miles east of Rome. Antony spent a good hour swearing, shouting and breaking things before Fulvia calmed him down enough to talk to him. When he had recovered sufficiently, he sent messages cancelling the Senate meeting, and with a trusted bodyguard, small but tough and well-armed, set off on horseback at a gallop for Alba Fucens.

When he arrived, to his astonishment, the small town was closed to him. He leapt from his horse and strode to the thick wooden gates, hammering on them with both fists.

'Open up for your consul! For your general!' he roared. Legionaries appeared on the turrets and the ramparts above him. He pointed at one at random. 'You, get down here and get these gates open. Right now!'

The young lad he had indicated looked uncertain, but the scarred veteran beside him yelled down, 'Bugger off, Antonius, before you get a pilum up your arse.'

Antony gaped at the insult as the legionaries erupted into raucous laughter. Swallowing hard in an attempt to prevent fury from overcoming him, he shouted, 'Are none of you brave enough to parley with me? To discuss your grievances like reasonable men?'

'Parley with my cock,' shouted one legionary, and then another called down, 'Send us in Fulvia, and I'll show her my grievances.'

The legionaries were in fits of laughter now, and as Antony stared up at them in impotent rage, the missiles began: soft fruit at first, then faeces, human and animal. Antony was too agile to let any make contact, but he withdrew out of range as the first stones arced out. When one of the legionaries actually tossed a pilum in his direction — a soft throw clearly aimed to fall short, but an outrage nevertheless – he gave up and remounted his horse.

'I will not waste my time on these fools and traitors,' he growled to his guards. 'Come on, back to Rome.' He spurred his horse with unnecessary severity, startling it into a gallop.

ante diem iv Kalendas Decembres DCCX AUC (28 November 44 BC), Rome

As soon as he was back in Rome, Antony announced a Senate meeting for that evening. This was technically illegal, but he was in no mood for niceties. That afternoon, he called an emergency council of the only people whose loyalty to him were beyond doubt – Fulvia and his brothers. Over well-watered wine and a frugal meal, they discussed strategy and tactics.

Gaius and Lucius were of the firm opinion that Octavian should be declared an enemy of the state.

'Get the Senate to declare a *senatus consultum ultimum* to allow you to deal with him as you see fit. Let's see Cicero oppose that.' The Senate's ultimate decree was the device which Cicero had used to execute the Catiline conspirators without trial, among whom was the three brothers' own stepfather.

Fulvia was more cautious. 'Going all out for Octavianus could be risky,' she said. 'We don't know to what extent his agents have suborned the other legions. And even without his treachery, they still love him as Caesar's son.'

'He is no more Caesar's son than I am,' scoffed Gaius.

'That's not what the soldiers and the people believe. And what's more, they now consider Caesar a god, and Octavianus the son of a god.'

Antony emitted a wordless growl from clenched teeth.

'Why are we wasting our time with this nobody?' he asked. 'He has no official position, no military experience. The real threat is in the north. Decimus Brutus has a host of battle-hardened legions in Cisalpine Gaul. I must deal with him as a priority, and I must do it before Pansa and Hirtius become consuls and undermine me. After he is defeated, I can squash Octavianus like the irritating gnat he is.'

Fulvia sat back, her lips pressed together in a straight line. Antony knew she didn't agree with him, but for all he respected her opinion, she did not have his experience of war and strategy. Gaius and Lucius enthusiastically backed him.

'Declare Octavianus an enemy,' Lucius insisted. 'Cut him off from his support, deal with your other Senate business, then take your legions north.'

That evening Antony sat in his curule chair, the only presiding consul now that Dolabella had departed for the East, as the senators assembled. He was turning the words of his speech over in his mind when one of the freedmen who helped ensure the smooth running of Senate proceedings approached him with a note. Antony took it and scanned the contents quickly. It was from a loyal tribune of the Fourth Macedonica Legion, stating tersely and apologetically that the legion had just declared for Octavian and was marching to join him.

Antony let out a cry of rage, screwed up the note and tossed it to the ground. The hubbub of the senators' conversation stopped abruptly as they turned to him quizzically. He forced himself to smile, and stood to begin the meeting with the traditional prayers. Once the customary preliminaries were out of the way, he strode out between the benches of the senators to start his speech. They all looked at him expectantly, well aware that the conflict between him and Octavian had become an open breach, and waiting to see how he would respond.

Giving himself time to think, Antony began by proposing a vote of thanks to Lepidus. In Spain, Lepidus had successfully negotiated a treaty with Sextus Pompeius, Pompey's son. Lepidus was a crucial ally for Antony, and having the Senate honour him would help tie him to Antony's cause. But little persuasion was needed – everyone knew that this treaty was actually a significant achievement that would help ensure peace in at least one quarter of the Empire, and with a potentially highly dangerous foe. Antony didn't allow any speeches on the subject, worried that it might allow the debate to drift into areas he preferred to avoid, such as the civil war between Caesar and Pompey. Instead, he went straight for a vote on the proposal to grant a thanksgiving in Lepidus' honour, which passed easily.

Next, he addressed the allocation of provinces for the following year. Although the Senate had agreed to honour Caesar's plans, Antony had decided he was sufficiently dominant to push through his own nominations. Traditionally and legally, the provinces were to be assigned by lot, but Antony had made sure that key allies were rewarded, and had manipulated the results. Most importantly, Gaius was to become governor of Macedonia, a key province for its position near Italy and as a bulwark against incursions from the east, where Marcus Brutus and Cassius were currently skulking. Further, Sabinus, one of the senators who had tried to defend Caesar from the assassins, was rewarded with Africa, which would help shore up Antony's pro-Caesarian credentials and send a warning to the Liberators.

There was little opposition, except from Marcus Pupius Piso Frugi, whose family home Antony had acquired cheaply three years previously during the civil war. Antony let him speak for a short while for the sake of form, then cut him off and called for a vote. The motion again passed easily.

Finally, it was time to address the problem of Octavian. Antony looked around the ranks of the senators. Allies and opponents, friends and foes, moderates and extremists, all waited expectantly for his words, his decree.

'You are aware of the treacherous actions of the so-called son of Caesar, Octavianus. That he illegally hired an army. That he invaded Rome. That he occupied the Forum with armed men, threatening to take control of our Republic by force, like Sulla or Cinna. For this, he should be condemned. For this, a *senatus consultum ultimum* should be declared, as is tradition for such threats against our country. I should take an army against this rebel who wishes to be a new Spartacus, who is a threat to our homes and our families.

'But who is he, after all? A boy with no heritage – he is from equestrian stock, and his father was a new man, and we all know how much trouble they can be.' He gave a pointed look towards Cicero's empty seat, which elicited a chuckle from the senators – everyone knew how prickly Cicero was about his own background, and the fact that he was the first of his family to serve in the Senate.

'He is a youth with no military experience. Having a talented adoptive parent does not bestow the same talent on the newly named child. If that were the case, Romulus and Remus would have been able to catch a hare in their jaws.' More muted laughter.

'What's more, he is a young lad with no political position. Nor should he have one – since his extreme youth makes it illegal, regardless of the exceptions that have been made in the past. And even then, Pompeius was twice Octavianus' age when he was elevated to consul by Sulla.

'So, I ask you, why should I concern myself with this distraction? The year, and my consulship, is nearly at an end. I will lay it down, as the law requires, and commend the office to my successors, Pansa and Hirtius. I will leave to take up my province of Cisalpine Gaul, and I will put down any rebellion and disorder I find there.' They all knew he was talking about Decimus Brutus.

'And so I say to you, let the boy do as he will. He is no concern of mine, and he should be no concern of yours.'

He sat back down to a ripple of applause and general approval. There were many in the Senate who believed, at least partially, in Octavian's cause – his right to inherit Caesar's money and name – and there were equally many who thought he had overreached. But ultimately, few wanted an open conflict so close to home, and if Octavian was declared an enemy of the state, they knew Antony would have to take the field against him. For all their self-interests and their partisan positions, few of the senators wanted to see further civil war, with all its damage to their wealth and the threat to their lives if they chose the wrong side, or even sometimes if they picked the right one.

After the meeting was dismissed, Gaius and Lucius came up to their brother privately.

'What happened? Why did you go easy on Octavianus?'

Antony told them about the newest defection, and they both cursed.

'It's not important. I have the Larks on hand, and they are as loyal as hounds, and I have the rest of my legions in Ariminum. I'll deal with Decimus Brutus, then I'll come back and put the child in his place.'

He embraced each of his brothers earnestly, kissed them on each cheek.

'I leave tomorrow. These are dangerous times. I beg you, please look after yourselves. I love you both.'

They returned his affectionate gestures and the words of love, and he bid them farewell. It was the last time the three of them would ever be together again.

Antony returned straight home after the Senate meeting, thoughts and emotions churning.

He sat with Fulvia until late into the night, drinking wine and discussing his position with her earnestly. He believed his words to the Senate were largely true. Octavian was a distraction, with Decimus being the much bigger threat. But he had an uneasy feeling about the boy. Octavian had surprised him once too often already. For all his youth, inexperience and physical frailty, there was something about him that made him hard to ignore; Antony had to concede that. If nothing else, his position as Caesar's heir made him a useful ally to any who wanted the support of the legions and the Caesarian supporters.

'Don't forget Cicero,' warned Fulvia, as Antony ruminated on his multiple enemies – Octavian, Decimus Brutus, Marcus Brutus and Cassius. 'Since that speech of his, and your reply, I think the rift between you has become impossible to bridge. But for all that you and I might dislike him, he still holds more respect than perhaps anyone in Rome. He may not want, or be able to take, power for himself, but he could certainly bestow it on another, and an alliance between Octavianus and Cicero might be formidable.'

Antony nodded.

'How can I keep track of these shifting alliances? I try to ensure peace between the factions after Caesar's assassination, then Octavianus comes in and stirs up the pro-Caesarians, demanding vengeance. He forces my hand so I have to declare against the assassins sooner than I might have wished, and he opposes me and turns my own men against me with money he doesn't have and lies that I am doing nothing to avenge Caesar. And now you warn me that he might ally with Cicero. Cicero? The man who rejoiced at Caesar's death allying with the boy who claims to wish to bring his assassins to justice? My head is spinning.'

'It's a good job you have me, then,' said Fulvia, smiling.

'But I won't, will I? Not after tonight – not by my side. You can only send letters, which might be intercepted and read.'

'But I will be here in Rome, protecting your interests, while you go and do what you do best. Make war.'

He leaned in and kissed her, letting one hand stray to her breast. 'Is that really what I do best?' he teased. She giggled and pushed him away.

'Be serious, Marcus. Now Caesar is dead, Rome has no general who is your equal on the battlefield. Your men know it, your allies know it, your enemies know it. You will prevail.'

'But I fear for you, Fulvia. Gaius is departing for his province soon. If something should happen to me...'

'Hush, Marcus. We aren't living in barbarian lands, or in the time of the kings. There is no honour in taking a woman's life, whatever her husband might have done.'

'But there are other punishments a vengeful Cicero or Brutus might inflict. They might confiscate all your property, throw you onto the streets. They might even have you stripped in public and whipped if they think you have been complicit in whatever crimes they trump against me. No, I will write to Atticus.'

'Atticus? Why?'

'Because he is a close friend of Cicero, because he is an honourable man, and because the world knows he has remained strictly neutral in every political and civil struggle in recent decades. He is rich enough to have a seat on the front rank of the Senate, his pick of offices and provincial postings. And yet he remains safely below it all, holding on to his equestrian status like a soldier grips his shield.'

'Fine,' said Fulvia. 'If it makes you feel better, write to Atticus, though I am not as defenceless as you make out. I have my own followers in Rome. It's just that they are rather less reputable than yours.'

Antony puffed out his cheeks and exhaled, relieved that Fulvia would be in at least a somewhat safer position. Besides, she had already outlived two politically active, populist husbands. He had a strong suspicion she would survive him, too.

'Happy now?' she asked.

Antony nodded. 'As much as I can be in the circumstances.'

'Good. Now, the hour is late. I am going to bed.' She stood up and walked to the door, then turned, and with an inviting smile, said, 'Coming?'

ante diem iii Kalendas Decembres DCCX AUC (29 November 44 BC), Tibur

The Fifth Gallic Legion had been raised by Caesar in Transalpine Gaul eight years previously to fight Vercingetorix's rebellion, and was the first legion levied entirely from non-citizens. It saw its first action in the brutal siege of Alesia, in which arena they had forged a close mutual respect with Antony. They subsequently saw battle in Dyrrhachium and in the battle of Thapsus against Cato, where they fought with such bravery against the enemy elephants that Caesar awarded them an elephant as their emblem, the only one of Caesar's legions not to bear a bull on their standards.

But it was the larks' wings that they sported on their helmets, a Gallic custom, that gave them their nickname of 'Alaudae' or the Larks. The legion was one of many that were retired after the Gallic wars, and the veterans settled in Italy, but Antony had reformed them, and the bored soldiers, many of whom had already burnt through their pensions, had eagerly answered his call. They were now arrayed in full ceremonial uniform outside their camp near the town of Tibur, the location of Antony's country villa, and perhaps more importantly, the site of a celebrated sanctuary of Hercules Victor, Antony's demigod ancestor.

Assembled before them was a host of senators and equestrians. Antony had made it known that he expected their presence, and was pleased to see that the majority of the Senate and the second rank of nobles, the equestrians, had chosen, through love, fear or pragmatism, to attend. Of course there were many notable absences: both Bruti and Cassius, obviously, as well as Cicero and Lucius Calpurnius Piso, and – annoyingly – Antony's uncles, Lucius Julius Caesar – who appeared to be wavering in his stance towards his three nephews – and Gaius Antonius Hybrida, who probably could not be bothered to attend.

Antony mounted a dais before the Larks and raised his arms for silence. The soldiers hushed instantly. A crow flew overhead, cawed twice, then circled back on itself. Antony pointed it out.

'A sign from the gods, blessing our venture. So speaks an augur of Rome.'

The soldiers and senators cheered respectfully. In fact, Antony had no idea what future the crow foretold, but he was fairly sure all the other augurs were simply guessing, too, or – more likely – manipulating the interpretations in their own interests, just as he did.

'Comrades, we have marched together, side by side. We have fought the enemies of Rome, both foreign and domestic. We have faced hardship and danger in Gaul and Greece. And though I was not with you, all Rome knows of your valour against Scipio's elephants, when you fought with our beloved Caesar in Africa. Tales are still told of how you faced down the charge of these fearsome beasts, that can crush a man beneath one foot. How you stabbed up at their eyes and their groins, how you blew your trumpets, until the elephants turned tail and ran back into their own lines. And this is why you bear the elephant on your standards and shields now.

'I could not wish for hardier, braver and more faithful soldiers at my back when I lead you into battle. Soon we march for Ariminum, to collect my other legions, the loyal men I brought over from Macedonia and the new recruits I have raised. Then we head north to take control of Cisalpine Gaul, currently held illegally by the faithless assassin Decimus Brutus. The man whom Caesar loved, whom he named as heir in the second degree. Who plotted his death, and held me outside the Senate so I could not intervene while the murderers plunged their blades into our general.

'When we reach Ariminum, I will have three legions following my standard, with more on their way. But who needs so many legions? Caesar had only one legion with him when he crossed the Rubicon. And I, too, only need one, as long as that legion is the mighty Alaudae!'

The legionaries broke out into spontaneous and wild applause. The clash as they banged their spears on their shields and the unrestrained cheers were deafening. Antony let the adulation peak, held it for a moment, then when he judged it was about to fade he made a sign for silence again. The soldiers reluctantly settled down.

'And now, I will administer the military oath. Repeat after me:

"'I swear that I shall faithfully execute all that the consul commands, that I shall never desert the service, and that I shall not seek to avoid death for the Roman republic!'"

The soldiers, in a reasonably co-ordinated unanimity, cried out the oath enthusiastically, and then Antony descended from his dais to walk among them, shaking hands with officers and legionaries alike, receiving so many embraces and claps on the back that he soon felt thoroughly bruised, despite his curaiss. When he had mingled for a long while, he remounted his dais, and turned to the assembled senators and equestrians.

'And now, Conscript Fathers and noble men of Rome,' he said, 'I will take your oaths, too.'

The elites of the city glanced at one another uncertainly. They had not been warned of this. But they stood there, clad only in togas, before five thousand heavily armed and armoured soldiers who were thoroughly fired up.

'Raise your right hands,' Antony said, 'and swear by all the gods that you pledge your loyalty to the people and Republic of Rome, and to the person of Marcus Antonius, consul, augur and proconsul.'

The assembled nobles did as they were told, though with considerably less enthusiasm than the soldiers. Antony knew what their oaths were worth. After all, they had sworn to protect the person of Caesar with their very lives not long before they participated in, or stood by and watched, his murder. Still, it strengthened his position to have their sacred vow of loyalty, since to turn against him would mark them once again as oath-breakers.

'I leave you now, nobles and Conscript Fathers, to take up the position of Governor of Cisalpine Gaul with which you entrusted me. I entreat you now, to take good care of the city I leave, under the undoubtedly competent hands of its consuls for next year, Aulus Hirtius and Gaius Vibius Pansa Caetronianus. Farewell.'

Hirtius and Pansa were the consuls nominated by Caesar for the following year, and Antony had seen no reason to change the dictator's wishes on this matter. Hirtius was a strong supporter of Caesar, having crossed the Rubicon with him, and had even added a final chapter to Caesar's *Civil War*, documenting his time in Alexandria. Antony counted him as an ally. He was a little less certain of Pansa, who had always been friendly to Antony, but was getting closer to Octavian in recent months, according to Fulvia. Nevertheless, Pansa was a moderate who wanted peace, and he was married to the daughter of Quintus Fufius Calenus, who was one of Antony's trusted friends.

Antony walked to the horse his groom held for him, leapt smoothly into the saddle, and began the journey north. He was just as uncertain about what lay behind him in the Rome he was leaving as what lay before him in the Gaul he was approaching. But the enthusiastic Larks marching behind him, already singing the old ribald songs about Caesar being the Queen of Bithynia, and some new ones about Antony and Cytheris, gave him confidence. With his own ability on the field, and men like that behind him, what could go wrong?

Chapter VI

Januaris DCCXI AUC (January 43 BC), Cisalpine Gaul

Things started to go wrong almost immediately, and then got worse. Antony had just crossed the Rubicon in a northward direction, and had sent an order to Decimus Brutus to vacate the province, when a pamphlet reached him containing the text of a speech by Cicero. The accompanying letter from Fulvia informed him that the speech had not been delivered orally, but was written as if it addressed Antony personally in a Senate meeting. Fulvia told him that Cicero was referring to this and his previous attack on Antony as 'Philippics', after the famous speeches given by Cicero's hero, the Greek orator Demosthenes, against Alexander's father Philip. If the first Philippic had been infuriating in its imputations and insinuations, this one was a staggering and vicious personal attack on Antony. Cicero began by praising his own career, then refuted Antony's accusation of being behind Caesar's assassination, saying that if it had been up to him, he would have ended not just one act but the whole play, which everyone took to mean he would have finished Antony off at the same time as Caesar. Then he savaged Antony's entire life, and those of all his friends and family: his father's insolvency; his friendships with Curio and Clodius; his tribunate. He even accused Antony of starting the civil war between Caesar and Pompey. He spoke of the time Antony vomited in public, his purchase of Pompey's house, and even brought up the time he had played a trick on Fulvia by surprising her dressed as a slave, while bringing her a love letter, something Cicero found particularly scandalous. He mentioned the time Antony toured Italy with Cytheris, professing as much outrage that Antony had legitimised her by using her real name of Volumnia, rather than her stage name, as that his mother was at the back of the procession His quarrel with Dolabella and offering the crown to Caesar at the Lupercalia were picked over, followed by accusations of forging Caesar's papers and a generally drunken and debauched lifestyle.

It was a masterful attack, because it was largely based on truth. Even Antony could not deny that. But Cicero had put the worst possible interpretation on almost every important event in Antony's life. Blatant lies were easy to counter, half-truths much harder. And the nature of the assault, the breathtakingly personal nature of the insults! Not just his abilities as a leader, nor charges of corruption, but a denigration of every aspect of his life and of those close to him.

His eyes were drawn to one line that Fulvia had underlined:

In truth, that wife of yours, who is not in the least avaricious, and whom I mention without intending any slight to her, has been too long owing her third payment to the state.

Third payment? He was hoping for her to be widowed a third time!

Antony closed his eyes and breathed heavily through flared nostrils. He did not rage, or shout, break plates or smash his head against a wall. A cold fury gripped him. This was a declaration of war. And though Cicero intended to take to the battleground of the Senate floor armed with words, Antony would use his own preferred weapons – swords and spears. First, he would take the province from Decimus Brutus, and if necessary smash his outnumbered legions in the field. Then he would return triumphant to Rome for a reckoning with Cicero, and at the same time put the young upstart who called himself Caesar in his place.

But Decimus Brutus had other ideas. He sent letters to Antony and to the Senate stating that he would not surrender his province, and that he would defend the liberty of Rome, and keep his army and his province, as was the will of the Senate. Then he slaughtered all his pack animals and smoked the meat in preparation for a siege, and retreated behind the walls of the city of Mutina, the chief city of Cisalpine Gaul, situated on a strategically important crossroads on the Via Aemilia that led from Ariminum to Placentia.

Antony invested the city, and set about building siege equipment and artillery. He was well versed in the art of siege warfare, as besieger, besieged, or in the case of Alesia, both. But he knew that to reduce a well-defended walled city took time – time in which the political situation in Rome could shift decisively against him.

He sent his youngest brother Lucius, who had brought up the delayed legion from Macedonia, to crush opposition in the surrounding territories, as well as to gather supplies and recruit further men, and he was pleased to see Lucius showed some talent for warfare, probably more than the middle brother, Gaius. Antony himself was furiously active, supervising the construction of the walls that ringed Mutina, preventing any movement to or from the city. He worked the new recruits ceaselessly to build up their fitness, fighting skills and discipline. He ran the legions through drill after drill, and took part in much of the training himself. When he wasn't dealing with administrative affairs of supplies and manpower, he was writing letters to influential senators and equestrians as well as foreign kings and rulers whom he might need to call upon for money and aid. And when it came time to rest, he relaxed with the off-duty legionaries, dining, drinking and dicing with them, swapping war stories with the veterans and entertaining the recruits with tales of heroism, and anecdotes about Caesar.

In January, letters arrived from Fulvia and others with more news from Rome. Towards the end of December, Cicero had made two more speeches, one to the Senate and one to the people, denouncing Antony as a Catilina and a Spartacus, and carrying a motion that when the new consuls took office they must consider the governorship of Gaul. At that moment, Fulvia told him, with Dolabella and Antony absent from Rome, and the new consuls not yet in power, Cicero was being widely recognised as the de facto ruler of Rome. How that peacock must be revelling in his renewed relevance, Antony thought with disgust.

On the Kalends of January, the new consuls Aulus Hirtius and Gaius Vibius Pansa took office and, according to a letter from Fulvia, instead of immediately giving the floor to Antony's opponents, Pansa had let his father-in-law Calenus – one of Antony's strongest supporters in the Senate – speak first. Preventing the debate moving immediately to stripping Antony of his proconsulship, he proposed that negotiators be sent to Antony and Brutus. Others spoke in favour of this proposal before Cicero was allowed his turn. He delivered another vicious attack on Antony, and stated that no negotiators should be sent unless Antony laid down his arms. He proposed, too, that all the laws of both Dolabella and Antony since they took office should be abolished. Then he went further, demanding the *senatus consultum ultimum* be declared against Antony. Next he moved on to praising Decimus Brutus, as well as

Lepidus, a clear tactic to try to split one of Antony's key allies from his cause. But his strongest adulation was reserved for Octavian.

'What god was it, who gave to the Roman people this godlike young man?' he asked, and after comparing him to a young Pompey, proposed he be given a seat in the Senate and propraetorial imperium, despite his young age.

Fulvia's letter continued:

> *The debate lasted three days. Calenus was strong on your behalf, and Pansa agreed with him on the need for negotiations. Calpurnius Piso said that no action should be taken against a consul such as yourself without proper legal proceedings. But it looked like you might yet be declared an enemy of the state. Each night of the debate, your mother and I dressed in mourning clothes and, with little Antyllus in my arms, went to the house of every undecided senator we had time to visit. Every morning, we stood outside the Senate house and on our knees we wailed our grief and lamentations at your treatment.*
>
> *Whether it was our actions that made the difference, I cannot say. But in the end, the Senate did indeed vote for negotiators to be sent. Calpurnius Piso and Lucius Marcius Philippus have been chosen, as well as Servius Sulpicius Rufus, despite his pleas to be excused due to age and ill health.*
>
> *Handle them respectfully, I beg you, Antony. Even now, Pansa and Hirtius are raising new legions, and it is said that Octavianus has five legions under his banner now, including the two Macedonian veteran legions, and he intends to use them in support of the Senate against you. My sources tell me that he has even been corresponding with Decimus Brutus in order to co-ordinate attacks against you.*
>
> *Have a care, my darling Marcus. Come back to me and to your son safely.*
>
> *Your loving Fulvia.*

Antony read the letter twice, then summoned Lucius and had him read it through, too. Lucius had a tendency to violent outbursts that exceeded even Antony's. In his younger days when travelling in the East, he had fought as a Murmillo gladiator for his amusement and, transported by battle rage, had killed one of his friends in combat in the arena, a stick Cicero didn't fail to use to beat him with. Lucius bitterly regretted the event, but Antony worried about his judgement and self-control, for all he valued his brother's loyalty and military ability.

Still, at this moment, he was Antony's closest confidant. Antony asked for Lucius' opinion on Fulvia's letter.

'Screw them all,' he said. 'They can say what they like. With your generalship and our legions, we have the ability and the strategic position to withstand whatever they throw at us.'

Antony sighed. Much as his natural inclination was to agree with Lucius, his vastly greater experience in political and military matters told him that things were not so simple. Loyalties could shift. The morale of the men could drop in prolonged sieges, with desertions common and mutinies not unheard of. And though he had no high opinion of the ability of Octavian or either consul to lead an army, numbers would tell in the end. Unless you were Caesar, who had a knack of winning when outnumbered. And Antony had to concede, though he was good – maybe very good – he wasn't Caesar.

'How many legions can they muster?' Antony asked, knowing the answer, but wanting Lucius to consider it.

'Decimus Brutus has three. Octavianus has five. I suppose the consuls might bring five or six more if it comes to it.'

'Fourteen legions. And what do we have?'

'The Larks, the Second, the Thirty-Fifth, the legion from Macedonia, and a lot of Moorish cavalry. But we can call on Plancus' and Lepidus' legions in Transalpine Gaul and Spain. And Publius Ventidius is currently recruiting three more.'

Publius Ventidius was a former mule driver who come to Caesar's notice, and been rapidly promoted. Now he was a general of some skill and influence.

'No,' said Antony. 'Even if we can rely on Plancus and Lepidus, and I hope we can, their men are not here. It doesn't matter how many legions you claim to have following you. The only ones that count are the ones present on the day of the battle.'

'So what are you saying? We should negotiate? Surrender?'

Antony rubbed his hand over his eyes. He was very tired. But the thrill at being once more in command of soldiers in war sustained him.

'We will listen to what the delegation has to say. But I have no hope they will offer anything to our advantage. It will come to a fight, I'm sure of it.'

'Then why so gloomy about our chances?'

'Not gloomy. I just need you to understand our position. When the odds are not in your favour, it is necessary to use skill to shift them. And politics will still have a role. It's unfortunate the mood in the Senate has shifted against us.'

'We still have many supporters there, Marcus. Quintus Fufius Calenus is a rock. Lucius Varius Cotyla is bravely outspoken on your behalf. And there are many other allies around the Empire – Plancus, Lepidus, Dolabella, Gaius.'

'Nevertheless, victory is far from certain, brother.'

Lucius put a hand on Antony's shoulder. 'You know I believe in you, brother. I don't doubt that we will prevail. Now, away with these doubts. When was the last time you got properly drunk?'

Lucius called for wine, and when it promptly arrived, he proposed a series of toasts, to Fortuna, to Caesar's shade, and to the resolute Fulvia and Julia. By the time Antony had drained cups to each of these, he was feeling much better.

Januaris DCCXI AUC (January 43 BC), Mutina

The legionaries heaved on the levers tensioning the catapult. They perspired with the effort despite the cool winter air. Once the arm was forced back to its full extent, it was loosed. There was a swoosh as the arm shot forward, then a thwack as it hit the padded buffer. The heavy stone in the sling at the end of the arm arced through the air, and smashed into the city wall with a crash audible several hundred yards away. The nearest legionaries let out a ragged cheer. Antony peered through the early morning mist to assess the damage. A chunk of masonry had been dislodged high up on the thick wall, but there was no sign of a breach.

'Good shooting, boys,' he said, clapping the artillery men on the backs. 'Keep at it.'

Antony had directed his bolt- and stone-throwers – the ballistae and catapults – to concentrate on a small section of wall, hoping to make a breakthrough and take the city before Octavian and the new consuls had organised themselves enough to march north against him. He had no desire to fight another Alesia, besieged from within and without. But though his engineers were busy building more siege weapons, so far he was having little effect on the city's formidable defences. Mutina had been besieged during Hannibal's invasion of Italy, sacked fifty years later by the Ligurians, and besieged again by Pompey in the aftermath of Sulla's death. As a consequence of its traumatic past, the city had spent a lot of time and money building thick walls and defensive towers, and it was no easy matter to reduce them. Further, the unusually severe winter was hampering Antony's efforts, with frequent squalls of snow and sleet, equipment icing over, and winter sickness laying swathes of his men low.

As was often the case with sieges, time might well be the decisive factor. Could Decimus Brutus' supplies hold out long enough for relief from Rome to arrive? Neither side could be certain, and so Antony pressed his siege engineers to maximise their efforts to allow him to force a battle before Octavian and the Senatorial forces could arrive.

One factor that had bought him time was the senatorial decision to send him a delegation, and hold from moving against him until negotiations had been concluded. And that day, as Antony watched the legionaries manhandling a heavy rock into the catapult's sling and begin once again to work the tension levers, an orderly rushed up to him with news that the embassy had arrived. He gave orders that they should be accommodated and made comfortable, then turned his attention back to the work of the catapult. He was in no hurry to meet them. He was the proconsul, and though his position was being challenged by the consuls, by Cicero and by Octavian, he was still the foremost power in Rome. No one could claim to rule Rome until they had dealt with him. By contrast, the senatorial ambassadors were supplicants, and as such they could wait on his pleasure.

The sun had passed its zenith when Antony deigned to grace his visitors with his presence. They had been waiting for him in a luxurious tent, supplied with every courtesy – food, wine, reading and writing materials – and when he entered they showed no sign of the impatience they must have been feeling. Instead, the two ambassadors, Lucius Calpurnius Piso and Lucius Marcius Philippus, stood, smiling, and bowed their heads in greeting.

'My honoured colleagues,' said Antony, holding his arms wide and embracing them in turn. He had to concede the Senate had demonstrated sound diplomacy in their choice of envoys. Calpurnius Piso, Caesar's father-in-law, had been of great help to Antony in the immediate aftermath of the Ides of March, and had spoken against Cicero's proposal to declare him an enemy of the state. But he had also given a harsh speech in the Senate opposing some of Antony's actions as consul, which had been strongly approved by Cicero and others of the Liberator-supporting optimates. Lucius Marcius Philippus was Octavian's stepfather, having married his mother – Caesar's niece Atia – after Octavian's father died. Although tied by marriage to Caesar, he had managed to stay neutral during the civil war. When Octavian had returned to Italy after the reading of Caesar's will, both Atia and Philippus had urged restraint, worried that his life would be endangered if he pressed his claims too forcefully. Antony wished fervently that Octavian had taken their advice – his life would have been so much simpler in that case.

The third delegate, Servius Sulpicius Rufus, was notable by his absence. His sympathies had been with Pompey during the civil war, but he had a reputation for being a highly respected jurist, honest and dedicated to upholding the law. Antony had never had any cause for complaint against this venerable old former consul and had been pleased to see his name on the list of ambassadors.

'You are one short, I think,' said Antony, smiling. 'Old Rufus is using the toilet, perhaps? Or taking a nap after his long journey?'

Piso and Philippus exchanged grave looks. Piso spoke in a solemn tone. 'I regret to report that Servius Sulpicius Rufus died this morning.'

Antony's face fell. His first thought was of sadness at the old man's passing, followed immediately by concerns as to what his loss would mean for the embassy.

'His health was very poor,' said Philippus. 'But he bravely took on this task knowing it could make an ending of him.'

'I will order a fine sacrifice to his departed spirit later,' said Antony. 'But first, we should get to business. Please, sit, and tell me what message you bring from the Senate.'

Philippus and Piso settled themselves in the chairs Antony indicated, and he sat opposite them, leaning forward expectantly.

Philippus sat back and folded his arms, and Piso gave him an irritated glance, obviously realising that Philippus had no intention of being the one to give Antony the Senate's ultimatum.

Piso cleared his throat, and recited from memory. 'Marcus Antonius, the Senate has reallocated the provinces. You are to be given Macedonia instead of Cisalpine Gaul for this year. The Senate therefore orders that you withdraw your men back across the Rubicon into Italy, but that you remain at least two hundred miles from Rome. There, you will await the deliberations of the Senate and the people of Rome, who will decide your fate, and you will submit yourself to their will.'

Antony had known in advance the terms of the Senate's demands, but to hear them laid out before him so starkly sent a cold anger through his veins. They did not even address him as 'proconsul'. Holding himself still, face expressionless, he said, 'You respectable men, who are honest brokers in this matter, do you really think this is an acceptable or equitable proposal? Is it just? I, Marcus Antonius, last year's consul, voted by the Senate to proconsulship of Cisalpine Gaul, must surrender it to the assassin Decimus Brutus, who has refused to relinquish his command when the Senate previously demanded it?'

Piso looked to Philippus, who opened his mouth to speak but could find no words.

'What of the boy, Octavianus?' continued Antony. 'He raises an illegal private army, he invades Rome. He induces mutiny in consular legions. And the Senate rewards him with a seat and propraetorial powers and votes bonuses to his legions? What madness is this?'

'I... We...' stuttered Piso.

'But why should I be surprised? The Senate has countermanded the *lex de provinciis consularibis* that allocates the province of Syria to Dolabella and Cisalpine Gaul to me, an act which they have no legal power to do. I wish that Sulpicius Rufus was here – he was an honest man, who would agree that the Senate's actions are illegal.'

'The Senate has the power to annul such a law by the process of *abrogatio*,' said Piso hesitantly.

'But it didn't, did it?' said Antony. 'And therefore its ruling is null and void.'

Piso and Philippus exchanged glances, but neither responded.

'How do you upstanding men find yourselves on the side of Cicero in this disagreement?' asked Antony. 'He rejoiced in Caesar's death.

Caesar, your son-in-law, Piso. Your wife's uncle, Philippus. This man, who claims to love liberty and the Republic, seems to be prepared to resort to any illegality to uphold the Republic's laws.'

Both of the delegates looked thoroughly unhappy now. Antony sat back and let the moment stretch, enjoying their discomfort.

'I understand the Senate has concerns,' he said after a while. 'And unlike my opponents, I am not unreasonable. I am prepared to surrender my rightful province of Cisalpine Gaul, but not for Macedonia. I will swap my province with Plancus, and take Transalpine Gaul. Further, I will retain my armies for a minimum period of five years. All my Acts are to remain valid. My legions will receive the same bonuses that the Senate voted to Octavianus' legions. And further, I will not vacate Transalpine Gaul until, if Marcus Brutus and Cassius Longinus are elected consuls two years hence, they have departed for their own allotted provinces.'

Philippus gaped at this list of demands.

'Marcus Antonius,' said Piso, voice strained. 'You cannot be serious. The Senate will never agree to this.'

Antony sat back and folded his arms, saying nothing.

'This is your answer?' asked Piso. 'It can mean nothing other than war.'

'Then I suggest you are persuasive on my behalf. But don't for a moment believe that I fear Octavianus or the new consuls. None of them has the slightest idea how to fight. Conflict will lead only to more Roman death and destruction of property, more misery, more expense. Cicero has set his heart against me, but the rest of the Senate need not follow that bitter old man.'

Philippus and Piso had no reply. After all, Antony was right. By the letter and spirit of the law, the Senate was acting both illegally and unfairly.

'I have military matters to attend to,' said Antony, standing. 'It is a pleasure to see you both, but I must leave you. It looks like there will be more snow this afternoon, so I suggest you make use of my hospitality tonight, and begin your journey to take my reply back to Rome in the morning.'

'We have messages from the Senate to take to Marcus Junius Brutus,' said the ambassadors.

'I'm afraid that will not be possible,' said Antony. 'Farewell.'

He left the two former consuls sitting with shoulders slumped, looking like a pair of slowly emptying pricked wine skins.

ante diem xviii Kalendas Maias DCCXI AUC (14 April 43 BC), Forum Gallorum

Antony advanced slowly down the Via Aemilia, seated on his bay gelding. Behind came his Moorish and Gallic auxiliary cavalry, armed with javelins and mounted on small, fast horses. Accompanying them were further lightly armed auxiliary foot soldiers – mainly spearmen and slingers. Somewhere ahead of them were the legions of the consul Gaius Vibius Pansa. It began to hail, and the little ice stones rattled as they bounced off helmets and shields.

Events had moved quickly since Antony had dismissed the senatorial embassy. Unsurprisingly, the Senate had rejected Antony's counterproposal out of hand. They passed the *senatus consultum ultimum* against him, though his uncle Lucius Caesar prevented them from declaring outright war. Antony was ordered to lay down his arms by the Ides of March, and all of Antony's Acts were repealed, although those the Senate liked were reinstated by Pansa.

In February, Octavian and Pansa advanced up the Via Aemilia, camping at Forum Cornelii and Claterna respectively.

Then terrible news arrived from the East. Marcus Brutus had raised an army and taken Antony's brother Gaius captive. Cicero, of course, was jubilant, and sent messages to Brutus exhorting him to have Gaius executed. Lucius took the news particularly badly, and Antony tried to reassure him that Brutus was an honourable man and would not treat a prisoner ill. Cassius, too, was active in the East, raising a vast army and taking control of Syria.

Dolabella, however, retained control of Asia, and when he took the city of Smyrna, he captured Antony's old friend and comrade Trebonius – the same man who, with Decimus Brutus, had prevented Antony from being at Caesar's side in the Senate on the Ides of March. Not content with simply holding Trebonius prisoner – or even giving him a clean execution, as befitted a Roman noble – Dolabella had chosen to torture Trebonius for two days with whips and brands, ostensibly to interrogate him about embezzlement of public money. He had then had Trebonius beheaded, and had the head paraded on the end of a spear, while his body was dragged through the streets before being dumped in the sea. Antony had always known Dolabella capable of cruelty, but these acts sickened even him, who had seen unimaginable butchery in battle. He mourned for his former friend, and feared for what Dolabella's actions might mean for himself and for his captive brother.

Cicero, of course, leapt on Dolabella's deed with savage delight. He delivered the eleventh of his Philippics at the end of February, describing Trebonius' demise, and painting Antony to be as foul and barbarous as Dolabella. Much as Antony wished to distance himself from the unpleasant little man, he could not afford to alienate such an important ally. But Dolabella was declared an enemy of the state, regardless, and Cassius took his army and marched against him.

In March it was proposed to send another embassy to Antony that included Cicero, but Cicero refused to go, and the idea was dropped. Lepidus and Plancus in Narbonese and Transalpine Gaul respectively wrote to the Senate urging peace, but were ignored. Antony himself wrote a final, long letter to the Senate urging compromise. Cicero brutally dismembered it line by line in his thirteenth Philippic. Negotiations were over. The Senate prepared for war, and Hirtius and Octavianus marched on Gaul with Pansa following on behind.

Antony knew that he would be in a dangerous position if Hirtius and Octavian linked up their forces with Pansa. His initial plan had been to force a battle with Hirtius and Octavian before Pansa could arrive. Then he got word that Pansa was advancing up the Via Aemilia with four legions. But Pansa's legions were new untested recruits, and he had almost no cavalry. If Antony could rout them with minimal loss to his own forces before the other Senatorial legions arrived, he could greatly improve his position. So he left Lucius and the Larks to both maintain the siege of Mutina and to stage some feints against the legionary camp of Aulus Hirtius, and he led the rest of his forces, which included the Second and Thirty-Fifth legions, two Praetorian cohorts and his auxiliary infantry and cavalry, down the Via Aemilia. It was in his bones and blood to confront danger head-on. While Caesar might have had a more subtle and strategic approach to war, Antony tended to boldness. But Caesar could be bold when the situation demanded it, and Antony was capable of subtlety.

So as he advanced slowly on Pansa's legions, his mind ran over and over the plan he had conceived in talks with Lucius and his senior commanders.

Antony had carefully chosen the site for this first major confrontation between his men and the Senatorial forces. The village of Forum Gallorum was situated on a section of the Via Aemilia where the road, which ran roughly north-west to south-east, narrowed, flanked on either side by marshes covered in dense reed beds. It was here, in the stinking bogs, concealed by the tall vegetation, that his veteran legions waited. The role of the cavalry at this stage was simply to draw the fresh, green recruits of Pansa's legions into the jaws of his trap.

He heard the clatter of hooves on cobbles, and moments later two of his scouts came galloping down the road. They drew up their horses before Antony, saluted, and without preamble reported, 'Enemy sighted, Proconsul.'

'Excellent. How far?'

'About two miles, just leaving their camp.'

'Good, good. We will be in contact with them soon. Dismissed.'

'Proconsul,' said the scout, and his tone made Antony pause, the wiry hairs on the backs of his arms standing up.

'What is it?'

'They were carrying the standards of the Martian Legion.'

Gods of Olympus, thought Antony. Hirtius must have donated one of his veteran legions to reinforce Pansa. He had not given the sickly old consul enough credit. He had predicted that Antony might try to intercept Pansa's inexperienced and poorly trained force, and had stiffened its backbone with five thousand grizzled and scarred old hands. Not only that, the legion he had chosen was the one whose centurions Antony had executed for insurrection, and who had then defected to Octavian.

Antony barked out orders to his cavalry commander to advance, but break off at first contact and draw Pansa's legions to the ambush site. Then he rode back to where his men were concealed. The road was on an elevated causeway through the marshes, and he could see the occasional glint of a helmet or the point of a spear on either side of the road. From horseback, he called out to the hidden legionaries that they would soon be facing the traitors of the Martian Legion, the oath-breakers who had betrayed their general and their comrades. Shouts of anger and outrage came back to him from the reed beds.

'I have no doubts you will show those back-stabbers how true, loyal Roman legions fight!'

Cheers broke out from both sides of the road.

'Mars will show us which legions he truly favours,' said Antony. 'But from now on, silence, and let Fortuna favour us this day.'

He dismounted and handed his horse off to a groom, then joined his elite Praetorian cohorts who waited beside the road a little west of the village. There he gave them a similar speech, and received a similarly angry response. This time, he could look into their eyes, and see the desire for revenge against those they considered to have betrayed not only Antony and Rome, but – more importantly – Caesar's memory. Then he formed them up in a line across the road, took position immediately behind the first rank, and waited.

The sun was hidden behind a thick cover of grey, and the morning brightened to give a flat, dull light to the landscape. The wind whipped around the elevated causeway, and the susurration of the reeds and the flapping of the flags on the standards was the only noise.

Then came the sound of horses at a canter, and soon after, Antony's cavalry came into view, withdrawing in good order. The Praetorian cohorts opened their line for the cavalry to pass through, then closed up again, interlocking their tall, curved shields. Within moments, the front rank of Pansa's forces appeared. It was the Martian Legion. If the raw recruits were with them, they must have been well to the rear, since they were nowhere in sight.

The Martian legionaries came on at a fast march, and Antony murmured to his men to hold their line. The front ranks entered the trap, where Antony's Second and Thirty-Fifth waited, hidden. Then, with a blast on a bugle and shouted orders, the legion halted. One of the leading centurions was peering into the marsh and pointing something out to an officer.

Antony held his breath. The bulk of the enemy legion had still not entered the trap. If they retreated now, surprise would be lost, and Antony would have to fight a conventional battle while outnumbered.

Behind him, the Praetorians raised their standards high in the air and, still in complete silence, stared at the enemy with an intense hatred.

The Martian legionaries glared back. Then, without orders from their commanders, they broke into a charge.

'Brace,' cried Antony, and his tribunes and centurions took up the refrain. He watched as the enemy advanced at a run, hobnailed boots pounding on the stones of the road, armour rattling. Yet both sides were almost silent, neither giving voice to the battle cries and taunts that usually immediately preceded an engagement. Was that because this was the first conflict between two of Caesar's legions? Was there to be no glory in this, just a grim job to be done?

When they came into range, the enemy legionaries halted and tossed their javelins, a ragged, rather unco-ordinated volley, since they had advanced without orders. Antony's Praetorians took most of the spears on their shields, and when the missile attack was over, they reached over to snap off the shafts that had lodged there. A handful of men did not have Fortuna on their side, and the javelins had found gaps in shield wall and armour, to bury themselves in flesh and shatter bone. Some had superficial wounds, some were badly injured and were hobbling or being dragged to the rear. A small number were dying or dead.

Pansa's legion, spreading out into a wide line, resumed their charge at a headlong run, and Antony's front line braced against the inside of their shields, while the rows behind dug their feet into the cobbles and shoved their shoulders into the backs of the rank before them. Even two rows back, Antony felt the collision of the opposing sides reverberating through the bodies of men, the hammer of the Senatorial cohorts ringing the anvil of Antony's Praetorians.

Antony felt his men give way. Two cohorts against an entire legion would not usually be expected to withstand such an impact, but the disordered nature of the charge, with many of the Martian Legion not yet engaged, allowed Antony's Praetorians to push back. Immediately, swords thrust out from both front ranks, reaching over the tops of the shields, seeking chinks where the steel could bite into the enemy. The noise crescendoed, grunts of exertion, cries of anger and pain, shouts of 'traitor' and 'coward' coming from both sides. Then another wall of sound, the battle cry as the first waves of Antony's Second and Thirty-Fifth appeared from the marshes like some muddy monster from myth, and charged into the fray.

If, as Antony's intelligence had suggested, they had been opposed only by the newly raised legions, the battle might have turned decisively at this point. Untested men might easily break when they realise they are trapped. But the Martian Legion were veterans of the Gallic and civil wars, and they had served under Caesar, just as Antony's legions had. What's more, they had a grudge against Antony and any who fought for him. So, with superb discipline and bravery, they extended their lines left and right, wading into the marshes to confront the ambushing forces. Eight cohorts of the Martian Legion threw themselves against the Thirty-Fifth on Antony's left, fighting with such ferocity that the larger force of the Thirty-Fifth gave ground. To the right, two Martian cohorts and Pansa's Praetorian cohorts stood firm against Antony's Second.

Antony could see Pansa's standard among the troops on the right, and thought he could briefly make out the face of the consul. But he had to turn his attention to the battle right before him, and trust his lieutenants to play their part. In fact, the high causeway divided the battle into three parts: that on the road, and those on each flank, with little scope for those fighting in one part to be able to see what was happening in the other arenas. Antony, in the middle, had a somewhat better idea of what was going on, but it was still as confused as any battle he had been in.

On either side of the road, legionaries stabbed and hacked at one another, up to their knees in the bog. All movement was impeded by the sucking, cloying mud that gripped their boots, and legionaries failed to avoid sword and spear thrusts because of the clutches of the marsh, or failed to make their own blows tell. Many fell, and though the ooze was only a couple of feet deep, the trampling boots of friend and foe pushed injured and clumsy alike beneath the surface to drown in the stinking darkness.

It was no swift contest, but a long, hard slog, lasting hours. Tens of thousands of men hacked and slashed at one another in foul conditions, exhausted by the fighting, contending simultaneously with treacherous footing and traitorous former comrades. On Antony's left, the Thirty-Fifth continued to give ground, though they still fought ferociously, and were, Antony judged, far from breaking. The centre where Antony fought was at a standstill, with Antony's two Praetorian cohorts confronting Praetorians sporting Octavian's insignia. Antony knew that Octavian, unsurprisingly, was far from this battle, but it was still highly irritating that he had supplied his men to fight with the Senatorial forces.

On Antony's right, though, the situation was wholly different. Although Pansa had placed himself on this flank with two veteran cohorts of the Martian Legion and Hirtius' Praetorian cohort, they were outnumbered in this entirely separate battle, and after brutal and savage hand-to-hand fighting, Antony's Second Legion began to prevail. Soon, the Senatorial left flank was crumbling under the pressure from Antony's right.

In normal circumstances, Antony could have exploited this victory and turned his victorious troops into the centre in a flanking movement, but the unusual division of the battlefield made this manoeuvre hard to pull off. Besides, there were large numbers of raw recruits in the Senatorial rear still to be dealt with, so Antony decided to concentrate his attention where the battle was still being fought the hardest – the centre and his left, and trusted to his commanders to look after the right.

In the centre, where Antony was throwing himself personally into the fighting wherever he thought his presence was needed, he had a local numerical superiority. Though Octavian's Praetorian cohort fought with brutal savagery, as the Senatorial left retreated, Antony could see the realisation that their position was becoming more exposed in the faces of his opponents. He exhorted his men to greater efforts, and at last they began to prevail, weight of numbers and the uplifting presence of Antony enough to make the difference between the two closely matched sets of warriors.

Once Antony was confident the battle in the centre was won, he extricated himself from the fighting, leaving the command to his general Marcus Junius Silanus, and gathered reports on the situation on his left. Peering over the side of the causeway, he could see for himself that the Martian Legion had struggled through the marshes and forced Antony's Thirty-Fifth back around five hundred feet. This left a hugely exposed flank, and Antony summoned up his cavalry commander and ordered in the Moors. From the firm footing of the road and causeway, they darted back and forward, harrying the Martian cohorts. One fateful javelin struck and killed the legate commanding the Martian Legion, and the shock of this disaster halted their advance. The Moors pressed home their advantage, and without a leader, the Martian Legion reluctantly began to retreat. The Thirty-Fifth had fought themselves to the verge of collapse, and despite orders from Antony, could not be persuaded to advance. So Antony sent a detachment of his cavalry to encircle the Martians – a tactic that, even if it failed, would often throw an enemy into a panic.

Not only did the Martian Legion not panic, but a Senatorial general, Servius Sulpicius Galba, led a counter-attack with lightly armed auxiliaries. He had been a legate under Caesar in Gaul, but had fallen out with him, firstly over debt, and secondly when Caesar slept with his wife. He had been one of the senators who had taken part in the assassination on the Ides of March, and clearly had a lot to lose if Antony prevailed. His intervention, while not decisive, was enough to prevent the annihilation of the Martian cohorts, allowing them to withdraw in good order.

But it was not enough to save the battle. The veteran Martian Legion and the Senatorial Praetorian cohorts were all now in full flight. On paper, the Senatorial forces with their legions of recruits still outnumbered Antony's men. But when they saw the hardened soldiers streaming past them down the road, the recruits broke, fleeing back down the Via Aemilia towards the Senatorial marching camp.

As Antony had seen so many times before, when a battle ended, no matter how long its duration, the ending always came quickly. Exhilarated by the completeness and scale of his victory, won despite the surprise of a larger than expected opposing force, he punched the air, then commanded his cavalry and any infantry fresh enough and whole enough to pursue the fleeing enemy. Sharing his jubilation, and unwilling to miss out on the spoils that came to a victorious army, even the most exhausted soldiers joined the pursuit.

Antony followed at a more leisurely pace on horseback with a personal bodyguard of well-armed cavalrymen. His horse picked its way through the debris and detritus of the battlefield. Despite how familiar this scene was, it never failed to make an impact. Here, there was a solitary helmet, chin strap snapped, a horizontal dent in it so deep that the wearer could not have survived. Over there was an arm, detached from its owner, a bronze bracelet still wrapped around the wrist, the inert fist still clutching a dagger. And just before him, a young legionary, surely no older than Fulvia's oldest, Claudius, lying on his back, staring sightlessly towards the heavens, with no outward sign of the injury that had ended him. The smell of blood and bowels hung in the air, and the cries of the wounded came from all around.

The *medici* rushed from one prostrate body to the next, and when they found one with survivable injuries they called for stretcher-bearers, who carried away the wounded on shields or stretchers improvised from cloaks with two spears. Later they would come back to retrieve the dead for burial. But already, the carrion crows were gathering, readying themselves for the feast to come.

There was no let-up from the signs of slaughter as Antony progressed down the road, but the nature of the casualties and their wounds changed. Whereas at the site of the battle, there was an almost equal mix of dead and wounded from both sides, and their injuries were mostly to the front, as Antony rode through the aftermath of the pursuit of his men against the fleeing legions, the shields and discarded standards exclusively bore the insignia of Senatorial units, and the wounds were now largely behind them: spear thrusts to the spine and kidneys; sword slashes to the back of the head and neck. It was hard to take satisfaction from the death of other Romans, but this was not Antony's first battle in a civil war, and so he swallowed hard to dislodge the lump in his throat and focused on what he had achieved.

Silanus caught him up, reining his horse in to match Antony's pace.

'A magnificent victory, Proconsul,' he said.

'Thank you, Legate,' said Antony. 'It certainly improves our position immeasurably. We have routed five legions today, and kept our own legions intact. That should give the Senate and that troublesome boy pause. And it will improve our boys' morale, and maybe persuade a few others to come over to our side.'

'What are your orders now?' asked Silanus.

'Let's assess the situation before us when we reach Pansa's camp, then I will decide our course.'

Pansa's legions had set up the standard marching camp before they set out that morning, a couple of miles from the site of the battle. Every Roman soldier carried equipment to construct a strong fortification, a task that took around four hours every night. It had been standard practice for two hundred years – since the wars against Pyrrhus – and had saved countless Roman lives ever since. With their ditches, embankments and tall palisades, they were a formidable defence that allowed the defending Romans to hold out against superior forces.

It was, predictably, to Pansa's camp that the survivors of the newly recruited legions and the Martian Legion retreated, and Antony had planned to assault it while its defenders were still exhausted and in disarray.

But when he arrived before the camp, he found his advance forces had paused. He manoeuvred his horse through their ranks and when he got to the front he saw the reason for the hold-up.

The Martian Legion, who had just fought so bravely, but was now shattered and mauled, had drawn itself up outside the camp walls, with grim resolution facing down Antony's legions. Antony whistled at the sight. Barely a single man among them was without some wound or other, and many looked as if they could barely stand from their injuries or extreme fatigue. Yet still they held position, preventing Antony from assaulting the walls, which were held by the raw recruits, directly.

'I wish they had stayed true,' said Antony to Silanus. 'What a body of men. They are truly worthy of Mars.'

'It's a shame we have to destroy them,' said Silanus.

Antony didn't reply, furrowing in his brows in calculation as he took in the state of his men and those of the enemy, and considered the hour, which was just past noon.

'No,' he said eventually. 'We could brush those brave men aside easily enough, and then what? A long siege to take the camp? I haven't left my brother enough resources to keep Decimus Brutus locked up in Mutina if Hirtius and Octavianus decide to attempt to relieve him. We need to take this victory back to Mutina and get our men back inside our own defences there.'

Silanus looked at the fortification with its scared, vulnerable men inside, penned like sheep inside the fold while a pack of wolves prowled the perimeter. Then he shook his head.

'It's a pity, but you're right, Proconsul.'

'Get the men rounded up,' said Antony. 'Let's go.'

He led his exultant legions north-west along the Via Aemilia towards Mutina, smiling at the victory songs swelling up behind him. The centurions tried to maintain discipline, but the fatigue, the injuries, and the spontaneous celebrations disrupted their marching order. Antony let them have their head. They would regroup properly at Mutina.

His thoughts turned to his next steps. Decimus Brutus' supplies were surely almost gone, and deserters from Mutina suggested the civilian population was already starving, with the troops on the verge of running out of food themselves. Antony needed to prevent Brutus from breaking out or being resupplied by Hirtius and Octavian, and now he had removed the threat from Pansa, while retaining the legions he had taken into the battle himself, he was in a strong position to do so.

Things were looking up.

—

They were a short distance north of Forum Gallorum, the afternoon was well advanced, and Antony was still lost in his thoughts when one of his scouts came galloping down the road towards him, reining in abruptly, his horse sweating and snorting through flared nostrils.

'Proconsul,' said the scout breathlessly, then swallowed.

'Spit it out, man,' said Antony.

'Soldiers,' he said. 'Lots of soldiers.'

Antony looked further down the road. Squinting, he could make out men marching at a forced pace towards them, standards waving.

'Who are they? Are they ours? How many? Come on, man, speak!'

'The Fourth,' he said. 'And the Seventh.'

Antony went cold. Two legions. Veteran legions. Fresh legions. He looked back at his own men, disorganised, ready to drop after their efforts from the morning's fighting.

'Form up,' he cried. 'Enemy sighted.'

The nearest officers and centurions stared at him in momentary disbelief, before their training took over. They scurried about, shouting orders, kicking and beating the men into some sort of defensive line. The enemy legions approached rapidly.

How had they got here? They had been around ten miles away at the start of the day, according to his intelligence. Pansa must have got a messenger to them at the start of the engagement, and they must have marched double pace to get there so fast. Antony had underestimated Hirtius once again.

Antony's tactical mind started working feverishly. He was always at his best in a crisis, and this was certainly a big crisis. He directed the defences as best he could. But his men were in a loose marching column, while the attacking legions were already drawn up into battle lines. There was simply not enough time to get his exhausted men into defensive formation.

Hirtius' legions smashed into Antony's leading troops like a mallet into a ripe melon, and the legionaries who moments before had been celebrating a hard-earned victory were crushed. Antony screamed at the top of his lungs for his men to hold, but it was hopeless. He pulled his cavalry back to hold it in reserve, and he galloped back to the cohorts further down the road.

The initial attack on the front of his column had met scant resistance, but there was enough fight in those men to momentarily impede Hirtius' advance. It was enough for Antony and his officers to organise a short double line of legionaries, with the bottoms of their shields wedged into the cobblestones and the turf on either side of the road, bracing them against the upcoming attack. Reinforcements trickled up from the stragglers, limping and staggering from their fatigue and injuries, and with grim resignation joined the defence, strengthening the centre and extending the wings.

The men were slow to get into formation, and they were in no state individually or collectively to mount a coherent defence. But these were Caesar's veterans, commanded by their beloved Mark Antony, and they were not going to surrender without putting up a Herculean fight worthy of their commander's ancestors. Antony's chest swelled with pride at the sight of his men, so close to the end of their reserves, fighting with desperate savagery for their lives, their comrades and their standards.

Antony rode back and forth, shouting encouragement, throwing himself into the fight when he saw that the line needed stiffening. But he could see the situation was hopeless. The opposing forces were similar in terms of experience and numbers, but Antony's men had been caught unawares and disorganised, and were nearly spent. Step by step, moment by moment, they were forced back. Antony tried to gauge the time by the amount of daylight – difficult, given the overcast sky – and wondered if his men could hold on, like a boxer trying to keep upright under a hail of blows, waiting for the sand in the hourglass to run down.

The answer, he soon found out, was 'no'.

As Antony had witnessed many times in his military career, as he had seen just earlier that day, there often came a point in a battle where one side crumbled like a stale honey cake. There was a tipping point where so many of the losing side were incapacitated or had fled that a viable defence was no longer possible. At that moment, realisation of the inevitability of defeat swept through the ranks like a scythe, and the defenders' only thoughts were of saving themselves. The problem was that a Roman legionary facing his enemy, even exhausted, was a formidable opponent, with his armour and his short stabbing sword and his shield interlinked with his comrades to left and right. A legionary running from his enemy was as vulnerable as a deer fleeing a hunter. More often than not, they cast their shields and swords aside, sacrificing defence for speed in the forlorn hope they would reach some elusive, possibly illusory safety. Their desperate prayers for salvation usually went unanswered – it was common in ancient battles for the vast majority of casualties to be inflicted after the battle was over.

When Antony saw the collapse begin, he stood his ground, roaring at the troops streaming past him to stand their ground, even grabbing some and attempting to thrust them back to the battle. But it was hopeless and he knew it. His bodyguards knew it, too, and they forcibly pulled him back, hustling him to his horse, and formed a strong defensive picket around him as he rejoined his cavalry.

He wondered briefly whether he should throw his superior cavalry forces into a counter-attack. But it would not be enough. Cavalry unsupported by infantry could not prevail against a legion, at least not in these conditions, where their room for manoeuvre was strictly hampered by the marshes either side of the causeway. Reluctantly, he led his mounted auxiliaries away from the battle, south-east down the road, away from Hirtius and his rampaging legions.

It was the marshes, though, that saved many of Antony's men. They disappeared into the reed beds and the bogs, submerging themselves up to their necks, holding still while the enemy hunted them. Screams and gurgles rang out intermittently as a hiding place was discovered and the fugitive was slaughtered, or pushed into the mud to drown. If the day had been younger, Antony would have been in a very real danger of being pinned between Pansa's legionary camp, to the south-east, and the two legions advancing from the north-west. But night fell, and Hirtius obviously decided not to risk losing his advantage by having his men flounder around in the dark marshes, possibly even against their own side in the confusion.

Caesar's Avenger

So Antony still had a full cavalry and a small force of infantry when the sun disappeared and the sky was a starless black. Hirtius marched his legions, almost completely intact, to Pansa's marching camp, where they were no doubt received with much rejoicing. The battlefield, with the wreckage of Antony's best two legions, was left to the defeated.

But it soon became clear to Antony that, grievous though his losses were, there were large numbers of survivors in the marshes – maybe spent, maybe badly wounded, but alive. Antony's bodyguard urged him to take the cavalry and ride straight for his fortified position at Mutina. Antony would not hear of it.

'These men gave their all for me. I will not desert them now.'

He set about organising search and rescue parties, working with urgency to make the most of the night. Now, his cavalry excelled themselves, the hardy horses and ponies picking their way through the treacherous footing to help haul trapped men out of the bog, and to round up survivors too injured or drained to help themselves.

Antony saw a legionary dragging himself slowly along the road using his spear as a crutch, one leg clearly broken at the thigh, with a shard of white bone protruding through bloody muscle. The legionary gritted his teeth, and every step was clearly agony, but he made no noise apart from the hissing of breath through his teeth. This was a man who would probably never fight again, may not even survive for long. But he was one of Antony's own, and Antony would not abandon him.

Dismounting, Antony called a couple of his bodyguards to assist him. Together, they wrestled the injured man, who could not prevent himself from crying out at the rough handling, into the saddle of Antony's own mount. Antony took the reins himself and walked beside the horse, leading the injured man along the road.

'What's your name, soldier?' asked Antony.

'Lucius Postumius, of the Second, General,' said the injured man, his voice faint.

'You boys fought like lions today,' said Antony.

'Fortuna was not with you today, General,' said Postumius.

Antony looked around at the dead and dying littering the road.

'I think you are right,' he said tightly.

'But your victory this morning was magnificent. Don't give up. The lads believe in you, General. We fight for you because we know you.' Postumius paused, breathing heavily for a moment and screwing up his features at a wave of pain. 'We know you love us, and we feel the same about you.'

Antony blinked, tears suddenly filling his eyes. He didn't reply, and the legionary became quiet. Antony realised that he had passed out, probably from blood loss or pain, and Antony walked on in silence.

His officers had set up a temporary camp at the village of Forum Gallorum, commandeering every hut and barn as shelter for the injured, as the medici and *capsarii*, the legionaries trained in bandaging techniques, hurried from man to man, doing what they could. A medicus, not realising who Antony was because of the darkness and the grime that coated him, checked the soldier over and tutted.

'This one won't make it. Chuck him over there and go and fetch me one who might survive.'

He went to move on, but Antony grabbed his arm, and the medicus' eyes widened as he realised who he was talking to.

'I'm sorry, Proconsul, but I don't think—'

'Treat him,' said Antony, his tone icy. 'Treat him as if he was my son.'

'Yes, Proconsul,' said the medicus, and he called a couple of orderlies to help him carry Postumius to a mattress, where he immediately began to work on his damaged leg. Antony watched for a moment, then remounted and rode back to the site of the battle to look for more survivors. He rode past a constant trickle of his men heading to safety, some largely uninjured but moving slowly and stiffly, some wounded but able to move under their own power, some being assisted or carried by comrades, an arm around them, or hoisted over a shoulder like a sack of grain, or dragged along on a shield that bumped over the cobblestones. Many of the cavalry had followed Antony's example and were walking beside their horses, which carried one or more badly injured men on their backs.

The rescue went on all night, the survivors gathering in Forum Gallorum, tending their wounds, gulping down water and bread, or simply falling asleep in sheer exhaustion. There was no attempt to construct a defensive fortification, and Antony did not enforce the custom. The men were in no state to dig ditches and erect palisades, and if Hirtius changed his mind and chose to attack, Antony could do nothing about it. Fortuna had let him down that afternoon, but maybe she would favour him that night.

When the first glow of dawn appeared in the east, Antony called a halt to the rescue and ordered the remnants of his army to get ready to march. The re-formed legions were painful for Antony to behold, with maybe half the number they had set out with the previous morning, though that was better than the complete loss that he had faced at one point. The men were dirty, dishevelled. Some trembled as they stood; others had a faraway look in their eyes, as if they were focused on some horror that no one else could see. Just as distressing, the two legions had lost both their eagles and a large number of other standards, a source of terrible shame for Antony and the legionaries alike.

He sighed and walked out before them.

'Men of the Second and Thirty-Fifth, you have suffered a misfortune,' he said. 'But the fact remains, I am so very proud of you. You executed my plan to perfection yesterday, and won a famous victory. We could not have predicted that Hirtius would find us so quickly.' Well, maybe he should have predicted that and been prepared, he thought. Maybe the outcome would have been different if his men had been marching as if they were in enemy territory, not carelessly celebrating. He put the thought from his mind. It was not a time for doubts and second-guessing.

'We took a beating. But last night showed the best of us. We pulled together, and we have re-formed a fighting force. We march now to my brother at Mutina, to your comrades, to our strong fortifications, where you can rest and recover and watch as Decimus Brutus and his men starve inside the city.'

There was a ragged chorus of cheers, weak, but as loud as the men could manage. He ordered the men to march out, then he moved up and down the line on horseback, praising individual bravery, calling out greetings to legionaries by name when he remembered them. He spotted the medicus to whom he had entrusted Postumius the previous night and called him over.

'What news of the man I brought you last night?' he demanded. 'Lucius Postumius of the Second.'

The medicus' brow furrowed momentarily as he tried to remember. He had obviously treated a lot of patients that night. But only one had been brought to him personally by Antony.

'Postumius? Oh, yes, broken femur. Didn't make it.'

Antony glared at the medicus, anger building at the dismissive way he had delivered the news. The medicus saw the expression and stuttered an apology.

'Sorry, Proconsul. I meant no offence. I did everything I could. His wound was too grave, he had lost too much blood. I'm sure he was a good man. But a lot of good men died yesterday.'

Antony stared at him, then pulled his horse off the road to spend a moment or two with his own dark thoughts. Then he rejoined the column to continue to encourage the troops with smiles and heartening words.

ante diem xvi Kalendas Maias DCCXI AUC (16 April 43 BC), Mutina

'It's good to have you here, Lucius,' said Antony, sitting in his tent. 'I'm starting to realise what a lonely place command is. I wonder how Caesar stood it for so long.'

'You're no Caesar, Marcus,' said his brother.

Antony raised his eyebrows.

Lucius smiled. 'Caesar was unique. You share many of his traits – your boldness in battle, your tactical astuteness, even your skill with oratory. But surely you would be the first to admit you are not the same. For a start, Caesar had incredible good luck. It wasn't just when he crossed the Rubicon that he had tossed the die. Fortuna favoured him more times than she should have. There were plenty of times it was only the intervention of the fickle goddess that saved him. You should be celebrating a stunning victory against superior forces because of your tactical brilliance at Forum Gallorum, but you are nursing a defeat purely because Fortuna turned her face away from you at the last minute.'

'Don't let the men hear that,' said Antony. 'They believe in luck, and won't follow an unlucky commander.'

'Don't worry, I'm not that stupid. Besides, you aren't completely unlucky. That Hirtius didn't press his advantage was a piece of good fortune that allowed you to rescue a sizeable fighting force, which even now is recovering its strength and preparing to fight again.'

'I hope they recover quicker than me,' said Antony, stretching and wincing at the pain from bruising and over-exertion in arms, legs and chest. 'I'm nearly forty now, I don't bounce back as quickly as I used to.'

'Stop fishing for compliments, Marcus. You know you are still in your prime physically.'

Antony gave a half-smile. His mood was still sombre, but Lucius was doing a good job of restoring his morale.

'So that's another way Caesar and I differed,' said Antony. 'He was fit, but he was really a skinny little specimen.'

'Quite,' said Lucius. 'And, to come back to my original point, you are no Caesar in your relationship with the men. They revered Caesar like a god. They love you like a brother. You share their hardships, you understand them. For all your distance in social and military rank, you are one of them. Do you think Caesar would have spent the night after the battle rescuing the wounded like you? He would have been in his tent, cogitating and strategising.'

Antony thought of the words of Postumius, coming to him now ironically after the legionary's death. He felt a surge of emotion bubbling up inside him again and took a deep slug of wine to suppress it. He had no desire to burst into tears in front of Lucius, though he didn't doubt that his brother would be sympathetic.

'Tell me, brother, what do your scouts and spies tell you is the situation inside Mutina and in the enemy camps?'

Antony had his own sources, but he wanted to hear Lucius' intelligence and interpretation.

'Decimus is surely days away from surrendering or attempting a breakout,' said Lucius. 'Deserters from the city tell us that the civilian population are dropping like flies from starvation, and the food is now almost gone, even for the legionaries.'

'We will redouble our efforts with the artillery,' said Antony. 'We may or may not make a breach before his food runs out, but the constant bombardment will keep up the attrition on his men and on their morale. If they try to break out and fight us, they will be demoralised and weakened by hunger. We will defeat them easily if we can keep the Senatorial armies at bay.'

'And how will we do that?'

'With our horse. You know my first command was in the cavalry, and I always have a soft spot for fighting cavalry actions. We have a superior number of mounted men, especially after those Gallic riders deserted from Octavianus. I plan to use them to harry the Senatorial forces and discourage them from coming close enough to engage.'

Lucius looked doubtful. 'Surely if they decide to attack, skirmishers will not dissuade them.'

'True,' said Antony. 'I just need to buy time. Time to defeat Decimus and take Mutina, and time for Ventidius to bring up the three legions he has recruited in Picenum.'

'Another way fortune has favoured you is that your enemy's only experienced military commander is bottled up in Mutina.'

'Maybe,' said Antony. 'But Hirtius has proven to be no fool. And Pansa may yet surprise us.'

'I doubt it,' said Lucius. 'Word is he took a mortal wound at Forum Gallorum. He still lives, but not for long.'

Antony sighed. More death. Pansa was an opponent, but he had been a moderate, and a strong supporter of Caesar. His passing would make negotiations with the Senate harder after this was all over.

'Have you heard about Octavianus?' asked Lucius.

'Very little, in fact,' said Antony. 'It seems like he kept himself well clear of any danger.'

'Quite so. When I was leading feints against his camp, I saw no sign of him or his standard, though Agrippa seemed quite active. But despite that, his men have hailed him Imperator after Forum Gallorum.'

Antony spat out the mouthful of wine he had just taken.

'They did what? That cowardly little shit took no part whatsoever in the battle.'

Lucius shook his head ruefully. 'He claims Caesar's legacy, and there is something about him that inspires loyalty in the way that Caesar did, despite his distance and aloofness from the soldiers.'

'Sometimes it feels like I don't understand men at all well,' said Antony.

'That's not true, brother. You understand their hearts and souls. But it feels like Octavianus has the knack of manipulating their minds.'

Not for the first time, Antony wished that he and Octavian were on the same side.

'Maybe it's time to sound the boy out again. Put our differences aside. I'll send him a secret message. At worst, it might give him pause while he considers an alliance. At best, it would split the Senatorial forces in two.'

'You certainly have nothing to lose.'

Antony called for a scribe and composed a carefully worded letter, sealed it, and gave it to a trusted scout to take covertly to Octavian. Then tiredness threatened to overwhelm him. He embraced Lucius and retired to his bed, falling asleep the instant he lay down.

Chapter VII

ante diem xi Kalendas Maias DCCXI AUC (21 April 43 BC), Mutina

Antony managed to avoid pitched battle with the Senatorial forces for seven days. He kept his two legions – the solid and untouched Larks, and a legion cobbled together from the remnants of the Second and the Thirty-Fifth – behind the circumvallation around Mutina, and used his cavalry to keep the Senatorial forces away from his defences.

Time was on his side. Decimus could surely not last much longer, and Antony had received word that his trusted general Ventidius had finally formed up his three newly recruited legions and set out to reinforce him. Those sorely needed men would greatly redress the imbalance in the opposing sides, with Antony currently badly outnumbered. But the new legions were four days away, even at a forced march. And the Senate was growing impatient. Dispatches from Rome and letters from Fulvia had told how the news of Antony's victory turned defeat at Forum Gallorum had been received in the city, with Cicero particularly exultant.

Antony knew that Hirtius, in particular, understood the need to defeat him before Decimus' surrender and Ventidius' arrival. So it was unwelcome news, but no surprise, when Antony's scouts reported that the legions of Octavian and Hirtius were on the move. He sent out his cavalry to harry them, but gave them strict instructions to avoid a full engagement. Further reports came to him of their movements as the morning wore on, and it soon became clear they were not aiming for the nearest part of his fortifications, to the south-east, but were working their way round to the north. It was a good plan, Antony grudgingly admitted. The ground to the north was soft and he had been unable to construct as formidable defences in that area. Spies or good scouting on the part of the Senatorial forces must have informed them of this weakness.

The cavalry did their best to ward off the Senatorial advance. They had a mix of heavy and light horse, armed with bows, spears and long swords. There was even a small unit of elephants who had defected to Antony from Octavian. With more freedom to charge and retreat in the open ground than in the battle on the Via Aemilia, they were effective at inflicting damage and forcing the advance to halt to repel their attacks. But then Hirtius and Octavian sent out their own cavalry.

In contrast to the foot soldiers, the Senatorial horse was much smaller in number than Antony's cavalry but stayed close to their light infantry, whose slinger and archer auxiliaries began to take a toll on Antony's troopers. Meanwhile, the legionaries marched onwards unimpeded.

Antony knew he now had no choice but to engage. If he let them strike at his poorly constructed walls to the north, defence would be hard. He was better to take the fight to them directly.

He dispatched messengers to Ventidius, urging him to make all possible speed. Further desperate messages were dispatched to bring every Antonian force from the surrounding area: every garrison of every nearby town loyal to Antony; every detachment foraging for supplies or harassing enemy supply lines. Antony knew they would be too few and too late to make a difference.

He formed up his two legions. He spoke to them of service and loyalty, of his pride in their bravery, and then, riding before them, he led them out of his encampment and into battle.

This was what the Senatorial forces had been craving since Forum Gallorum: a chance to assault Antony's numerically weaker army in open battle, without having to reduce his defences first. With almost palpable glee, the legions of Hirtius and Octavian swung inwards to meet Antony.

The battle was brutal and utterly devoid of tactical nuance that could have swung the result for either side. Try as he might, Antony could think of no ruse, no stratagem that might give him an advantage, and soon he was too firmly occupied with directing the battle to attempt to devise a new plan.

The newly constituted legion made up of survivors of Forum Gallorum fought with impressive courage, given the mauling they were still recovering from, and the fresh Fifth defended the ground around Antony's headquarters ferociously. It was here that Antony chose to station himself with his loyal bodyguard, while his brother Lucius and Silanus commanded the amalgamated Second and Thirty-Fifth.

As was usual for Antony, he was soon involved in the fighting directly, leading charges with his elite bodyguard whenever he saw a part of the line that was wavering. His own sword was quickly bloodied, and his bodyguard took many casualties attempting to defend him, since whenever he entered the fray, his standard both boosted the morale of his own men and attracted furious assaults from enemy soldiers thirsting for the glory and inevitable rewards of killing or capturing the great Mark Antony.

The air was filled with all the noises of bloody conflict – screams, shouted orders, yells of rage – and all the smells – metal and leather, the sweat, the blood, the stench of voided bowels and spilled guts. Both sides must have begun to tire, given the intensity of the fighting, but it was not evident to the eye as they redoubled their efforts.

Then Antony saw a new movement of soldiers off to his right. He pointed and asked one of his bodyguards, who had younger eyes, to tell him what he saw.

'It looks like a large number of cohorts of the Third,' he said. 'And they have the eagle of the consul with them.'

Hirtius was bringing up a large force, and it was aimed directly at Antony's headquarters.

Antony gave orders to rebalance the line, to pull back enough men to confront the new threat, dispatching a message to Silanus to send reinforcements to his location.

Before Antony could fully reorganise his defence, Hirtius' fresh troops had smashed through Antony's initial defences and penetrated deep into his camp. Antony led the Fifth against them, screaming exhortations to fight for their lives. Antony fought now in the front line, stabbing, parrying, thrusting, and his loyal Larks closed around him, fighting like demons to repel the attack.

The battle hung in the balance. A collapse here, and everything would be finished for Antony.

But the Larks did not let him down. Inch by inch, foot by foot, they pushed Hirtius' Third Legion back. Antony moved to another part of the line to encourage the resistance, and suddenly he found himself just a few yards from Aulus Hirtius. They locked gazes and the consul looked at him with eyes full of a profound sadness. He lifted his sword in a salute, and Antony respectfully returned the gesture. Then they returned to the fighting. Hirtius, elderly, in poor health, fought beside his men like a twenty-year-old, and Antony could not help but admire his tenacity.

Then, before Antony's eyes, a sword thrust made its way past Hirtius' guard, punctured his cuirass and slid deep into his chest. He looked down with what Antony could only describe as an expression of resignation and, without a sound, slid to the ground.

The death of the consul sent the fighting to a new pitch of intensity as the Larks surged forward in savage joy, and the Third howled their outrage and threw themselves once more into the fray. The battle line ossified into an immovable front for some time.

Then a new force appeared. This time, Antony did not need anyone else to tell him whose banner he was looking at. Octavian himself, with his bodyguard and a small number of reinforcements, charged into the battle that was raging over Hirtius' body. Though Octavian himself hung back, his men were able to force enough of a breach to retrieve the corpse of the consul and the standard. They brought them back to Octavian, who shouldered the eagle himself, and retreated from the battlefield to great acclamation from his men. Antony shook his head at the boy's audacity. He could imagine how the tale would be retold – how Octavian, almost single-handed, had recovered Hirtius' body and the eagle at great personal risk. Once again, Antony wished the boy was on his side.

With the eagle and the consul's body recovered, the fight went out of the Third. The Larks pushed on, forcing them out of the camp, and Antony was able to repopulate his defences. But just as it looked as if he was going to be able to hold against the assault, a great shout of warning went up to his rear. He looked behind him and saw, to his disbelief, the gates of Mutina opening and a force of legionaries sallying forth.

Screaming orders, he pulled detachments away from the fight before him, and sent for other units to be brought over to face the new threat. The force from Mutina – which showed the standard of another of Caesar's assassins, Pontius Aquila – was meagre, in both number and physique. The prolonged siege and the privation had clearly taken their toll, and when Antony's forces engaged them, they were unable to put up a strong fight. Soon, they were pushed back inside the city, and

Aquila was dead. But they had done their job, forcing Antony to pull men from other parts of the battle where they were sorely needed.

Leaving the fight, which seemed currently to be at an impasse, Antony took himself to his headquarters and summoned Silanus and Lucius. His two generals arrived, both blood-spattered and bruised, looking grim-faced but firm.

'I need your opinions. Can we hold?'

'Of course,' said Lucius. 'One consul is dead, another is dying somewhere far away. Decimus has been unable to break out. And we have repulsed the Senatorial attack.'

'But at what cost?' asked Silanus.

Lucius rounded on him with a glare, but Antony held up his hand.

'Let him speak, brother.'

Silanus swallowed and took a moment to choose his words.

'On balance, I would say the day is ours, though our opponents would no doubt disagree. But as Lucius says, to have killed both consuls, or as good as, would surely mean that the war is won. The siege holds, and with Decimus Brutus still bottled up inside Mutina, the command of the Senatorial forces is now in the hands of an entirely inexperienced boy.'

'But?'

Silanus nodded, as if agreeing with his own decision.

'But we cannot hold.'

'Are you mad?' burst out Lucius. 'We have won. You said so yourself.'

'I fear it a victory worthy of Pyrrhus. Look at what we have lost. Look at the forces that remain to us. Brave, loyal, veteran, yes. But terribly depleted, and beyond exhaustion. If the Senatorial forces continue to hold today, and I don't see how they can't, then our men will collapse, maybe this hour, maybe this day, maybe tomorrow, but certainly before we can hope for aid from Ventidius or anyone else.'

Antony stroked his beard, considering Silanus' words.

'Brother,' urged Lucius, 'do not do this. Seize the moment. Victory today, and there will be no further opposition. Italy is yours.'

'This is Gergovia,' said Antony. Lucius looked confused, but Silanus understood. He had been with Caesar in Gaul at the great man's famous defeat. Antony had joined Caesar for the first time shortly afterwards at Alesia, but he had learned much about the battle. Caesar had been besieging the hill fort, but was attacked by a relieving force led by

Vercingetorix. The Roman legions had had some victories, but had worn themselves out, and were unable to resist Vercingetorix's cavalry charge. Caesar had taken the decision to retreat and keep his forces intact rather than risk annihilation, allowing pragmatism to rule over his immeasurable pride. If Caesar could do it, so could Antony.

'We pull back,' said Antony.

Lucius groaned, but Silanus nodded his sad approval.

'Where will we go?' asked Lucius, not hiding his disappointment.

'We cross the Alps, to Lepidus and Plancus.'

'Will they support you?' asked Lucius.

'The gods alone know,' said Antony. 'Lepidus still wants to avenge Caesar's death and is no fan of the Senate. And Silanus here is his brother-in-law. I think he can be persuaded. If he falls into line, Plancus will likely follow.'

'But can we get away? If we leave our defences and Decimus Brutus and Octavianus pursue us, we could be overtaken and destroyed.'

'That is a possibility,' said Antony. 'But we have two reasons for hope. Firstly, our strength is still in our cavalry. We may need to leave some of our infantry behind, even resign ourselves to seeing them recruited into the Senatorial ranks. But we then have the speed to outrun our enemies, and more infantry can always be recruited.'

Lucius looked doubtful. 'And the second reason for hope?'

'With our apparent defeat, and both consuls dead, command of the Senatorial forces devolves to Decimus Brutus as the most senior. But the legions are loyal to Octavianus. And for all his pragmatic co-operation with the Senate to try to be rid of me and become the chief Caesarian, he still desires to avenge his adoptive father, and his legions want the same. He will not co-operate with the assassin Decimus.'

At this, Lucius brightened. 'You think you may persuade him to your cause?'

'Perhaps. Or at least that he might stand by. Now get your men ready for the march. We travel light and fast, and we leave at nightfall. Meanwhile, I have time to write one last letter to young Octavianus.'

ante diem iii Kalendas Maias DCCXI AUC (29 April 43 BC), Parma

Withdrawing from a battle was a skill often overlooked. But a successful retreat required boldness, acute tactical awareness, and a little luck.

Antony had all three when he lifted the siege of Mutina and led his battered forces up the Via Aemilia. It was bold to pull out in the face of superior numbers and to abandon part of his army. But he was tactically astute in the timing of the withdrawal, taking his enemies by surprise, and using his brother Lucius and the former tribune Lucius Trebellius Fides, commanding the cavalry, to harry the enemy and screen their retreat. And he was lucky that Decimus Brutus and Octavian did not immediately pursue him. At least, it was partially luck. His last letter to Octavian, suggesting their goals were aligned, and warning him of how he might expect Cicero and the Senate to treat him once he had served his purpose of removing Antony, had perhaps stayed the young man's hand from inflicting the killing blow. Antony defeated but still in the field could be the ideal situation for Octavian. The Senate needed Octavian to keep Antony at bay, as Octavian held what was currently the most powerful army in Italy. Moreover, Antony was now no longer consul, and his abandonment of Cisalpine Gaul to Decimus made it hard to press his claim that he was still proconsul.

Yet Antony felt far from defeat. His withdrawal from Mutina had not been a desperate flight, but a calculated stratagem. He had with him the Fifth Alaudae – his faithful and ferocious Larks – plus the remnants of the Second and Thirty-Fifth, and the mauled but intact Praetorian cohort commanded by Silanus, as well as his powerful Gallic and Moorish cavalry. Moreover, Ventidius was still on his way with his three freshly recruited legions, and as Antony's general marched north and west, he had the opportunity to conscript more. The parties sent out to round up new recruits were efficient and resourceful, and soon the ranks of legions and auxiliary units were being swelled by the urban poor, released prisoners and freed slaves.

Supplies were a problem. The late spring weather was favourable, and the land was fertile, but much of it was given over to vineyards, when what Antony really needed was grain for the men and fodder for the animals. Morale, too, was an issue. Trusted officers reported back to him about the mutterings in the ranks, even among the Larks. Defeated, mauled and exhausted, this was not an army that was prepared to endure much hardship.

Antony marched on foot with the legionaries and auxiliaries, sharing their basic and meagre food, making grim jokes about their situation.

His mere presence – his personality and charisma – was enough to sustain them for the time being, but he knew it could not last forever.

When they reached Parma, a city that had already surrendered to Lucius, he called a council with his senior officers: his brother, Lucius Antonius; Marcus Junius Silanus, the brother-in-law of Lepidus; and Lucius Trebellius Fides, the former Caesarian tribune who had supported Antony since Caesar's assassination. They stood in Antony's command tent, around a table across which a large map was spread.

Antony ordered his personal slaves to pass around cups of water and plates of bread and dried fruit. None of them raised their eyebrows or made any complaint about the poor fare. They had all followed Antony long enough to know that he would never feast if his men were going without.

Antony took a long drink from his cup. The water was brackish, with a sour aftertaste, but it quenched his thirst.

'Trebellius,' he said. 'What news of our pursuers?'

'My scouts say that Brutus is camped at Regium Lepidi. They couldn't be sure of numbers, but they counted at least eight legion eagles.'

'Eight?' said Lucius. 'He must have taken command of the consular armies.'

'Is he getting ready to march?'

'There was no sign of that at the last report. He might be waiting for instructions from Rome, or corresponding with Octavianus.'

'And what of the boy?'

'He hasn't moved an inch,' said Trebellius.

'Good lad,' said Antony. 'Maybe my letters have had some effect.'

'Or maybe his Caesarian legions object to supporting the most egregious of Caesar's assassins,' said Lucius.

Antony nodded.

'So Decimus Brutus has upwards of eight legions. Octavianus has… what, eleven? Ahead of us, Lepidus has seven, and Plancus and Pollio have around thirteen. We have the Larks and the legion formed from the Second and Thirty-Fifth, brought back up to strength by the new recruits, the Praetorian cohorts and the cavalry, plus Ventidius' three legions – if he can reach us. It's clear that we need to reach Lepidus, Plancus and Pollio and ensure they support us.'

'My brother-in-law is wavering,' said Silanus. 'I have written to him urging him to throw his full support behind you, but he is prevaricating. I think he is trying to avoid being on the losing side.'

'I'll deal with Lepidus,' said Antony, 'once I meet him face to face. But we have a long and difficult march ahead of us. Do we have enough supplies? And will the men follow?'

The three officers looked at one another, not wanting to be the first to speak the hard truth. It was Lucius who broke the silence.

'Brother, we do not have enough grain and meat for the men, nor other basic necessities like fodder and clothing, and we are low on arms – javelins, arrows, even swords and shields. Our monetary reserves are hardly healthy, too, and we know what happens when the men don't get paid.'

'We can forage and raid for food,' said Antony. 'As for the rest, these things don't grow on trees.'

'But they do sit in stockpiles in cities,' said Lucius.

'We can empty the warehouses, yes,' said Antony, 'but even that wouldn't be enough.'

'Then you must bleed the city dry.'

Antony narrowed his eyes. 'Just what are you suggesting, Lucius?'

'Let the men have Parma.'

There was a long pause. Antony turned away and looked out of the flap of the tent. Many of the legionaries were bustling about, sharpening weapons, cooking over open fires, chopping stakes to reinforce the camp defences. But others were sitting slumped on the damp ground, or stretched out, unmoving, blank-eyed, gazes distant. Some were shaking. Some were crying. Antony looked back at his officers' grim expressions. Much as the very idea made him sick, he knew there was no alternative. Lucius' suggestion would restore their supplies, their treasury and the men's morale.

He let out a long sigh. 'Give the men Parma,' he said, and dismissed the officers.

Later, as he lay in bed, he could hear the screams from the dying town, and the smoke that had drifted over the camp filled his nostrils. He closed his eyes and tried to shut out the images of brutalised women and children that flickered behind his eyelids.

ante diem v Nonas Maias DCCXI AUC (3 May 43 BC), Vada Sabatia

'You wouldn't believe how good it is to see you, Ventidius,' said Antony, shaking his loyal general's hand firmly, then pulling him into a close embrace.

'Me, or the legions I bring?' asked Ventidius with a smile. He had a weather-beaten face and a rough country accent, and was as wonderful a sight as Antony could imagine at that moment.

'Both are very welcome,' said Antony.

Publius Ventidius was one of those rare officers who had risen through the ranks of the Roman legions. As a boy from rural Picenum, he and his mother had been captured during the Social War and he had been paraded in Strabo's triumph through Rome, carried in his mother's arms. He had gone on to become a mule driver for an army bakery, then a trader in livestock, and it was in this capacity that he had caught the eye of Julius Caesar, who was preparing to campaign in Gaul. Caesar, with his eye for a good man, had persuaded the no-nonsense Ventidius to join up by offering him a staff posting dealing with the baggage train and the myriad problems that accompanied it. He had served so well that Caesar enrolled him in the Senate and then made him Tribune of the Plebs. Caesar also awarded him the rank of praetor for the current year, which Antony had ensured was honoured posthumously, gaining Ventidius' loyalty in the process. As soon as his term started, he had begun recruiting legions from the veterans in the region of his birth on behalf of Antony.

And at last, when they were desperately needed, those legions had arrived.

Antony had opened up a decent gap between his men and Decimus' legions. After the destruction of Parma, his rejuvenated men had marched swiftly along the Via Postumia to Dertona, where he had turned south along a minor road to join the coastal road, the Via Aemilia Scauri, along which his scouts told him Ventidius was marching. It was at Vada Sabatia, a small town and military outpost on the coast of the Ligurian Sea, that the two armies linked up, and the rejoicing on both sides was loud and protracted.

Antony ushered Ventidius to his command tent, and treated his friend to a generous cup of wine and a meal of freshly caught fish and roast vegetables. He ordered that his men be given extra rations, too, in celebration of their good fortune.

Lucius, Silanus and Trebellius joined them for the meal, and they reclined around a table and picked at the simple but tasty repast. Antony drank well-watered wine, and noted with disapproval that Lucius was drinking his wine neat. Maybe he himself was being a bit hypocritical, Antony thought, given his own penchant for the grape, but he was well able to control his vices when the situation called for him to be clear-headed, and though he did not criticise his brother, after all the good service he had done him in recent months, he resolved to keep an eye on Lucius' behaviour.

Antony and his generals filled Ventidius in on the battles of Forum Gallorum and Mutina from their point of view, since Ventidius had only heard the story distorted by the propaganda of the Senatorial faction. Then Ventidius brought them up to date with the news from Rome, which was much more recent than Antony had had access to.

'When news first arrived of your victory at Forum Gallorum,' said Ventidius, 'all Rome seemed to panic. Rumours abounded that Cicero intended to seize power in a coup, and your close supporters discussed at a council whether they should have him assassinated. Then came news of Hirtius' victory later that day, and public feeling shifted back towards Cicero and they acclaimed him like he was the conquering hero himself.

'Cicero delivered another of his speeches to the Senate against you – the fourteenth. He calls them "Philippics", I believe.'

'Typical of Cicero's modesty,' commented Lucius. 'Comparing himself to Demosthenes.'

Ventidius shrugged. He had not had the education of the noble-born men in whose company he was eating and drinking, but he did not seem to let it bother him.

'He proposed a thanksgiving for Decimus Brutus, and then said that you should be declared a public enemy. He brought up the destruction of Parma by you and your brother, I'm afraid, Antonius, and called you a second Hannibal.'

'He has called me many things now,' commented Antony.

'Then he talked about how the crowd had greeted him the day before, and then denied that he was boastful! He followed that up by talking about all the senators who envy him, and said that the Roman people know that it was Cicero who had fought for liberty and the Republic. Then he proposed honours to the Martian Legion and the Senatorial leaders at Mutina, and again that you should be declared an enemy of the state.'

'How was he received?' asked Antony.

'I'm sorry to say the Senate took his side,' said Ventidius. 'They held off declaring you a public enemy. At least at first. But when they received news of your defeat at Mutina and the lifting of the siege, you and all your followers were declared public enemies and all property belonging to us was confiscated.'

There was a long silence as each considered the consequences of this for themselves. One thing was certain now: there was no going back. They had all joined their fates with Antony's, and they would live or die with him.

'Fulvia?' asked Antony with trepidation. 'The children?'

'Safe, to my knowledge,' said Ventidius. 'Here, I have a letter from her for you.'

Antony took the scroll and tore it open. It was dated the same day Antony was declared an enemy of the state. He devoured it quickly, breathing a sigh of relief as he digested its contents.

> *My love, I fear for you, but I trust in you. I know your resolve and steadfastness. You will take this reversal in your stride and come out the stronger for it, I have no doubt.*
>
> *Do not fear for us. Atticus has been true to his word. He has protected us from any harm, and has taken us into his house, which is protected by a strong private bodyguard. The children and I are quite safe, and your mother, too.*

She repeated some of the news that Ventidius had already given them, then added a report of the Senate meeting the next day, which Antony read out to his generals.

'"Once the Senate heard that Pansa and Hirtius were dead, and that you were defeated, they took everything into their own hands. Decimus Brutus was given command of the pursuit against you, and was instructed to take supreme command of all the Senatorial troops, as well as proposals to transfer the Fourth and Martian legions from Octavianus to Brutus. It was decreed that Dolabella be stripped of his command and his legions given to Cassius, and also Sextus Pompeius was to be made commander-in-chief of all the naval forces of the Republic! Lepidus and Plancus were ordered to assist in the fight against you. What's more, Octavianus was to be denied a triumph, but given only an ovation. It's even been widely reported, though he denies it, that Cicero quipped that young Caesar should be raised, praised and done away with."'

Antony looked at the generals, and slowly, smiles crossed each of their faces.

'Can they really be so stupid?' asked Silanus incredulously.

'Of course they can,' said Lucius. 'So there it is. They've lost Octavianus.'

'And their loss may well be our gain. But to treat with him, I need to face him as an equal. And much as it pains me to say it, right now, he is my superior, at least numerically. I need Lepidus' legions.'

ante diem v Kalendas Iunias DCCXI AUC (28 May 43 BC), Forum Iulii

When Antony's legions arrived, bruised, footsore and hungry, on the banks of the river Argenteus near Forum Iulii in the south of Gaul, he did not order fortifications to be raised. He had finally thrown off Decimus Brutus' troops by letting a false report be captured that his soldiers had refused to continue west, and had instead demanded that he turn north and cross the Alps. Decimus had taken the bait and sent detachments north, where they had been ambushed and thrown into retreat by cavalry under the command of Trebellius. Antony continued westwards as planned, and a frustrated Decimus finally gave up the pursuit. Meanwhile, Plancus had been approaching from the north, and from further away, Gaius Asinius Pollio was bringing two legions from Spain. Lepidus, Pollio and Plancus were all ostensibly commanded by and loyal to the Senate, and Antony was at risk of being pinned by a four-pronged fork made up of Decimus and the three proconsuls. But Antony hoped that their loyalty to him, their friendship and, of course, their self-interest would be greater than their allegiance to the Republican cause.

So when he arrived on the opposite bank of the river from Lepidus' encampment, it was a deliberate ploy that he did not throw up defences. It allowed his men to roam freely outside the boundaries of the legionary camp, and similarly for Lepidus' men to do the same, and wander without hindrance into Antony's camp. It was a terrible idea if he planned to face Lepidus in battle. But if it came to a fight against Lepidus, with Pollio and Plancus no doubt throwing their lot in with him, then Antony stood no chance. Instead, he was gambling everything on the actions of Lepidus in particular, and on the amity of the legions who had fought for Caesar in this very country.

But when Antony first arrived and sent embassies requesting a meeting with Lepidus, the proconsul of Gallia Narbonensis turned him down flat. He informed Antony that though he had no wish to wage war on him, the Senate had commanded him to do so. Antony reminded Lepidus of their friendship and the favours he had bestowed on him, and warned him that should he, Antony, fall, so would everyone else who had enjoyed Caesar's friendship. Lepidus vacillated, but did not come over to Antony, stating he had no wish to defy the Senate.

Antony was not entirely surprised. Lepidus had always been a weathervane, turning in the direction the wind was blowing like the statue of the Triton on the newly built Tower of the Winds in Athens. It didn't matter. It wasn't Lepidus himself that he needed to persuade. And his men were assisting him in this matter, fraternising with their opponents across the river, at first tentatively, then when there was no reprimand from Lepidus or Antony, more openly, until they decided to make the whole process simpler and built a bridge of boats across the river. The soldiers spent the night in each other's camps, sitting around camp fires, swapping stories of battle, plunder and sexual conquest. Antony moved among them, particularly pleased to find legionaries of the Tenth among the visitors.

Antony seated himself on a low stool among a group of soldiers eating and drinking around a glowing brazier. The gibbous moon was low in the sky and, together with the flickering flames, illuminated faces enough that it took only a few moments before the men realised who had just joined them. They leapt to their feet, but Antony motioned them to settle back down.

'I'm not here to be treated like your commander,' said Antony. 'I just want to eat some of this rancid food, drink some of this vinegar, and listen to the nonsense you men spout about your exploits.'

The men laughed, instantly at ease, and Antony asked after their units. Eight of them constituted a *contubernium* from one of Ventidius' newly raised legions, but they were all veterans who had been persuaded to come out of retirement out of loyalty to Antony and Caesar, and for the promise of reward and a relief from boredom. Except for Audax, who had got the local gang boss's daughter pregnant, and had jumped at the chance to join up to avoid having his testicles fed to the pigs. Another two were soldiers of the Tenth Legion, and Antony recognised one.

'Aulus? No, Albinus, right?'

'Albinus, that's right, Proconsul,' said the man, pleased at being remembered.

'I'm not likely to forget you, am I, even if I'm hazy with names sometimes. You know that in Rome, all the senators are followed around by a *nomenclator*, a slave specifically trained to remember everyone's names and whisper them in the forgetful senator's ear.'

The men laughed, then stared in disbelief when they realised he wasn't joking. Antony took a swig of the wine, which really did taste like vinegar, made a face, then drained his cup in a single go, which earned some cheers and claps on the back.

'So, Albinus of the Tenth. You were in Britannia, correct?'

'Correct, Proconsul.'

'And Alesia. And Dyrrhachium.'

'Impressive. And after Pompeius' defeat?'

'The Tenth were disbanded and settled here in Gallia Narbonensis. When Lepidus reformed us, I jumped at the chance to join up again. You wouldn't believe how boring farming is.'

Several of the others nodded their agreement. Many of the currently serving legionaries on all sides had been disbanded after the civil war, taking up civilian lives with greater or less success, only to be re-recruited when it became obvious hostilities were going to break out again.

'How are things in Lepidus' camp, legionary?' asked Antony.

Albinus looked to his colleague from the Tenth, who shrugged.

'No complaints,' said Albinus neutrally. 'Though I am an *optio* now.'

'Congratulations on your promotion,' said Antony. 'Lepidus is a good man, isn't he?'

The two legionaries of the Tenth grunted a tepid agreement.

'Maybe not in the top tier of generals?' suggested Antony.

They nodded more enthusiastically.

Antony sighed. 'Lepidus is my friend. As are the soldiers in his command. We really should be united against the true enemies, the murderers of Caesar.'

Now all the soldiers voiced angry assent.

'Perhaps there is something you men can do to help bring that about.'

ante diem iv Kalendas Iunias DCCXI AUC (29 May 43 BC), Forum Iulii

Early the morning after he arrived, with fingers of sunlight peeking out between the gaps in the foothills of the Maritime Alps, Antony set out, on foot and alone, for Lepidus' camp. He wore a plain, dirty tunic, his hair was unkempt, and his beard was grown long in mourning, showing his grief at both the loss of Caesar and the pass to which he had been brought by the actions of Cicero and the Senate. Unlike Antony, Lepidus had fully fortified his position, as military doctrine demanded. The rectangular camp was surrounded by a deep ditch lined with stakes, and a tall palisade. Wide gates were positioned in the centre of each wall at the four cardinal compass points, barred closed and guarded by watch towers.

Antony made his way around to the north of the camp, greeting passing patrols cordially. They invariably did a double take on recognising him, then saluted and wished him good fortune. At the north gate, he knocked three times. As he waited, his heart beat strongly against the wall of his chest. His nerves made themselves felt by a growling in the pit of his stomach, which was not entirely caused by the terrible wine the night before. But they were tempered by the thrill of anticipation.

He heard the scrape of a bar being lifted, then the gate swung open, just wide enough for one man to enter. Antony squeezed his bulky frame through the narrow gap, and was greeted by Albinus.

'Good morning, Proconsul. Welcome to the legionary camp of the Tenth.'

'Thank you for inviting me, Optio.'

'Come and meet my comrades.' Albinus led Antony to a small group of legionaries who had gathered expectantly on the inside of the camp defences.

'These are the lads from my contubernium,' said Albinus. 'All good men. Except Secundus, our cook. His meals could choke a demon.'

'Go screw yourself,' said the man whom Antony presumed was Secundus, as the rest of the contubernium laughed.

'And this is our centurion, Ferox.'

Ferox, a large man whose frame was just the right side of being fat, with russet hair streaked with grey and a forearm criss-crossed with livid scars, reached out and shook Antony's hand vigorously.

'It's a great honour, Proconsul,' he said. 'A great honour.'

'The honour is mine, Centurion, believe me.'

Antony looked around him. The small group of men with Antony at its centre was drawing curious glances from the other legionaries going about their business, carrying slop buckets, chopping wood, sharpening weapons, polishing standards. One by one, legionaries drifted over to see what the fuss was about, and as they realised who was now in their midst, they called out to colleagues to come and see. Before long, Antony was at the centre of large crowd of enthusiastic legionaries, all wanting to shake his hand, give him their best wishes, and ask him when Caesar would be avenged.

When Antony judged his audience was sufficiently large, he leapt nimbly onto a barrel so he could address them.

'Comrades, fellow soldiers, friends. Thank you for your warm welcome. You cannot know what a pleasure it is for me to be among you, after all the trials and tribulations of the last year. We should have been looking forward to an unparalleled era of peace and prosperity under my beloved friend, Gaius Julius Caesar. He was on the verge of marching east and settling the threat to our eastern borders from the Parthians, when small, jealous men, men whom he had honoured, lifted up, forgiven past betrayals, even named in his will, men like Gaius Cassius Longinus, Marcus Junius Brutus, Marcus Tullius Cicero and the most ungrateful Decimus Junius Brutus, whom Caesar loved like a son, these men slaughtered him like a common criminal. Murdered him in the presence of the Senate, who had sworn an oath to protect him with their lives.

'I was there, comrades, and maybe I could have saved him, if Decimus Brutus had not deliberately delayed me while his friends carried out the infamous deed.

'Yet afterwards, despite my soul crying out for vengeance, I acted on behalf of the Republic, and I called for peace and conciliation. Though I lusted for the blood of the assassins, my responsibility as consul was to the Senate and the people of Rome, and I did my best for a country weary of decades of civil war. And I would have succeeded in keeping the peace, too, if not for Cicero and his friends, and their insistence on driving a wedge between me and the Senate, who have declared me an enemy of the people, when all I have done is for the good of Rome.'

The legionaries were spellbound as he spoke, his powerful oratory emphasising his points. Now, when he paused, they broke out in jeers and boos directed at all those who had done Antony wrong – the assassins, the Senate, Caesar, and most of all Decimus Brutus, who, as one of Caesar's favourites, was seen as having betrayed the dictator more cruelly than anyone.

'I have been forced to take up arms once more,' said Antony. 'And you men must make a decision. In Rome, the Senate continues to recruit new legions and bring others from the provinces. In the east, my colleague Dolabella is being opposed by illegitimate and illegal armies raised by Marcus Brutus and Cassius, and soon they will turn their attentions to Rome. Will we let our great city, our country, fall to the men who killed Caesar? Will we let them bring back the corrupt institutions and practices of the past? Will we let them take away the rights of the legionaries to their rightful awards of land and bonuses?'

This last hit home particularly, and outraged shouts of 'No!' echoed around the camp.

Antony paused and looked out around the mass of legionaries, hanging on his every word. He had them, he knew. It was only now, as the relief flooded over him, that he realised how anxious, how uncertain he had been over this gamble. But it had paid off. It was time to seal the deal.

'What say you then, that we end this foolish separation? That we join our forces together, so we can unite against the real enemies. For Caesar!'

The roar reverberated around the camp, echoing back off the hills, such was its volume.

A bleary-eyed figure, looking as if he had only just woken and had hastily donned his military uniform, made his way through the ranks, who parted respectfully for him.

'Marcus Antonius,' said Lepidus, looking up at Antony, who was still perched on his barrel.

'Marcus Aemilius Lepidus. Sincerest greetings.'

Antony called out for another barrel to be pulled over, and though Lepidus looked reluctant, Antony extended his hand and hauled Lepidus up so the legionaries could view them as equals.

'Proconsul,' said Antony in a voice loud enough to carry across the attentive soldiers, 'I come with the proposal that we join forces against the assassins of Caesar and the enemies of Rome. Your men seem to approve the idea. What say you?'

Lepidus looked out around the massed, expectant faces, knowing that he had no choice: that Antony had suborned his army by pure force of personality.

'How could you doubt?' asked Lepidus. 'Of course, I agree.'

As the two generals shook hands, the noise from the delighted legionaries reached new heights. Antony raised Lepidus' arm into the air, and, hands joined, saluted the troops as if they were victors in the arena.

When the noise died down enough for Antony to be heard again, he spoke once more.

'I am so grateful for your loyalty, Proconsul,' said Antony. 'I accept your proposal that I take command of our forces, and obviously I nominate you second-in-command.'

Lepidus gaped at this audacious move, but the cheering legionaries drowned out any protest. Antony leaned forward and whispered in his ear.

'Don't feel bad, Lepidus, old friend. It was inevitable that I take command. But fear not, this is very much a joint enterprise. Together, we will rule Rome again, just like after the Ides of March. Today has been very much to the benefit of both of us.'

Lepidus didn't reply, but Antony pumped his hand further, then called to the soldiers, 'The proconsul and I have much to discuss. For now, celebrate this union of allies. But be prepared. Battle may not be far away.'

He leapt down from his barrel lightly, and offered his hand to help Lepidus down. Lepidus refused the help and jumped down himself, turning his ankle as he landed, so he was limping slightly as he made his way with Antony to the command tent. Behind them, despite the early hour, the legionaries were breaking out the wine and preparing for a blow-out party. Antony himself, having gone from almost utter destruction a month ago to finding himself now in sole command of a huge army, felt that a drink or two might be in order.

Chapter VIII

Sextilis DCCXI AUC (August 43 BC), Forum Iulii

Antony's war council had greatly expanded since the siege of Mutina, when he had only Silanus and his brother Lucius as senior generals that he could turn to for advice. Now, seated around the table, in addition to Silanus and Lucius, he had Ventidius and Lepidus. Importantly, he had now been joined by Lucius Munatius Plancus, the governor of Transalpine Gaul, and Gaius Asinius Pollio, governor of further Spain. Besides them, the diminutive Lucius Varius Cotyla and the former tribune Lucius Trebellius Fides had come from Rome to take up positions in his army, though both, somewhat less senior than the others, were absent from this meeting, busy with their assigned duties.

After Lepidus and Antony had joined forces, Plancus, forty miles to the north, always nervous, had prevaricated. He had written to the Senate assuring them of his loyalty, and had invited Decimus Brutus to meet him. Antony and Lepidus had moved some detachments north and Plancus had quickly retreated to the Isara river, where Brutus brought his army up and camped with him. Together, Brutus and Plancus could muster fourteen legions, and though only four were veteran, it was not in Antony's interests to force an engagement, particularly if he hoped to bring those legions under his own standard.

A stand-off between the two sides persisted, with messengers buzzing around between Brutus and Plancus, Lepidus and Antony, and Cicero and the Senate, like particularly industrious honeybees. In his missives to Rome, Plancus called Lepidus and Antony traitors and red-hot rebels. Further, he chastised Octavian for allowing Antony to join up with Lepidus and not assisting Brutus. Octavian, whom Antony had carefully left out of his speech to the Tenth, not wishing to alienate Caesar's heir, but not wishing to show him too much deference either, was, as far as Antony knew, in his own negotiations with the Senate while he stayed with his army in Cisalpine Gaul. Yet Plancus' letters to the men he called traitors were much more moderate, and it was clear he was hedging his bets.

Cicero, having successfully passed a motion to have Lepidus, too, declared an enemy of the people, pressed Plancus and Brutus to push on and crush Lepidus and Antony. Decimus Brutus called for Cassius and Marcus Brutus to bring their legions from the East to reinforce him, leaving Dolabella so they could concentrate on the real threat: Antony. But nothing happened until August, when Pollio arrived with two legions from Spain.

Although Pollio had reservations about Lepidus, he had a good relationship with Antony. He had been with Caesar and Antony at the start of the civil war with Pompey, and he had assisted Antony in his struggles with Dolabella when Antony was Caesar's Master of Horse and Dolabella was a rabble-rousing tribune. And Antony had never forgotten the gentle way Pollio had written to him, breaking the news of the death of his best friend Curio in battle in Africa. It was Pollio, then, who had persuaded Plancus to throw his weight behind Antony, both for the sake of friendship and loyalty, but more importantly, because he thought Antony would win. Certainly the two fresh Spanish legions that Pollio added to Antony's cause tilted the scales even further, and Decimus Brutus' and Plancus' legions combined would not be enough to confront Antony and his allies.

So Plancus informed Decimus and his legions of his decision to join Antony, and Decimus' legions, tired, traumatised from the battles and siege at Mutina, fed up with marching through the Alps on a wild goose chase trying to catch up with Antony, and in any case never particularly supportive of Decimus Brutus, the assassin of Caesar, promptly defected, the veterans and cavalry to Antony, the new recruits to Octavian. Plancus graciously allowed Decimus Brutus to leave with a small escort of guards and informed Antony of his decision, much to Antony's relief and delight.

Summer was at its height now, and though it seemed there had been an expectation that Antony would immediately march on Rome, he had preferred to bide his time, secure in his Gallic stronghold, recruiting, training, preparing for the right moment. In the meantime, he corresponded frequently with Octavian, who was getting ever more frustrated with the Senate's position.

'Friends,' said Antony, opening the proceedings, 'shall we begin?'

'Perhaps a prayer and a sacrifice first,' said Lepidus.

Antony shrugged. He wasn't sure if Lepidus was being truly devout, superstitious, or was reminding everyone present of his important position as Pontifex Maximus. Antony was happy to indulge him, and they all traipsed outside and waited patiently while Lepidus slaughtered a white ram on the camp altar and dedicated it to Fortuna and Mars. They returned to Antony's tent while a butcher dragged the carcass away to be divided among some of the men lucky enough to get some extra meat added to their bland diet.

'Thank you, Lepidus,' said Antony once they were all seated again. 'And thank you all for coming. It's good to meet you all together. Let's begin with a round-up of our strength and the strength of our opponents. Silanus?'

'The number seems to be ever-changing, Proconsul,' said Silanus, 'and of course counting eagles is not the same as counting men – many legions on both sides are not at full strength. Still, we can be confident of our own number. Between the legions you brought from Mutina, those that I recruited in Picenum, the legions controlled by Plancus, Lepidus and Pollio here, plus the units that were previously commanded by Decimus Brutus, I put our count at twenty-three legions.

'By contrast, Octavianus has eight legions, and the Senate has one, with two more on their way from Africa.'

Antony was, of course, aware of the figures, but it was pleasing to hear them spoken aloud in front of his lieutenants. He was once again, without doubt, the most powerful man in the Empire, stronger than the Senate, stronger than Octavian, stronger even than the combined forces of Marcus Brutus and Cassius, who were busily recruiting in the East.

'So what is your plan, Proconsul?' asked Plancus, sitting back, arms folded. 'Are we to wait in Gaul until Cicero dies of old age?'

Antony gave him a smile. 'If there is one thing I learned from Caesar, it is to prepare thoroughly and patiently, and when the moment comes, to strike with surprise and overwhelming force.'

The proconsuls and legates around the table nodded sagely in agreement. None of them were militarily naive, with Ventidius, Pollio and Plancus all having served with Caesar in Gaul and during the civil war, and Lucius and Silanus fully involved in the action around Mutina.

Lepidus, despite holding more prestigious positions in the past than any of them except Antony, was actually the least experienced, and had often resolved the conflicts he was involved in by negotiation rather than battle. Yet they all deferred to Antony, whom Caesar had favoured and who had shown himself to be both skilled and lucky in battle.

'But before we march on Rome, I want to see the situation between Octavianus and the Senate resolved. The boy is undoubtedly playing both sides, the Senate and us both, but he has been polite in his letters to me even though we are nominally opponents, and he even offered me help in dealing with Decimus Brutus' legions. I turned him down, of course.'

'What do you think he intends?' asked Lucius.

'I'm not sure exactly what motivates him,' said Antony. 'It seems on the surface that he wants to avenge Caesar and gain power for himself. But the waters run deep in that one. I want him on my side, but I don't entirely trust him. And despite our strength, it would be no mean feat to swipe aside his eight legions, not to mention the risk of further defections from our own legions, given the love they hold for Caesar's heir.'

The expression on Antony's face, as if he had sucked something sour, showed the others how he felt about that.

'But what if he joins up with the Senate's legions?' asked Lepidus nervously. 'Or worse, Brutus and Cassius bring their legions over from the East, as Cicero keeps imploring them.'

'Calm yourself, Lepidus,' said Antony. 'Firstly, Cassius and Brutus can't come to Italy with Dolabella still in the East – they would lose their power base. As for the Senate's legions, they are so few in number and poor in quality, they do not concern me. Yes, we could strike at Octavianus now, and deplete both our strengths. But Octavianus is no fool. He knows that he is not strong enough to resist Brutus and Cassius when conflict between them comes – and it will come – without me. We need to let Octavianus' plans in Italy play out. Then it will be our turn. Then, he can join us, or be annihilated.'

The generals looked mollified, and Antony congratulated himself on appeasing them all. Lucius and Ventidius were the most bellicose, anxious for the fight. Lepidus and Plancus wished to avoid all bloodshed if possible, especially if it put them in personal danger. Antony seemed to have successfully steered a middle ground that kept them all happy.

'You seem not to have factored in Decimus Brutus,' said Plancus, with a hint of acidity. 'He is still at large.'

'Ah,' said Antony. 'There I have news for you.' He made a motion to an attendant orderly, who disappeared out of the tent. 'When Decimus left you, Plancus, he pressed east with a bodyguard of Gallic horse, hoping to reach Marcus Brutus in Macedonia. But most of his bodyguard deserted, and with only ten men left, he disguised himself as a Gaul and headed towards Aquileia. He was captured on the way by bandits and bound, but when he asked after the name of the chief of the tribe who had taken him prisoner, he discovered it was one Camilus, a man he had had good relations with in the past. He asked to be brought before Camilus, who greeted him cordially and chastised those who had subjected such a great man to this indignity.

'But while Camilus hosted Decimus Brutus as an honoured guest, he was secretly writing to me, informing me of his captive and asking me my wishes.'

Antony looked around the table at the expectant faces. He sighed. 'What could I do? Order his release and grant him clemency? Caesar tried that tactic, and look how that ended. Demand he be brought to me? That would have been a long and arduous journey, and I didn't want to risk Decimus Brutus escaping, and raising more opposition.

'So I asked Camilus to kill him, and send me proof of his death.'

The orderly returned with a wooden box about the size of a hat. The generals around the table looked at it with suspicion and mounting horror.

'This arrived this morning,' said Antony. 'I have not yet opened it.'

He took a breath, then flicked the latch on the box and lifted the lid. A stagnant smell of decay met his nostrils. He looked on its contents for a moment, then turned and tilted it, so all could see. Decimus Brutus, beard coated with congealed blood, the dried meat and tubes of his neck exposed, looked up at them with a faintly disappointed gaze.

A groan went around the table. Antony unexpectedly felt tears well up, threaten to overflow. Decimus Brutus, praetor, proconsul, consul-designate, had been his friend. But he had also been a traitor, who had murdered one who loved him in the cause of some rarefied concept of liberty. Antony refused to cry for such a man. He wiped his eyes angrily with the sleeve of his tunic and closed the lid, gesturing for the orderly to take it away.

'His remains will be buried with all honours due a man of his rank,' said Antony firmly. 'But though I mourn the loss of another comrade, I will not regret his fate. And the same fate will come to all who had a hand in the death of Caesar.'

Lepidus looked nauseous, Plancus looked sad, but all the generals looked resolute. Antony had everyone's cups filled, and they toasted Caesar's memory and drank deeply.

Kalendis Septembribus DCCXI AUC (1 September 43 BC), Cisalpine Gaul

Antony finally gave the order for the legions to march towards the end of the month of Sextilis. Spirits were high throughout the ranks, from the legates down to the lowest auxiliaries. Meanwhile, Antony received regular news from Rome from various sources. Quintus Fufius Calenus, the former consul, who was a strong supporter of Antony and consequently hated by Cicero, was a frequent correspondent, as was Antony's mother, Julia. Less frequent – and less welcome – were the letters from his mother's brother, Lucius Julius Caesar. Antony's uncle had been decidedly lukewarm in his support since Caesar's assassination, often supporting the Senate as it became increasingly anti-Antony, but at least acting as a brake on some of its most violent proposals against his nephew. His messages to Antony alternated between dutiful expressions of familial love and reproof at Antony's actions, in particular his defiance of the Senate and his enmity with Cicero. Antony paid his words little heed, deeming it rank hypocrisy, given the firm support Lucius Caesar had given his cousin Gaius Julius Caesar throughout his civil war against the Senate and Pompey.

But it was the correspondence from Fulvia that he particularly looked forward to, and he still felt a little flutter in the pit of his stomach when mail arrived from Rome with her seal on it. Early in September, Antony received a letter from Fulvia and the first lines made him whoop with joy.

ante diem xiii Kalendas Septembres

Dearest Marcus,

> *I must start by bringing you the news I know you have been anxious for. I am dictating this letter to my scribe from my bed, since I am too weary to write in my own hand. But I know you will forgive me when you learn that the reason for my fatigue is that yesterday I gave birth to a healthy baby boy.*

Antony immediately stopped reading, punching the air and yelling out for his slaves to fetch his brother immediately. Lucius arrived moments later, breathless and anxious.

'Brother, what's wrong?'

'You're an uncle once more,' said Antony, and Lucius grabbed his brother in a hearty embrace, and then called for wine.

After they had each drained a cup, Lucius asked, 'What will you name him?'

'I thought I would call him Iullus, in honour, of course, of the great man.'

'It's an unusual name, but it will be well received,' said Lucius.

'It will. And it will remind the world that Octavianus is not the only relative and heir of Caesar.'

Lucius smiled, then nodded to the abandoned scroll on the table. 'It's a letter from Fulvia?'

'Yes. I haven't actually finished reading yet.'

Lucius had his cup refilled and took a seat, putting his feet up on the table.

'Tell me all, brother.'

'In a moment.'

Antony read the remainder of the letter in silence.

> *As you know, Octavianus has been playing both sides, corresponding with you and with the Senate, although he disdains to have anything to do with the assassins in the East. Throughout the summer, he has been working on Cicero to help him gain power in Rome, even suggesting that they hold the vacant consulship jointly. But the Senate seems to have taken Cicero's quip about raising, praising and discarding Octavianus literally. They seem to believe he is an irrelevance, which I think you and I both know is to greatly underestimate the devious boy. Octavianus lost patience, and he sent a deputation of four hundred unarmed*

soldiers into the Senate to ask for the donatives they had been promised, for Octavianus to be made consul, and interestingly, a demand that the decree of enemy of the state against you be repealed. The senators were outraged and told them angrily to leave, and one senator even struck a soldier. The lead centurion left and returned wearing his sword, which he showed to them, saying, 'This will decide matters if you don't.'

Cicero responded, 'If that's how you make a request, then I'm sure you are right.'

When the soldiers reported back to Octavianus, he realised finally that the Senate had no intention of honouring their previous promises to him, so, like the man he claims to be his father, he crossed the Rubicon, though with eight legions instead of one, and marched on Rome.

The reaction here was rather wonderful to watch as the optimates panicked to a man. They sent messengers offering him the consulship and wagons loaded with gold for his troops. Octavianus merely had his cavalry turn the wagons aside so his legions weren't distracted, and marched on.

Then two legions arrived from Africa, and the Senate, deciding they would be enough to defend the city, sent messengers rescinding their offer of the consulship. The senators attempted to take poor Atia and Octavia hostage in a crude attempt to force Octavianus to desist, but this shows how little they understand the boy, and in any case, they took refuge in the Temple of Vesta. As soon as Octavianus approached the city, the legions defending it defected to him, and he entered Rome with his bodyguard, where he was received like a returning hero by the masses.

The senators fell over themselves assuring him of their goodwill, and Cicero arranged a private meeting with him to make sure he knew that it was he who had proposed Octavianus for the consulship. But the Senate met at night amid rumours that the Martian and Fourth legions had defected from Octavianus. Cicero greeted each senator as they arrived, and they agreed to send a party to recruit more legions from Picenum. Then they learned that the rumours about the defecting legions were false, and Cicero fled in a litter.

> *Two days ago, Octavianus and his cousin Quintus Pedius took office as consuls. He immediately had his formal adoption by Caesar ratified – I suppose this means we should call him 'Caesar' now, too, though it will be a hard habit to master – and he has repealed the status of public enemy for you, Lepidus, Plancus and Dolabella. Octavianus has set up a special court to try all the assassins and everyone who had been forewarned of the plot, and they were quickly judged guilty.*
>
> *What a wonderful reversal of fortunes, Marcus, for you and our family. We are feted everywhere we go in the city now, and those clients of yours and mine who were less than steadfast have crawled back out from under their rocks and show up every morning to show their respects. When you return to Rome, we will discuss which of our supporters deserve rewarding, and which we should perhaps be having some frank discussions with.*
>
> *I have to say, Octavianus does have the luck of his adoptive father as well as his cunning. If you had not survived and restored your position with your legions, he would have no allies, and would have been crushed by Brutus and Cassius when they returned to Italy. But with your current strength, they cannot confront you, giving Octavianus a free hand. Now, it's up to you to make sure you do not let him get the upper hand. I would suggest you make cause with him – after all, Brutus and Cassius remain a significant threat – and you and he have common interests. Together you would be just as powerful as Caesar and Pompeius were, although perhaps you need a Crassus as a go-between. And, of course, never forget how that alliance ended.*
>
> *It is time to feed your son again – he has a wonderful healthy appetite. Send all my love to Lucius,*
>
> *Your beloved Fulvia*

Antony handed the letter to his brother, who read it in turn. When Lucius looked up, he was smiling broadly.

'What do you think?' asked Antony.

'I think the Senate's power and authority have evaporated. And though Octavianus is consul, you control the most powerful army in the Empire. You should march on Rome yourself, and put Octavianus in his place.'

'Perhaps,' said Antony. But he knew, out of Fulvia and Lucius, whose advice he trusted more.

A few days later, as Antony progressed towards Italy, he received a letter from Octavian, congratulating him that he was no longer a public enemy and suggesting they should meet. Antony replied in similar terms, congratulating him on his election, promising friendship and co-operation and agreeing to a meeting. It would not be easy to come to an accommodation with the boy after all the bad blood between them. But it would be worth it. And Antony was confident that whatever terms they came to, he would be first among equals.

October DCCXI AUC (Late October 43 BC), Bononia

Antony advanced along the coast road into Italy with seventeen legions at his back, leaving six legions with his trusted general, little Varius Cotyla, to ensure peace in the provinces. Octavian, whose strength also numbered seventeen legions, now that they had been further augmented by the six newly recruited legions that had defected from Decimus Brutus, marched slowly north up the Via Flaminia. As the massive armies approached each other, messengers scurried back and forth between the two camps, negotiating the fine details of their momentous meeting.

It had been agreed to put Lepidus in charge of the first encounter between the leaders of the Caesarian faction to take place for around a year. Octavian and Antony had both recognised the need for an intermediary – a Crassus, as Fulvia had put it. Lepidus' seniority, his legions, his ancestry, coupled with the vanity that made him so easy to manipulate and his complete inability to inspire loyalty from his men, made him the obvious choice. He went about his task with an ostentatiousness that amused Antony, though he had to admit ultimately that Lepidus performed his task well.

The agreed venue was a small island in the river Lavinius near the town of Bononia, not far from Mutina. Antony and Octavian approached the river from opposite directions with five legions each and camped on their own sides of the river. Lepidus had bridges built to the island from both banks, then had tents pitched and a dais raised that could be seen by both armies. When all was in place, Antony and Octavian approached their respective bridges, each with a small Praetorian escort, and waited while Lepidus went onto the island and made a dramatic show of searching for traps and ambushes. When he was satisfied, he waved his cloak in the air to signal the all-clear.

Antony looked across the river to where Octavian stood. Their eyes locked, and though it was hard to tell at this distance, he thought he saw Octavian smile. Antony raised his hand in salute, then set foot on the bridge, Octavian mirroring his steps. When they reached the island, both of them mounted the dais, and with Lepidus looking on like the celebrant at a wedding ceremony, Antony reached out to shake Octavian's hand. He made sure to grip the young, slender man's hand firmly – not enough to hurt, just enough to remind him of his physical superiority. Octavian returned the shake with surprising strength, making Antony wonder if he had been exercising his arm specifically in preparation for this moment. They embraced, then raised their linked arms to the air. The armies on both banks roared out their approval, and they let the applause last, before taking seats on the dais. Octavian, as consul, now had the highest ranking magistracy of the three, and so, as had been previously agreed, he took the central seat, acting as chair of the meeting. But in reality, it was a meeting of two near equals and one hanger-on.

For a while the two men sat quietly, sizing each other up. Since they had last met, Octavian's face had firmed up, lost some of its puppyishness, and he had put on a little muscle, though he was still a sapling to Antony's mature oak. Antony wondered how he himself had changed. If there had previously been any suspicion of him letting his body go to seed with his lifestyle, a year in the field had hardened him once more, so his muscles rippled when he flexed, and there was not a pound of fat on him.

Lepidus, becoming uncomfortable at the silence, said, 'It's been quite a year.'

Octavian inclined his head. 'It's certainly had its moments.'

'There have been one or two ups and downs,' said Antony.

Then all three men burst out laughing, and the tension was broken.

Lepidus offered them cups of wine, and they drank, though Antony noticed that Octavian only took a small sip, and he reminded himself that he would need to keep his wits about him in this negotiation.

That said, most of the plans had been thrashed out in messages and meetings of representatives prior to them getting anywhere near Bononia. They were all wise enough to know that the meeting would be pointless if the preliminary approaches suggested they had no common ground, which fortunately wasn't the case. But there was still plenty of detail to decide upon, and Antony settled himself in for a long day, pulling his cloak around him to ward off the chill autumn air.

'Shall we start with some broad principles?' suggested Octavian.

Antony gestured for him to continue.

'We are all firm Caesarians, correct? Despite the... compromises we have all had to make for political reasons.'

Antony conceded the point. Much as he had hated to see Octavian cosying up with Cicero and the Senate, he had been forced into similar actions in the immediate aftermath of the Ides of March, for self-preservation as much as political ideology.

'So we agree that is intolerable that the assassins Marcus Junius Brutus and Gaius Cassius Longinus hold the eastern half of the Empire, enriching themselves and growing their armies?'

'That goes without saying,' said Antony. 'Their position is incompatible with our loyalty to Caesar's memory, and to our own personal safety.'

'Good. So we take the fight to them? We sail our legions to Greece?'

Antony sat back and stroked his beard. The boy was eager for war. Antony approved.

'I agree,' said Antony. 'As soon as we are ready, I will march against the assassins.'

'I said "we",' said Octavian.

'Young man—' said Antony.

'Call me Consul, or Caesar,' snapped Octavian.

Antony closed his mouth and regarded Octavian through narrowed eyes. Then he continued.

'Consul, would it not be more prudent for you to consolidate our hold on Italy while I do what I do best – make war?'

'And give you control of the vast majority of our legions? We are negotiating an alliance here, and I believe we are all acting in good faith. But that doesn't make me naive. It must be a joint command.'

'All three of us?' asked Lepidus hopefully.

'No,' said Antony and Octavian in unison.

Antony patted Lepidus' thigh. 'If Octav— the consul and I are to go east, we need someone trusted and legally empowered to rule Italy while we are gone. And who better than you, with your dignitas and your experience in the role?'

Lepidus reluctantly allowed himself to be mollified.

'That's agreed, then,' said Octavian. 'You and I, Antonius, will lead our legions against the assassins as soon as we are in a position to do so. It's a good start. But there are other matters we need to attend to before we reach that point. Namely, the legal authority and the funds.'

'For the first,' said Antony, 'I believe you have a proposal?'

'Since you abolished the role of dictator, rightly or wrongly, we can't resurrect that title. Not that it would serve us in any case – which of us would be prepared to be Master of Horse to the other's Dictator?'

'Go on,' said Lepidus.

'My tame tribune Titius will formulate a law in the Senate for us. We will be elected as *tresviri rei publicae constituendae* – the Three Men to establish the State. Our stated purpose will be to restore the function of the Republic, and end civil war by defeating the assassins.'

'And what powers will we have to enable us to do this?' asked Antony.

'Full powers,' said Octavian. 'Legislative and executive, for a five-year term, with sole right to appoint all consuls, other magistrates and governors of the provinces.'

Antony stroked his chin. It was dictatorship in all but name, though divided three ways. This was never something he had aimed for. Power, yes, in order to take the choicest provinces for himself, and to ensure his safety and the safety of his family after Caesar's death. But this supreme, absolute form of power? It was dangerous. And highly seductive.

'So be it,' said Antony. 'As Caesar – your father Caesar, I mean – said at Pharsalus, "They chose this."'

'Precisely,' said Octavian. 'We have both been abused by the Senate, just as my father was. All I wanted was my rightful inheritance, my father's name, and recognition of my authority. Neither of us wished to be in this position.'

Antony nodded.

'So we must decide on the split of the provinces and the magistracies for the coming years,' said Octavian.

'Do we need to be so specific at this stage?' asked Antony.

'We do,' said Octavian. 'We must not leave this island until every last detail has been agreed by the three of us. I want there to be no doubts, no room for misunderstandings or disagreements going forward.'

Antony sighed. It was going to be a very long meeting.

'Very well. Let's start with Spain.'

The negotiations carried on for the rest of the day, and it was dark when Lepidus suggested they pause proceedings for the night and continue the following day. Antony gratefully accepted the suggestion. Octavian was pedantic, stubborn and clearly highly intelligent. He had prepared thoroughly for this meeting, and had come armed with figures and statistics, while Antony had arrived with only a vague idea of what he wanted, and consequently felt as if he was constantly playing catch-up. If he proposed an ally for a position, Octavian always seemed to have a long list of reasons that person would be unsuitable, be it incompetence, unpopularity or a history of illegality. When Octavian proposed one of his allies, Antony did not have such ammunition to hand, and he had to be creative in finding reasons for refusal, or had to simply dig his heels in and say no. Octavian showed no signs of frustration when Antony was obstinate, simply moving on, though often later circling back to his arguments for or against a particular candidate.

A yellow crescent moon peeked over the trees, and Lepidus lit a couple of lamps and dished out the meal the army cooks had prepared – cold meats, olives, nuts, some fruit, and some wine from Picenum of a decent vintage. Antony stuffed some nuts into his mouth and watched Octavian picking delicately at the olives.

'Tell me, honestly,' said Antony. 'What did you think when you learned Caesar had made you his heir?'

Octavian shrugged. 'That it was no more than my due.'

Antony exchanged a look with Lepidus, then shook his head. Antony could hear the young man's wheezy breathing. His build was such that Antony wondered he could lift a sword. His smooth, beardless face still had hints of adolescent acne. And yet here he was, treating with Antony and Lepidus as an equal. A consul of Rome, no less, despite his extreme youth. Caesar had famously lamented when he was thirty-two that by his age, Alexander had conquered the world, while he had done nothing memorable. Yet his heir, just turned twenty, was calmly and skilfully making himself one of the three rulers of Rome, the most powerful empire in existence.

Even so, Antony was confident that he was going to be the dominant party in this triumvirate. How could it be otherwise? He had the seniority, the political experience, the military skill and the love of his men.

'Don't you worry about coming into all this power at your age?' he asked. 'You have discovered for yourself how hard it is to trust people in politics. But you are not old enough to command the respect and authority you need on your own.'

'I trust to my own acumen. And where I have deficiencies, I recognise them, and use the attributes of loyal friends to fill the gaps. I am fortunate to have had Marcus Vipsanius Agrippa and Gaius Cilnius Maecenas as friends ever since we were at school together. Maecenas always gives me sound political advice, and Agrippa's grasp of military tactics and strategy is formidable. Perhaps even equal to yours, Antonius.'

Antony scoffed, but he resolved to learn more about this Agrippa. If relations did sour between him and Octavian in the future, it would be sensible to know his potential enemies. That wasn't something Antony felt he had to worry about for the time being, however, not with Brutus and Cassius threatening them from the east.

'And Cicero? Another loyal friend and advisor?'

Octavian pursed his lips.

'You know full well what Cicero said about me.'

'I do,' said Antony. 'And I'm sorry to say it came as no surprise. Cicero has always had only his own interests at heart, whatever he says about liberty and the Republic. As soon as he heard of my... withdrawal from Mutina, he will have set his sights on a consulship, a return to his glory days of the rebellion of Catilina, with you as his puppet to keep the legions pliant.'

'As you say, I am young. Perhaps I was naive. But I assure you I am learning very quickly.'

Antony smiled. 'I don't doubt it. And for that reason, I'm glad we are on the same side.'

He tilted his cup towards Octavian, who tapped it with his own. Lepidus looked put out, so they both clinked their goblets against his own, too.

'Colleagues, I think I will retire,' said Octavian eventually, when he had finished his meal. 'I suggest we recommence our discussions at dawn.'

'I concur,' said Lepidus.

Antony sighed. It was a bit early, but he might as well go to bed himself. It might have been intriguing to talk to Octavian for longer, but he had no desire to sit up drinking and chatting with the tedious Lepidus.

'Until dawn, then. Sleep well.'

—

Antony was woken by Lepidus shaking his shoulder and offering him some bread and water. He rolled out of his tent, blinking in the early morning light. Octavian was already seated at the central chair on the dais, sipping from his cup and breakfasting lightly. Antony dashed down his water and devoured half a loaf of bread while pacing around the tiny, marshy island. The soldiers in both camps were already up and starting their daily duties: relieving the night watch; clearing out the latrines; checking the defences; preparing breakfast. He took a deep breath, his nostrils filling with the scents of the army – the manure of the horses and pack animals, the sweat of men, the aromas of onions, garlic and garum drifting out of the kitchens. There was really nothing like it, and if he had to choose between a life in his luxurious Roman villa, with all the slaves, the well-stocked wine cellar, the parties and gaming and theatre, and a life on the march with the legions, he would struggle to decide. He realised how fortunate he was that he could have both.

He waved to the bodyguards at the end of the bridge across the river to his camp, and they saluted sharply, grinning broadly at the acknowledgement from their commander. Then he took his seat with Octavian and Lepidus, and the negotiations began again.

It was nearly noon by the time they had finished deciding all the provincial and magisterial appointments for the next five years, Lepidus documenting every agreed position on a wax tablet with a neat, careful hand. The final agreement divided up the provinces that were not controlled by Brutus and Cassius between themselves. Cassius had recently defeated and killed Dolabella, and the two Liberators were undisputed rulers in the East, so to attempt to award themselves the Eastern provinces would be clear fantasy.

So Lepidus kept Gallia Narbonensis and Nearer Spain, and had Further Spain added to his purview. Octavian was given Africa and Sicily – important grain-producing regions – as well as miscellaneous other islands. Antony kept Cisalpine and Transalpine Gaul. He was content. While he was not given any extra provinces than had already been previously voted for him, it confirmed his as the most senior of the three: the two large Gallic provinces commanded the most legions, and Cisalpine Gaul was the key to Italy, as exemplified by the two marches on Rome from across the Rubicon in a few short years by Caesar and his heir. Pollio would surrender Further Spain to Lepidus, but would run Cisalpine Gaul as Antony's legate. Octavian, to some extent, had the roughest deal, since Sicily was largely controlled by Sextus Pompeius and his fleets, and he would need to be dealt with before Octavian could take possession of the rich island.

For the magistracies, Antony's disreputable uncle and ex-father-in-law Gaius Antonius Hybrida was given the prestigious position of censor – technically in charge of the membership of the Senate. It was agreed that Octavian would resign the consulship in favour of Ventidius, allowing Antony to reward his loyal lieutenant and complete the man's dizzying rise from donkey driver to consul of Rome. Plancus was consoled by being designated as consul for the following year, with Lepidus instead of Decimus as his colleague. The following year, Antony's brother Lucius would be consul, and his colleague would be Publius Servilius Vatius Isauricus, who had supported the Senate against Antony and whose daughter had been betrothed to Octavian. Servilius had switched his support to Octavian, despite the fact that Octavian had broken off the engagement, and this was Servilius' reward. The final consuls agreed upon for the penultimate year of the term of the triumviral agreement were Pollio and Gnaeus Domitius Calvinus, the high-born Caesarian general. Antony and Octavian would jointly take the consulship, both for the second time, in the final year of the triumvirate.

Antony was well satisfied with the outcome. Anyone looking at the result of the negotiations would have to conclude that he had come out the best, with the strongest personal position, and his closest allies taking the lion's share of the rewards. Not that this wrote off Octavian in the long term, and no doubt there would be much politicking and jockeying for position to come. But it seemed to guarantee five years of peace, strong leadership of Rome, and security for Antony and his family.

Next, Lepidus suggested they consider the two armies who were watching their deliberations from afar. Without much argument, Antony and Octavian agreed that eighteen of the richest cities in Italy should be forced to offer up some of their best land on which to settle the veterans when they were disbanded. All three of the newly minted triumvirs knew that their entire authority rested on their legions, and that the legions knew this, too. There could be no short-changing the army.

The final agreement was to have a tie of marriage to seal the deal. Antony and Lepidus were already married, and Lepidus' oldest son was already betrothed to Antony's daughter, young Toni. Antony therefore offered his stepdaughter Claudia's hand in marriage to Octavian, the original suggestion actually coming from Fulvia. It was a good match. The Claudii were a venerable family, and as the daughter of Fulvia and Publius Clodius, Claudia was well loved by the common people.

Lepidus laboriously copied out his notes onto a scroll and all three of the triumvirs signed their names to the document. Octavian, as consul, then took the document and read out the terms to the expectant armies. His words were greeted by cheers of relief that war had been averted, excitement and the prospect of their beloved generals ruling Rome together, and, of course, delight at the personal rewards of land, on top of a repeated commitment to pay the donatives they had already been promised. The three new rulers of Rome went among their men, accepting their good will and congratulations. Antony prepared for an evening of drinking among the legionary tents.

But a messenger found him downing a cup of rough wine with two centurions, and told him that Octavian wished to meet with him and Lepidus once more on the island.

With trepidation, Antony excused himself to his drinking companions and made his way back to the dais on the island. Lepidus and Octavian were waiting for him.

'What is it?' he asked suspiciously.

'Not here,' said Octavian. 'Would you join me in my tent?'

Antony was on the alert, suddenly aware that he had not so much as a dagger hanging off his belt. But there were only the three of them on the island, and guards had been stationed at the end of both bridges to keep it that way. Knowing that he could easily overpower Lepidus and Octavian, even if they came at him together, he agreed, and ducked inside Octavian's tent.

The three of them were seated, and Antony waited expectantly.

Octavian looked grave.

'Colleagues, we have come to a historic agreement today. We have stabilised Rome after the chaos caused by my father's murder. And we have in our hands the military might and the legal authority to deal with the assassins Brutus and Cassius once and for all.

'But there is one problem. We don't have enough money.'

Antony sat back, and he let out a relieved sigh. Money? Is that all this was about?

Antony had always had a casual relationship with money. He liked to have it, but having spent so much of his life in profound debt, he wasn't particularly bothered by its absence, provided he had a good line of credit. And who would not extend credit to the three triumvirs now? But Octavian would not accept this argument.

'It's not enough,' he said. 'Firstly, the three of us have all already used up much of our personal funds raising our armies, and most of the usual lenders in Rome have lent as much as they are prepared to.'

'It's true,' said Lepidus. 'Even my personal banker is showing reluctance to extend my credit further, despite my letters telling him of the improvement in my personal circumstances.'

'Fine,' said Antony. 'We tell the men we will pay them after we defeat Brutus and Cassius and take possession of the wealth of the Eastern provinces.'

'Do you really think they will be that patient?' asked Octavian.

Antony had to concede that the young man was right. The legions had learned that defiance and insurrection could bring punishment and shame, but it could just as easily bring great reward. Antony did not want to risk the legions deciding they would down swords until they had been paid.

'Then we milk the rich,' said Antony. 'We can tax the senatorial and equestrian orders.'

'Yes,' said Lepidus. 'Property taxes. Taxes on their capital wealth. Heavy fines for non-compliance.'

Octavian shook his head. 'Yes, we can do all those things. But it's not enough.'

'So what do you propose?' asked Antony.

Octavian looked at the two older men, and said one word that chilled them both.

'Proscriptions.'

–

It was Sulla who first introduced proscriptions to Rome, as a method of taking revenge and making money from the aristocracy who had made him an enemy of the state during his struggles with Gaius Marius. Its after-effects were felt for a generation, with the loss of status of some of Rome's oldest families only being reversed when Caesar took power. The term 'proscription' still made rich men shudder some forty years after they were imposed. And now the triumvirs were bringing them back.

The negotiations were long and unpleasant. The three triumvirs took it in turns to propose names. The initial suggestions were straightforward, the assassins being the most obvious targets. Thus Marcus Brutus and Gaius Cassius Longinus came first. Unfortunately, they were protected by large armies in Greece, so their inclusion was purely symbolic, although could be used later to justify war. After this, they worked their way through other obvious enemies like the assassin Casca, Lucius Cornelius Cinna – the ally of Caesar who had rejoiced at his death, and in whose place the poet Helvius Cinna had been mistakenly murdered by an angry mob – and Quintus Aponius, who had served under Trebonius. Next came those who had not particularly done them ill, but had a fatal combination of senatorial sympathy and significant wealth.

Then came those who had personally wronged them. And for Antony, one man had done more harm than anyone to him and his loved ones.

'I propose Cicero,' he said.

Lepidus gasped. Octavian went quiet and turned pale.

'You ask much,' said Octavian. 'He is our foremost intellectual. Our greatest ever orator. He is beloved by the nobles and the common man.'

'I think you overestimate the common folks' opinion of him. They see him as cowardly and vainglorious.'

'Nevertheless, would not killing him be like destroying a precious treasure that belongs to Rome? It may not be a legacy we wish for. Besides, he was kind to me when I first arrived in Rome.'

Antony scoffed. 'You know full well that he was gentle with you purely out of self-interest. He wished to use you and discard you. As for legacy, do you feel our renown will be served by having a living Cicero criticise our every edict and act in beautifully crafted prose?'

Octavian looked doubtful.

'This is not a matter I will be moved on,' said Antony firmly. Cicero had actually been the first name that had sprung to his mind when proscriptions were mentioned, though he had bided his time to bring him up. 'Need I list his offences against me and mine? He had my mother's husband executed without trial. He refused to allow us his body for proper burial. He opposed Caesar at every turn. He joined Pompeius, and despite Caesar's forgiveness and affection for him, he rejoiced at his death. And then he launched these so-called Philippics, directed not just against me but also those I care deeply about. Lucius. Fulvia. Even my first wife, Fadia.' Not to mention his beloved Cytheris, his long-term actress mistress whom Caesar and society had forced him to abandon. 'Like Caesar, I am a forgiving man, and I can tolerate most assaults on my person. But not against those I love.'

Octavian rubbed his smooth chin and looked at Lepidus, who looked actually scared at the prospect of doing away with the most respected intellectual in Rome's history.

'Very well,' said Octavian. 'But we don't want this to look like personal score settling. We are supposed to be acting for the good of the Republic. We need to show that we are prepared to make personal sacrifices. It is known that Cicero was, at least for a time, a friend and protector of myself. I will add the name of Thoranius, who cared for me after my father died. Who of yours will you give up, Antonius?'

Antony gave Octavian a hard stare. It was obvious this wasn't an idle suggestion, nor was he bluffing. He really wanted Antony to sacrifice someone important to him. Was Cicero's death worth more than the life of someone close to him? He thought about the text of the Philippics, none of which Cicero had dared to speak to his face. The vile way he had twisted almost every aspect of Antony's life. Fulvia's fury and devastation at her portrayal. Not to mention how Cytheris must have felt on being dragged into it.

'We can put my uncle on the list.'

'Hybrida?' Octavian frowned. 'The cruel, incompetent father of your cheating wife? That doesn't seem much of a sacrifice. Besides, we've only just agreed to make him censor.'

'No,' said Antony. 'My other uncle, Lucius Julius Caesar. My mother's brother.'

'Antonius,' said Lepidus, looking shocked. 'Are you sure?'

'It's obvious. He has been a strong supporter of my career. He helped me get my first posting with Caesar. He is beloved of my mother. But latterly, he has let me down. When I was at my lowest, he even declared I should be made an enemy of the state. He is my choice.'

'Very well,' said Octavian. 'We add him to the list.'

'And what about you, Lepidus?' asked Antony.

Lepidus looked surprised. 'What about me?'

'Oct— Caesar here has given up Cicero, and his former guardian, Thoranius. I have given you my uncle. Who will you sacrifice for our cause?'

Lepidus looked despondent, but after a few moments said, 'I suppose you can have my brother, Lucius Aemilius Paullus. I never really liked him anyway.'

Paullus had supported Caesar, but only after being heavily bribed, and had recently spoken out against the alliance of his brother and Antony.

'That will be acceptable,' said Octavian, and Antony nodded agreement.

'Are we done?' he asked, feeling weary and dirtied by the grubby negotiations.

Octavian shook his head. 'It's not enough. We should invite Plancus and Pollio to join us. They can add their own enemies to the cause. That will maximise our gain. This is a one-time event, we cannot repeat this, so we need to be sure it fully serves its purpose. Besides, having Plancus and Pollio on board will bind them further to our cause and prevent them from claiming in the future that they opposed this.'

Pollio and Plancus were duly brought into the meeting, and after they had got over their shock about the proposals, they enthusiastically joined in by adding a number of personal enemies to the ranks of the proscribed. They, too, were invited to make personal sacrifices, and Plancus suggested his brother, while Pollio, a little too enthusiastically, gave up his father-in-law, Lucius Quintius. Ultimately, when the list was finalised, it had the names of around three hundred senators and two thousand *equites*.

Chapter IX

ante diem vi Kalendas Decembres DCCXI AUC (26 November 43 BC), Rome

The three triumvirs entered Rome on three successive days, each accompanied by one legion and Praetorian cohort. It was not a triumph, since they had no enemy over whom to declare victory, nor did the three men try to represent it as such, but the gathered crowds treated their entry as a huge celebration. Though there were no prisoners to parade, no actors portraying scenes from great battles, no gladiatorial games, the people took advantage of the events to break out into spontaneous parties and celebrations. The feeling on the streets seemed to be one of genuine joy: that peace had come to Rome; that the two most beloved of Caesar, Antony and Octavian, were united at last; and that together they would continue Caesar's wise rule, and bring vengeance on Caesar's murderers. Inevitably, the mood among the senators and equestrians was vastly different.

Antony could not deny Octavian, as consul, the right to march into Rome first. So he had taken the final day for his entrance, in what was very clearly an expression of 'last but not least'. The people were still in full holiday mode, and after he had marched to the Forum, Antony took to the rostra and gave them a short address, full of vague promises of rewards and gifts, a pledge of friendship and co-operation with Octavian, a long, measured rant against their enemies in the Senate, and a promise to rain bloody vengeance upon the so-called Liberators and all who supported them. Then he came down from the rostra and walked among the crowds to receive their acclaim. He was still wearing his armour, sword and dagger at his belt, and was accompanied by a small bodyguard. He was not foolish enough to ignore the fact that a desperate Senate might have planted assassins among the people, but he was the only one of the three to have been confident enough in his own strength and the love of the common man to mingle with them so openly.

His first port of call after his entry into Rome was, of course, his own house. Fulvia was waiting in the atrium for him, with the children and the household staff all lined up to formally welcome him home. As soon as he walked in, Fulvia began to speak.

'Beloved husband, it is my joy and pleasure to greet you on your return and—'

Antony rushed forward and scooped her up in his arms, hugging her tight and kissing her firmly on the lips. He stepped back to look at her. She had clearly had her personal slaves spend a long time on her makeup, hair, dress and perfume, though Antony's attentions had mussed her up somewhat. Not that she seemed to care, grinning broadly, both at his return and his enthusiastic greeting. Antony went among his children and stepchildren, embracing them and offering them words of love and admiration at how much they had grown during his absence.

Then one of the nursemaids stepped forward, holding a tiny bundle. She held it out for him, and he took little Iullus into his arms for the first time, looking down into the blinking eyes of his infant son. He stared for a long while, and was suddenly overcome with emotion. His face flushed, and tears sprung to his eyes. He carefully handed the baby back to the nursemaid, put a hand on Fulvia's table, and said gruffly, 'What's for dinner?'

ante diem v Kalendas Decembres DCCXI AUC (27 November 43 BC), Rome

Antony rubbed his eyes with the heel of his palm, and for a moment was tempted to keep them closed and briefly doze. It had been a long day, and a long night. Though he had made sure he dined in peace with his family, he soon had to attend to the huge queue of visitors at his door – relatives, friends, clients, many of them genuine well-wishers, though most still having some ulterior motive, a favour, a request, or just taking the opportunity to ingratiate themselves with their once more supremely powerful patron. There were less welcome visitors, too: those senators and equestrians who had opposed him, but now saw which way the land lay, and had come to beg forgiveness. Some of these he received courteously. Others he turned away, unable in good conscience to look them in the eyes, knowing their fate. The night he had spent making love to Fulvia, then talking for hours, bringing her up to date with the details of the negotiations, plotting and planning with her, then making love again.

Lepidus, seated next to Antony, nudged him with his elbow, and Antony started, realising that he must have been drifting off. He was seated on a bench in the front rank of the senators. Technically he held no magistracy at that moment, though everyone knew his real position. The meeting of the Comitia Tributa, taking place on the Campus Martius not far from Antony's house, had been called the day before, instead of with the required three days' notice, though no one dared to complain. Octavian, as consul, chaired the meeting, the sole purpose of which was to hear and vote on the proposal of Octavian's tame tribune, Marcus Titius, to enact a law which would be known as the *lex Titia*.

Octavian called the meeting to order, and Titius rose to announce his bill. The law formalised the legal position of the triumvirate for a period of three years. All three men were to be given consular imperium and were given full control of the executive and legislature. Their Acts were automatically valid without the approval of the Senate, and there was no power of veto. They were given the power of life and death over every single citizen of the Empire, with no right of appeal. They were also given the rights to use public funds as they saw fit. However, the bill made it clear that this was no perpetual dictatorship in the fashion of Caesar or Sulla. It was a collegiate arrangement between three powerful men, and it stipulated a term of five years to repair the Republic, although the position of triumvir had no fixed term and would extend indefinitely.

The law was passed without opposition. Antony now possessed more power than he had ever held – than, in fact, almost anyone had ever held, except Caesar and Sulla. Admittedly, he had to share it with two other men, but there was no doubt in his mind, or in the mind of the majority of Romans, that Antony was the senior partner in this alliance, teamed up as he was with an ineffectual and unpopular general and a youthful, inexperienced boy.

As soon as the law was passed, Octavian renounced his consulship in favour of Ventidius, and the three of them processed to the

Forum to give speeches from the rostra to the jubilant crowds. As they walked, Antony gave Octavian his condolences at the passing of his mother, Atia, who had died as they were returning to Rome after the negotiations at Bononia. Atia had always opposed Octavian's ambitions since the death of Caesar, fearful that they would endanger his life. But Antony consoled him that she had lived long enough to hear the outcome of the triumviral treaty, and had died knowing that Octavian's position was secure and that he was safe. Octavian accepted Antony's good wishes calmly and with little outward display of emotion. Antony couldn't tell if the young man was numb – overwhelmed by the magnitude of what he had achieved, coupled with the loss of his mother – or if he really was that cold. He suspected the latter.

The next morning, the day after the triumvirate officially came into existence, the triumvirs announced the proscriptions.

Before they had even arrived at Rome, they had sent a dozen names of the condemned deemed to be most at risk of flight, Cicero among them, together with soldiers nominated to find and execute them. Octavian's cousin, the consul Pedius, went beyond his remit, announcing to the city that these were the only men in danger – which he had, in fact, been led to believe. It had been a handy lie for the triumvirs, who had no desire to arrive in a Rome that was in a state of panic, nor to alert the rich men to the true extent of the slaughter to come. When Pedius found out the truth of what they intended, his heart failed and he died on the spot. Octavian, at least publicly, did not shed a tear.

Antony ordered the gates of the city closed, set soldiers to watch the harbours, and then sent patrols throughout Rome to find the doomed nobles. The triumvirate posted the names of an initial one hundred and thirty, with more to be released at regular intervals. Whitened boards were set up in the Forum and other places, and fearful rich men and curious crowds gathered around to read the morbid notices. Each name was accompanied by a detailed justification, blaming the condemned for betraying Caesar and Rome and making public enemies of the triumvirs.

Antony, Octavian and Lepidus all gave speeches attacking the proscribed to ram the point home. Many of the common people believed and approved, not least because the triumvirs had offered huge rewards to anyone bringing them the head of one of the condemned

– twenty-five thousand *denarii* for a free man, and liberty for a slave. That had been Octavian's shrewd idea, not only aiding the capture of fugitives, but implicating the masses themselves in the crime.

For a crime it was, Antony had no doubt. He was a tough man, used to violence and bloodshed, but it did not sit well with him that they had resorted to this tyrannical measure. Nevertheless, he was also a realist, and he recognised the need for the money this operation would provide, as well as allowing them in one stroke to be rid of all their enemies who may make life difficult for them in the future. It was Fulvia who had pointed out the real genius of Octavian's plan. They were not simply killing off a few troublesome politicians or potential rebels, not purely raising money by an unorthodox, if not unprecedented, method. When the list of names was read from beginning to end, it constituted a cull of the old order. The noble families that had overthrown the kings, defeated Hannibal and Pyrrhus, and built the Rome they all knew, were being erased. This, more than anything Caesar had brought about, was the real end of the Republic, and if something came afterwards that bore the name Republic, it would be like the ship of Theseus – looking the same, but its constituent parts entirely replaced.

Antony wondered what the new empire he was shaping would look like.

–

For the rest of the year, chaos and slaughter reined, and the streets of Rome ran with blood. Stories of the executions titillated those too lowly to be implicated, and terrified those who weren't. Antony, with a ferociously busy schedule of official ceremonies, speeches, meetings of the Senate, private audiences, administrative duties, and dealing with a constant stream of correspondence, could not insulate himself from the consequences of the proscriptions. Fulvia kept him fully informed of every detail she heard, and he couldn't help notice with a little distaste that she seemed to be taking a grim delight in the bloody demise of those who had wronged her.

The first magistrate to be killed was the tribune Salvius, a former ally of Antony, whose veto at the beginning of the year had initially prevented Antony from being declared a public enemy. Suspecting it was his last night, Salvius threw a huge banquet for his friends and family. The centurion leading the execution squad burst in mid-meal and, grabbing Salvius by the hair, cut off his head. He then departed, warning the guests not to move or they would suffer the same, and so they stayed late into the night, reclining in stupefaction by the headless corpse of their host. Next came the praetor Minucius, who was discovered by the soldiers, disguised and hiding in a shop. Another praetor, Annalis, who was hiding with a client in the outskirts of Rome, was betrayed by his own son, whom Octavian rewarded with a fortune and promotion to the aedileship. It did not serve the faithless young man well – he immediately got drunk, got in a fight with some soldiers and was killed.

Two men of the Egnatii, father and son, were killed with a single sword stroke while embracing each other. The son of Arruntius was persuaded to flee by his condemned father and was accompanied to the city gates by his mother. She then returned to Rome to bury her husband. When she discovered her son had died in a shipwreck, she starved herself to death.

Throughout Rome, cellars, attics and even midden heaps concealed fugitive nobles, many hidden and protected by their loyal family members and slaves, others betrayed by theirs. To obtain a reward, the head of the proscribed victim had to be brought to the Forum, where it was displayed on a spear for the crowds to gawp at, and for the deeper thinkers to reflect on the capricious nature of fortune.

Despite preferring to have the whole business handled at a distance, it was impossible for Antony not to be exposed personally to the horrors. A host of supplicants, relatives and friends of the proscribed assailed his doors and tugged at his robes when he went into the city, begging for mercy for their loved ones. For the most part, he hardened his heart to their cries. Having already agreed the necessity of the measures, he was not one to show overt weakness.

But there were exceptions. Lucius Caesar sought refuge in the house of Antony's mother, Julia, and when the soldiers arrived to take him, Julia barred their way, baring her breasts and crying, 'You shall not take my brother until you first kill me, who suckled your general.' As soon as the soldiers departed, she marched to the Forum, where the three triumvirs were handing out bounties, and loudly harangued Antony for his villainy in condemning his own uncle.

Antony looked down on her from the rostra with a mixture of shame, pity and anger.

'You are a good sister,' he said. 'But perhaps not such a good mother. Where were you when my uncle declared me an enemy of the state?'

She ignored his comment, and threw herself to her knees, tearing her clothes and ripping at her hair. Lepidus turned away in embarrassment and Octavian pursed his lips in annoyance, but neither made a move to intervene, making it clear the decision was Antony's alone. He commanded his mother to silence and said in a loud voice, 'Very well, since my beloved mother asks it, I will pardon my uncle Lucius Caesar and remove his name from the list of condemned. But I suggest, Mother, that in future you consider more carefully where your loyalties should lie.' Then he stood and strode back home, feeling unbearably sad.

Soon after this, his conscience was assaulted once more when the wife of a senator called Ligarius presented herself to him. She had hidden him, but he had been betrayed by the one slave she had entrusted the secret of his location to. No doubt overcome by feelings of guilt, she had followed his severed head to the Forum, crying out that since she had sheltered her husband she, too, should be killed. When the soldiers ignored her, she came directly to Antony and accused herself of breaking the law of the proscription. The best Antony could do was pretend he had not heard her, and he had some soldiers gently remove her. Later he found that she, too, had starved herself to death.

But for every example of nobility and self-sacrifice, there were a dozen showing the cruelty and treachery of human nature. The proscriptions were used by traitorous friends and family across the city to settle scores and gain personal advantages. Many who were on the original list were betrayed by those they trusted, but others had their names added to the list after family members appealed to the triumvirs to have them condemned. In some cases, men were simply murdered without sanction, and then their heads were brought to the Forum in hope of a reward. Sometimes, those names were added to the list retrospectively, and occasionally the murderers were punished.

On more than one occasion, Antony found himself duped. He was petitioned on behalf of the wife of one Septimius, not to pardon him, but accusing him of conspiracy against the triumvirs and requesting to have his name added to the list. Antony agreed, and it was only later that he found out, through Fulvia, the true motivations behind the denouncement. Septimius' wife was having an affair, and she wanted him out of the way. Septimius was oblivious to this, and when he heard of his condemnation, he fled to his wife, who promptly locked him in the house until the executioners arrived. She married her lover the same day her husband was killed.

Once even Antony's own wife went behind his back. Without him knowing, she had the name of a man called Rufus added to the list. He had a large property near Antony's own house, and while Antony had been in Cisalpine Gaul, Fulvia had tried to buy it. Rufus had refused, insulting her, mocking her and telling her that her husband would soon be dead at the hands of Octavian and Decimus Brutus. When Rufus' head was brought to Antony, he realised what had happened and instructed the head be taken direct to Fulvia, saying it was nothing to do with him. Demonstrating the bloody-mindedness that he both loved and hated, she had the head placed on the front of their house instead of in the Forum.

Many of the proscribed decided to take their own lives, with sword, poison, or by throwing themselves into the Tiber. Lucius Quintius, Pollio's father-in-law, escaped by ship, but threw himself into the sea and drowned. One rich equestrian threw open the doors of his house and beseeched his family, friends and slaves to take away whatever they wished. When the house was empty, he burnt it down with himself inside. Some drew swords and fought against their murderers until their last breath.

In a separate measure, the triumvirs, prompted by worries from Octavian that there would still be a shortfall in the funds needed for their war against the assassins, issued an edict that the richest fourteen hundred women in Rome should submit a valuation of their wealth, and the triumvirs would then determine what proportion they should contribute to the public coffers. This provoked almost as much outrage as the proscriptions, if not more so, and the women formed deputations which went to the houses of the womenfolk beloved of the triumvirs – Antony's mother, Julia, Octavian's sister, Octavia, and Fulvia. Fulvia, in typical spirited fashion, threw them out with her words warming their ears, remembering how recently many of these women had turned their backs on her, when Antony was declared a public enemy. Julia and Octavia received them more sympathetically, but the triumvirs were not swayed by pleas from these relatives, who were less forceful than Fulvia.

The deputation therefore marched on the Forum, where the triumvirs were issuing decrees and bounties in return for the heads of the proscribed. Heading the group of noble women was Hortensia, the daughter of Cicero's great rival for the accolade of best orator in Rome, Hortensius. She had inherited her father's gift, and the speech she gave pleading the women's naivety in all matters political, and their innocence when it came to past decrees and Acts directed against the triumvirs, was well received by all. Of the three triumvirs, it was the more traditional and conservative Lepidus who was most outraged by this flaunting of the natural order of things, and he ordered the Lictors to drive the women from the Forum. But the crowd protested vigorously, and Antony ordered the Lictors to stand down. They promised they would consider the women's case again, and the next day they reduced the number to be taxed to four hundred, making up the shortfall by raising further taxes on the male wealthy.

Many of the proscribed escaped Rome, taking on disguises as varied as slaves and praetors. Lepidus' brother managed to flee, probably with Lepidus' assistance, and he went east to join Brutus. The search for the proscribed spread to the rest of Italy. Many were captured in their country estates, or in the mountains, the woods or the marshes.

Some of those who managed to get out of Rome travelled south to Rhegium at the tip of the Italian peninsula, where they put up a successful resistance against the men sent to capture them. When a larger force was sent, they crossed over to Sicily and joined Sextus Pompeius, who was in control of the island.

But one man continued to evade the hunt. Much to Antony's frustration, and Fulvia's outright fury, Cicero remained at large. He had fled the city before the triumvirs even arrived, and then when he found he had been proscribed, he attempted to flee Italy in a small boat. Unfortunately, his constitution could not handle the seasickness, and after incessant vomiting had weakened him, he was forced to ask for the ship to return to shore. His brother and nephew, both named Quintus and both also proscribed, unselfishly returned to Rome to try to raise cash, and were quickly captured. They died bravely. Cicero's nephew found a hiding place for his father, and when he was taken, would not reveal the location even under torture. But his father heard of his son's capture and gave himself up. Each of them begged to be killed first, so they were taken to separate locations and, on a pre-agreed signal, executed simultaneously.

The news of their deaths saddened Antony. He had served with the senior Quintus Tullius Cicero under Caesar in Gaul and had never had a personal problem with him, despite Antony's long enmity with his brother. Quintus had been a brave and effective commander, despite an occasional cruel streak, and the manner of his passing and the passing of his son did not surprise Antony, though it did cast the triumvirs in an even worse light.

But it was Cicero that he wanted – the only one of the proscribed, in fact, that Antony wished to see dead for their own sake, regardless of the monetary rewards. So Antony sent a search party south, led by a military tribune called Popillius who had once been defended by Cicero, but who was a loyal adherent to Antony, and a tough and ruthless centurion called Herennius.

And then, seething in frustration, he waited.

ante diem vi Idus Decembres DCCXI AUC (8 December 43 BC), Rome

The number of severed heads arriving in the Forum on a daily basis had slowed to a trickle, and the first to have been mounted on spikes were turning green and beginning to smell. The triumvirs had paid out a fortune in bounties and rewards, but the value of the confiscations that now filled the treasury had been vast. Unpleasant and morally unsound as the process had been, Antony had to concede that Octavian had been right. The proscriptions had fulfilled their purpose, and now they could pay their men properly, recruit and equip new legions with promises of decent signing-on fees and salaries, and even consider a few projects to improve Rome herself.

The work of ruling Rome was arduous and time-consuming, even though the workload was divided in three. Octavian was the most diligent, while Lepidus – when he did make an effort – was largely ineffectual. Antony was between the two: fairly hard-working, but also aware that the time would soon be upon him when he must leave Italy again for months or years, endure brutal conditions and fight for his survival. He therefore made sure he made plenty of time for himself, dining with Fulvia and the children, seeing plays at the theatre and chariot races in the arena, drinking with old army friends and, despite Fulvia's disapproval, throwing lavish banquets and parties, attended by all levels of society from senators down to mimes, although not, of course, by Cytheris.

That morning, with the cold December wind whipping around the Forum, Antony was the only triumvir seated on the rostra. Octavian had been ordered to bed by his physician on account of a productive hacking cough, and Lepidus was spending a few days at one of his country villas. Antony sat on his curule chair, his toga pulled tight around him, dispensing judgements on legal matters, receiving petitions for pardons for the proscribed and others condemned to death or exile, and deciding on administrative matters, from how much money to allocate to sewer maintenance to ensuring the adequacy of the grain supply.

The civil servant was droning on about the need to open new lead mines, and Antony's attention was drifting, when he noticed a commotion among the crowd at the far end of the Forum. A small group of soldiers were marching purposefully towards the rostra, barging the civilians out of the way, who were crowding around them in curiosity. News from the East? Antony wondered. A report of an unwelcome rebellion in some province or other? Or perhaps another head of a proscribed man. He felt an uneasy sensation in the pit of his stomach, but it was tempered with excitement and possibility.

The leading soldier, a military tribune by his cloak, halted and opened a drawstring on a leather bag. At that distance, Antony had to strain his eyes, but, held by its thin hair, a head was slowly pulled out and lifted in the air. Antony stared. Could it be...?

The tribune, Popillius, approached, the centurion Herennius by his side, and the features of the head came into focus.

The open, blank eyes of Cicero regarded Antony sightlessly.

A wave of emotion swept over Antony, and for a moment the world spun around him.

Disbelief gave way to elation. He slowly stood, holding on to the chair for support to stop him falling, and beckoned the tribune and centurion to him.

'Proconsul,' said Popillius, 'I present to you the head and right hand of the proscribed criminal, Cicero.'

Trembling, Antony stepped forward and took the head from Popillius, holding it at arm's length in front of him. Eyes wide, he gazed at the dead face of his lifelong enemy. All the injuries that this man had heaped on him and his family came flooding back: the execution without trial of his stepfather Lentulus; preventing Lentulus' burial; his opposition to Antony's career at every step; and, most recently, the hateful, spiteful attacks on him, and worse, on those he loved – Fadia, Fulvia, Cytheris, Curio, Clodius. Antony was not a vindictive man. But for Cicero he made an exception.

He held the head up for the crowd in the Forum to see. They looked on in silence.

'This man has wronged me throughout my life. More than that, he has wronged Rome, over and over. Today, we celebrate the removal of this thorn in the side of the Republic.'

He thrust the head into the air, and there was a ragged chorus of cheers, mainly from the soldiers. The civilians remained quiet, giving off an air of confusion. Cicero had always evoked mixed feelings, but generally he was considered well for his long career and his skilled oratory. Moreover, many important men owed him their lives or their freedom after he had pled on their behalf in the courts, although of course there were many others who had been on the wrong side of his rhetoric.

'Go and fetch Fulvia,' Antony said to an aide. Then he said to Herennius, 'Nail the head and hand up on the rostra for all to see.'

By the time a ladder, hammer and nails had been found, Fulvia had appeared, flushed and out of breath.

'Give it to me,' she said, and Herennius, who had been about to wield the hammer, passed the head over. Fulvia took it off him, and her face twisted in anger. She drew out a pin and began to stab the tongue that had spewed such hatred towards her and hers, furiously and repetitively, animal cries of anger and distress emerging from somewhere deep in her chest.

After a moment, Antony gently took the head from her, then hugged her. She turned to him and wept into his chest. Antony passed the trophy back to Herennius, and he got on with the business of attaching it to the rostra with long nails, the thud of the hammer as it drove the iron into the skull echoing around the Forum.

Antony put an arm around Fulvia's shoulders and led her home. No doubt there would be a celebration when the fact sunk in that their perennial antagonist was dead. But it would certainly take a long time for Antony and his family, and indeed all of Rome, to adjust to a world without Cicero.

Januarius DCCXII AUC (January 42 BC), Rome

The new year was greeted with the usual festivities. Some hundred years previously, the new year had been celebrated on the Ides of March, but there had been a legislative change to appoint consuls on the first day of January, and Caesar in his calendar reforms had decreed the first of January would be the official new year and a public holiday. To give the year as an auspicious start as possible, everyone was kind and generous to one another, exchanging handshakes, greetings and gifts with family, friends and neighbours. Doors were decorated with green branches, and lanterns when night fell, and huge feasts with copious wine and games of dice were indulged in, while itinerant jesters and jugglers went from door to door begging for alms in exchange for tricks and jokes.

On this particular new year's day, the Senate was summoned to swear an oath to support and uphold all of Caesar's decrees. None refused. Caesar's divinity was confirmed, and Octavian now styled himself 'son of a god', while Antony was inducted as the first priest of the cult of the divine Caesar.

But serious work still needed to be done. Sextus Pompeius still ruled the oceans and held Sicily, and Crassus and Brutus continued to plunder the East, raising money and men with the ultimate aim of confronting the triumvirs. It was Octavian's task to deal with Pompeius, but, unwilling to leave Rome for fear of Antony consolidating his power further, or perhaps just lacking sufficient resolve, the youngest triumvir sent a deputy in his place to command a fleet against Pompeius. Unfortunately, this underling was roundly defeated. Octavian reluctantly decided to take command in person. But before he was able to confront Pompeius, Antony found his fleet at Brundisium, where it was preparing for the expedition east, under attack by Republican ships commanded by Gnaeus Domitius Ahenobarbus, son of the Pompeian senator Lucius Domitius Ahenobarbus, whom Antony had killed at Pharsalus.

Antony dispatched messengers to Octavian to bring his fleet to reinforce Antony, and also to Cleopatra, who was safely in Alexandria, to try to draw off Republican ships with an attack of her own. Without reference to Octavian, who he knew would have opposed the measure, he declared Caesarion the legitimate son of Cleopatra and co-ruler of Egypt. Although this was short of Cleopatra's wish that he be declared Caesar's son, it went a long way to ensuring the boy's safety.

Fortunately, Cleopatra decided, despite her uncertainty of the future of Caesarion with Octavian in power, that her chances were better with the triumvirs than the Liberators, and she accepted the proposal and did as she was asked. Octavian and Antony were able to defeat the split Republican navy, although unfortunately Cleopatra's flotilla, which would have reinforced Antony, was lost in a severe storm without ever engaging the enemy.

It was then that the worst news arrived from the East. Brutus had been holding Antony's brother Gaius captive for some time. He had been treating him kindly, but then Brutus discovered that Gaius had been inciting the legions to mutiny in favour of him and his triumvir brother. This discovery, fresh on the reports of Cicero's murder, had pushed Brutus to revenge.

It was Fulvia, pale-faced, who told Antony of his brother's execution at the hands of Caesar's assassin. Antony had known it had to be a possibility, but he had somehow never believed Brutus would do it. He raged, cursed, broke statues and tore tapestries.

When Lucius came charging in, alarmed by the rumours he had heard, Antony's own tempest had begun to dissipate. But if anything, Lucius' reaction was worse. He sank to his knees, howled, gouged his nails down his cheek, tore his hair. Then he leaned forward and began to bang his head on the hard mosaic floor until his forehead turned bloody.

'Marcus,' cried out Fulvia. 'Stop him. He is going to hurt himself.'

Antony stepped forward and put his arms around Lucius, pulling him gently to his feet. Lucius fought him, all sense of reason lost, and when Antony tried to restrain him, Lucius punched him hard in the nose. Barely feeling the pain, Antony drew his arm back and slapped Lucius across the face with such force it knocked him on to his backside. He sat there, legs spread, hands behind him, completely stunned. Antony put his hand out, and Lucius allowed himself to be helped up.

'Look at me,' said Antony, voice calm but cold. He took his brother's chin in his hand so Lucius had to meet his gaze. 'This is no longer about punishing Caesar's murderers. It is not about the good of Rome, or even the future and well-being of you and me and our families. Now, this is personal.'

Lucius nodded, once more in control, but his face a mask of misery.

'Lucius, I swear by Jupiter, by Apollo, by our Hercules and all the rest of our ancestors, that we will be avenged. Do you trust me?'

'Always,' said Lucius.

'Good. Because the time has come. We will take the fight to the enemy.'

Chapter X

Sextilis DCCXII AUC (August 42 BC), Dyrrhachium

The first half of the new year had been one frustration after another for Antony. As agreed, Lepidus remained in Rome to look after their interests in the city and Italy as a whole, and Antony and Octavian marched out together at the head of a massive force of twenty-eight full-strength legions. The well-trained recruits and experienced veterans sang and cheered as they marched to Brundisium and prepared to cross the Mare Adriaticum to Greece, morale soaring to the heavens as they finally got their wish to take the fight to Caesar's murderers.

But soon, Antony and Octavian found their progress blocked in exactly the same way Caesar had. In fact, the situation was all but identical to six years previously, the lead up to the battle of Pharsalus. Then, Caesar, the usurper, had superior land forces and control of the West. The faction preferred by the Senate under Pompeius had superior naval forces and control of the East. It was the same now. Antony had managed to sneak eight legions across to Macedonia under Gaius Norbanus Flaccus and Decidius Saxa, but before Octavian could arrive from Sicily, the Liberators' admiral Murcus, who had been blockading Egypt until Cleopatra lost her fleet, arrived and blockaded Brundisium. Just as before, Antony was faced with the problem of split forces, with a superior enemy navy preventing them from joining together in Greece.

But Fortuna was once more on his side. When Octavian's warships arrived, having abandoned the fight with Sextus Pompeius, Murcus retreated, and the triumvirs were able to ferry their vast army across. Though fifty warships under Gnaeus Domitius Ahenobarbus were dispatched by Brutus and Cassius to reinforce Murcus, he was too late, and nor did Sextus Pompeius attempt to make things difficult for them by leaving his Sicily stronghold.

So by the beginning of Sextilis, Antony and Octavian reached Dyrrhachium on the Epirus coast. After the long and complicated task of disembarking their titanic army, with all its artillery, warhorses, pack animals, ammunition, food and fodder, Antony took Octavian for a tour of the port, pointing out the locations of key moments of the battle between Caesar and Pompey. Octavian had been just fourteen years of age at the time, but had studied his divine father's commentaries and other reports of the battle in detail, and paid close attention to every word Antony spoke, as if attempting to wring every lesson he could from the older man. At times like this, when they were talking strategy and tactics, and Octavian was treating Antony's military experience with due respect, he enjoyed his young colleague's company.

But that evening he felt snubbed when Octavian sent his apologies that he could not fulfil his promise to dine with Antony on account of poor health. Antony had to console himself with the company of Octavian's trusted friends and advisors, Agrippa and Maecenas.

'Why do you follow him?' he asked bluntly, after the serving slaves had cleared away the first course of anchovies and fresh asparagus. Antony knew that when they marched, such delicacies would be harder to come by, and though he was always happy to share the conditions of his men, camped as they were in a well-supplied port, there seemed no need at this stage to deny himself the comforts of life.

Maecenas took a delicate sip of wine, deferring to Agrippa.

'He is my commander,' said Agrippa bluntly, his voice deep and carrying a provincial accent he refused to disguise. 'And he is my friend. What other reason do I need?'

Maecenas raised his eyebrows and gave a small smile, inclining his head towards Agrippa as if to say the tough young soldier spoke for him as well.

'Very well...' Antony regarded the two men. 'Let me phrase it another way. Why do the men follow him with such loyalty? I know why they love me. They see me as one of their own. I fight beside them, I eat their food, I share their camp fires and their jokes. And they know my ability in battle, as a general and as a soldier. But Octavianus? He has won nothing. He has shown no martial strength or skill, either with his own right arm or with his brain. And yet they adore him, to the point that some deserted me. Me! To join him! Tell me why.'

Agrippa frowned, as if the question made no sense. To Antony, it seemed that he was as faithful to Octavian as a hound. He could not conceive of anything but loyalty to his childhood friend. It was admirable, and Antony couldn't help but like Agrippa for his steadfastness and his bluff soldierly demeanour. But it didn't answer his question.

It was Maecenas who spoke up.

'You're right,' he said. Maecenas was the complete opposite of Agrippa. Where Octavianus' general was broad, Maecenas was slight. Where Agrippa was deeply spoken, Maecenas' voice was lighter. And in contrast to Agrippa's aversion to culture and philosophy, Maecenas had a reputation as a sponsor of the arts and a deep thinker. 'They don't see Octavianus as one of them, not in the way they view you. But they didn't see Caesar that way either. When you circulate among the men, they respect your authority, but they know they can joke about women and farting, and they can drink and brawl. With Caesar, it was always like a king, or a god, deigning to grace the mortals with his presence. They love you. They worshipped Caesar.'

'Literally, now,' said Agrippa.

'Quite,' said Maecenas. 'And Octavianus is Caesar's adopted son and designated heir. You see how they feel about the dictator, even now. How much they are motivated to avenge his death. It devastates them that they can't march behind Caesar any more. But they can follow his son.'

Antony nodded. It did actually make sense.

'But there is more to him than a name and a legacy, you know,' continued Maecenas. 'He is the most intelligent man I have ever met. For all Cicero's self-aggrandisement, he did not have half Octavianus' wit. Nor his bravery.'

'His bravery?' scoffed Antony. Agrippa scowled and opened his mouth to speak, but Maecenas smoothly cut in.

'He isn't cut out to be a fighting man like you, Proconsul,' he said. 'His health and physique don't allow it. But I tell you, he has ice water in his veins. How many men of his age would have dared to raise a private army, and successfully faced down both you and the Senate? How many would demand the consulship so young? How many could rise to rule Rome as one of three before their twentieth birthday? Not Pompeius. Not even Caesar. And I tell you this, my friend… The one who you still call "boy" when you think he can't hear you, will some day rise higher than either of those great men.'

Maecenas calmly reached out for his cup of wine and drank. Agrippa sat back, arms folded, apparently satisfied that Maecenas had said all that needed to be said. Antony pursed his lips, eyes narrowed. He had no reply to Maecenas' words. He could not refute them. Nor was he stupid enough to try. Quite the opposite. Whether Maecenas intended it or not, Antony took his words as a warning. Octavian was a formidable personality. And while, at this juncture, he was largely acknowledged as Antony's junior in practical terms in the triumvirate, Antony feared that Octavian's ambition would not allow that to last.

But that was a worry for another day. For the time being, they were united as allies in a common cause. There would be no conflict between them until after the assassins were defeated. And if Octavian was reasonable, perhaps they could continue to rule as colleagues for many years to come. After all, Octavian did seem to have an eye for detail, and would be skilled at administering the Empire. With Antony's military abilities, they seemed to be a match made by the Olympian gods.

'We should talk supply chains,' said Maecenas.

'I would prefer to discuss strategy,' said Agrippa.

Antony waved a dismissive hand. 'There will be plenty of time for such things. Let's arrange a meeting with your commander tomorrow, when he is feeling himself. In the meantime, please, drink and eat. I think you – Maecenas, in particular – will find life on the campaign trail tougher than you expect, so make the most of it now.'

Agrippa and Maecenas exchanged glances, then nodded and smiled their acceptance. Antony clapped his hands for the next course, and settled back to attempt to enjoy the evening, putting the Liberators out of his mind, at least until his meeting with Octavian the following day.

–

But Octavian did not emerge from his quarters the following day. Agrippa and Maecenas brought the young triumvir's apologies personally to Antony, and he could tell from the worried looks on their faces that this was no flimsy excuse. Octavian really was ill.

'I should see him,' said Antony.

'No,' said Maecenas. 'The physicians say he should not be disturbed.'

'What is it? His chest?'

'Perhaps. His breathing is certainly harsh, and he is sweating out a fever. They are purging him, but it is yet to show a benefit.'

Antony sighed. This was a problem. After Maecenas' words the night before, Antony was not sorry to hear of his colleague's frailty. In fact, in many ways, his future would be brighter if Octavian were to succumb to whatever ailed him. Someone more ruthless than Antony – say, Octavian himself – might have arranged a little poison to help him on his way to the Styx. But that was not Antony's way, and besides, he still thought they could work together.

At that moment, though, they needed to be getting underway. Summer had nearly run its course, and the campaigning season would soon come to a close. Antony did not wish to have to overwinter in hostile enemy territory. They needed to force a battle before then.

'Fine. I'll take his legions and head east. He can catch up when he feels better.'

'No,' said Agrippa.

'No?' asked Antony, surprised.

'Octavianus' legions stay with him. As will I. If you must march, you can take your own legions and those of Lepidus.'

Antony prepared to argue, but Agrippa's face was set, and he could see it would be pointless.

'So be it. I will go on ahead. But I warn you, if my colleague delays too long, I will be greatly outnumbered, and the victory will be all the more to my glory, and the less to your commander's. And if the assassins defeat me, your commander's fall will not be far behind.'

'He is aware of this,' said Agrippa, and turned to head back to be at Octavian's side.

Antony sighed and summoned his legates and outlined the position.

'Octavianus is indisposed,' he told them bluntly. 'So we march without him.'

There were some tuts and pursed lips among Antony's senior officers, but none seemed particularly surprised.

'This is the strategic situation,' he continued. 'Sending Norbanus Flaccus and Decidius Saxa ahead of the main force seems to have caught the assassins by surprise. They have taken their eight legions into Thrace, and occupied the passes of the Corpilii and Sapaei tribes, which are the only known routes from Asia into Greece. They are holding them at bay until we can reinforce them. But the enemy forces are vast. Cassius and Brutus have between them seventeen legions – not full strength, but some eighty thousand men nonetheless. In addition, they have perhaps seventeen thousand horse and mounted archers from Gaul, Lusitania, Spain, Arabia, even Parthia. We know, in fact, that the son of the traitor Labienus has been sent to Parthia to ask for an alliance with this most dangerous enemy of Rome.

'By contrast, we have only thirteen thousand horse, mainly Spanish, Gallic and German, but with Octavianus' army we have nineteen legions numbering about one hundred and ten thousand. Unfortunately, my colleague has not given me permission to lead out his army, so we march with only half our strength. But we cannot wait. Our supplies are greatly limited by the enemy navy controlling the passage from Italy, and failing to force an engagement before the weather halts the campaigning could see us starving this winter.

'So, we march, today. If Octavianus does not join us before we engage in battle, we will be facing a greatly superior force. But I am confident. Our men fight for a just cause, their morale is strong, and they are of the highest calibre.'

Antony looked at the faces of his officers and they returned his gaze with grimly resolute expressions. Antony nodded, satisfied at what he saw. Then he drew a coin out of his purse and held it up so they could see. It was a gold denarius. On one side was a portrait of Brutus in profile. On the other side, two daggers flanked a pileus – the cap of freedom. Under these symbols were the letters 'EID MAR', short for Ides of March. It could not be a more blatant and shameless celebration of the assassination, showing as it did the weapons of the murder, the motive and the date.

The officers had been aware of the coin's existence, but it was the first time they had seen one. Antony passed it round, and they examined it with various expressions of anger, disgust and disbelief. Then Antony took it back, made a show of wiping his backside on it, then threw it to the floor. He ground it into the dirt with his heel, and then, for good measure, spat on it.

'Any questions?' he asked.

There were none.

'In that case, we march.'

September DCCXII AUC (September 42 BC), Amphipolis

Antony led his legions on a rapid march to secure Amphipolis, a coastal town in Thrace that had been founded by the Athenians and then conquered by the Macedonians and Romans in turn. It would be a strong base for further operations, and a safe haven to retreat to if the worst happened, with its walls protected on three sides by the river Strymon. Although he hoped for minimal resistance from the city, Antony was prepared for a siege. However, when he arrived, he found the city gates flung open, and when he entered he was greeted by his legates Gaius Norbanus Flaccus and Decidius Saxa. While the legions set to building their encampments, his two generals updated him and his other senior officers over some welcome refreshments.

'We took the passes as you instructed, Proconsul,' said Norbanus. His impeccable accent belied his provincial Etruscan origins. His grandfather had served under Antony's grandfather in the campaign against the pirates and had been the first of his family to achieve the consulship. Like Antony's grandfather, Norbanus' grandfather had perished in Sulla's proscriptions, but the young Norbanus had found favour and promotion under Caesar and had become a loyal follower of Octavian after the Ides of March. 'The assassins did not even attempt to dislodge us, and we were hopeful that we could hold the passes until your arrival. Unfortunately, their Thracian ally Rhascupolis found a way through.'

The area in which the two vast armies were approaching each other was in a region of Thrace claimed by two quarrelling brothers, Rhascus and Rhascupolis. Rhascus had declared for Antony and Rhascupolis for Cassius, and each had donated three thousand horse to their respective causes.

'We occupied the two known passes,' continued Saxa, a Spaniard who had been supporting Antony since Mutina. 'But there was a third route that was considered impassable, because of its dense forests and lack of water. Rhascupolis showed them if they could carry enough water for their march, and hack their way through the forests, they could outflank us. And they nearly succeeded. But at the end, when their forces, at the limit of their endurance and out of water, reached the river, their shouts of joy reached us. Rhascus took out a reconnaissance party and discovered the enemy, and was able to warn us in time for us to escape overnight and reach Amphipolis.'

'We have been reinforcing the defences since we got here,' said Norbanus. 'Our fortifications are strong, but we are truly pleased to see you.'

'You have both performed admirably,' said Antony. 'You will both be in line for honours when this business is concluded.'

The two generals smiled, grateful but weary.

'But I see only half our army,' said Norbanus. 'Where is the young Caesar?'

Antony looked grave. 'My colleague is unwell,' he said.

'And his legions?' asked Saxa.

'They remain with him in Dyrrhachium.'

The generals exchanged concerned glances, but said nothing.

'I hope he will join us,' said Antony. 'But we will prevail with or without him. Tell me about the disposition of the enemy.'

Saxa, who as well as being a competent general was a skilled surveyor, sketched out a map showing what they knew of the movements and positions of Brutus and Cassius. After their bold march through the harsh terrain, they had arrived at the city of Philippi. They had then proceeded to position their forces on the high ground either side of the strategically vital road, the Via Egnatia, Brutus to the north and Cassius to the south. South of Cassius' position was an impenetrable marsh, and north of Brutus were impassable hills. Antony looked at Saxa's etchings with interest, stroking his beard thoughtfully. One of his first victories had involved him crossing waterless desert and impenetrable marshes to conquer Pelusium on behalf of Cleopatra's father. To Antony, the word 'impenetrable' was just a challenge.

Antony began to outline a plan, asking for input from his officers, who helped him to refine it. When he was happy, he gave the orders to prepare to set off for Philippi the next day.

September DCCXII AUC (September 42 BC), Philippi

Antony left one legion at Amphipolis under the command of his legate Lucius Pinarius Scarpus, a grandnephew of Caesar's. With the other legions and his cavalry, he set off east along the Via Egnatia towards Philippi. Despite lacking Octavian's legions, his army, now swollen by the eight legions of Saxa and Norbanus, seemed enormous when

Antony, riding at the head of the endless snaking columns, looked over his shoulder.

But when he arrived at the wide plain west of the city of Philippi, he was confronted by a force even bigger. The encampments that looked down on the plain from north and south were truly vast, and full of activity as men – the size of ants from the distance he surveyed them – scurried about, building new defences, training, and performing the countless mundane tasks that kept a legionary camp operational. Antony heard his officers draw breath at the sight, and a chill ran down his own back. Had he been too impetuous, confronting the assassins without the assistance of Octavian and his army? But he had chosen to advance for sound reasons – logistics, timing, surprise. There was no point second-guessing himself now.

So he gave the order for his legions to advance into the middle of the plain and pitch camp a bare mile from the enemy. It was an audacious move, with his clear numerical inferiority, and he knew what effect it would have on the leaders of the Liberators – amazement at his contempt for their position, and no doubt some element of fear.

Immediately on halting, Antony's legions set about what Roman legions, particularly those who had served under Caesar, did better than anyone. They began the construction of their defensive position. While some were detailed to dig a large trench in front of their position, others hastily threw up a palisade, utilising the stakes that each legionary carried as part of his kit. Once the obligatory initial defences were in place, they began to construct towers along the walls in which they could install archers and ballistae. Next came the wicked traps and obstacles that would impede an enemy attack – the lilies and tombstones and the caltrops strewn across the open ground that would cripple horses and advancing men alike. Antony had learned from Caesar, the master, and used every trick he knew to shore up his position. Caesar had held out against vastly superior forces when fighting Vercingetorix and Pompey. Antony could do the same.

But Brutus and Cassius did not attempt to attack. Just as at Pharsalus six years before, the Republican generals held the superior defensive positions, and with time on their side, amply supplied by sea and by the Eastern provinces, they saw no need to rush an engagement. Perhaps they were not aware how weak Antony was since he had not yet been joined by Octavian. Perhaps they did know, but feared Antony's military reputation. Either way, Antony was able to reinforce his position at leisure, while all his opponents did was to extend their lines, filling in the gaps between their camps and the marshes and hills with strong defences.

Antony's attention was now forced to turn to the logistic situation. His men were almost entirely dependent on their own supplies, with very little capacity for foraging or resupply. They didn't even have access to fresh water at first, although that was quickly solved by his skilled engineers, who dug enough wells to amply supply the men, horses and pack animals. He pored through reports of supplies of grain, salted meat and animal fodder and, with the aid of his senior centurions, calculated how long it would be until they were exhausted. He considered imposing rationing, but that would be an admission to his men that they were in for a long siege, and it would affect morale. He knew from experience what a short step it was from dissatisfaction to desertion and mutiny.

The only realistic option for victory here was to force an engagement. For that, he really needed Octavian's men, and he sent several messages, pleading that if he would not come in person, that at least he would send his legions.

Ten days after Antony arrived at Pharsalus, his scouts reported a large body of men approaching along the Via Egnatia from the west, bearing Octavian's standards. Antony surmised that Octavian had acceded to his request and sent his legions on without him. But Octavian was not going to let his ill health provide Antony with the opportunity to take all the glory for defeating his father's assassins. At the head of Octavian's legions, flanked by an honour guard, came a litter bearing the sickly triumvir.

Relieved as Antony was to welcome the new legions, he was disappointed to find that his colleague had accompanied them. Still, he greeted Octavian with good grace and feigned enthusiasm, and immediately called a conference with all the senior generals present to update Octavian on the situation.

The united Caesarians now held a numerical superiority and all agreed that it was time to bring the Republicans to battle. But Brutus and Cassius held the better defensive situations. They could not be assaulted without great losses, and the Caesarians were in no position to starve them out with a prolonged siege – quite the contrary, in fact.

Every day, the Caesarian army marched from their defences onto the open plain, in full battle array, waving their standards and taunting the enemy. Every day, the Republicans sat securely behind their defences, refusing to be drawn out. It was a temporary stalemate, but Antony knew that unless he could force an engagement, they would have to withdraw and retreat to the coast, where they would likely find themselves besieged with a vast army to feed.

Antony pored over Saxa's latest maps and the reports from the scouts outlining the enemy positions and defences. Agrippa was energetic and thoughtful in his suggestions, but he did not have Antony's experience, and Antony vetoed his suggestions, which, though often having some intriguing tactical nuance, mainly involved a costly frontal assault. His thoughts went back to the discussion of the impenetrable marshes to the south, and a plan began to form in his mind. If he could somehow forge a way across the marshes, he could reach the enemy rear and cut off their supply route. That would completely change the strategic situation, and would give the Caesarians a fighting chance of enforcing an effective siege, or making the assassins give battle.

He ordered Saxa to send scouts into the marshes to survey them. When they reported back he summoned his engineers, and together they roughed out, then refined a stratagem. Every day, he continued to send the legions out onto the plain, but though the number of units appeared to be the same, Antony had actually drawn large detachments from each cohort to help the engineers. In secrecy, while his visible forces distracted the enemy, his engineers and their legionary labourers worked to create a narrow causeway across the marshes. As silently as possible, they cut down reeds for a foundation, lined the edges with stones and sunk piles to bridge the deeper parts. A cover of reeds was left untouched to screen them from enemy eyes.

After ten days of intense labour, Antony was at last able to send a sizeable force across the causeway, where they suddenly appeared on Cassius' supposedly protected southern flank and began to build fortifications.

Cassius' immediate response was to begin to build his own fortifications to the south. For a couple of days, Antony read reports and examined with his own eyes the construction work of Cassius' engineers. Then, on the morning of the third day of October, with his legions already lined up as usual on the plain, he realised what Cassius intended.

The new wall was at right angles to his main defences, and must have been designed to cut the new fortifications of Antony in two and isolate those caught inside, who could be eliminated at will.

Antony could not allow this to happen. Though his own engineering works were not complete, they were sufficiently advanced to allow him to attack Cassius directly.

Finally, it was time to fight. And time to avenge Caesar.

Chapter XI

ante diem v Nonas Octobres DCCXII AUC (3 October 42 BC), Philippi

Antony received the message from Octavian, stating that the young man was still too ill to lead his troops in person, phlegmatically and without surprise. He hoped that his colleague would have entrusted to a competent general the command of his forces that confronted Brutus in the north. It was not something Antony had time to worry about. Because now he was leading his own legions against Cassius.

Cassius was certainly more skilled and experienced in command than Brutus, having fought at Carrhae for Crassus, in the civil war for Pompey, and then later for Caesar. But he hadn't been at Pharsalus, and had refused any further action against the Pompeians in the later stages of that war. By contrast, Brutus had been present at Pharsalus, but played no real part in the fighting and had done little else of importance militarily. Octavian, of course, was the least experienced of all the four generals in the field that day, and that would remain the case as he ducked out of yet another battle due to his health. That made Antony by far the most seasoned and capable general at Philippi, and the troops on both sides knew it. It was a great boost to his own men's spirits, while the opposing troops, not entirely sure they were on the right side – since they were opposing Caesar's son and heir, as well as his right-hand man – feared Antony's proven abilities as a commander.

So Antony put thoughts of the dispositions to the north – the Caesarian left flank – out of his mind. He could not influence the outcome there. All he could do was aim to inflict as profound a defeat as possible on Cassius here in the south on the right flank, and hope that Octavian's deputy, whoever that was, could at least hold Brutus' legions in place. One win and one draw would be enough to secure an overall victory.

Acting with his usual speed and decisiveness once his mind was made up, Antony ordered his legions facing east over the plain, who had been waiting vainly for the Liberators to come out and fight, to wheel right and advance in the direction of Cassius' new fortifications. He ensured the men were liberally equipped with ladders and grappling hooks to storm the new wall that Cassius' engineers were building.

As soon as they were in range of Cassius' slingers and archers, Antony, leading from the front on foot, gave the order to charge. With a terrific roar, off the leash at last, his men broke into a run.

It was a brutally difficult assault. Cassius was stationed on high ground, so Antony's legions had to run uphill. Although their heavy marching packs had been left behind in camp, each man still wore chain mail and a helmet and carried a pilum, a dagger, a gladius and a shield. Legs pumped, hobnailed boots stomped into the dirt, hearts pounded and breath quickly became laboured with the exertion. And all the while, they had to defend themselves from a vicious hail of arrows and slingshots.

Antony had never neglected his training, even when he had been living his most luxurious of lifestyles. Since Caesar's death, he had been in a constant state of war or preparation for war, and was at a peak of fitness impressive for a young man, let alone one of forty. That said, his heavy physique favoured feats of strength and short sprints rather than endurance, and he felt his heart would burst as he ran on. His legs burned, the air rasped down his throat, and all the while he fended off the missiles with his shields. All across the front line men fell with howls of pain, crippled, fatally wounded or killed outright. Nearby, his personal bodyguard, who had to look to their commander's safety as well as their own, were hit particularly hard.

But soon they reached their first goal: the defensive line of Cassius' men stationed in front of the incomplete wall. Antony's furious legions, their hearts and voices crying for violent revenge in Caesar's name, loosed their pila, then smashed into the Republican defenders. Their discipline had held, the rigorous training and the leavening of the new recruits with liberal quantities of veterans ensuring strict compliance to orders. Consequently, they hit the enemy line as a single unit, shields to the fore. The front line of the Republicans, despite being braced by the ranks behind them, could not withstand the impact and crumpled under the force of the hammer blow.

Antony, in the second rank, yelled out his encouragement, marauding up and down his line, ensuring his men heard his voice and saw his standard, so they knew he was with them, sharing their danger and hardship. The Republicans were pushed back, step by step, and more Caesarians piled in behind their own front line to add their weight to the effort. As with most Roman-on-Roman combats, it was largely a shoving match, with some hacking and slashing at the very front. But the momentum was with Antony's men.

As his men pushed forward, Antony extricated himself from the combat to survey the situation. As far as he could tell, Cassius had nine legions to his ten. What was more, Cassius' legions were under strength, while Antony's boasted almost a full complement. But even this couldn't explain Antony's overwhelming numerical superiority. In the brief moment he had to assess the situation, he surmised that Cassius had been taken entirely by surprise by the sudden assault, and that his forces were distributed inside the camp and across the defences, instead of being concentrated to fend off the attack.

Antony heard noises echoing across the plain from the north, and saw that Brutus' army had advanced against Octavian's position. They seemed to be in poor order, though, a ragged charge reflecting Brutus' inexperience and the heterogeneous make-up of his manpower. A good commander should easily repulse them. Antony smiled grimly. They had finally managed to engage the forces of the assassins, and he could stop worrying about how long his supplies would last. Now, he just had to worry about winning.

He yelled out a series of orders, and his senior centurions co-ordinated the direction of the assault to part the defending Republicans, so they could reach Cassius' transverse wall. As soon as a sufficient gap had been created, Antony led a group of reserves forward, hauling their scaling equipment and entrenching tools with them. Sheltered beneath the shields of their colleagues, legionaries used their shovels to fill in the defensive ditch. Then ladders were thrown up against the towers defending the palisade, and Antony's own archers and slingers sent up a barrage to keep the defenders' heads down.

Antony was not the first through the enemy defences – he was happy to give that honour to a younger man seeking glory and advancement. Besides, though he was brave, he was not stupid. Being first was hugely dangerous, and not only was his own safety important to him; he knew that his men would collapse without his personal leadership. Still, he did not hesitate for long, and once the first of his men had taken a defensive tower, Antony took his turn to scamper up one of the scaling ladders. From there, he was able to wave to his men, his standard-bearer and trumpeter by his side, his scarlet cloak conspicuous, and a cheer of delight echoed through the Caesarian ranks.

Grappling hooks shot out and soon the palisade was being hauled down. The defenders behind the ruined wall fought bravely, but Antony's men, their tails up, piled through. Antony was close on their heels, and after a short period of intense fighting, he found himself confronting the walls and main gates of Cassius' camp. As more of his men swarmed forward, he caught sight of movement in the marshes to his south. A large detachment of Cassius' men, who had been labouring further south in the marshes to create their defences – partly explaining the surprisingly small number of men defending the wall – came charging to the aid of their comrades.

Antony looked around him, gauging the size of the force that had made it through the first defence with him. It was smaller than the enemy reinforcements, but the enemy charge was disorderly. He could not allow them to get themselves organised.

'On me,' he cried, and his trumpeter sounded the charge once more. This time, Antony led the way, and his men closed around him, anxious to both keep their commander safe and share his glory. Soon, they reached the first of the reinforcing Republicans. But there was no line of interlocked shields to meet them, the way a Roman legion should receive a charge. The legionaries, lacking a formation, fought like undisciplined barbarians, and Antony's men, with their shields protecting one another, advanced inexorably: step, stab, twist, withdraw; step, stab, twist, withdraw.

Soon, the muscles of Antony's right arm were protesting at the effort as his gladius thrust out time after time, glancing off a helmet, batted aside by a shield, or sinking wetly into meat or innards. He could feel the battle lust transporting him once more, as it hadn't for such a long time, and he relished it. This was who he really was – a warrior, not a politician. Joy welled up inside him, and he voiced it in a wordless roar.

The Republican reinforcements collapsed and fled back to the marshes. Antony called his men back from pursuing them. They were no longer a threat, and the overall battle was far from won. He looked around. On the far side of Cassius' transverse palisade, vicious fighting continued as the bulk of his army continued to subdue the Republican defenders. Before him was Cassius' encampment, its heavy gates and more formidable defences, which Cassius had had much longer to construct, blocking Antony's advance.

Antony had just a handful of cohorts with him. But Cassius made no attempt to sally forth and strike him while he was vulnerable. Why not? he mused. Perhaps because Cassius had not felt it necessary to keep a strong force in the camp, since it was so well fortified, and instead had lined up most of his men to oppose Antony's and Octavian's displays of force out on the plain. Surely by now Cassius had realised his mistake and was hurrying more legions back to plug the gaps in his defence.

Antony made his mind up. It was always in his nature to take the bold choice. And he knew Caesar would have felt the same. His centurions organised the men for another assault, giving them a few brief moments to catch their breath, bandage their wounds and haul the wounded away to the rear. Then he gave the order to advance against Cassius' camp.

The defences were more daunting than the hastily constructed palisade of the transverse wall, and all the usual unpleasant traps were there — ditches lined with stakes, covered holes with spikes at the bottom, caltrops. But Antony's men knew what they were doing. They advanced steadily, probing the ground before them, sheltering under shields to keep out a rather feeble drizzle of arrows and bullets, filling in ditches as they went. Before long they had reached the walls, and had thrown ladders up by the towers that defended the gates.

Antony watched with pride as they scrambled up, the first wave inevitably taking severe losses. Some of the ladders were pushed back off the walls with long poles, the attackers tumbling to the ground in a flurry of broken bones and broken heads. But more came behind, and before long they had established a foothold on the walls. Antony's suspicions had been correct — Cassius had left the camp lightly defended. Even Antony's small detachment, once they were able to engage hand to hand, soon overwhelmed the defenders on the walls and the towers around the gates. Moments later, the heavy gates let out a great creak, and slowly swung open. With a mighty roar, Antony waved his sword high and pointed it into the camp.

Antony's legionaries rushed forward. There was no need for a carefully formed-up front line now, nor was it possible to maintain one when entering a fortification through a narrow ingress. Antony ran, outpaced by the fastest of his men, but still near the front as they entered Cassius' camp. The battle degenerated into vicious hand-to-hand fighting. Antony hacked and slashed around him, wishing the terrain had enabled him to bring up his horse, but content nevertheless to be in the middle of the tumult.

An auxiliary thrust forward with a spear, and Antony sidestepped and thrust his gladius into the man's guts. A Republican legionary appeared on his right, and Antony withdrew his sword enough to parry his new opponent's thrust. They exchanged blows, their swords taking chunks out of each other's shields. The Republican legionary was bearded, with blood and spittle not fully obscuring his grey whiskers. A veteran, Antony thought, and with some skill.

But there were few men who matched Antony in physical size and strength, and he used this to full advantage, his blows forcing the man backwards, shattering his shield, then knocking his gladius out of his hands. He sank to his knees, and Antony prepared to accept his surrender. But the legionary, with a look of defiance and hopelessness, whipped the dagger from his belt and slashed out. Antony leapt back, the tip of the weapon lightly grazing his thigh. He moved back in and thrust downwards, his gladius sliding down the side of the veteran's neck and into his chest. With a low groan, the man sank back in a pool of blood.

A loud cry warned Antony of a new attack, but as he yanked on his sword to meet it, it caught, perhaps on rib or clavicle. From the corner of his eye, he saw a spear thrusting with enough force to penetrate his mail and skewer him. He let go of his gladius, but knew in that instant that he had been too slow to avoid the blow.

His attacker suddenly flew to the side as one of Antony's bodyguards barrelled into him. The spear thrust went harmlessly wide, and the Republican legionary landed on his back, the wind knocked out of him. Antony's bodyguard, too close to use the point of his gladius, instead pummelled him in the face with the hilt until the man stopped moving, his head a bloody, unrecognisable mess. Antony retrieved his sword, then put out his hand to help his bodyguard to his feet. There was only time for a brief word of thanks before they both rejoined the battle.

For a while, Cassius' men held out bravely. But more and more of Antony's men made their way through the gap in the transverse wall and through the gates, and the advantage swung decisively to Antony. It still took time to mop up the last of the resistance, but by mid-afternoon, Cassius' camp was in Antony's hands, and Cassius had withdrawn the remainder of his forces to the east, to the hills in the direction of Philippi.

Now Antony was able to catch his breath and survey the extent of his victory. Some of his men sat or lay, completely exhausted. Many bore injuries of varying severity, from mere scratches to amputations, fractures and fatal gut wounds. Many were dead. But many more were celebrating wildly, and singing Antony's praises to the heavens. Cassius' legions were shattered, many dead, the rest fled. Of Cassius himself there was no sign.

Antony looked to the north. Don't let me down, Octavianus, he thought. Even if you aren't leading yourself, please let your men have made a decent show of themselves. But the vast extent of the plain, and the huge clouds of dust thrown up by both flanks of the battle, prevented even an educated guess of the outcome in the north.

Cassius' main camp was firmly in Caesarian hands, but without knowing if Brutus' legions were intact, Antony was uneasy. His men were now busy tearing down the enemy headquarters and looting every building, tent and body for every last coin of booty. It was their due, but if Brutus suddenly appeared out of the dust clouds with his legions in battle order, they were in trouble. Antony had seen jubilant victory turn to disaster at Forum Gallorum, and had no desire for a repeat. So he sent out the order that the men should gather what they could and return to their own camp, where they could regain their strength behind their powerful defences.

Reluctantly the legionaries and auxiliaries complied, and started back to their own lines, so laden down with bounty that they looked more like porters than soldiers. Antony lingered on the battlefield, surveying the wreckage, pride at the victory and sadness at the cost in Roman lives tugging his heartstrings equally. To the north, he could make out movement through the dust clouds: a body of cavalry making its way south, though still very far off. He could not tell if they belonged to Octavian or Brutus. It didn't affect his decision to withdraw – if it was Brutus, he could defend his own camp better than this unfamiliar and damaged fortification. If it was Octavian, there would be precious little left for his men to plunder, Antony's own men having taken the lion's share. He gave one last look around, then marched back to his own camp.

—

Antony spent the afternoon mingling with the men, touring the sentry posts, the hospital, the work parties improving the defences, the stables and the stores and the blacksmiths, offering profuse thanks and congratulations for their efforts that day, and promising huge – though unspecified – bounties. Messenger after messenger brought him intelligence from his scouts, from the prisoners and deserters from Cassius' camp, and eventually from Octavian's side of the battle. As the true picture slowly emerged from the fog of war, Antony's ebullient mood evaporated.

It turned out that Octavian had been too sickly or too negligent to appoint an overall commander to his legions, not expecting an outright attack. He was taken completely off guard by Antony's bold attack in the south. Some of Brutus' legions, seeming to sense the lack of leadership in Octavian's legions, had taken it upon themselves to charge into battle. Brutus had not specifically ordered this, and his men's attack was ragged and disorganised. But this disorder meant that two legions had bypassed Octavian's front line completely and smashed into his camp, quickly overwhelming it and putting to the sword everyone they could reach, including two thousand Spartans who had just arrived in a response to Octavian's appeal.

Meanwhile, Brutus' main force had engaged Octavian's legions, who were working more or less independently, each legate trying to hold their men together while desperately seeking orders. It was a terrible performance by the Caesarian leaders on the left flank. Their men, by contrast, had fought bravely, unlike Cassius' men, who fled, but as a consequence they were cut down where they stood. Initial reckonings suggested Octavian had lost at least three legions.

Fortunately, instead of immediately turning south to take Antony's flank, while Antony was still engaged with Cassius, Brutus' men had stopped to plunder Octavian's camp. By the time Brutus realised what was happening in the south, and sent reinforcements, Antony was already on his way back to safety.

At this point, it seemed that, despite Antony's stunning victory in the south, Octavian's incompetence and unfitness in the north had nullified the advantage. It meant the outcome appeared to be something of a draw, at least initially.

Of Octavian himself, there was no word. He had gone missing early in the battle, and no one had laid eyes on him since. Antony alternated between wishing his fellow triumvir was safely dead, where he could no longer mess up in battle or threaten Antony politically, and hoping he was alive, since Brutus was still in the field with his full army, and Antony needed Octavian's influence to ensure his legions were able to continue the fight.

'Curse that boy,' he raged to Norbanus and Saxa in his tent as another report of casualties in Octavian's ranks arrived. 'He should have stayed in bed in Rome, and let his mother nurse him better.'

The two legates looked at the floor, having nothing constructive to add. They knew as well as Antony that Octavian's weakness had cost them a complete victory that day. Battle would have to be joined again, and more Roman lives would be lost on both sides, regardless of who was the eventual victor.

Antony sighed.

'Saxa, get some reports of our casualties and what our effective fighting strength is now. Norbanus, find out what our supply situation is. We have taken a vast sum of gold from Cassius' camp, but you can't eat gold. How long have we got before we need to join battle again, or retreat?'

The two legates nodded and made to leave, when one of Antony's guards poked his head inside.

'Proconsul,' he said. 'There is a legionary who is demanding to see you. He says he has something you must see.'

Antony scowled, then nodded. 'Send him in.'

The grizzled veteran legionary, blood-spattered and covered in dust, entered and saluted briskly, standing smartly at attention despite his obvious fatigue.

'What is it, soldier?' asked Antony, trying to outwardly seem patient.

In answer, the legionary shucked off his backpack and drew out some fine robes and a sword, offering them to Antony with an expectant expression.

Antony took them and turned them over. The sword had an ornate jewelled hilt, and the robes were of finest rare silk.

'What are these?' he asked.

'They belonged to Cassius, Proconsul. I took them from his body. His head was nearby.'

Antony stared in disbelief.

'Cassius is dead? How?'

'The survivors said he took his freedman with him and instructed him to kill him. There was another suicide, too – a man called Titinius. Apparently he killed himself when he realised he had arrived too late with news of Brutus' victory to save Cassius.'

Antony whistled and looked at Norbanus and Saxa, who were smiling in satisfaction. This changed everything. The day was no longer a dubious draw. Even if Octavian was dead, and both sides had lost a general, the Republicans would miss the talented Cassius much more than the Caesarians would miss the weak Octavian. Antony grinned.

'So,' he said to his legates. 'I think we can count the day a victory after all. Let's take some wine. We celebrate. But not for long. There is still much to do.'

pridie Nonas Octobres DCCXII AUC (6 October 42 BC), Philippi

The next day there was still no news of Octavian's whereabouts. His body had not been found, but neither had he returned. Was he fleeing back to Rome, thinking all was lost? Antony assumed overall command of all the Caesarian legions, with no dissent from officers or men. He assembled the combined forces and from horseback, in his deep, booming voice, he gave them the finest of his oratory.

'Yesterday,' he said, 'we achieved a great victory.'

He could see the expressions of the soldiers in the front ranks: uncertain, dubious, even outright sceptical, especially those who had been on the left.

'Does it not seem so? Do you think that the enemy gathered a huge army in the East merely to sit behind fortifications in the Thracian desert? Yet that is what they do. They built their defences because they were afraid of you, and they sit behind them now, terrified. They do not accept our challenges to come out and fight, and though we will offer them battle again today, I guarantee they will not accept, because they know their defeat is certain.

'And what's more, their oldest and most experienced general took his own life yesterday in despair when he realised he was utterly defeated. I tell you again, we were the victors.'

The men seemed to accept this argument, and he could see nods in the ranks, as their backs became visibly straighter.

'Further, we are getting ever stronger. Domitius Calvinus is bringing us two legions of reinforcements from Brundisium, and will arrive any day.

'Yesterday, one of our camps was plundered, and yet we must not be concerned about this for a moment. Wealth doesn't comprise the property we hold in our hands, but is found in conquest, by which we can restore not only our own properties stolen from us, but also all the enemy's riches. In any case, we took at least as much from them as they took from us. In fact, it was doubtless more, since we travelled with only what we needed, while they had all the treasures they had extorted from the peoples of the East with them.

'Any gains that our own generals accrued, we will gladly redistribute to you in compensation for your own losses yesterday, when we defeat the enemy. I will go further, and tell you each man will receive five thousand denarii, the centurions five times as much, and the tribunes twice as much again.'

Spontaneous cheers broke out at this. Money was always a great motivator.

'Now we will offer them battle again, and if they do not accept it, we will force them, for are we men not stronger than their walls?'

The legions roared enthusiastic affirmation.

'Then let us go, and prosecute this war swiftly, that the peace we gain may be of the longest duration.'

Antony led the men, thoroughly whipped up for battle, out onto the plain and lined them up in battle formation. Brutus saw them approach and assembled his own men. But he held them on the high ground in a defensive formation, and refused to offer battle.

The legionaries yelled out catcalls and insults, calling them cowards and traitors and demanding they come out to fight. But as Caesar had found in his war with Pompey, it was hard to force an army to fight that did not want to, and Brutus' legions, through equal measures of discipline and fear, held their ground. Antony kept his legions drawn up for most of the day. The men soon tired of chanting and just set their minds to enduring the long, boring hours of waiting.

It began to rain. A cold, torrential downpour that initially disturbed the dust of the plain, then turned it into a quagmire. Eventually, sure that Brutus was not going to come down, and sensing his men's increasing unrest, Antony ordered them back to their base.

As usual, spies and deserters were able to bring back snippets of information from the enemy camp. Antony was taking a light meal that evening with Norbanus, Saxa and a sullen Agrippa, when an Athenian from a unit of Brutus' Greek allies was brought to him. He had crossed the enemy lines as soon as dark fell, to defect to Antony in disgust at Brutus' behaviour.

'Morale is very bad,' he said in a well-educated Attic Greek, suggesting he had had some schooling and maybe a previous position of civilian or military responsibility. Antony, as most noble Romans, but also as a one-time resident of Athens, understood this language and spoke it fluently. 'He has already offered his men countless riches to keep their loyalty, but they know that this is a hollow promise if he cannot win, and many do not believe he can, though he tells them all they need to do is hold their nerve and your supplies will run out, deciding the result.'

Antony glanced at his generals, who looked solemn. Brutus was not wrong, and if he stuck to this strategy, it would be a real problem.

'So in order to bribe them further, he has offered them to sack the cities of Thessalonike and Sparta when the battle is won, and take all their loot for themselves.'

Antony whistled. That was both a reward of immense value, and a brutally cynical strategy, involving the mass slaughter of the civilians of the two huge Greek cities.

'Though Athens and Sparta are traditional enemies, I have no wish to see a great city reduced to ash, and fellow Greeks put to the sword, for the sake of this faithless Roman.'

Antony clapped him on the shoulder.

'You are a good man,' he said, 'and you will be rewarded. What more can you tell me about the situation over there? How are the men feeling?'

'Some of them want to fight, especially those who were under Cassius, and wish to avenge their defeat. What's more, they are jealous of Brutus' legions, who were victorious and gained much personal wealth. Brutus' legions, on the other hand, are happy to maintain a defensive position and retain what they have gained.'

'And Brutus himself?'

The Athenian shrugged. 'I am a lowly auxiliary, I have no personal knowledge of him. But perhaps I can relate two happenings to you that might be of interest.'

Antony nodded for him to continue. The Athenian licked his lips and glanced at the cup of wine that Antony held. Antony waved a hand for a servant to offer the deserter a cup for himself, and he took it gratefully and drained it quickly.

'As you know,' he said, 'Brutus took many prisoners from your northern camp. Freemen and slaves. The freemen, he has spared for now. The slaves, he has had killed, every single one.'

'What a waste,' said Norbanus, shaking his head.

'It makes sense, though,' said Saxa. 'They are just mouths to feed. The freemen, the soldiers and civilians, he may turn to his cause.'

Antony tasted a sourness in his mouth at Brutus' callous actions. It should not surprise him, though, he realised. After all, this was the man who had killed Antony's own brother.

'You said you had two tales to relate?' he said.

The Athenian hesitated. 'Maybe the second is not so important to waste your time with.'

'I'll be the judge,' said Antony. 'Speak.'

'Well, among the prisoners were an actor called Volumnius and a jester called Saculio. Despite their position, they made ceaseless jokes and speeches about Brutus, mocking him relentlessly. Brutus seemed to ignore them at first, but his friend Messala said they should be flogged, stripped naked and sent to you. But the general Casca said that they should not be joking while the rites of Cassius' funeral were still being celebrated, and that how Brutus dealt with them would reflect how his level of respect for Cassius was perceived. Brutus snapped back at him, asking why he was bothering him with this, and saying Casca should do what he thinks best. Casca had the men led away and killed.'

Antony stroked his beard. Maybe it was a minor detail, but it spoke volumes to Brutus' state of mind: distracted, irritated, anxious to hand off decisions to his subordinates, even if the result was savage. It gave Antony further hope, though whether it would translate into an impetuous move by Brutus would remain to be seen. He would still have to do all he could to force the issue, before his time ran out.

The next day, and every day thereafter, Antony lined up his men and offered battle to Brutus, who continued to refuse. Not that there was no action at all. Skirmishers and small parties harassed each other's work parties who were repairing, reinforcing and extending their defences. Brutus sent out night attacks, probing for weaknesses, and Antony did likewise. Brutus even managed to divert a small river to flow through Antony's camp, causing some damage before his own engineers were able to redirect it. It added to the miserable conditions, with the rain and mud and the falling temperature dampening his men's enthusiasm.

Three days after the battle, there was a commotion and there were cheers on the outskirts of the camp, and Antony came out from his tent to see what was the matter.

Standing in the parade ground, surrounded by cheering soldiers, was Octavian, pale, shaky and caked in mud. Antony stared in disbelief for a moment, then, gathering himself, he strode forward and embraced his fellow triumvir, to an even greater acclamation from the men.

Once the young man had been attended by the physicians, bathed and fed, Antony visited him in his tent. Maecenas sat by his bedside, while Agrippa stood near the door, arms folded, expression unreadable.

'What happened?' demanded Antony, not trying too hard to keep a suggestion of accusation out of his voice.

Octavian's voice was hoarse. Whatever illness had prevented him from being present at the battle seemed to have resolved itself, though he was clearly weak, and had a streaming cold.

'I was warned,' he said, then coughed and took a sip of water.

'Warned? Warned about what?'

'My physician,' said Octavian. 'He had a vision in a dream. The goddess Minerva told him I was in grave danger, and while I was too ill to resist, he led me out of the camp before the attack even commenced.'

Antony stared at Octavian in disbelief, then looked to Maecenas and Agrippa, neither of whom would return his gaze.

'And where have you been since?'

'Recovering my strength,' said Octavian. 'And now I am here, and ready to resume my command.'

Antony barked out a laugh. 'Colleague, you don't look ready. I suggest you make sure the men know you are well and confident of our victory, and leave all the fighting to me.'

Octavian glared at him defiantly for a moment, but he did not seem to have the strength to resist, and he weakly nodded acquiescence.

'I will leave you to your recuperation,' said Antony. 'Maecenas, I have some supply matters to discuss. Will you walk with me?'

Maecenas looked uncertainly to Octavian, who nodded his agreement. Maecenas accompanied Antony out of the tent.

Once they were out of earshot, Antony demanded, 'What really happened?' He knew that the loyal and stubborn Agrippa would give Antony nothing, but Maecenas was slightly more pliable. Even so, he played dumb at first.

'It is as Caesar told you. Minerva intervened to save his life.'

'Octavianus does not believe that, and neither do you.'

'Caesar is my friend—'

'And he is my ally, and his well-being is as vital to me as to you. But I must know. We are fighting for our lives here. If I am to lead our legions effectively, I must understand to what extent Octavianus is capable of commanding his own men.'

'Agrippa and I will not let him go astray,' said Maecenas defensively. 'Nor would we ever betray him.'

'I don't doubt that. Whatever you say goes no further. It is not in my interest to have the men doubt his fitness to lead them.'

Maecenas halted, looked down at the ground, as if weighing up his options. Then he looked up and said bluntly, 'He ran away, and has spent the last three days hiding in the marshes.'

Anger surged up inside Antony. How dare he? He was supposed to be Caesar's heir. The men loved him, would lay down their lives for him. And this was how he repaid them? He clenched his fists, fighting the urge to march back into Octavian's tent and shake him, smack him around the head, until the boy cried for his mother.

'Why do the men adore him so?' Antony fumed. It was a rhetorical question, but Maecenas took it literally, despite the fact that they had had this conversation before.

'First and foremost, Caesar chose him. But there is much more than that. He is clever, cunning, far-seeing. He knows what to say to them, what to do. He may not be a great general, but any idiot can send a legion into battle... no offence.'

Antony visibly bristled, and Maecenas realised he had gone too far.

'Marcus Antonius, you are a brilliant tactician. But my friend has always been one step ahead of everyone else, ever since we were at school together. Only a fool would bet against him.'

Antony swallowed his ire. 'Just keep an eye on him. Don't let him embarrass himself.'

Maecenas nodded his agreement and Antony left him, trying to turn his mind to more important matters.

Later that day, news arrived that Domitius Calvinus' fleet of reinforcements, with its two legions – which included the mighty Martian Legion, cavalry and auxiliaries – had been intercepted by the Republican admirals Murcus and Gnaeus Domitius Ahenobarbus. Despite ferocious fighting by the accompanying triremes and the soldiers on board, almost every ship had been captured, sunk or burnt. It was a complete disaster, and the only way the Caesarians could mitigate it was to try to prevent the news from reaching Brutus.

That night the temperature plummeted, and the mud on the plain froze to ice.

ante diem x Kalendas Novembres DCCXII AUC (23 October 42 BC), Philippi

Antony kept his eyes fixed on Brutus' front line, watching for any signs of action. It was mid-afternoon, and just as on every one of the last score of days since the first full engagement, Antony had offered battle. But today was different. Instead of remaining safely behind his fortifications, Brutus had brought his army out of its camp. Still, he remained just in front of his walls, on high ground, with an easy escape route behind him. Antony could attempt an assault, but by the time his men had scrambled up the steep slope, either they would be too tired to fight, or

Brutus would have withdrawn. Antony needed Brutus to fully commit to battle, and to descend onto the plain to fight him.

There were parallels with Pharsalus, that great confrontation between Caesar and Pompey. Brutus, playing Pompey's senatorial, Republican role, might be advised to attempt to wait for Antony, playing Caesar's anti-senatorial, anti-Republican part, to collapse through exhaustion of his supplies. No doubt, like Pompey, Brutus was under considerable pressure to attack from men, officers and senators in his ranks, even if it was disadvantageous. And it seemed that, like Pompey, he was demoralised and uncertain.

But the situation was not the same. Because in one respect, Antony had been more successful than Caesar. He had not been passively waiting a move from Brutus over these last days, but had been actively working to isolate him and block his supply lines.

The first tactical success was due to a simple mistake on Brutus' part, a symptom of his inexperience relative to Cassius. There was a small hill just south of Cassius' camp. It was within bowshot of the Republican defences, but Cassius had occupied it to prevent the Caesarians taking it. Perhaps Brutus thought he could hold Antony's legions off with his archers, but he had miscalculated, and a few days previously, Antony had sent four legions by cover of night to seize the mount and erect a wicker screen that would protect the defenders from arrows. By dawn it was firmly in Antony's hands.

With this position, Antony was able to send ten legions south of Brutus' camp, and another two legions a mile further east. It was a risky tactic, since he had committed almost all his forces to the encirclement, leaving only a skeleton force of infantry, together with his cavalry, to defend his own camp. But the rewards were huge. If Antony could complete the manoeuvre, Brutus would be trapped against the mountains with no way to resupply, while, by contrast, the riches of the East would be open to the Caesarians. If it failed, Antony and Octavian would have to disperse their forces for the winter, with a view to starting from scratch the following spring.

Brutus might be inexperienced, but he was no fool. He could see his danger just as clearly as Antony. This was why Antony held his men out in the field for longer that day, despite the bitter wind whipping around them. Brutus had to engage, and the longer he left it, the worse his position would be.

But the day wore on, and still Brutus hesitated. Had his courage failed him?

Then at last Antony saw some movement in Brutus' ranks. He squinted, and moments later, to his disappointment, he realised it was just a single rider. But as the man neared him, he discovered it was not just any rider, but a man called Camulatus, one of Brutus' finest cavalry officers. He was deserting to Antony!

Antony rode to meet him with a small guard, wary of a trick. But Camulatus was genuine in his defection.

'What brings you to my ranks, Decurion?'

'Proconsul, please accept my service,' Camulatus said, out of breath from the hard ride and, no doubt, some nervous excitement. 'I can serve that man no longer. He has just put to death every captive he took from you, for fear they will be a burden to him in the battle to come.'

Antony looked up to the hill where Brutus' standard was held high. Antony had done some things he was not proud of himself, but Brutus seemed to be truly unconcerned with what human misery he caused.

'You are welcome, Decurion,' he said. Addressing one of his personal guards, he said, 'Take this man to the rear and have him questioned – gently, mind you. Decurion, I will thank you in person at a later date, but as you can see, for now I am rather busy.'

Camulatus nodded, relief at his reception evident on his face. But Antony had already forgotten him. For it seemed that the defection of Camulatus, who was renowned on both sides for his bravery and his loyalty, had finally stirred Brutus. On the hillside, trumpets blared, standards waved, shouted orders echoed down to the plain. And at last, Brutus committed his army to battle.

The front between the two enemies' armies had shifted in the past days since the previous battle, with Antony's efforts to bypass Brutus' defences to the south forcing Brutus to confront his opponent to the south instead of the west. Antony's right flank was therefore in the south-east and his left flank was to the north-west, with Brutus facing him to the north-east. It was on the left flank that battle was first joined. Here, the legions that had defeated Octavian's wing were craving battle, anxious to repeat their previous success, and raced ahead of their comrades.

Antony remained in command of the entirety of the Caesarian legions. Octavian had remained too sickly to challenge this situation, and rather than take part in the battle in a subordinate role, he had decided to largely stay in his tent, his ongoing illness the reason given for his absence. Antony wondered how much of his malady was real and how much imagined, brought on by the stress of combat, or even feigned to avoid having to fight.

At that moment – presumably because it was now obvious that this was going to be the decisive day of the campaign – Octavian appeared from the rear, and was brought to Antony in a litter. Antony greeted him distractedly. It wasn't a bad thing for the troops to see the so-called son of the man in whose memory they were fighting, so Antony allowed Octavian to show himself, then suggested he keep well out of the way for the rest of the day.

Now, with Cassius dead, it was Antony versus Brutus, man on man, Caesar's avenger against Caesar's assassin, as if they were gladiators facing off in the arena.

Antony ordered a legion from his left wing, one that had previously been commanded by Octavian, forward to counter this first Republican attack. The width of the front line was greatly constrained by the parallel fortifications running from east to west, and so this first attack was on a narrow front. The Republican legion did not pause to shoot arrows or sling stones, but charged straight into the attack, crying out for 'Liberty' and 'The Republic'. The Caesarian legions yelled back, 'Revenge for Caesar.' Then the two legions smashed together.

Even Antony was startled by the brutality of this encounter. Both legions were composed mainly of veterans, but they each seemed to have forgotten that their enemies were Roman soldiers too, and they fought as if they were confronting the vilest of barbarians, without a sliver of mercy. The accustomed sounds of battle – shouts, screams, clashes – seemed accentuated in that narrow space. Soon, a stream of dead and wounded were being carried to the rear, and reserves sent into the gnashing jaws of the enemy to be ground up and spat out. The extent of the slaughter was staggering.

Battle had not been joined for long before the terrific ferocity of the encounter began to show results. Unfortunately, it was the Caesarian flank that started to give way, slowly being forced back. Antony hesitated, waiting for the right moment to commit further forces. His senior commanders became uneasy, and Agrippa voiced their concern.

'Why don't you reinforce them? They are going to collapse.'

'Wait,' growled Antony. 'And don't question me.'

Brutus clearly saw the battle shifting his way, and decided to press home his advantage. He sent in more legions, and at the same time, his cavalry came charging down the hill, attempting to roll up the Caesarian left flank. It was almost impossible for a legion to hold against a strong enemy on two fronts. And if the left collapsed, the Republican cavalry could penetrate directly into the Caesarian rear, sowing panic which would rapidly turn into a rout.

'Proconsul,' said Agrippa, voice tight with anxiety. 'Marcus Antonius. Do something!'

Antony ignored the young general. He directed a relatively small proportion of his cavalry and some extra cohorts to reinforce the left wing, which was still being forced backwards, but kept the majority of his vast army out of the fight, content for the front lines to simply exchange the odd javelin or arrow. His expression remained impassive, but his heart beat fast. Had he judged these men right?

'I think the retreat is slowing,' said one of the younger tribunes, who had excellent eyesight. 'Yes, for sure. They are holding.'

Antony nodded curtly. He had trusted the heart of those legionaries of Octavian, who would not willingly taste defeat a second time. They had not let him down.

Now Antony sent a sizeable force against Brutus' left flank, on the other side from the first engagement, attempting to encircle him. Brutus, already stretched on his right flank, was forced to commit his reserve to his left, to prevent Antony doing to him what he had just attempted himself. The opposing legions collided, and began the same relentless hand-to-hand combat. Blood was soon mixing into the muddy ground.

Antony waited until Brutus' reserve was fully committed, then he summoned his bugler.

'It's time,' he said. 'Sound the charge.'

The horn blared out its call, quickly picked up by the other trumpeters. Standards were hoisted high. Centurions screamed to advance. The restless legions, who had been waiting like hunting hounds straining to be let off the leash, yelled out their fury and excitement, and charged.

But this was no disorganised, headlong rush into the enemy ranks. These soldiers were highly trained, most of them experienced, and they jogged forward, careful not to exhaust themselves or to allow their front to become ragged. At the last moment, with a huge roar, they put their heads down, accelerated to a sprint, and crashed into the Republican centre.

It was like a wrecking ball hitting a shoddily built Suburan *insula*. Brutus had concentrated most of his forces on the Caesarian left, and having failed to break through there, his centre was now as thin as papyrus.

It broke.

The Republican centre was forced back, so rapidly that the front lines retreated faster than the two reserve lines, so they became entangled. The cohorts were squashed together, and each Republican legionary lost the sense of safety that came from a strong line with shields to the left and right. In the blink of an eye, the centre of Brutus' army was transformed from a single cohesive unit to a disordered mass of individuals, fighting or fleeing according to each soldier's personal mettle. Antony wasted no time in exploiting the collapse, and, mounted so that he could respond rapidly to changes and roam about at will, he led up further reserves himself. The chaos in the Republican lines spread from the centre to the flanks as the Caesarian legions forced their way through the middle of the battlefield.

Antony rode up and down the lines, directing his officers to exploit gaps as they arose, to concentrate men on pockets of resistance, while avoiding getting too bogged down. At one point, Antony caught a glimpse of Marcus Porcius Cato, the son of Caesar's obstinate old opponent, fighting with a group of loyal men around him, refusing to take a single step backwards. He quickly disappeared from view, overwhelmed by a mass of Caesarian legionaries. Antony doubted he would survive. How many other men would be lost that day, he wondered, Republican or Caesarian, high-born or lowly?

But it was not yet time to count costs. He directed Octavian's legions to seize the gates to Brutus' camp. There, they were subjected to heavy missile attack, from the defensive towers and the garrison within, but they bravely held their ground, and prevented the majority of Brutus' forces from reaching safety. He also dispatched his reserve cavalry to run down those fleeing the battlefield to the east, particularly hunting the Republican leadership, Brutus above all.

There were too few defenders to hold the southerly camp, which had previously been commanded by Cassius, and soon Antony's men had scaled the defences and opened the gates. The Caesarian legions poured in to begin the process of systematic plunder and massacre.

For the rest of the day, Antony marauded across the battlefield, encouraging and cajoling, though his jubilant men needed little motivating by this stage, except to remember to save the looting until the battle was over. He was intent on ensuring that Brutus' army was totally destroyed, and that there would be no third battle.

But Brutus, by some combination of skill and luck, managed to extract four legions, more or less intact, and led them up the mountain behind the town of Philippi.

Night fell and Octavian retired to bed. Antony ensured the southern Republican camp was firmly in his hands, giving the camp command to Norbanus, and then set up defences to the north, facing the camp that had originally been commanded by Brutus, and was still in enemy hands. His men ripped down the Republicans' own defences and used them to build their own barricades, reinforcing them with shields and javelins taken from the dead, and even using the corpses of the enemy to heighten the walls.

Then they waited.

Antony was delighted, but could not bring himself to celebrate. Not until Brutus was dead or in his hands, would he genuinely believe it was all over, and that Caesar was avenged. He walked or rode up and down his lines, congratulating his men, sharing their food and drink, all the while wondering what Brutus would do. He was trapped, with a tiny force in comparison to Antony's army. Surely he must surrender now.

Hope rose in him when a small squadron of cavalry came riding up, crying out they had captured Brutus. Antony stood, frozen in anticipation, staring through the night gloom, as they brought up a hooded figure. How should he behave towards his opponent, he wondered. Haughty? Magnanimous? He had no time for further consideration. Triumphantly, the cavalry decurion pulled back the hood to reveal...

'Greetings, Marcus Antonius. Apologies for the deception.'

Antony sighed. 'Greetings, Lucilius,' he said, recognising the man as an officer and friend of Brutus.

'Lucilius?' asked the decurion, dismayed. 'He told us he was Brutus.'

'Don't worry,' said Antony. 'You weren't to know. Besides, I don't know what I would have done if it had been the man himself. Lucilius, I presume you did this to cover Brutus' escape?'

Lucilius inclined his head.

'You are a loyal man. And I would rather have you as a friend than an enemy.'

He stepped forward and, to Lucilius' surprise, embraced him warmly.

'Take him under guard,' Antony said the decurion, 'but ensure he is fed and given every courtesy.'

'Yes, Proconsul. Sorry, Proconsul.'

Antony waved the apology away, and returned to wandering from camp fire to camp fire, mingling with his exhausted, bloody, victorious army.

ante diem ix Kalendas Novembres DCCXII AUC (24 October 42 BC), Philippi

The sun rose over a scene of pure carnage. Antony, who had not slept, had received prisoner and casualty reports throughout the night, though at this stage he knew they would be far from accurate. They had taken several thousand Republicans prisoner, with more being rounded up all the time. But there were many more dead – tens of thousands on both sides. This was one of the largest battles in the history of Rome, certainly the largest ever between two Roman armies, and despite grieving at the losses, Antony could not help being awed by the fact that it was he, the son of a disgraced father and an executed stepfather, who had led his side to victory. Further, with Octavian so inconspicuous, no one could doubt that the result was solely due to Antony. It cemented his place as the foremost man in the Roman world.

The twists and turns of fate were strangely brought home to him when one of his cavalry officers presented him with a particularly beautiful and unusually large stallion captured from the enemy. Antony accepted the gift with thanks, and he stroked its thick, glossy mane thoughtfully.

'To whom did this horse belong?' he asked.

'To Cassius,' said the officer.

Antony stroked his chin.

'I recognise him,' he said. 'Cassius must have taken this horse from Dolabella when he defeated him. But I happen to know from where Dolabella acquired him. A man called Gnaeus Seius brought it to Rome from Argos. It was reputed to be bred from the line that my ancestor Hercules took there. I had the sad duty of having to order the execution of Seius for plotting against the state.

'And now, after three unlucky masters, he comes to me.'

'My deepest apologies, Proconsul,' stammered the cavalry officer. 'I never meant to bring you a gift of such ill omen. I will take it away and have it sacrificed to the gods.'

'You will do no such thing! This marvellous beast is mine now, and you can see, I am a lucky man. Besides, I am an augur, and a priest of Caesar. I will sacrifice to Fortuna to remove any trace of bad luck.'

The cavalry officer bowed and retreated, but Antony saw him surreptitiously turn and make a sign in the direction of the stallion to ward off evil spirits. Antony patted the horse affectionately, and gave it to a groom to be fed, watered, checked over by a *veterinarius* and stabled. For a moment, Antony wondered if he was being hubristic, the heady feeling of glory overwhelming good sense, which suggested he should have nothing to do with that animal. But he also knew that what was bad luck for one, was good for another, and with the legend of his forebear Hercules mixed into the story, not to mention the fact that the horse was such a fine mount, he made his mind up to keep him.

As it transpired, the acquisition of the horse did not affect his luck that day. Antony was making the preparations to take the camp still held by Brutus' men, after which he intended to pen Brutus in at the top of his mountain with his four legions and starve him out. He doubted they would last long, since they had been unable to take enough stores with them to endure a lengthy siege. As he surveyed the camp defences, assessing the weakest point against which he would direct his assault, one of his tribunes approached him.

'Proconsul, a messenger wishes to speak to you.'

'From Brutus?'

'No, but he is from his ranks.'

Antony gestured for the messenger to approach. The young man came forward and bowed deeply.

'Speak,' said Antony.

'Proconsul, I bring you this message from Strato, dear friend of Brutus.' He relayed the words from memory.

'"Proconsul, I regret to inform you that this morning, Marcus Junius Brutus took stock of his position. Seeing it was hopeless, and wishing no further Roman blood to be spilled, he begged me to take his life. I am ashamed to say at first I refused, but when he summoned a servant to perform the task, I consented and thrust the sword into his side. He neither flinched nor groaned. Thus ended the life of the greatest of Romans."

'Strato concludes by offering the surrender of the legions and bidding you ascend the mountain with whatever forces you see fit. He assures you there will be no further resistance.'

A strange mix of feelings swept over Antony as, accompanied by a Praetorian cohort of elite infantry and a screen of cavalry, he made his way up the mountainside to the position Brutus had held that morning. Relief predominated. His struggles were finally over, and his position was secure. There was also some sadness, if only a little. Brutus was many things – sometimes cruel, often indecisive – but in the end he had chosen honour over friendship and personal advancement. Antony could not forget that it was Brutus who had insisted that he had been spared on the Ides of March. Nor could he forget that it was Brutus who had murdered Antony's beloved brother, Gaius.

But when he reached Brutus' body, placed on his back, wrapped in his fine purple robe, Antony could feel no anger. He looked down at the lifeless corpse of the leader of the Senatorial faction, the so-called Liberators, and sensed that this was a turning point in the history of Rome. Though he and Octavian would continue to utilise the machinery and the trappings of the old state to govern, the Republic was surely finished for good.

He gave orders for Brutus' body to be prepared respectfully for cremation, and for the ashes to be returned to his mother in Rome, Servilia. Antony had always been considerate to defeated enemies, such as his old friend turned foe Archelaus, and he felt no desire to change this stance now.

After all, at long last, Caesar was finally avenged.

–

Unfortunately, Octavian was not as magnanimous towards the vanquished. The young man ordered Brutus' head cut off and sent to Rome, to be placed at the foot of Caesar's statue. Happily or not, depending on one's perspective, the head was lost at sea, falling overboard during a great storm in the crossing back to Italy. Antony knew nothing of this when he sat beside Octavian's bedside later that day. Any doubts he had about his fellow triumvir feigning illness were dispelled. Octavian looked dreadful – pale, sweating, shivering. Always lean, he had lost even more weight, so he was beginning to look skeletal. The superstitious side of Antony urged him to make a sacrifice to the gods later, to remove the taint of associating with one who looked like a lemur returned from the underworld to haunt the surface.

To his credit, Octavian did not let his physical infirmity prevent him from strategising with Antony, and his mental faculties seemed as sharp as ever. Antony lounged in a comfortable chair, drinking deeply from a fine Falernian wine plundered from the Liberators' camp, while Octavian sipped from a cup of water, occasionally spluttering and holding a cloth to his mouth, which came away tinged with blood. Agrippa and Maecenas sat close to Octavian, Maecenas in particular attentive to the sickly man's needs.

For his own part, Antony had Norbanus and Saxa as confidants – they had certainly earned their place by his side. But he missed the counsel of his allies. Fulvia was in Rome, of course, as was his brother Lucius, who was preparing to take up the consulship for the following year. Ventidius and Calenus were in Transalpine Gaul and Pollio was in Cisalpine Gaul. Plancus and Lepidus were the current consuls in Rome. But he did not feel particularly in need of sage advice. All his serious opposition was vanquished. His only real potential threat came from his ally Octavian, and the way he looked, he doubted the boy would survive the winter.

Their most pressing problem was what to do with the vast army they had accumulated, numbers inflated even further by incorporating a large proportion of the surrendered Republican legions. Rome could not afford their upkeep, so they must be disbanded and settled in a way that was acceptable to the veterans and avoided an uprising, while not bankrupting the state, whose finances were already stripped bare by the fund-raising needed to prosecute the war against the assassins. A huge – and hugely unpopular – project of land redistribution would be required. Antony was greatly relieved when Octavian volunteered to return to Italy and take care of the problem himself. So the lad could still be of some use, he thought. Antony, for his part, undertook to travel east, to settle matters in the provinces that had declared for Brutus and Cassius, and raise funds to send back to Rome to keep the state afloat.

Then the conversation turned to the allocations of the Western provinces, which had proved so important in deciding the fate of both Caesar's and Antony's fights against the Senate. Sextus Pompeius in his stronghold in Sardinia and Sicily remained a problem that had been postponed after Antony had called on Octavian to assist him against the assassins. Antony mused whether Lepidus could be prevailed upon to broker a peace with Sextus, since he had had some success in that matter in the past.

Maecenas made a sucking sound with his lips.

'You have something to add?' asked Antony.

'I think you need to be wary of Lepidus.'

'Why so?'

Maecenas looked cagey, and spoke carefully.

'I have certain... sources in Rome. They tell me that Lepidus has been secretly colluding with Sextus.'

Antony frowned. Octavian looked impassive. The news was clearly no surprise to him. Antony didn't like others having secret intelligence that was not available to him, but he could not ignore it.

'What do you think of this, Octavianus?' he asked.

'I think...' said Octavian, coughed weakly, and then started again. 'I think that Lepidus is untalented, incompetent and untrustworthy, and he is long past being of any use to us.'

'Perhaps,' said Antony. 'Yet we cannot discard him completely. For one thing, our legal power comes largely from our triumvirate. If we dissolved it, we would have to force new motions granting us authority through the Senate. It should be a formality, but it's a distraction we don't need.'

'Let him keep the title, then,' said Octavian dismissively. 'We will simply take away his provinces and his legions.'

Antony looked around the room and saw there was a general agreement at this.

'Very well. Let us divide up the Western provinces between the two of us.'

A little back-and-forth negotiation then took place, but soon both triumvirs were happy with their allocations. Octavian would take Spain, Numidia, Sardinia and Sicily – though, of course, he still needed to take Sardinia and Sicily back from Sextus and his powerful navy. Antony took Africa and Transalpine and Narbonese Gaul. Cisalpine Gaul was incorporated into Italy, and Italy itself was designated common territory for both triumvirs for the purposes of administration and recruitment. Lepidus was stripped of all his territories and his army, but he was given the possibility of receiving Africa as a province at a later date, to prevent him turning against them.

Maecenas drew up a document to this effect, and Antony and Octavian signed the deal in front of the witnesses. Antony was well pleased with the outcome. Gaul and Africa sandwiched Italy, giving him a strong foothold in the West, but the matter of the Eastern provinces had not even come up. Various Roman generals in the past had shown what could be achieved by using the riches and manpower of the East – Sulla, Pompey, Brutus and Cassius, for example, although only the first of these had ultimately used the resources effectively. Besides, Antony was looking forward to renewing his acquaintance with the East, having fond memories of his studies in Athens and his blooding on the battlefields of Syria, Judaea and Egypt.

On top of this, Antony had one eye on his legacy. It was all very well building a reputation on defeating Romans, and the legion had no tougher opponent than another well-trained, experienced legion. But there was no honour in killing compatriots. In the East was the real prize: the Parthian Empire, which still held the eagles of Crassus' defeated army as trophies. It had been Caesar's dream to conquer Parthia, and it was now Antony's ambition. If he could leave Octavian to mop up the mess in Italy, he could have free rein to build an army that would topple Rome's most dangerous remaining foreign enemy. It would take years to prepare, but Philippi had bought him that time.

With the meeting concluded, Antony went back to his own tent and began preparations for the journey to Athens, the first stop on what he hoped would be a delightful tour of the East. He could already taste the exotic foods, the fine wines, and feel the soft beds with the bodies of Eastern beauties nestled up against him. He closed his eyes, and within moments was fast asleep.

Chapter XII

Martius DCCXIII AUC (March 41 BC), Ephesus

Ephesus was one of the great cities of the world. It had passed through the hands of Greeks, Lydians, Persians, Macedonians, Seleucids and Egyptians before ending up under Roman rule, but despite all the conquests, had remained largely intact through these upheavals. Its ancient Temple of Artemis was considered to be one of the Wonders of the World. Now, as Antony entered the city, as its newest ruler, the inhabitants hailed him as a god.

Perhaps, he admitted to himself, he had encouraged this attitude a little. He was preceded into the city, first by his six legions to emphasise his military power, and then by dancers dressed as Bacchantes, the cultists of the Greek god of wine, Dionysos, called Bacchus by the Romans. Boys and men dressed as satyrs, with horns and furry tails, paraded alongside him. The Ephesians waved *thyrsi* – staffs topped by a pine cone and decorated with grapes and berries – associated with the Dionysiac traits of prosperity, fertility and hedonism. Harpists, flautists and pipers played, and the whole city was lavishly decorated with ivy and vines. As he passed, the crowd called him Dionysos, the Bringer of Joy, the Liberator, the Roaring Wind, the Winnower and Goat-slayer, this last because the goat tended to damage vines, to the wine god's disapproval. When they gave him another of Dionysos' titles, Pig-plucker – 'pig' being a euphemism for female genitalia – Antony smiled, wondering if his reputation preceded him. He had, after all, hardly been celibate since Philippi; he missed Fulvia, but he was a man, not a eunuch!

He had overwintered at Athens, and had quickly resolved to relax and enjoy the good things of life, which he had been deprived of almost continuously since Caesar's death nearly three years previously. Actors, mimes, dancers and courtesans had flocked to his court, and Antony had indulged himself extensively, hosting and attending parties, but not neglecting the cultural opportunities the city provided, such as visiting the theatre and attending lectures by philosophers and other intellectuals. He took on the Greek style of dress, much more flamboyant than the austere Roman toga, and he kept up his physical strength by spending part of every day in the gymnasium.

But though he was resolved to enjoy the fruits of his victory by having an enormous amount of fun, he did not neglect his official duties. Perhaps more mature now than when he had ruled Italy in Caesar's absence, he had received apologetic delegations from cities and territories that had supported the assassins, and deputations from potentates and minor kings, wishing for him to settle disputes and confirm lines of succession, or just to shower him with gifts in the hope of favourable treatment in the future. More than one ruler had sent one or more of their wives to him, knowing his reputation with the ladies. Antony was too polite to decline such a gift, and many of his nights were spent entertaining these high-born queens and princesses, and more often than not giving them a pleasurable lesson in the Roman techniques of love.

There was a more serious side to his duties, though, which mostly involved imposing onerous taxes on territories already heavily bled by Brutus and Cassius. Soon after he had settled himself and his retinue in Ephesus, commandeering the villa of one of the richest men in the city for his temporary home, he announced further taxation. The next day, he received an Ephesian orator called Hybreas.

'My lord and king,' he said after the usual Eastern-style prostration and obsequious greetings. 'It is my understanding that you wish to impose a second levy on the province by the end of the year.'

Antony looked down from his gilded throne at the kneeling supplicant, whose arthritic old knees seemed to be giving him some discomfort. 'Please stand, my venerable guest.'

Hybreas struggled to his feet with the aid of a stick.

'You are correct,' said Antony. 'Unfortunately, the rebellion of Caesar's assassins, the damage they have done and the costs of opposing them have led to the requirement of raising large sums from across the Empire. It is a regrettable but necessary measure.'

'I understand,' said Hybreas. 'It is a truly miraculous thing you do, worthy of the god you are hailed as.'

Antony cocked his head to one side.

'What do you mean?'

'To take a second annual tax in a single year is a prodigy. If you can do this, no doubt your divine powers will cause there to be a second summer, and a second harvest.'

Antony chuckled.

'You make a good point. But I'm sure the province can find reserves. Even if the stores are depleted, they can be replenished in better times.'

Hybreas shook his head sadly. 'In all seriousness, my lord, you must know that the province of Asia has already provided you with two hundred thousand talents. There is no more to give. If you have not received this sum, I suggest you look to those who took it from us.'

Antony looked at him thoughtfully. He had not scrutinised the accounts in detail, and it would be easy for the tax farmers and other civil servants to squirrel away some of the proceeds for themselves. He resolved to have someone look into it.

'You amuse me, Hybreas, but you argue well, too. I am persuaded. I will not levy the second tax.'

Hybreas bowed deeply.

'You are generous and wise, my lord.'

'I would wish to be wiser and more generous,' said Antony. 'For the former, that is only in the gift of the gods. For the latter, my hands are tied by fortune and fate.'

He dismissed Hybreas with a gift of gold and fine art.

Later that day, he received a deputation of a different kind. Her name was Glaphyra. She was a queen of the client kingdom of Cappadocia, and she had some intriguing connections. Antony's advisors informed him that she had obscure origins, but had become a *hetaera*, a kind of high-class courtesan. Hetaerae were highly respected in Greece, playing the role of conversationalist, artist, musician and dancer, as well as being a sexual companion. In fact they were even allowed to attend *symposia*, the intellectual discussions after banquets from which Greek wives and daughters were prohibited, since hetaerae were often highly educated.

In Glaphyra's case, she had risen even higher, and had married her lover, Archelaus, the high priest of the city of Comana, a position second in rank to the Cappadocian king. This was the son of the same Archelaus whom Antony had befriended in Syria, and who had gone on to marry Cleopatra's sister Berenice, before being killed in his battle against Cleopatra's father, Ptolemy Auletes, fought by Antony and Aulus Gabinius. Antony had fond memories of Archelaus, and agreed to receive his daughter-in-law both for old times' sake, and since she was an important royal in her own right.

Glaphyra was preceded into Antony's audience chamber by a herald, who flamboyantly proclaimed her as, 'Queen Glaphyra, mother of Archelaus Sisines, the son of Archelaus, the second of that name, and rightful ruler of Cappadocia'. But there was no doubt who was the supplicant here, and it was in the power of the man on the throne to grant or deny her requests at his whim.

Still, when Glaphyra entered, Antony sat up and took notice. A tall elegant Greek with light tan skin, a long, thin nose and high cheekbones, she was a beauty by any standards. Her bearing was both regal and sensual, and she was wearing a fine silken dress that both concealed and accentuated her slim figure. Her curled dark hair was pinned up and styled intricately, her eyes were darkened with kohl, and her perfume filled the room without being overpowering. She bowed deeply, then lifted her head to regard Antony with a slight smile on her lips.

'Queen Glaphyra,' he said. 'You are most welcome.'

'Lord Antonius, Proconsul, Triumvir, Augur, Priest of Caesar, Son of Herakles, Beloved of Dionysos, God and Saviour, thank you for deigning to allow this humble servant into your presence.'

There was a twinkle in her eye that suggested she knew she was overdoing the honorifics, but Antony had no doubt that, as a former hetaera, she was used to playing up to men's egos. He wasn't going to indulge that game.

'You may call me Antonius,' he said. 'I trust your journey was uneventful?'

'It was pleasant, Lord Antonius,' she said, not fully conceding to his request.

'And to what do I owe this visit?'

'First and foremost, my lord, I wished to show my loyalty and devotion to the new ruler of the Empire.'

He decided not to point out that he was, in fact, co-ruler with Octavian. When he left Philippi, it had felt as if he was by far the senior partner in that relationship, and all the titles, honours and flattery bestowed on him on his travels had only reinforced his opinion that he was the de facto ruler of the Empire and all the states that owed it allegiance.

'Your good wishes are much appreciated,' said Antony.

'As a small token, perhaps I could offer you a gift.'

'Of course,' said Antony. Glaphyra gestured to her herald, and he summoned two slaves, bald-headed eunuchs, who struggled under the weight of an ornate wooden chest suspended between two wooden poles. With visible relief, they placed their burden at Antony's feet, and the herald threw open the lid with a flourish.

The chest was full to the brim with gold and silver coins, jewelled necklaces, bracelets and anklets, as well as plates and statuettes made from precious metals. It was a fine gift for one man, enough to have allowed a young Antony to pay off his prodigious debts and still be rich. Now, it was barely enough to make a ripple in the surface of the ocean of public debt that Rome was drowning in. Still, it was nice enough, and he smiled graciously and thanked Glaphyra politely. She seemed a little put out that he wasn't overwhelmed with gratitude at her generosity, but recovered quickly.

'I knew your father-in-law, Queen Glaphyra,' Antony said. 'I counted him as a friend, though we ended up on opposite sides of Egypt's civil war.'

'My husband, his son, Archelaus the Second, did not see his father after he left Cappadocia, of course, but they corresponded, and my father-in-law spoke well of you.'

'Archelaus is well?'

'My husband passed away last year, I regret to say, soon after the Divine Gaius Julius Caesar saw fit to take away his role of high priest of Comana and replace him with the usurper Lycomedes. But it is on behalf of my son, Archelaus Sisines, that I petition you. The high priests of Comana have long been considered the proper kings of Cappadocia, but others have ruled in their stead. Until recently, the Cappadocian king was Ariobarzanes the Third, who was surnamed "Friend of the Romans" for his support for your people. But the traitor Gaius Cassius Longinus had him executed last year, and he was replaced by his brother, Ariarathes the Tenth, who I can assure you is no friend of Rome.

'My son, who should be on the Cappadocian throne in any case, would be a much stronger ally to Rome, and an ally to you personally.

I plead, for the sake of your friendship with his grandfather, that you install him as king of Cappadocia.'

Hearing the word 'grandfather' made Antony feel suddenly old. His friend Archelaus would have had an adult grandson if he was still alive. And how old did this make the queen before him? Probably a similar age to himself, maybe slightly younger. Well, either she looked good for it, or her maids had done an amazing job with her make-up.

He decided he had done enough governing for the day.

'The hour advances, and you must be weary after your trip,' he said. 'Would you care to join me for dinner? We can discuss your petition and the problem of Cappadocian succession further over a fine wine and some good food.'

Glaphyra smiled warmly, and Antony knew her pleasure was genuine. Not only did this mean she would have the exclusive ear of the most powerful man in the world for an evening; she would also get to experience all the charms Antony could bring to bear. And what woman could resist that?

Aprilis DCCXIII AUC (April 41 BC), Ephesus

Antony tried to concentrate on the letter in his hands, but Glaphyra was making it very difficult. He sat up in bed, eyes scanning the papyrus, but she held him from behind, her slight breasts pressed against his back, her fingertips caressing his wiry chest. He gave up, tossed the letter to one side and turned to her, his lips finding hers, hands exploring.

Afterwards, he dismissed her so he could concentrate.

He had only intended to spend one night with her, but he soon discovered a single night was nowhere near enough to explore every delight she had to offer. Besides, he enjoyed her intellectual company when they weren't in bed together, and he took to spending all their leisure time together. She was not his first paramour, of course, with Cytheris being foremost among the others. But Glaphyra combined Fulvia's brain and wit with Cytheris' beauty, and brought her own invention to the bedroom. It was a heady mix that he found himself falling for.

But he had other matters to attend to, and his days were a constant whirl of audiences, meetings and councils, leaving only his nights for partying and entertainment. Still, he found time to reward his friends. Installing his loyalists in important positions in the Eastern provinces had helped ease his administrative burdens – Saxa was made governor of Syria and Plancus governor of Asia – but the weight of his duties and the volume of his tasks were still crushing. And it was not just the useful and important friends that Antony looked after. His personal trainer, a former slave whom he had freed, and who now took the name Marcus Antonius Artemidorus, requested that Antony confirm the Company of the Victors of the Sacred Games in its traditional privileges of exemption from military service and taxation, and Antony was happy to grant his friend's wish.

Among the many rulers from whom he had to obtain oaths of loyalty to him and to Rome, Cleopatra VII of Egypt was one of the most important. They had corresponded in friendly terms regularly since the death of Caesar, and she had tried to send naval assistance against the Liberators. Though the attempt had failed, Antony had been pleased by the commitment it showed. Now, he decided it was time for her to pledge her allegiance more formally. He could have travelled to Alexandria himself, but there was still so much work to do in Asia and the neighbouring provinces.

One of the problems Antony had inherited was the mess in Judaea, which never seemed to be at peace. Antony's old comrade from his time in Syria, Antipater, had been a strong ally of Caesar during his struggles in Alexandria. Caesar had rewarded him by making him the first Roman Procurator of Judaea, with Hyrcanus, the king, submitting to Antipater's will in all practical matters. However, when Cassius took control of the province, he had forced Antipater to side with him. Cassius was a harsh master, and whole cities were sold into slavery in an attempt to satisfy his rapacious demands. Then Antipater was assassinated, and his sons Herod and Phasael, who had been serving as provincial governors of Galilee and Jerusalem respectively, continued in his place.

Unfortunately, Herod seemed to have maintained good relations with Sextus Pompeius, since his father had supported Sextus' father in the civil war between Caesar and Pompey the Great, up until Pompey's death. Antony had liked Antipater, and he knew and respected Herod, and had no wish to depose him, but he could not tolerate disloyalty. It was yet another problem to solve.

Another reason for Antony to stay in the region of Asia Minor was his ambition towards Parthia. Since Crassus' humiliating defeat at Carrhae, Rome had cried out for vengeance against the Eastern empire. Caesar had been murdered three days before he was due to depart for his campaign against the Parthians. Antony, as Caesar's military successor, felt it incumbent on him to carry out Caesar's plans, and besides, Parthia was the only foreign enemy that he felt worthy of his time and efforts.

He decided therefore to summon Cleopatra to him, rather than visit Egypt in person. Antony had become accustomed to the rulers of the East, no matter how grand and powerful, attending him the way one of his clients in Rome would come to his house to pay their respects and confirm their loyalty. That said, it felt like time to move on from Ephesus. He needed to show his face and demonstrate his power in more cities and territories, to reinforce his claim to be overlord of the East. Besides, he wanted to see more of the East. The culture of the Hellenic world greatly appealed to him, artistic, intellectual and hedonistic. It was much more fun than the austere and frankly boring Roman tradition, as exemplified by Cato and Cicero.

His next stop would be Tarsus in Cilicia, the former stronghold of the pirates who Antony's father had failed to defeat, and which had been finally conquered and incorporated into the Empire by Pompey. It was close to Syria, which would be his staging post for the Parthian invasion, but was not an unreasonably long sea journey for Cleopatra to undertake, especially if she stopped at Cyprus on the way to reprovision. He summoned a scribe and drafted a letter to Cleopatra, demanding her presence in Tarsus, then tasked his secretaries with organising the moving of his court to a new city, with all the upheaval and detailed planning that entailed.

Then he went to Glaphyra to tell her she would not be accompanying him. She had been a wonderful distraction, but it was time to move on. And from what he knew of Cleopatra, Antony doubted she would be happy to have another queen present, attempting to outshine her.

Cleopatra had always been pleasant company, but had never been a romantic target for him. When they first met, she had been too young. At their second meeting, she was Caesar's paramour and firmly out of bounds. Technically, she had been married to her younger brother, Ptolemy XIV, as Egyptian tradition dictated, but she had had him poisoned soon after the Ides of March, and elevated Caesarion, her son with Caesar, to be her co-ruler.

So now this attractive, intelligent, powerful and fabulously wealthy woman was available. Perhaps she would be the next Glaphyra – a pleasant distraction for a month or two. Antony felt a little frisson of anticipation.

Sextilis DCCXIII AUC (August 41 BC), Tarsus

It had been a long time since Antony had been refused, and he was not used to it. Nor was he accustomed to being kept waiting. And yet his first letter to Cleopatra had resulted in a polite but firm rebuff. His follow-up letters had been more insistent, even suggesting that he was dissatisfied with the amount of aid she had provided the Caesarians in their wars with the Liberators. The implied threat was no more successful than his previous demands. Finally he remembered who he was dealing with – a proud woman who ruled an immensely powerful nation, but whose personal position was always precarious. He summoned a new aide, Quintus Dellius, a rather unreliable young man who Antony nevertheless liked for his sarcastic sense of humour. Dellius had travelled east with Dolabella, deserted to Cassius, and then begged to join Antony after Philippi. Antony had been using him for diplomatic missions, finding his easy manner and silver tongue highly effective. Dellius was therefore dispatched to Alexandria on a mission to persuade Cleopatra to meet Antony.

'Remind her of our pleasant encounters in the past,' Antony told him. 'And feel free to hint that the space beside me in bed is currently empty.'

Either Dellius had been successful, or Cleopatra had decided she had played hard to get for long enough, for in high summer, in sweltering heat, Antony finally awaited her arrival in Tarsus. He had been told she would arrive by boat, and had prepared a lavish reception for him. He himself was mounted on a gold throne on a dais in the marketplace on the river Cydnus, by which she would arrive. Then he and his huge entourage of noble officials, military officers, priests, dancers, actors and entertainers, together with crowds of citizens, waited, as the hot sun sank lower and lower towards the horizon.

Antony sipped well-watered wine cooled with crushed ice transported huge distances from the mountains, and badgered the slaves to fan him harder.

'Where is she?' he grumbled to Dellius, who waited beside him.

'She will be here soon, Proconsul,' Dellius assured him, though he did nothing to hide the uncertainty in his tone.

A murmur spread through the crowd of the local populace, whispers turning to cries of excitement. People drifted away, a few at first, then more and more, until the marketplace was soon emptied of everyone except those who dared not abandon Antony. He looked around in bewilderment, and then sent Dellius to find out what was happening. He returned soon afterwards, and said simply, 'I think you should come and see for yourself.'

Antony, out of favour with Caesar at the time, had been present in the crowd when Cleopatra entered Rome in splendour and glory. He should have anticipated that she would have something similar in mind. He followed the hurrying citizens down to the river, and when he got there, he caught his breath.

Cleopatra had processed up the river in the most enormous and sumptuously decorated barge Antony had ever seen. The sails were dyed purple. The poop deck was gilded. The rowers hauled on silver oars. The air was filled with the smell of incense from burners placed along the riverbanks, which were lined with crocuses. Haunting oriental music drifted across the awed spectators: beautiful melodies and harmonies from pipers and flautists of a skill that even the unmusical Antony could appreciate. Serving maidens dressed as sea nymphs and the Graces were stationed at the ropes and the rudder.

And in the middle of it all, fanned by young boys dressed as Eros, beneath a gold-spangled canopy, reclined Cleopatra, clothed as a goddess, draped in a loose, flowing blue dress.

Antony could do no more than stare in wonder at this heavenly spectacle, almost hypnotised as the barge drifted into dock and was made fast. Whispers flew around that Aphrodite had come to Tarsus to visit Dionysos, but Antony did not feel like a god himself at that moment, but a humble supplicant before an all-powerful deity.

He shook himself, and sent Dellius to Cleopatra, inviting her to attend him for a dinner banquet. Dellius returned promptly with her counter-proposal that Antony and his officers and advisors come to dine with her on the barge. Antony had rarely felt more helpless, and he acquiesced as meekly as a lamb being taken to a sacrifice. Keeping his back straight, suddenly desperately worried that he might stumble – or even trip and fall into the water – he boarded the barge and entered Cleopatra's presence.

She remained reclining as he approached, and it occurred to Antony that she should be prostrating herself before him. But it seemed an impossible demand on his part, and so he stopped before her and bowed his head.

'Queen Cleopatra Thea Philopator, Daughter of Ra, Mistress of the Two Lands, I greet you.'

'Marcus Antonius, Proconsul, Triumvir, you are welcome. Please, you and your men, join me inside.'

She was lifted by her slaves and carried into the huge cabin. Antony followed her inside, and stopped abruptly in amazement. It was now dusk, but the cabin was brightly illuminated by lanterns, arranged on all sides in rectangles and circles, angled in different directions to create a mesmerising display of light. Gold and purple tapestries hung from the walls, and twelve long tables were set with the most exquisitely beautiful gold and jewelled vessels.

Cleopatra smiled softly at Antony's expression, and said quietly, 'All this is for you, my lord Dionysos.'

Antony could not help but note the implication that she had included herself in those gifts. He gestured to his men to take their places, and they stumbled forward in wonder as they were shown to their couches by stunningly beautiful slave girls. Antony was ushered to the couch at right angles to Cleopatra, and he lay down so their bodies were aligned, feet away from each other, heads close.

He could see her more clearly now, and his eyes roamed unabashedly, taking in every detail. The skin of her face was whitened lead, her cheeks made rosy with a light rouge. Her lipstick was red, and her eyebrows were plucked, eyes heavily outlined in kohl, the corners elongated. Her eyelids were shaded with yellow saffron, replicating the golden allure of a goddess each time she blinked. The back of her hair was pinned up in a bun with gold, pearl-tipped hairpins, but the sides fell loose in long, thick ringlets around her shoulders and neck.

Her dress was a Greek-style silk blue *chiton* – a sleeveless dress revealing one shoulder – and her cork-bottomed sandals were gilded.

She was decorated in a long necklace of pearls, wrapped around twice, and two earrings made from the largest pearls Antony had ever seen. Emerald-studded gold bracelets hung loose from each wrist. And then there was her scent: a mix of complex and heady aromas that included myrtle and rose, and made him dizzy when he inhaled.

She was not pretty in any conventional sense. If Antony had been in any state to assess her objectively, he would have found her nose overlong, her figure a little ordinary, her lips not particularly full. But none of that mattered – it did not even register. To him and every man – and, no doubt, quite a few of the women – present, she was simply stunning.

Slaves brought the finest wines and delicacies, and the Epicurean in Antony appreciated the expense, skill and effort that had gone into preparing the banquet. But he would have eaten mouldy bread and drunk stale water if it meant he could spend the evening in the company of this unearthly woman.

He could not even contemplate where to start a conversation, and Cleopatra appeared to tease him for a while, aware that he was tongue-tied but waiting for him to speak first. At length, with a subtle turning up at the edges of her mouth, she took pity on him.

'We have both come a long way since our first meeting, don't you think, my lord?'

Antony cast his mind back to the spotty adolescent he had first encountered at the beginning of his military career: the charismatic but plain child who he suspected had a crush on Antony, the handsome young Roman cavalry officer. She had been of not the slightest interest to him then; he had his sights fixed on the wives and daughters of the local dignitaries.

'A long way,' he agreed.

'My late father and I were always aware of our debt to you in aiding us to regain his throne.'

'It was my pleasure to be of service.'

They were in fact, good times, he recalled: his first battles, a long way from his debtors, proving himself much more than the son of an incompetent father and stepson of a disgraced senator.

'And of course, I enjoyed your company in Rome, when I was there with Caesar. I was sorry I did not have a chance to say goodbye, but in the end I thought the situation meant I should look to the safety of my son, first and foremost.'

'I understand, of course. How is young Caesarion?'

'The pharaoh is in good health, thank you. He is six years old now, and showing promise in the schoolroom and the gymnasium.'

'With two such remarkable parents, how could he fail to be outstanding?' Antony said.

Cleopatra smiled, then laid a hand on his.

'Before we go on, can we put to rest this silly misunderstanding between us?'

'Misunderstanding?'

'You said that I did not offer you sufficient aid in your fight against my beloved Caesar's murderers.'

'Ah, that. Look, it may be that my information was not accurate...'

'Then let me inform you. I did nothing to assist those murderers. I refused Cassius' demands for aid and funds. I, in fact, sent assistance to Dolabella, of which you may be unaware due to his unfortunate passing. And I sent a fleet to Greece to help your fight, though it sadly did not reach you.'

Antony waved a hand dismissively. Even if she had told him that she had given every last gold coin and soldier to Brutus' cause, he suspected he would have forgiven her at that moment. As it was, her account was both believable and acceptable. He understood she had troubles in her own country, with pretenders such as her sister Arsinoë, currently claiming sanctuary in the Temple of Artemis in Ephesus, vying to take the Egyptian throne.

'Then the matter is closed. You have been a loyal ally to Rome and me, and Rome and I will repay you.'

Cleopatra fluttered her golden eyelids and smiled her gratitude, and Antony's heart skipped a beat.

'Perhaps that is enough talk of matters of politics for now,' she said. 'Would you care for some more crocodile liver?'

At the end of the evening, Antony had a litter bear him home. His head was spinning, and he was unsure if the cause was Cleopatra's wine, or the queen herself.

–

Cleopatra turned down Antony's dinner invitation a second time, and so he dined on her barge again the following night. If anything, the queen outdid herself, with everything more expensive, bigger, better, although the first impression was still hard to beat.

The following night, she deigned to attend a banquet in her honour at the palace he had taken over in Tarsus, and though he went to every effort to impress her with the cuisine and decor, he knew it was a pale imitation of what she had achieved. She was magnanimous in her praise of his hospitality, but he could see in her eyes that she was humouring him, and she could tell he knew. As with most things in his life, he decided to face the matter head-on.

'I apologise, my queen,' he said, 'that my fare is so poor in comparison to the bounty you brought from the Nile. I am just a coarse soldier, and do not have your sophistication and intelligence.'

Cleopatra knew full well that Antony was, in fact, an enthusiastic admirer of Hellenic culture, highly educated and quick-witted. But she went along with the conceit of the rough soldier boy entertaining the princess, and both played up to their role, until they both broke down in fits of laughter. Eventually, Cleopatra announced it was time for her to retire to her barge.

'Surely it's too late for you to travel through this dangerous city?' suggested Antony.

'Have you not made it safe with your power and wise rule?'

'Of course, but there is always the risk of some villain prowling the streets. Or a falling roof tile.'

'But I have nowhere to stay.'

'I'm sure there must be a spare room somewhere in this huge palace,' said Antony, giving her a lopsided grin.

They became lovers that night, and Antony fell instantly in love. The entire experience was magical, from the first kiss, to the sweaty, breathless cuddle afterwards. And if he was any judge of women – and he prided himself that he was – Cleopatra was also well satisfied. Several times. Of course, as far as Antony knew, her only comparison to him was Caesar, who, although he himself was a lover of some renown in his day, was getting rather elderly and beginning to develop the illness that plagued him for the rest of his life by the time he began his affair with Cleopatra.

Antony spent every night from then on in her company, and increasingly his days, and as their closeness increased, he let her attend some of his meetings and formal occasions, seated at his right hand, as if she was his queen. They took to dressing as Dionysos and Isis, the Egyptian equivalent of Aphrodite, for fun at first, but when they realised how seriously the Eastern nobility viewed their newly appropriated personas, they made sure to play up to the expectations, attending religious ceremonies and sacrifices, and having plays and games performed in their honour. The more conservative Romans pursed their lips at Antony's behaviour, but the Greeks and others of the East loved the way he clearly respected, admired and took part in their culture.

Occasionally, he thought of Fulvia, and still enjoyed the letters from her. He felt a twinge of guilt, not at taking a lover, but at actually falling in love with someone else. But at the same time, he felt helpless to resist, nor did he want to. Besides, Fulvia was a very long way away, and he had not seen her for a very long time.

They had not been lovers for long when Cleopatra, after one particularly extended period of love-making, sat up and sighed.

'What's wrong?' asked Antony, suddenly anxious that he had displeased her.

'I love it here, my lord, by your side. But I fear for my country. Just today, I had intelligence that my sister Arsinoë intends to leave Ephesus and travel to Alexandria to supplant me, with the aid of my governor in Cyprus, Serapion.'

'I will not allow that!'

'It is my problem to resolve,' said Cleopatra regretfully. 'Not yours or Rome's.'

'Your problems are my problems, my love. What would you have me do?'

'You know what my family are like. You have seen how they behave. I will never be safe while Arsinoë lives.'

'Then she dies,' said Antony.

A tear rolled down Cleopatra's cheek. 'My poor sister. But she brought this on herself.'

'She did.' Antony impulsively summoned a messenger. He quickly dispatched a directive to his officials in Ephesus, ordering the execution of Arsinoë, then lay down and went to sleep.

He had actually forgotten this event when he received the news that Arsinoë had been torn from her religious sanctuary in the Temple of Artemis and cut down on the spot, with Serapion, who was hiding in Tyre, being dispatched soon after. Antony had a vague sensation of being manipulated, aware that this was not the way he would have handled the situation if left to his own devices. But what was done was done, and Cleopatra was delighted with the account.

Nevertheless, soon afterwards, she announced that she must return to Alexandria.

'Egypt is not a settled country, my lord,' she said. 'If I am absent too long, I fear for unrest, especially after the death of my sister. There are those who wish me ill, and covet my possessions, you know.'

Antony protested, but she would not be moved. Reluctantly, he bid her goodbye, but promised that, contrary to his previous plans, as soon as he had wrapped up his affairs in Tarsus, he would join her.

For the next month, he worked hard, eschewing parties to get his tasks finished so he could go and visit his new beloved. A number of cities in the East that had been under Roman influence had taken the opportunity to declare independence or ally themselves with Parthia, with a tyrant often seizing power from the Roman-approved administration.

One of these was Palmyra, a city situated near the Euphrates, which acted as the border with the Parthian Empire at that point. On the pretext that they had failed to aid the Caesarian cause – but really because, with Octavian still desperately in need of funds to keep the West settled, Antony wished to plunder the riches the city had acquired by trading between the two empires, and also to reward some of his newly integrated legions with the promise of booty – he dispatched a cavalry force with the aim of sacking the city and bringing back the treasure he was told it held.

Unfortunately, the Palmyrans had got word of the approach of the army, and they abandoned the city and crossed to the far side of the river with all their possessions, setting up a strong force of archers to repel any pursuit. Antony's cavalry, finding the city abandoned, burnt a few buildings and returned empty-handed. It was frustrating to Antony, and what was worse, he began to receive reports that the Parthians, inundated with the angry rulers that Antony had expelled, were becoming restless. He was a long way from being ready for war, and besides, his ardour for military campaigning had receded as his mind was occupied with thoughts of Cleopatra.

With some diligence, but perhaps a little over-hastily, Antony completed his reorganisation of the East, in some cases confirming arrangements of local rule made by Caesar, in others, replacing the ruler with someone he felt more efficient or trustworthy. Some cities were rewarded for their loyalty and help, a score being declared free – although not, of course, exempt from taxation. Some hostile tyrants were expelled – for example, Marion of Tyre, who had warred against Judaea. In other cases, cities that had been overly enthusiastic in their support of Cassius and Brutus were deprived of their freedom and old dynastic rulers favourable to Antony were restored. Ultimately, Antony, informed by his deep knowledge of the Orient, and by his numerous contacts and friends from his time in the region, made a swathe of changes to the Eastern provinces and the states that were in the Roman sphere of influence. It was arduous and painstaking work, for though he was anxious to complete the arrangements, he was acutely aware that a successful invasion of Parthia would require a settled and compliant East.

Finally, he was content. Syria, Judaea, and the territories that bordered Parthia would always be restless, and waiting until the East was at peace would be as interminable as waiting for the end of poverty or disease. So, as confident as he could be with the loyal and competent Saxa governing Syria, taking only his Praetorian Guard, Antony set sail for Alexandria.

Januarius DCCXIV AUC (January 40 BC), Alexandria

The winter climate in Alexandria felt like late spring in Rome, and high summer in Gaul. The temperature was pleasant, and the rainfall was light. Antony, conscious that Caesar had taken an extended holiday in Egypt with Cleopatra after the end of the war with Pompey and the subsequent Alexandrian war, felt fully justified in taking a break himself. He continued to indulge his love of Greek culture, attending lectures and plays, exercising in the gymnasium and hosting symposia with philosophers. He also indulged his hedonistic side fully, drinking, gambling, even occasionally going out at nights dressed as a slave and getting into drunken fights. The Alexandrians, already well disposed to him, remembering his previous honourable conduct when he had been in Egypt under Gabinius, adored him.

It was Cleopatra, of course, who dominated his attention. They spent the majority of their time together, and she was happy to join in his fun. She diced with him, got drunk with him, watched him exercising, went hunting with him, and even dressed as a serving girl to accompany him out on his nocturnal high jinks. She threw him banquets, took him on cruises, went riding in the countryside with him, and took him to bed every night, so he had neither the inclination nor the energy to so much as glance at the beautiful Egyptian women in the queen's court.

Cleopatra was twenty-one years of age, and though she had the life experience of one twice her age, her girlish sense of fun complemented Antony's sense of humour. One day, she took him on a fishing trip on the Nile. Angling was not a pastime Antony had practised much, not considering it as worthy a pursuit as, for example, hunting boar or sparring with gladiators, but rather as a necessity for commoners to obtain food. Still, he was competitive in everything he did, and quickly became frustrated when the Alexandrians – and even some of his Praetorian escorts – hauled in numerous flapping fish on the end of their hand-held lines, while he got not a hint of a bite. Even worse was Cleopatra's gentle mocking at his failure.

'Oh, Marcus,' she said, putting a hand on his arm and giggling. 'You can't be good at everything.'

Antony stalked off to the other end of the boat, and an idea struck him. He slipped a coin to one of the boatmen, and then went back to his line. With the quietest of splashes, the boatman dived off the boat, and placed one of the freshly caught samples on Antony's hook. When Antony felt the tug, he hauled in his line, hand over hand, and cried with delight at the large silver fish dangling there. Cleopatra looked at the catch, dangling, suspiciously still, then clapped her hands and congratulated him. He repeated the trick several more times, until Cleopatra suggested that they had caught enough for the day and they should retire.

The next day, they went fishing again, and Antony wondered if perhaps he could succeed on his own merits. Surely his lack of success the previous day had just been bad luck. He baited his hook, cast his line out and waited. After a few short moments, he was rewarded with a firm tug, and with excitement, he pulled the line in, and took hold of the sizeable fish. Then he blinked, staring at his catch. The fish was a large herring, dried and salted.

He looked up at Cleopatra in confusion. She broke down in peals of laughter, and everyone around him, from boat hand to soldier to slave, joined in the hilarity. Antony flushed red, anger mounting inside him as he realised how he had been duped. But the rage dissipated in a moment at the sight of Cleopatra's delight at the joke and, ever the joker himself, he could see the humour. He laughed, a chuckle at first, then a deep belly roar, and he strolled around the boat, parading his catch.

He came back to Cleopatra and kissed her tenderly.

'You got me,' he said. 'Well played.'

'As I said yesterday, you can't be good at everything. And you should not resort to deceit to pretend otherwise. That is not who you are.'

He bowed his head, accepting the gentle admonishment.

She put a hand on his knee.

'Who you are,' she said earnestly, 'is a conquering general. Perhaps it's time to put aside the fishing tackle and play a game to your strengths – the sport of hunting cities, countries and continents.'

Antony looked into her eyes. The business of state had been far from his mind of late, but maybe she was right. He had always balanced the high-living part of his personality with the ambitious soldier, and maybe he had allowed his hedonism to dominate for too long. He and Cleopatra had even formed an exclusive club called the Guild of the Inimitable Lifestyle, the members of which threw regular, extravagant and fabulously expensive banquets for one another. On the one hand, the activities of the guild and other events helped to bind the Alexandrian nobility to him and Cleopatra, in a style that was very Hellenistic. But Antony was aware that, despite his regular exercise, he had had to loosen his belt more than once since Pharsalus, and that was always a sign that he had been away from the legions for too long.

When they returned to Alexandria, he sat down and sorted through the correspondence from Rome that he had been neglecting. What he read caused a little ball of anxiety to settle in his stomach. He had assumed that his representatives in Italy and the West – Ventidius, Plancus, Manius (who was a procurator and long-term ally of the

Antony family), but above all, his wife, Fulvia, and his brother, Lucius – would look after his interests. Instead it seemed that his brother, in particular, was stirring up trouble. Fulvia reported that Octavian's land confiscations in favour of the veterans had provoked outrage. Lucius, as consul, initially upset that Octavian was taking all the credit with the veterans and excluding Antony, had taken up the cause of the dispossessed. Fulvia had tried to dissuade him, not least for fear of alienating the veterans, but ultimately, with Lucius acting as Antony's spokesperson and de facto deputy in Rome, she had to back him.

Octavian had reacted angrily, divorcing Fulvia's daughter, Claudia, and returning her to her mother, claiming that despite two years of marriage, her virginity remained intact. Then Lucius claimed he had been the victim of an assassination attempt engineered by Octavian. Antony did not know whether to believe this; he was still suspicious that, despite his denials, Octavian had tried to have him murdered in the year of Caesar's murder, so he would not put it past him. Whatever the truth, the fact was that Lucius was furious, and he informed Antony that he had taken his supporters to the city of Praeneste, around twenty miles south of Rome, while Octavian waited north of Rome, and Fulvia had gone to Lepidus.

Antony read the letters out to Cleopatra, and she listened thoughtfully. For all their fun times together, he had come to respect her wisdom and intellect, especially in political matters. After all, it was not possible to rise to the Egyptian throne without political cunning and a ruthless will to win, and she had learned assiduously from her father and the rest of the Ptolemy family.

'Well?' he said. 'What should I do?'

'What is in your heart to do?' asked Cleopatra.

Antony stood up and paced, indecisive.

'Octavianus and I still need each other. It's a good alliance, for us and for Rome. My stupid brother and my ambitious wife are going to undo it all.'

'Then stay out of it.'

He looked at her in surprise.

'How can I? My family is preparing for conflict with my co-ruler. Surely I need to take a side?'

'But that would be fruitless. These letters are dated nearly a month ago. And how long would it take for your reply to reach Rome at this time of year? Fifteen days, twenty? By the time you have responded, the matter will likely have been decided. And if you back the wrong side, your position will be weakened.'

'You're saying I should abandon my wife and brother?' asked Antony.

'Not abandon, of course not. But this is a problem of their own making, and it is not your duty to solve it for them. If they prevail, your position will be much stronger, without you having to lift a finger. If they fail, you can deny all involvement, and continue your alliance with Octavianus.'

Antony considered her words. It felt wrong. He was a man of action, and his instinct was to intervene – perhaps even to set out directly for Rome with whatever forces he could draw on. But Cleopatra was right. Whatever he did now would be far too late. Perhaps if he had overwintered nearer the West – if he had not allowed himself to be distracted by Cleopatra and had paid more attention to the worsening situation in Italy – he could have been in a position to respond. But that was not the case, and there was no point in wasting time with what ifs.

'Very well,' said Antony. 'I will await the outcome. But in the meantime, I must prepare to leave Alexandria and attend to problems elsewhere in the Empire. As you said, it's time to put aside the fishing tackle.'

Chapter XIII

Martius DCCXIV AUC (March 40 BC), Alexandria

Cleopatra may have had her own agenda for wishing Antony to stay out of the conflict in Italy. Perhaps she wanted Fulvia, her rival for Antony's love, defeated and maybe executed by Antony. Or maybe she wanted the destruction of Octavian, who claimed to be Caesar's son, when in fact Caesar's only biological son was her Caesarion. Whatever her motivations, though, she was right. It was far too late for Antony to do anything about the situation Lucius had provoked.

As he prepared to leave Alexandria for Syria in the early spring, letters arrived from Lucius, Fulvia and his other supporters, and once he had read them all and decided which conflicting versions of events were most reliable, he was able to piece together what seemed to have transpired.

Whatever the exact truth of the matter – who was at fault, who had said what to whom, who had done what and why – it was clear that Lucius and Fulvia had inflicted a disaster on Antony's cause.

Lucius had begun his year as consul the previous year by celebrating a triumph for a previous victory over some Gallic tribes. The Senate had been opposed, but Fulvia had used her influence to force the measure through. From then on, Lucius appeared to have taken his role as consul and as the leader of the Antonian faction in the West ever more seriously, and with Fulvia constantly warning both surviving Antonius brothers about Octavian's untrustworthiness and cunning, Lucius had decided to oppose Octavian. This meant taking the side of the landowners who were being expelled from their Italian properties by the thousand to make room for veteran settlements, despite the fact that this put Lucius at odds with the legions, the treaties and agreements between the triumvirs, and in the end, the triumvirate itself. Antony did not think his brother was a true believer in restoring the Republic, but nevertheless he began to use the slogans of Republicanism to gain support.

The Italian towns that had never fully recovered from the brutality of the Social War a generation or two earlier took Lucius' side. Encouraged by Manius, Fulvia had thrown her support behind her brother-in-law, to the detriment of her son-in-law, Octavian.

Octavian himself appeared to have been remarkably conciliatory at first, and his letters to Antony pleaded a strong desire to avoid conflict, while begging Antony to rein his brother in. Even the manner of Octavian's divorce of Claudia, declaring her still a virgin, could have been seen as an attempt to lessen the blow, since it improved her future marriageability, even at the expense of doubts about Octavian's own potency. But each time Octavian agreed to Lucius' demands, Antony's brother pushed harder, until the very existence of the triumvirate – Antony's and Octavian's main legal excuse for power – was threatened.

Perhaps Lucius had simply been playing a dangerous game of escalation to improve his own standing in Italy at Octavian's expense, without wanting outright war. If so, he had miscalculated. The cities that were suffering from the land reallocation under Octavian decided to take Lucius at his word. They rose up against Octavian's agents, expelling and even executing them. Open rebellion against him was clearly intolerable to Octavian, but his move to punish Lucius' allies forced Lucius to react. Summoning his legions, he occupied strategically important cities. Octavian marched against him, but was repulsed by one of Lucius' generals. He moved instead to besiege the important city of Sentinum, sending a delegation to Antony at this time – which arrived far too late – stating that it was only with the greatest reluctance that he was taking up arms.

Lucius then marched on Rome, which was held by Lepidus with two legions. Lucius quickly defeated these, and addressed the Roman citizens, saying that both he and his brother renounced the legitimacy of the triumvirate, promising to bring it to an end and restore the Republic. The Senate, delighted to have a chance at restoring its power, declared Octavian and Lepidus enemies of the people. But Octavian abandoned the siege of Sentinum and moved his legions directly into a Rome left undefended by Lucius.

Lucius and Fulvia campaigned to raise legions to support their cause, although their task was made more difficult by the fact that

Lucius' public stance was so antagonistic to the veterans receiving their promised rewards. In fact, many, anxious about opposing Caesar's son and heir, and having no direct instructions from Antony, defected to Octavian, and Lucius moved north with the aim of linking up with the pro-Antonian generals in Gaul – Ventidius, Pollio and Calenus.

Octavian now dispatched Agrippa north to deal with Lucius, and he proved, Antony had to grudgingly admit, an exceptional general. Ventidius and Pollio, in the absence of direction from Antony, shadowed Octavian's forces but did not intervene, and Calenus was apparently too ill to leave Gaul at all. Lucius was forced to retreat to the city of Perusia, north-west of Rome, where Octavian and Agrippa besieged him.

Fulvia, with an energy, strength and efficacy that stunned and outraged a Rome that abhorred any suggestion of violence from a woman, urged Ventidius and Pollio to come to Lucius' aid, and helped Plancus, who had declared for Lucius, to raise more troops, with which they wiped out one of Octavian's legions in a crushing battle near Rome. She wrote, too, to Sextus Pompeius, still firmly in control of Sicily, urging him to use the opportunity to strike against Octavian.

But in the end, they all held back, unable to agree a plan of action between them, leaving Lucius penned into Perusia with insufficient supplies for the winter. The siege held tight, and the morale of Lucius' soldiers and the inhabitants of Perusia plummeted, assailed by starvation and the taunting of the besieging troops. Octavian ordered the slingshots to be embossed with mocking slogans, such as 'I'm aiming for Fulvia's clitoris', or 'Lucius Antonius, you are doomed, baldy' – Lucius having not retained his hair as Antony had. Octavian himself, either having fun, or deciding that it would boost the morale of his men, penned a poem with the lines, 'Because Antony fucks Glaphyra, Fulvia sentences me to this punishment: I must fuck her, too... I don't think so, not if I'm wise. "Fuck me or fight me," she says. Well, isn't my cock dearer to me than life itself? So let the trumpets sound!'

Fulvia was the only one of his correspondents with the courage to report Octavian's poem to Antony, and he could almost hear the disappointment in her voice as he read her words, both at the repugnant attack on her, and that Antony's philandering had given Octavian such an opportunity. Antony bridled at Octavian's hurtful words against Fulvia, but he also noted that there had been very little in the way of direct condemnation of him personally. In fact, reading between the lines, it seemed that Octavian was attempting to portray Antony as a man burdened by fate with an unworthy brother, who was guilty of nothing more than choosing his wife poorly. It was a glimmer of hope, that maybe Octavian was not aiming for a more widespread war with Antony and his representatives in the West.

The final letters describing the whole sorry saga were written soon after it ended, and arrived long after the whole matter had been decided. Starved into capitulation, Lucius had surrendered. Octavian had treated him magnanimously, with respect to his position as both consul and Antony's brother, and had sent him to Spain as a legate, where Octavian's loyalists could keep an eye on him. Lucius' legions were absorbed into Octavian's army and the citizens of Perusia were spared. But the decurions who comprised the town council were executed, with a single exception – a man who had served on the jury that had found against Caesar's assassins. The city itself was pillaged and razed by Octavian's jubilant soldiers. Octavian had managed to combine a show of mercy and conciliation with a lesson that rebellion would be harshly punished.

At least Lucius had made it clear to Octavian that Antony had played no part in his rebellion, and Octavian had chosen to accept him at his word. Neither Antony's mother, Julia, nor Fulvia trusted Octavian, however. Julia sought refuge with Sextus Pompeius, and Fulvia went east for Athens, escorted by Plancus and a huge honour guard of three thousand cavalry.

The events had played out to Antony in a punctuated epistolary form, with some gaps as letters were lost, and some delays as storms impeded messengers. Eventually, though he was able to take stock, and he was dismayed. His stupid, impetuous younger brother, who had the gall to call himself 'Pietas' because of his fealty to Antony, had almost ruined everything. As for Fulvia… What was she thinking? He would never have expected his intelligent, resourceful, powerful wife to commit herself to such a foolhardy enterprise.

Cleopatra had little advice to give Antony. He did not blame her. What could she say? At least she did not criticise Fulvia – it would have been a bad look, and would probably have put his back up. Anyway, Antony had quite enough fury with Fulvia on his own part, without anyone else adding fuel to the fire.

With some help from Cleopatra, he drafted letters of reprimand to Lucius and Fulvia and conciliation to Octavian, but he couldn't decide whether to send them. So far from Rome, the situation there still so uncertain, he could not be sure he was saying the right thing. So he remained silent, leaving a nervous Octavian and Rome to guess what his response would be. In the meantime, he accelerated the plans for his departure from Alexandria.

Antony was almost ready to leave when even worse news arrived. A Parthian army, led by Pacorus, the son of the Parthian king Orodes, had invaded Syria. He was assisted by Quintus Labienus, the son of Caesar's old second-in-command, who had been in Parthia seeking reinforcements for Brutus and Cassius at the time of the battle of Philippi, and had remained there on hearing of the news of his commanders' defeat.

The Parthian army first invaded Phoenicia, where it was unsuccessful in capturing the large Syrian city of Apamea. However, many of the surrounding Roman garrisons had served under Brutus and Cassius and readily defected to Labienus.

Antony's governor, Saxa, had had insufficient legions to counter the large invading force, and besides, Labienus had inherited much of his father's tactical brilliance. The loyal Roman forces were defeated in battle, the Parthians able to add yet more Roman eagles to the collection they had started after Carrhae. Saxa withdrew his remaining legions under cover of darkness, but Labienus pursued them, slaughtering most of the fugitives. Saxa himself made it to Antioch, but that great city quickly surrendered, and Saxa fled to Cilicia, where Labienus captured him and put him to death.

Labienus declared himself Imperator and ruler of Cilicia, while Pacorus took Syria for his own kingdom, with only Tyre holding out, aided by superior naval forces.

Antony vacillated. The loss of provinces under his watch to their chief enemy was a humiliating blow, and a dangerous situation for all the East. It was not so long ago that Mithridates had stormed through the Eastern Empire, massacring Roman citizens wherever he found them. Antony needed to shore up the defences against the invaders, and accelerate his own invasion plans. The nearest large Roman army was in Macedonia, but the legions there were hard-pressed by raids from northern tribes, and he could not afford to withdraw them. He would have to rely on auxiliaries raised from local client kings. Ideally, he would command them in person.

But there was the problem in Italy that his idiot brother had caused. And in the end, what was more important to his career and his position – a province that had only been added to the Empire a couple of decades before by Pompey, or Rome itself?

A letter from Fulvia, begging him to meet her in Athens, made up his mind. Rome came first.

The day came for him to leave. He would not head straight for Athens, but would first head to Tyre to see to the defences in that city, then to Asia Province to install suitable lieutenants and ensure recruitment was in full swing. After that, he would deal with Fulvia.

On the dock of the Royal Harbour, under the gaze of the fabulous lighthouse, Cleopatra laid on a lavish farewell banquet, with fine wines, exotic dishes and an excess of dancers and musicians. Seeing her in all her splendour, as completely in her element as a fish in the ocean, Antony was almost tempted to stay. But that would mean abandoning everything that he had struggled for all his life. She was wonderful. But she wasn't worth that.

She walked him to his ship, holding his hand, and at the gangplank, she kissed him. Then she took his hand and laid it on her belly.

'Marcus,' she whispered to him, 'I didn't want to tell you until your departure was irreversible. I didn't want you to think I was trying to hold you here against your will. But now you are about to embark, it's time.

'We are going to have a baby together.'

Antony stared at her, then hugged her, squeezing her shoulders but carefully avoiding her abdomen. He kissed her deeply, stood back and looked at her, then kissed her again.

Cleopatra smiled, uncharacteristically shy.

'You're pleased, then?'

He laughed. 'Can't you tell?' Then he became more sombre. 'I'm even more sorry that I must leave now.'

'I understand,' she said. 'You know that. Just promise that, one day, you will come back.'

He kissed her one last time.

'I promise.'

Iunius DCCXIV AUC (June 40 BC), Athens

Antony sailed into Athens with around two hundred warships, but few soldiers beyond his personal Praetorian cohorts. He could not possibly strip the Eastern borders in the face of this dangerous Parthian incursion – he already felt guilty for not being able to organise the defence in person. Lacking an army could be a problem if conflict with Octavian came about, but he reckoned his allies held about twenty-four legions in the West, including eleven under the steadfast Fufius Calenus in Transalpine Gaul. He would not make the same mistake as the hubristic Pompey, who had said that he only needed to stamp his foot for soldiers to spring up all over Italy. But he could be confident that, even if Octavian's forces slightly outnumbered his, his own superior generalship and his reputation, unmatched since Philippi, would give him the advantage.

Hopefully, it would not come to war. But before he sent any envoys to Octavian brokering peace, Antony needed to talk to Fulvia, and hear the truth from her mouth.

It was not Fulvia who greeted him as he entered the city, accompanied by his lictors and his Praetorians, but his mother Julia. He greeted her warmly, pleased to see her looking so fit, despite being well into her seventh decade. Beside her was Lucius Munatius Plancus, who had escorted Fulvia from Italy. Antony greeted Plancus somewhat coolly – he had taken part in Fulvia and Lucius' private war without Antony's approval, and Antony hadn't decided yet what the consequences of that would be.

'Mother,' he said, turning back to Julia. 'You were properly received by Sextus Pompeius?'

'I was,' she said. 'He treated me with respect and kindness, and when he learned Fulvia was to meet you here, he had his father-in-law, Lucius Scribonius Libo, escort me here with a strong guard to ensure my safety.'

Antony recognised Libo, standing respectfully back from the reunion between mother and son. He went over to him and embraced him firmly.

'I must thank you and your daughter's husband, Libo, for your care of my mother. I owe you both a debt of gratitude.'

'Please, think nothing of it. How could an honourable Roman possibly behave otherwise to such a noble matriarch?'

'We have much to discuss, I think,' said Antony. 'But forgive me if we must leave that until a later moment. I am anxious to see my wife.'

Julia had a litter on hand, and they were conveyed together to the residence Fulvia had taken in the wealthy district of Alopeke, a little south-east of the city. His lictors and bodyguard cleared the road before them, and kept the curious from approaching too close. Antony tried to get his mother's opinion on the actions of Fulvia and Lucius, but she refused to be drawn, beyond pleading with him not to be too harsh on them.

Fulvia received him in the atrium of her villa, dressed in a simple stola, her hair pinned up, wearing no jewellery and with only a light foundation for make-up. She looked thin, he thought. Her cheeks were pinched, and her collarbones prominent. Her expression was anxious, but beyond that, she seemed sad, and very tired.

Emotions warred in Antony, delight at seeing her after so long mingling with a simmering resentment at what she had done in concert with his brother. She held out her hands for him, and he took them, kissing her chastely on each cheek, an act which made her stiffen, as if he had slapped her.

'Walk with me,' he said, and led her into the ornate gardens at the rear of the house.

The early summer sun in Athens was strong. One of Fulvia's maids held a leather parasol over her to protect her from the heat, but Antony sent her away. He wanted to speak to Fulvia in complete privacy.

'May I sit, Marcus?' asked Fulvia. 'I am weary.'

Antony gestured to a bench next to a fountain shaded by a walnut tree and Fulvia sat down, tucking her dress under her. Antony remained standing, looking down at her. It felt as if there was a chasm between them, and it was such an unfamiliar sensation. This woman had been his friend and confidante for almost as long as he could remember. Widow of his two best friends. Then his beloved wife, his strongest supporter and his most trusted advisor.

Of course, he had no doubt she resented his affairs, especially with Glaphyra and Cleopatra, which were common knowledge in Rome. But she was a practical woman, not a dewy-eyed idealist. It was a rare Roman man who took no lovers besides his wife, especially when they were separated for months or years, as Antony and Fulvia had been. No, that was not the problem. It was the fact that she knew she had displeased him, for the first time.

'Explain to me,' he said. 'Lucius I understand. He has always been the impetuous one. But you? You're the intelligent one. You always have the plans, the stratagems, you see into the future with such clarity. So how did you get drawn into this. What were you thinking?'

She looked down at her lap, summoning her thoughts, her lips moving as if she was rehearsing the words she would speak. Eventually she looked up at him, and her eyes were wet with tears.

'You're right,' she said. 'I should have known better. I'm so sorry.'

Antony folded his arms and waited for her to continue.

'It was Lucius' idea. But he did it for you. He idolises you, you know.'

'That doesn't make him less of a fool. If Gaius had still been alive, he would never have let Lucius behave like he did.'

'Perhaps, but he still only wanted to advance your cause. He doesn't trust Octavianus. And in that respect, I am sure he is right. Octavianus wants absolute power. He is just biding his time.'

'Nonsense,' said Antony. 'He wanted vengeance for Caesar, which we achieved. He wanted to be recognised as Caesar's son, which he has. Now, he just wants to hold on to what he has, the same as I.'

Fulvia shook her head. 'Being trusting can be an admirable trait, Marcus, but it can also be a fatal flaw.'

She suddenly grimaced, and put a hand to her side. Antony stepped forward, concerned, but she waved him away.

'Could I have something to drink, please?'

Antony waved over her maid to bring a cup of cool water. Fulvia took a couple of sips, then continued.

'Lucius made mistakes. He thought he could be you, as a general and a politician. He thought he could confront Octavianus and win. But he has neither your experience or ability. And matters got out of his control. He wasn't seeking war, just to advance your position, and his.'

'You could have stopped him,' Antony said. 'You should have stopped him. How could you join in a war with my ally, my legal co-ruler, without my orders, without my permission, without even informing me of your intention?' His voice was getting louder.

'What was I to do?' Fulvia shot back. 'Sit back and let your brother be destroyed? He would not listen to me. You were thousands of miles away. I had no choice.'

'Then you should have made sure you won!' shouted Antony. 'Now you have left me in a worse position than before. Trust with Octavianus is broken. If it cannot be repaired, if we cannot forge a new treaty, then it will be civil war, all over again. All that death and destruction, not to mention the chance that I will lose!'

'You won't lose, Marcus,' she said, her voice small.

'Fortuna is fickle, Fulvia. Every battle is a throw of the die, a chance to fail. And are you even aware of the situation in the East? Parthia has invaded. They have overrun Syria. We might lose the East, and I am forced to return to Italy to attempt to clean up the mess that you and my brother have made!'

Fulvia turned even paler at this – the news of the Parthian incursion had obviously not reached her.

'Marcus, I'm so sorry.'

Antony turned his back on her. He looked at the sumptuous villa – its marble colonnades, bright frescoes and intricate mosaics. Wouldn't it be nice to just stay somewhere like this? Retire from public life, as Sulla had done, away from the strife and the constant, interminable struggle just to keep what was his. But he knew that would never satisfy his ambitions. He had a deep lust, not for power, but for glory – for adulation by the soldiers and the people and the wealthy – and for the freedom to indulge his high living.

'I expected better of you,' he said, calmer now, no longer angry, just feeling a profound sadness at her betrayal. 'You will accompany me to Italy. We will leave immediately. I will attempt to patch things up with Octavianus. And I will prepare for war, in case I fail.'

'Can we not rest in Athens? Just for a few days?' asked Fulvia, and her voice seemed uncharacteristically plaintive. 'I have only just arrived, and I am not sure I am up to another big journey so soon. Besides, I would like to spend some time with you.'

'You can rest when we get back to Rome,' he snapped. 'Besides, you will be taken by boat and litter. I'm not asking you to walk.'

'Marcus, I'm dying.'

Ice flooded his veins. He turned back to her slowly, his mouth open. He wanted to deny it, but now he looked – really looked – he could see she spoke the truth. The weight loss, the pallor, the fatigue. She wasn't just sad, or tired. She was very ill.

He sunk to his knees before her and grabbed her hands.

'What is it? What's wrong? Surely something can be done?'

Fulvia shook her head sadly.

'The physicians say I have a tumour in my womb. They can ease the pain with their concoctions, but there is no cure.'

'How... How long?'

'They cannot say. But it is growing fast. A month or two, perhaps.'

Antony gaped at her.

'I'll stay with you,' he said. 'Until the end. I can send envoys to Octavianus from here. Offer apologies and reparations...'

'No,' said Fulvia. 'You will not. You will go to Italy, and you will defend your interests and those of our children.'

'But—'

'Marcus.' The old Fulvia was reasserting herself now. 'You will not endanger everything we have striven for over so many years because of sentiment. When I die, I want to know that your position will be secure, and that Antyllus and Iullus, and Antonia, not to mention Claudius and Claudia and young Gaius Curio, will all be safe. Because if you allow Octavianus to take power, he will destroy you, and our entire family.'

Antony opened his mouth to protest, but he knew she was right. There was too much at stake for him to delay.

Suddenly, he was forced to contemplate returning to Italy to begin a difficult negotiation without her. Fulvia had not always been physically at his side, but her counsel had always been available to him by letter or messenger, since long before they were married.

'I can't do it without you,' he said, hating how weak and vulnerable that made him sound, but unable to hide his feelings from her.

'You can, and you will,' she said firmly. 'You should ally yourself with Sextus Pompeius. You and he would make formidable allies. You should end the threat from Octavianus once and for all.

'But if you wish to make peace with Octavianus, blame everything on me. He has no love for me, and he will believe it readily enough. Even if he harbours doubts towards you and your involvement, he does not want war, and I will make a convenient scapegoat for you both.'

'But your reputation...'

'Matters nothing, compared to my love for you and our children.'

Antony looked down and squeezed his eyes shut, tears dropping to the dry ground. Fulvia stroked his curly hair, then put a hand under his chin and lifted his face to hers. She kissed him gently. Antony put his arms around her, held her gently, and wept.

Chapter XIV

Iulius DCCXIV AUC (July 40 BC), Mare Adriaticum

Antony left Fulvia at Sicyon, near the colony of Corinth that Caesar had founded on the ruins of the old city. He looked back from the stern of his flagship, watching her until she was gone from his sight. Then he retreated to his cabin and howled out his grief. His lictors remained outside, waiting for the storm to pass. When he had cried himself dry, he re-emerged, and called for wine. With the concerned persons of Plancus and Libo looking on, he started to drink.

Every time the effect of the wine receded, the grief overwhelmed him, so he stayed drunk for the entirety of the four-day voyage between Sicyon and the island of Corcyra, where his ship put in. Here, he allowed himself to sober up, and to some extent the vicious hangover helped distract him from his misery.

In Corcyra, he received three important letters, and as he read, the messages brought him back to his senses as if a bucket of cold water had been thrown over him. The first was from the son of Quintus Fufius Calenus, Antony's strong ally who commanded eleven legions stationed in Nearer Spain and Transalpine Gaul. He regretted to say that his father had died of an illness. Octavian, on learning of this, had marched north and demanded that the son hand over the legions and command of the provinces to him. The young Calenus felt that he had no choice and had meekly acquiesced.

Antony was stunned. It was a flagrant breach of their triumviral agreement. Those legions and provinces were Antony's, and Octavian had taken them without even the courtesy of appearing to ask his permission. It also hugely shifted the balance of power in the West in Octavian's favour. Antony still had a large number of legions nominally under his command in the East, but with the ongoing Parthian invasion, he couldn't utilise them for his own purposes.

The second letter came from Ventidius. After the brief war that Lucius and Fulvia had waged against Octavian, Ventidius had moved his legions to the south-east of Italy. From here, he discovered that Octavian had sent his cavalry commander, Publius Servilius Rullus, to reinforce Brundisium. Ventidius suggested that Antony refrain from landing there, and gave him a list of other ports further north that would be less problematic to dock at.

Everything seemed to indicate that Octavian was preparing for war, even though Antony could barely understand it. He sought the advice of Plancus and Libo. Plancus suggested he avoid a confrontation until he had gathered more strength. Libo suggested he go straight to Sicily to link up with Sextus Pompeius' strong navy.

As Antony vacillated, wishing that he had Fulvia's counsel, or even Cleopatra's, a third letter arrived. This was from Asinius Pollio, stationed at his base at the mouth of the river Po, where it entered into the northern Mare Adriaticum. He wrote that he had persuaded the rebel Republican admiral Gnaeus Domitius Ahenobarbus to meet with Antony. To that end, Ahenobarbus was sailing with his full fleet westwards towards Antony's position. Pollio urged Antony to receive him and hear what he had to say.

This was a real conundrum. Domitius Ahenobarbus had been with his father Lucius Domitius Ahenobarbus at the siege of Corfinium, the only real resistance to Caesar's march into Italy after he crossed the Rubicon. He had been present with his father on the Pompeian side at Pharsalus, and though Antony had no reason to believe that he had been part of the Ides of March conspiracy, he had followed Brutus to Macedonia, and was legally declared one of Caesar's murderers. He had been put in charge of a Republican fleet, and it was he that had sunk the fleet with the Caesarian reinforcements on the day of the battle of Philippi.

But perhaps worst of all was the fact that Antony had personally killed his father in hand-to-hand combat at the battle of Pharsalus. Could the son forgive him for that? Or was this just an elaborate ruse to gain his revenge?

As always, Antony chose the bold option. With Plancus' predictions of doom ringing in his ears, he ordered his fleet to put out to sea and sail west.

The Mare Adriaticum between Italy and Greece was a long stretch of sea, its waters lapping the coasts of both peninsulas from north to south. Two lone ships attempting to meet would have struggled to find each other. But for two large fleets, stretched out widely, it was a much simpler proposition to rendezvous.

Half a day's sailing out of Corcyra, the lookout on Antony's flagship sighted ships, and as they drew nearer, it was confirmed that it was Ahenobarbus' large fleet. Antony had two hundred ships with him, but he had not put out to force a naval engagement. Ordering the majority of his vessels to heave to, he sailed on with a mere five ships. Ahenobarbus, by contrast, came on with his full fleet.

'Proconsul,' said Plancus, standing with Libo at Antony's side, fingers interlinked in front of him, knuckles white, 'perhaps we should turn back to the safety of our own lines.'

'Why would we do that?' asked Antony, eyes fixed on Ahenobarbus' oncoming ships, the flagship of the Republican admiral in the midst of his armada. Their oarsmen were rowing hard, and they were coming on fast.

'What if he wishes you harm? We are helpless. Why not send forward one ship in advance to test his good faith?'

Antony shared Plancus' doubts as to Ahenobarbus' intentions, but he would not let his subordinates see this.

'I would rather die from Ahenobarbus breaching a truce than have my life saved by playing the coward.'

'But—'

'Not another word,' snapped Antony. Plancus looked helplessly at Libo, who shrugged. Ahenobarbus' fleet came nearer and nearer, slicing through the waves, sails full, oars rising and dipping rapidly. Plancus began to tremble, clutching the rail of the ship, pale and looking as if he would vomit. His wide eyes were fixed on the vicious rams fixed to the prows as if they were the axes of his executioners. Although Antony despised his lack of courage, he knew he was right to be afraid. If Ahenobarbus did not reduce his speed soon, his ships would smash into Antony's tiny advance flotilla and send them to the bottom of the sea. Of the many ways Antony thought he might die – an enemy's spear, an assassin's knife, a poisoner's potion, or simply overindulgence – drowning, though an ever-present risk with any sea travel, was never a fate he had genuinely envisaged for himself.

Until now.

Ahenobarbus came on, and Antony's breath quickened in his chest. Had he miscalculated? He steeled himself, back straight, and trusted himself entirely to Ahenobarbus' good faith, to Fortuna and to Neptune.

Slowly, inch by inch, Ahenobarbus' flagship pulled out ahead of the other ships.

'What is he doing?' gasped Plancus. 'Does he want to engage us single-handed?'

They came within hailing distance, and Antony ordered his lictor in the bows to demand Ahenobarbus lower his ensign. There was no reply, and Ahenobarbus' flagship came on, bow first, ram aimed at Antony like an arrow.

Then suddenly, in an impressive manoeuvre of seamanship, Ahenobarbus sheared off, the ship cutting an arc through the water to present its vulnerable side to Antony's own ram. The flag came down, and the oars were all hoisted to point vertically in a splendid naval salute.

Antony felt the breath whoosh out of him in relief. As he watched, a small rowing boat put out from the flagship, and moments later, Ahenobarbus was being hauled up onto the deck, where Antony awaited him.

The two men stood silent for a moment, looking into each other's eyes, measuring each other. Then Antony stepped forward and embraced Ahenobarbus, kissing him on each cheek. Ahenobarbus dipped his head.

'Marcus Antonius, Triumvir, Proconsul, I offer you my service and the service of my fleet and legions.'

'You are most welcome, Admiral,' said Antony, 'and I gratefully accept.'

He ordered wine to be brought. 'Let us drink to our new alliance.'

Ahenobarbus accepted the cup, and they both drank deeply.

Antony offered a cup to Plancus, who took one sip and then vomited loudly over the side.

Iulius DCCXIV AUC (July 40 BC), Paloeis

Ahenobarbus invited Antony to his base at Paloeis on the western Greek coast. Here, he drew up his two legions, and there, possibly bribed to do so, they hailed Antony as Imperator. Technically, it was a title awarded to a victorious general that entitled him to a triumph, but more frequently it was becoming used simply as an acclamation for a powerful commander. Still, Antony received it gratefully, and the men seemed genuinely pleased to see him. After all, their chances of victory, riches and a happy retirement were immeasurably greater under Antony, the most powerful man in the Empire, than under the rebel Ahenobarbus.

They dined at Ahenobarbus' villa, Antony and Ahenobarbus, with Plancus and Libo also present. The first and most important item on the agenda was to reconcile Antony's and Ahenobarbus' differences. They had fought on opposing sides for many years, and had inflicted many injuries on each other's causes. The largest, though, was Antony's slaying of Ahenobarbus' father at Pharsalus, and Antony addressed this head-on.

'Your father was a brave man,' he said. 'When we fought, he had some twenty years on me, but far less experience in battle. Yet he did not flinch from the fight. Nor did he accept my surrender when I offered it. He died with honour. You should be proud.'

Ahenobarbus considered his words.

'I hated you for a long time for your actions that day, Antonius,' he said. 'But over the years, I have come to understand that war is not always, maybe even not often, personal. You and my father fought for different causes, and I should not consider it a fault of yours that you bested him. And I thank you, on his behalf, for your kind words now.'

Antony held up his cup of wine, and proposed a toast to the departed spirit of Lucius Domitius Ahenobarbus. They all drank.

All three present with Antony were men that he now felt he had common cause with and could trust, and he discussed openly the situation in Italy as his correspondents had described it.

'So you think it will be war?' asked Ahenobarbus.

'People I trust believe that Octavianus wishes only power for himself. For my part, I believe co-operation with him is possible and preferable. But I must prepare for the worse possibility. And if it comes to open conflict, what forces do I have and who can I rely on?'

'Octavianus has around forty legions now,' said Plancus, seeming overawed by the number.

'But no ships,' said Ahenobarbus. 'And no time to build any.'

Libo nodded. 'Between you two and Sextus, we have an overwhelmingly powerful navy that can blockade the whole of Italy.'

Antony looked doubtful. He was a land commander by experience and preference.

'Wars cannot be won by navies alone. Ask the dead spirits of the Carthaginians.'

'But they can be used to swing campaigns,' said Ahenobarbus. 'Legions can be moved rapidly to the sites of confrontations, concentrating forces locally, even if the enemy has larger overall numbers. And they can stop supplies and reinforcements from getting through.'

'And you do have powerful allies,' said Libo. 'Ventidius and Pollio are loyal, and they command considerable armies. You have Ahenobarbus' two legions. And my son-in-law Sextus has eighteen legions under his control.'

Antony nodded. Eighteen legions had not been enough for Sextus Pompeius to risk confronting the combined forces of the triumvirs, but if he allied with one triumvir against the other, his intervention would likely be decisive.

'But which side will Sextus take?' asked Antony. 'After all, Octavianus has taken his aunt for a wife.'

This was a blatantly political move that Octavian had undertaken shortly after Lucius' surrender. Scribonia, Sextus' aunt by marriage, was forced to divorce her husband to marry Octavian, who was several years her junior. Initial reports suggested it was not a happy marriage.

'I don't think you need to worry about that,' said Libo. 'It is a weak family alliance, and Sextus' natural inclinations are to side with you. He has no love or trust for Octavianus.'

Antony nodded. 'Then, when our conference is finished, Libo, please return to Sextus with all my good wishes, and tell him that if it comes to war, I would be honoured to have him fight by my side.'

'And if it is peace?'

'Then I will do everything in my power to arrange an accommodation between Sextus, Octavianus and myself.'

Libo did not seem entirely satisfied, but agreed to take the message to Sextus.

'You haven't yet corresponded with Octavianus since your wife and brother's... disagreement with him?' asked Ahenobarbus.

'I don't see any point in negotiating from a position of weakness. I will talk face to face with him in Italy, with an army at my back.'

'But what of Lepidus?' asked Plancus.

The other three men looked at Plancus, then at one another, and then they all burst out laughing. The conversation then turned to politics, to plans to issue coins commemorating the reconciliation of Ahenobarbus and Antony, and a heated discussion of the relative merits of Italian wine compared to the Greek vintages that Ahenobarbus had supplied.

For the next few days, Antony answered as much of his copious correspondence as he could, reassuring allies, dealing with the most important and pressing of provincial administrative matters that had to be resolved, and giving orders to co-ordinate the defences in the East.

Then, when he was as prepared as he felt he could be, he gave the command for their fleet to set out for Brundisium, where he would discover whether it was to be war or peace.

Sextilis DCCXIV AUC (August 40 BC), Brundisium

The combined fleet of Ahenobarbus and Antony, the flagship of each displaying their ensigns prominently, approached the Italian port of Brundisium. Antony had unpleasant memories of the place, besieged there during the war between Caesar and Pompey, with an angry Caesar demanding he cross the Mare Adriaticum with reinforcements, despite bad weather and a cork-tight naval blockade. Boldness had won that contest for him, and it was with boldness now that he sailed directly into the harbour of Brundisium, despite Ventidius' warning.

They docked uneventfully, and Antony supervised the disembarkation of his cohorts and Ahenobarbus' two legions. Their supplies were meagre, Antony having had little time to gather all the resources for war, and Ahenobarbus restricted to what he could seize by coastal raids. But they were in Italy, now with all its manpower and agriculture to hand.

Antony organised the legions to begin construction of a camp, then, taking his lictors and Praetorian cohorts, he marched to the city.

When he arrived at the walls, he found the formidable gates closed tight against him. His lictor stepped forward.

'In the name of Marcus Antonius, proconsul, triumvir, imperator, priest of the Divine Julius Caesar, open the gates and permit us entry.'

There was no reply, and the gates remained closed.

The lictor looked back at Antony for instruction, and Antony gestured impatiently for him to try again.

'By order of Marcus Antonius, proconsul, triumvir, imperator, priest of the Divine Julius Caesar,' cried the lictor at the top of his lungs, 'open the gates immediately.'

There was still no reply. Then a head appeared, peeping over the wall of one of the towers that defended the gates.

'My name is Publius Servilius Rullus,' he called down. 'Cavalry commander sworn to Gaius Julius Caesar Octavianus, proconsul, triumvir, imperator, son of the Divine Julius Caesar.'

Antony immediately bridled at the title. Being the son of the Divine Julius Caesar certainly sounded more impressive than being merely the deified dictator's priest.

'Open the gates, Rullus,' called up Antony, 'and we will say no more of this misunderstanding.'

'Regretfully, I cannot do that, Proconsul,' said Rullus. 'My orders are to hold this port against enemy threats. And I cannot help but notice that, though you might be an ally of my commander, you sail alongside the colours of Gnaeus Domitius Ahenobarbus, the proscribed rebel.'

'An understanding has been reached with Domitius Ahenobarbus,' said Antony.

'I have no knowledge of this,' said Rullus.

'That's because it is none of your damned business,' yelled Antony, outraged that this junior officer was defying him. 'Now open up,' he roared, 'or I will have your head on a spike!'

'I will send a message to my commander, and await his orders,' said Rullus. 'Hopefully, we will be able to permit you entry when he replies. But I will not surrender this city until I have specific instructions to that effect.'

He disappeared from view, and for a few moments, Antony shouted impotent curses at the impassive walls. Then he rounded angrily on Plancus and Domitius.

'This is a flagrant breach of the triumviral treaty,' he said. 'Italy is neutral territory. Any one of us can move freely here, recruit legions and gather supplies. Octavianus is forcefully denying me the most important port on the east coast.'

'It seems he cannot be trusted,' said Ahenobarbus.

'What now?' asked Plancus.

Antony inhaled deeply, let his breath out slowly, and took stock. His mind worked quickly, running through his options, considering all the intelligence he had about the disposition of Octavian's forces and his own. Brundisium was reportedly garrisoned by only five cohorts. But Antony had little artillery and no equipment for an immediate assault on the strong walls. There was no prospect of quickly taking the port. But that did not mean he was powerless. He shot out a series of orders.

'Take control of the island in the harbour.' He knew from his previous siege that holding the tiny island gave a powerful control over any ships coming and going.

'Send a detachment north to Sipontum, and seize it if possible.' Sipontum was a small port town just north of Brundisium, and it would give them another base for their fleet if Brundisium proved too tough a nut to crack.

'Seal off the harbour approaches and begin the construction of siege works. I want a ditch and palisade around the entire city. No one is to enter or leave, by land or sea.'

'Send orders to Ventidius and Pollio to have their legions ready to march.'

And finally he dictated a letter.

'To Sextus Pompeius. I, Marcus Antonius, triumvir, call upon you to fulfil your offer of alliance in the case of conflict. I request your aid against the treacherous actions of Octavianus, who sends men against me, and fortifies Italian cities against me, in defiance of our sworn treaty.

'I beg you, bring your legions to Bruttium, ready for battle. For all the signs point to one conclusion.

'It is to be war.'

Chapter notes

As in the previous book, I have organised my historical notes by chapters, to help the reader look up specific queries without using footnotes that would interfere with the reading experience. These notes are intended to provide sources, or just to expand on aspects of ancient Roman history and culture that I think are interesting. I hope you find them useful. For more regular posts about Roman history and Roman fiction, please follow me on Facebook at Alex Gough Author, where I'm most active, Bluesky (@alexgoughauthor.bksy.social) and subscribe to my Substack https://gougha.substack.com/ for my newsletter about Rome and writing, or https://alexgough71.substack.com/ for my free e-zine 'Roman Lives, Life in Rome' which discusses fascinating Romans and how the Roman people lived.

Chapter I

Pompey's house in the Carina district is discussed in Mann (1926).

The contemporary sources are contradictory on Lepidus' precise whereabouts at the time of the assassination. See Tempest (2017), note 14 to Chapter V.

Caesar never actually spoke one of his most famous lines (the other being *veni vidi vici*, of course). '*Et tu, Brute?*' comes from Shakespeare's *Julius Caesar*. According to Suetonius and Dio, Caesar either didn't speak when he died, or said to Brutus, '*Kai su, teknon.*' If he did speak these Greek words, the implications are interesting – did he see Brutus as his figurative or even real child? (This latter is very unlikely, though others in Rome may have believed it.) Tempest (2017) analyses the Greek phrase further, noting that *teknon* doesn't necessarily mean biological child but was a term used by older to younger men, similar to our term 'kid'. She notes further that '*kai su*' is also used on curse tables to ward off evil and reflect it back onto the recipient. Thus Jeffrey Tatum notes an alternative translation of Caesar's last words is, 'See you in hell, punk!'

Tiberius Claudius Nero was the husband of Livia, who divorced him to marry Octavian. He is the father of the emperor Tiberius. Interestingly, three Roman emperors descended from him also bore the name Tiberius Claudius Nero: the emperors we now refer to as Tiberius, Claudius and Nero!

The Athenian amnesty of 403 BC – in 403 BC, a brutal oligarchy in Athens was overthrown and democracy restored. An oath of reconciliation was sworn to prevent vengeance because of past wrongdoing.

'Conscript fathers' is a collective term for the Senate, a translation of the Latin *patres conscripti*.

Some date Piso's speech about Caesar's funeral to a second Senate meeting on 18 March.

Junia Tertia, also called 'Tertulla', the wife of Cassius, had a miscarriage which Cicero refers to in his letter to Atticus on May 11 44 BC.

The Praetor Peregrinus was the magistrate for foreigners and administered the law regarding foreigners within the Empire. The Praetor Urbanus (Urban Praetor) was concerned with the administration of the law in Rome.

Chapter II

Tatum claims Antony must have known that Octavius would be the main beneficiary of Caesar's will, due to Caesar's favour and relation to him, but Huzar argues that as Antony was Caesar's closest friend and commander, and that as Caesar had no legitimate sons or grandsons to inherit, Antony would have expected to be the principal beneficiary.

The volcano that erupted around the time of Caesar's death led to unusual cold and famine. Etna was active at this time, and Forsyth

(1988) discusses this eruption. However, other volcanic eruptions around the world might have been responsible for the climatic change, such as Alaska's Okmok volcano.
(edition.cnn.com/2020/06/22/world/volcano-ancient-rome-scn/index.html).

As far as I can tell, the names of the Vestal Virgins in 44 BC were not known. They tended to only be named in history when they were accused of breaking their vows.
https://feminaeromanae.org/ListofVestals3.pdf

Mark Antony never gave Shakespeare's 'Friends, Romans, Countrymen' speech, but near contemporary accounts are contradictory and may also be fictionalised. Appian, Cicero and Suetonius are sources.

Chapter III

Comitia Centuriata – the Centuriate Assembly.

Comitia Tributa – the Tribal Assembly.

Chapter IV

The date of the reconciliation between Antony and Octavian on the Capitoline is uncertain, but probably took place between the Games of Apollo and the Senate meeting on 1 August.

Tibur – modern-day Tivoli.

Cicero's speech is known to posterity as the first Philippic, named after the series of speeches given by the Greek orator Demosthenes against Alexander the Great's father, Philip. Note that Cicero's first Philippic was delivered in person in oral form in the Senate in Antony's absence. However, the written version we have is likely edited by Cicero for publication later on, so we can't be sure exactly of the wording that he spoke out loud. This contrasts with his second Philippic, which was never delivered to the Senate in person and was only ever circulated in written form.

We don't have the text of Antony's rebuttal to Cicero's first Philippic, but we can piece together some of the content from Cicero's second Philippic.

'Better to be feared than loved' – Caligula, Antony's great-grandson, later said 'Let them hate me as long as they fear me.' The line 'It is better to be feared than loved' is often attributed to Machiavelli, but he didn't quite say this. His opinion was that 'one ought to be both feared and loved, but as it is difficult for the two to go together, it is much safer to be feared than loved, if one of the two has to be wanting.'

'Let arms yield to the toga' – Latin: *Cedant arma togae*, meaning 'let military power give way to civil power', is the motto of Wyoming.

The statue to Caesar and the scuffle with Canutius are mentioned in Cicero's letter to Cassius. Cicero, *Epistulae Ad Familiares* 12.3.

The authenticity of the assassination attempt on Antony was much debated in ancient times. Plutarch and Appian think it was Antony's invention, with Appian pointing out that it was not in Octavian's interest to be rid of Antony at this moment, since Antony protected Octavian against the Liberators. Cicero claimed to believe it, mainly because he approved of the action. Suetonius believed it, but he always believed the worst in people as long as it made a good story. If it was true and not an invention of Antony's, it is plausible it was engineered by one of Octavian's intimates, since Octavian's outrage at the accusation seems genuine. Maecenas is a possibility, but the more aggressive Agrippa would be a more likely candidate. Feel free to discuss!

The blood spraying Fulvia's face is a detail from Cicero's third Philippic.

Chapter V

Alba Fucens – modern-day Massa d'Albe.

Pompey was first made consul at the age of thirty-six after being granted a triumph for his victory in the Sertorian war in Spain. The legal minimum age for consul was forty-two.

The military oath is recorded by Vegetius, who wrote in the late Roman Empire. In it he uses the Latin word *imperator*, which is usually translated as 'emperor'. However, in Republican times, this was a title awarded to a general by his troops. It is possible that the form was unchanged from Republican times to late antiquity, but I have chosen to replace 'imperator' with 'consul' to avoid confusion with the modern interpretation of the word imperator/emperor.

'Queen of Bithynia' was a homophobic slur directed at Caesar for his supposed affair with the king of Bithynia, Nicomedes IV, when he was a young man. In Roman times, being homosexual was not frowned upon, but being the passive partner in a sexual relationship, whether hetero- or homosexual, was considered shameful. See Trafford (2021) for a detailed discussion.

Chapter VI

Placentia – modern-day Piacenza.

Cicero's two speeches in late December were the third and fourth Philippics, and his speech to the Senate on 1 January 43 BC was the fifth Philippic.

Abrogatio – Tatum notes that the Senate lacked the power to terminate the *lex de provinciis consularibus*, which allocated Antony and Dolabella their provinces. Laws passed by violence or that were inauspicious could be annulled by the process of *abrogatio*, but there is no evidence that they did this. The Senate therefore broke the law of the Republic for the purpose of upholding the laws of the Republic against Antony.

Forum Gallorum was a village in northern Italy on the Via Aemilia.

Forum Cornelii – modern-day Imola.

Gallia Narbonensis – Narbonese Gaul, modern Provence. Caesar wrote that all Gaul was divided into three parts, inhabited by the Belgae, Aquitani, and 'our Gauls'. After the conquest of Gaul, though – and to a large extent before the conquest – the Romans referred to the three parts of Gaul as Cisalpine Gaul (the near side of the Alps), Transalpine

Gaul (the far side of the Alps) and Narbonese Gaul (although at certain times the names Narbonese Gaul and Transalpine Gaul were used interchangeably). This latter was also referred to as *Provincia Nostra* ('Our Province'), after which the modern region of French Provence is named.

Claterna – a town between Forum Cornelii (Imola) and Bononia (Bologna).

Forum Gallorum – Appian says that Antony blocked the road with his Praetorian cohorts, while Galba says that Antony showed only his light troops and cavalry. My version attempts to reconcile these two contradictory reports.

The Praetorian cohorts were bodyguards of officials in the Roman Republic, first recorded as being used by the Scipio family around 275 BC. Later, Augustus would form them into the Praetorian Guard, an elite legion dedicated to the protection of the emperor.

The senatorial general Servius Sulpicius Galba was the great-grandfather of the Emperor Galba, who succeeded Nero and was the first emperor of four in AD 69.

Chapter VII

It has been speculated that Pontius Aquila is an ancestor of the Pontius Pilate who washed his hands of Jesus' fate.

Pyrrhic victory – a victory that causes so much damage to the victor it might as well be a defeat. The saying, still in use today, comes from Pyrrhus of Epirus after his victory over the Romans at the Battle of Asculum, when he is reported to have said that one more such victory would utterly undo him.

Antony's retreat from Mutina was described by Plutarch as one of extreme hardship, during which his troops drank stagnant water and ate bark, wild roots and 'animals never tasted before'. Although many modern historians repeat this story, others say that this is pure poetry by Plutarch, foreshadowing future events. De Ruggiero makes a strong point that the fertile land in this region in the late spring was not likely to be too difficult a problem for hardened veterans. Nevertheless, leading a weary, defeated and pursued army was no mean feat and should not be downplayed.

Regium Lepida – modern-day Reggio Emilia.

Vada Sabatia – modern-day Vado Ligure.

Forum Iulii – modern-day Fréjus in south-eastern France.

The phases of the moon for the last 6000 years can be found at https://astropixels.com/ephemeris/phasescat/phasescat.html.
It's getting details like this right that makes writing historical fiction such a time-consuming affair. O, to be writing chick lit, where the only research you have to do is finding out which handbag is currently in fashion. (And now I've gone down a rabbit hole as to whether it should be 'O' or 'Oh'.
https://www.theparisreview.org/blog/2015/08/27/what-happened-to-o/.)

Isara river – modern-day Isère.

Chapter VIII

Bononia – modern-day Bologna.

The formation of the Second Triumvirate is described in Appian's *Civil Wars*, Book IV. Although universally referred to as the Second Triumvirate, this was technically the first triumvirate to be formalised by law, since the alliance between Caesar, Pompey and Crassus was only ever informal.

Chapter IX

Much of the detail of the individual deaths in the proscriptions comes from Appian.

Rhegium – modern-day Reggio Calabria.

Chapter X

For a detailed account of the Battle of Dyrrhachium, see *Caesar's General*, the previous book in this series.

The Ides of March coin is one of the rarest of ancient coins, and one of only three gold versions in existence sold in 2020 for $3.5 million. However, it was subsequently found to have been looted from the field in Greece where Brutus' army was camped, and in 2023 was returned to Greece. For a more detailed discussion of the moral quagmire of museums holding artefacts that were taken from other countries, see James Acaster's humorous piece on the British Museum ('No, you can't have it back. We haven't finished looking at it yet!').

The ruins of Amphipolis are located in the modern Greek municipality of Amfipoli. It is mentioned in the Acts of the Apostles that Saint Paul passed through this town.

Chapter XI

'Porters rather than soldiers' is a quote from Appian.

I couldn't find any reference to a specific commander of Octavian's legions at the first battle of Philippi. Perhaps there was none, which explains his legions' disorganised performance on the day. If Agrippa had been in charge, a stronger resistance might have been made, or even a victory achieved.

Speeches recorded in the ancient histories are frequently completely fictional, although perhaps based on truth. For Antony's speech to his men here, I have taken elements from Appian and invented others.

Appian states that Antony offered five thousand drachmas to each soldier. I have converted this to denarii for consistency. In checking that one drachma = one sestertius, I came across an amazing online calculator that gives the conversion of ancient currencies (Jewish, Greek and Roman) and compares them to modern-day dollar equivalent https://testamentpress.com/ancient-money-calculator.html).

We know little about Camulatus except that he was a good soldier and rider. I have given him the rank of decurion, similar in rank to a centurion but a leader of cavalry instead of infantry.

According to Plutarch's life of Brutus, Roman forces of such a size had never encountered each other before Philippi, although this might have been eclipsed later by the scale of the Battle of Lugdunum in AD 197, between Septimius Severus and Clodius Albinus. The total number of casualties at Philippi is unknown, but was certainly in the tens of thousands.

The horse with the unlucky masters is noted in Gellius, *Noctes Atticus*, Book iii. It struck me as a much-coveted prize that brought its owners ill luck, just like Tolkien's One Ring. The phrase 'That man has the horse of Seius' came to mean a man with bad luck.

Strato is described on Wikipedia as a fictional character from Shakespeare's *Julius Caesar*, but he is attested in Appian as the man who assisted Brutus' suicide. I could not find any more information about him.

Although the Roman Republic is considered to have ended in 27 BC, when Octavian took the title Augustus, I think it's safe to say that for all practical purposes, the possibility of restoring the Republic ended at Philippi, with the death of Brutus.

Chapter XII

Cappadocia was a client kingdom of Rome situated in modern Turkey.

See *Caesar's Soldier* for Antony's friendship and conflict with Archelaus.

Parthia was an empire centred in modern Iran that took over the territory of the Seleucid Empire, that had inherited Alexander's Eastern conquests. As Parthia expanded west and Rome expanded east, conquest became inevitable, with the terrible defeat by the incompetent Crassus at Carrhae being the biggest battle between the two empires up to the events of this book. The Parthian Empire persisted for a couple more centuries until wars with Rome and internal struggles weakened it to a point that it was superseded by the Sasanian Empire, which turned out to be an even bigger thorn in Rome's side than the Parthians had been. The final battle between Rome under Caracalla and Parthia is described in the final (for now?) book of my Imperial Assassin series, *Emperor's Fate*.

Cleopatra's lavish meeting and banquet for Antony at Tarsus is described in both Plutarch and in Athenaeus' *Deipnosophistae* ('The Dinner Philosophers'), an unusual book describing a series of banquets held for various philosophers and intellectuals. He quotes from the lost Civil War history of Socrates of Rhodes, who was a contemporary of Antony.

The description of Cleopatra's dress is drawn from a detailed speculation by Dr Joann Fletcher in her book *Cleopatra the Great*.

Chapter XIII

The Perusine War deserves much more attention than I can give it here, but both for reasons of space and because Antony was not a key player in the events, I have summarised them in letter form. Schultz's *Fulvia: Playing for Power at the End of the Roman Republic* and Tatum's *A Noble Ruin*, as well as the paper 'The Perusine War' by Reinhold, deal with the conflict in more detail (see bibliography).

As is often the case, the timeline of what happened when, and exactly when Antony knew of certain events that happened far away, is confusing and contradictory. I have tried my best to make the chronology accurate.

The Social War was fought between Italian cities and Rome from around 91 to 87 BC. The grievance was not that the cities wanted to be independent of Rome, but the opposite – they wished to join Rome on an equal footing.

Sling bullets with these slogans on have been discovered. The tactic has been used in countless wars, even in modern times – it was reported in the *Washington Post* in 2022 that Americans were paying to have slogans written on Ukrainian rocket shells destined to be fired at Russian positions.

Octavian's poem about Fulvia is recorded in Martial's epigrams.

Tiberius Claudius Nero fought on Lucius' side and afterwards went over to Sextus with his wife Livia, future wife of Octavian, and their son, the future emperor Tiberius.

The invasion of Syria in 40 BC aided by Labienus is described in the most detail in Cassius Dio.

Various theories have been put forward as to the cause of Fulvia's death. Heartbreak over his affair with Cleopatra seems unlikely. Poisoning by Octavian's agents has to be a possibility, especially since the relatively young and fit Lucius died in Spain at around the same time. But Antony would never have forgiven Octavian if he had suspected this, so I chose to attribute her death to natural causes. Opium was known to the Romans for its analgesic properties.

Antyllus and Iullus were Antony's sons by Fulvia, Antonia was his daughter by his cousin Antonia Hybrida. Claudius and Claudia were Fulvia's son and daughter by Clodius, and Gaius was her son by Curio.

Chapter XIV

Mare Adriaticum – the Adriatic Sea.

Sicyon – Ancient Greek city state near Corinth.

Corcyra – Corfu.

Gnaeus Domitius Ahenobarbus was Nero's great-grandfather, while Antony was the grandfather of Nero's predecessor Claudius. The character of Enobarbus in Shakespeare's *Antony and Cleopatra* is based on him.

Paloeis – This seems to have been a place in Greece but I could not find its modern location.

Scribonia is often described as elderly. She was, in fact, around seven years older than Octavian, and was about thirty when she married him, perhaps elderly by the standards of the day. Nevertheless she was young enough to bear him a daughter, the wayward Julia the Elder.

Sipontum – modern-day Siponto.

Bruttium – modern-day Calabria. This area in the south of Italy was once controlled by the Greeks, and its people were called Italoi. Over time, a variation of this name was used to indicate the whole of the peninsula.

Antony was nominated to be the *flamen Caesaris*, the Priest of Caesar, before Caesar had even died. Caesar was deified in 42 BC, making Antony the *flamen Caesaris*. However, this wasn't agreed by Octavian until the treaty of Brundisium in 40 BC, with the inauguration taking place in 39 BC.

Glossary

Abrogatio — Annulment of a law or legal procedure.

Aedile — An elected official responsible for maintaining public buildings, ensuring the accuracy of weights and measures, and organising public games.

Agnomen — A fourth name given to a Roman, often for some exploit. The Scipio who defeated Hannibal was called Publius (praenomen) Cornelius (nomen) Scipio (cognomen) Africanus (agnomen).

Agora — The main central open area in a Greek city, serving political and economic functions. The origin of the word agoraphobia.

As — A small value copper coin, worth a tenth of a denarius.

Atrium — The first room in a Roman house after the entrance, and one of the most important, a place for meeting guests and conducting ceremonies.

Auctoritas — A Roman virtue. Prestige, necessary to be respected in command and to be able to exert influence in society.

Ballista — An artillery weapon that could launch large stones or bolts over great distances.

Bucinator — The man who blew the *bucina*, a curved brass instrument.

Bulla — Charms worn around the neck, usually worn by boys until they reached manhood.

Campus Martius — The Field of Mars. An area that was used in the Republic for training and assembling troops. Later it was developed with various building projects.

Capsarius — A trained combat medic who could provide first aid and basic care, often under the direction of a *medicus*.

Cella — The inner chamber of a Roman temple.

Centurion — Commander of a century of men, originally numbering a hundred, but in late Republican times numbering eighty.

Chiton — A type of tunic.

Circumvallation	Field works around an enemy fortification to help maintain a siege.
Colonia	A settlement of Roman citizens.
Comitia Centuriata	The Centuriate Assembly, one of three voting assemblies in the Roman Republic.
Comitia Tributa	The Tribal Assembly, a voting assembly consisting of all the citizens, organised by tribes.
Consul	One of two annually elected leaders of the Roman Republic.
Contio	A public meeting in which the magistrates could inform the people of important news and events. It often took place after a Senate meeting.
Contravallation	Field works outside a circumvallation to protect the besiegers from attack from without.
Contubernium	A unit of eight soldiers who shared a tent. Not to be confused with the quasi-marital relationship between a freeman and slave, which has the same name.
Corona muralis	The mural crown awarded to the soldier who first climbed the wall of a besieged fortification.

Cubiculum — A small room in a private house that acted as a bedroom, as well as a place for private meetings.

Cursus honorum — The course of honours, the ladder of offices that senators in the Republic had to ascend to reach the ultimate prize of being elected consul.

Curule chair — A foldable, transportable chair. Magistrates with imperium were entitled to use this chair.

Decurion — A Roman cavalry officer in charge of a *turma*. Also an official in provincial towns.

Denarius — A Roman silver coin worth 10 asses.

Dignitas — A Roman virtue, incorporating dignity, charisma and respect.

Equestrian/equites — The second highest rank of nobility among Romans, behind the senatorial rank (Latin, *equites*, sometimes called knights in English). Originally the cavalry was drawn from the equestrians, but by the time of the late Republic, it was a purely honorary title. Equestrians were wealthy and provided many of the senior officers of the legions.

Familia — The extended Roman household, including slaves, ruled by the *paterfamilias*.

Fasces	Bundles of wooden rods carried by lictors as a sign of their authority. They could be used to administer corporal punishment, although when more severe danger threatened, the lictors could carry axes within the fasces, which symbolised the consuls' power to administer capital punishment. Origin of the word fascist.
Fibula	A pin or brooch.
Forum boarium	The original cattle market in ancient Rome, and the site of the first gladiatorial contest in the city.
Garum	A highly popular sauce made of fermented fish guts. May have tasted like soy sauce, and provided a large dose of umami flavour to whatever it was poured over.
Gladius	The standard legionary short sword.
Hetaera	Upmarket Greek courtesan.
Imperator	A commander in the Roman army. In the late Republic it was an honorary title, with a victorious general often acclaimed Imperator by his troops. The general was allowed to use the title until his triumph. Later it came to be associated with the word emperor.

Imperium	A form of authority associated with certain magisterial posts.
Impluvium	A pool that captures rainwater from the roof, often found in the centre of the atrium.
Infamis/Infamia	*Infamia* was a loss of social standing, and one subject to *infamia* was known as *infamis*. Certain professions were automatically *infamis*, such as prostitutes, actors, dancers, gravediggers and gladiators. Certain criminals and people caught in specific sexual situations might also be considered *infamis*. The status of *infamia* meant the loss of many legal protections that were owed to the other Roman citizens.
Insula	A block of flats, often cheaply and poorly constructed, with the upper floors tending to house the poorest.
Interrex	Literally 'between kings'. In archaic Rome, he acted as a regent. In the time of the Republic, he was appointed to hold the election of the new consuls when the previous consuls had been unable to do so during their time in office.
Lararium	A small shrine to the household gods, the Lares.

Legate	Senior Roman military officer, often in charge of a legion, usually of high political rank.
Lictor	The attendants and bodyguards of a consul or other magistrate.
Lituus	The sacred wand of the augur.
Lora	A cheap, bitter wine made from the leftovers of the grape-pressing process, such as the skin, husks and seeds.
Mare Nostrum	The Mediterranean Sea, literally 'our sea'.
Medicus	A physician.
Mos maiorum	The customs of the ancestors. It was important to Romans to follow the traditions of their forebears.
Murus gallicus	The Gallic wall, a form of defence constructed of earth, stone and wood.
Nomenclator	A slave whose job was to remind their master of the names of people they met.
Nundinum	A Roman week, consisting of eight days (or nine, in the inclusive Roman way of counting). Markets were generally held once every *nundinum*, and a market day was called a *nundinae*.

Optimates — The 'best people', the conservative faction in Roman politics.

Optio — Second-in-command of a century.

Palla — A headcloth or shawl worn by women.

Patera — A bowl, part of the legionary's marching pack.

Paterfamilias — The head of a family, with absolute power within the household.

Peristylium — The garden of a Roman private house, enclosed, often with ornate gardens, often colonnaded with various small rooms leading off.

Pileus — A felt cap that was a symbol of the goddess Libertas. It was placed on the head of a slave during the ceremony of manumission.

Pilum — The standard Roman legionary javelin.

Pilus posterior — Deputy to the *pilus prior*.

Pilus prior — The senior centurion in a cohort.

Pomerium — The sacred boundary of Rome, originally and traditionally the area within the line ploughed by Romulus on the founding of the city. It had religious and legal significance. For example, holders of proconsular power could not cross the pomerium into Rome,

	the dead could not be buried within its boundaries, and there were restrictions on the carrying of weapons.
Pontifex Maximus	The chief priest of Rome, a title still used today by the Pope.
Populares	The liberal popular faction in Roman politics.
Primus pilus	Commander of the first cohort and most senior centurion in a legion.
Principium	The headquarters in the centre of a Roman legionary camp.
Pronaos	The inner area of a temple that leads to the *cella*.
Propraetor	A form of promagistracy. A propraetor wielded the power of a praetor.
Quadrireme	A large warship.
Quindecimviri sacris faciundis	The fifteen members of the college who guarded the Sybilline books.
Regifugium	An annual religious festival held in February to mark the flight of the last king from Rome.
Rostra	A platform for speeches in the Forum, built from ships' rams captured at the Battle of Antium.

Scutum	A large, curved rectangular shield, made of sheets of wood glued together, covered with canvas and leather, around three feet tall and weighing 10 kg.
Senatus consultum ultimum	Extreme and final decree of the Senate. The Latin term is a modern derivation from Caesar's description of the decree in his *Civil War Commentaries*.
Sestertius	A coin worth quarter of a denarius.
Signifer	Standard-bearer.
Spatha	A long sword, probably used by cavalry in the Republican period, coming to replace the *gladius* in the late Empire.
Stola	A traditional female item of clothing, a long sleeveless robe.
Strophium	A breast band, serving as a type of bra.
Symposium	The part of an Ancient Greek banquet, after the meal, involving drinking, dancing, poetry and conversation.
Terminalia	A religious festival celebrating Terminus, the god of boundaries, held in February the day before the Regifugium.

Thyrsus	A staff tipped with a pine cone, carried by adherents of Bacchus.
Toga Praetexta	A white toga with a broad purple stripe worn by free Roman boys and some magistrates.
Toga Virilis	A plain white toga worn by free adult males.
Tribunus angusticlavius	A junior military tribune, usually of equestrian rank, wearing a narrow stripe on their tunic or toga.
Tribunus laticlavius	A senior military tribune, usually of senatorial rank, wearing a broad stripe on their tunic or toga.
Triclinium	Dining room, taking its name from the three couches surrounding a central table on which diners reclined.
Trireme	A warship.
Triumvir	One of three in authority. The so-called First Triumvirate between Caesar, Pompey and Crassus was an informal agreement and not called the Triumvirate at the time. The Second Triumvirate had official legal status.
Turma	A cavalry unit, thirty strong, commanded by a decurion.

Vestibule   The entrance hall to a private house.

Veterinarius   A Roman soldier who performed the functions of a veterinary surgeon, working mainly with the horses.

Via Lactea   The Milky Way.

Bibliography and references

Appian (2020) *The Civil War.* Translated by McGing, B. Cambridge, Mass: Harvard University Press.

Athenaeus, (1859) *Deipnosophistae.* Meineke, A. ed., (Vol. 3). Teubner.

Baca, A. B. (1966) 'The Identity of Gallus' Lycoris', *The Classical World,* 60, pp. 49–51

Ball, W. (2016) *Rome in the East,* 2nd edn. Abingdon: Routledge.

Beard, M., Crawford, C. (1999) *Rome in the Late Republic,* 2nd edn. London: Duckworth.

Betts, E. (2017) *Senses of the Empire: Multisensory approaches to Roman culture.* Abingdon: Routledge.

Bevan, E. R. (1927) *The House of Ptolemy.* London: . (available at https://penelope.uchicago.edu/Thayer/E/Gazetteer/Places/Africa/Egypt/_Texts/BEVHOP/home.html)

Broughton, S. (1951 & 1952) *The Magistrates of the Roman Republic,* Vols. I and II. New York: American Philological Association.

Bruschi F. (2011) 'Was Julius Caesar's epilepsy due to neurocysticercosis?' *Trends Parasitol.* 27, pp. 373–4.

Bumpus, K. (2004) 'Early Life of Mark Antony.' Honors Thesis. Paper 264. Southern Illinois University.

Caesar, G. J. (1951) *The Conquest of Gaul.* Translated by Handford, S. A. Harmondsworth: Penguin.

Caesar, G. J. (1967) *The Civil War.* Translated by Mitchell, J. F. Harmondsworth: Penguin.

Carandini, A. (ed.) (2017) *The Atlas of Ancient Rome.* Translated by Halavais, A. C. Princeton, NJ: Princeton University Press.

Cary, M., Scullard, H. H. (1975) *A History of Rome.* London: Macmillan Press.

Cicero, M. T. (1969) 'Against Sergius Catilina and The First Philippic Against Marcus Antonius.' In Cicero, *Selected Political Speeches*, translated by Grant, M. London: Penguin.

Cicero, M. T. (1977) Epistulae Ad Familiares: Volume 1, 62–47 BC (Vol. 1). Cambridge University Press.

Cicero, M. T. (1969) 'The Second Philippic Against Marcus Antonius.' In Cicero, *Selected Works*, translated by Grant, M. London: Penguin.

Collins, J. H. (1952) 'Tullia's Engagement and Marriage to Dolabella.' *The Classical Journal*, 47, pp.146–168.

Cook, S. A., Adcock, F. E., Charlesworth, M. P. (1932) *The Cambridge Ancient History: Volume IX*. Cambridge: Cambridge University Press.

Cowell, F. R. (1948) *Cicero and the Roman Republic*. Harmondsworth: Penguin.

D'Amato, R., Gilbert, F. (2021) *Armies of Julius Caesar 58–44 BC*. Oxford: Osprey.

De Ruggiero, P. (2013) *Mark Antony: A plain blunt man*. Barnsley: Pen & Sword.

Dighton. A. (2017). 'Mutatio Vestis: Clothing and political protest in the late Roman republic.' *Phoenix*, 71(3/4), pp.345–369.

Dixon, K. R., Southern, P. (1997) *The Roman Cavalry*. London: Routledge.

Dunn, D. (2016) *Catullus' Bedspread*. London: William Collins.

Edwards, I. E. S., Gadd, C. J., Hammond, N. G. L. (1970) *The Cambridge Ancient History*, 3rd edn. Cambridge: Cambridge University Press.

Everitt, A. (2001) *Cicero: A turbulent life*. London: John Murray.

Everitt, A. (2006) *The First Emperor*. London: John Murray.

Feufere, M. (2010) *Weapons of the Romans*. Stroud: History Press.

Fields, N. (2008) *The Roman Army: Civil Wars 88–31BC*. Oxford: Osprey.

Fields, N. (2018) *Mutina 43 BC: Mark Antony's struggle for survival*. Oxford: Osprey.

Fletcher, J. (2011) *Cleopatra the Great: The woman behind the legend*. New York: Harper Collins.

Frisch, H. (1946) *Cicero's Fight for the Republic*. Copenhagen: Gyldendalske Boghandel.

Gellius, C. (1927). *Attic Nights.* Translated by Rolfe, J. C. Cambridge, MA: Harvard University Press. (available at https://penelope.uchicago.edu/Thayer/E/Roman/Texts/Gellius/?*.html)

Goldsworthy, A. (1996) *The Roman Army at War, 100 BC–AD 200.* Oxford: Oxford University Press.

Goldsworthy, A. (2002) *Caesar's Civil War.* Oxford: Osprey Publishing.

Goldsworthy, A. (2003) *In the Name of Rome.* London: Weidenfeld & Nicolson.

Goldsworthy, A. (2003) *The Complete Roman Army.* London: Thames & Hudson, London.

Goldsworthy, A. (2006) *Caesar.* London: Weidenfeld & Nicolson.

Goldsworthy, A. (2010) *Antony and Cleopatra.* London: Weidenfeld & Nicolson.

Goodman, M. (2007) *Rome and Jerusalem.* London: Penguin.

Goodman, R. & Soni, J. (2012) *Rome's Last Citizen: The life & legacy of Cato, mortal enemy of Caesar.* New York: Thomas Dunne.

Graber, R. B., Richter, G. C. (1987). 'The Capon theory of the cuckold's horns: confirmation or conjecture?' *The Journal of American Folklore,* 100, pp. 58–63.

Grant, M. (1972) *Cleopatra.* London: Phoenix Press.

Grant, M. (1974) *Caesar.* London: Weidenfeld & Nicolson.

Grant, M. (2008) *Roman Cookery.* London: Serif.

Forsyth, P. Y. (1988). 'In the Wake of Etna, 44 B.C.' *Classical Antiquity,* 7(1), pp. 49–57.

Frederiksen, M. (1966). 'Caesar, Cicero and the problem of debt.' *The Journal of Roman Studies,* 56(1–2), pp. 128–141.

Hersch, K. K. (2020) 'Violence in the Roman Wedding.' in Beneker, J., Tsouvala, G. (eds) *The Discourse of Marriage in the Greco-Roman World.* Madison: Wis: University of Wisconsin Press.

Holland, R. (2004) *Augustus, Godfather of Europe.* Stroud: Sutton.

Holland, T. (2003) *Rubicon.* London: Abacus.

Holmes, T. (1923) *The Roman Republic and the Founder of the Empire.* Oxford: Clarendon Press.

Hughes, J. R. (2004) 'Dictator Perpetuus: Julius Caesar – did he have seizures? If so, what was the etiology?' *Epilepsy Behav.* 5E: pp.756–64.

Hughes-Hallet, L. (2006) *Cleopatra: Queen, lover, legend.* London: Pimlico.

Huzar, E. G. (1978) *Mark Antony.* Beckenham, Minn: University of Minnesota Press.

Huzar, E. G. (1985) 'Mark Antony: Marriages versus careers.' *The Classical Journal,* December 1985/January 1986, 81, 2, pp. 97–111.

Jeppesen-Wigelsworth, A. (2013) 'Political Bedfellows: Tullia, Dolabella and Caelius.' *Arethusa,* 46, pp. 65–85.

Joyce, C. J. (2008) 'The Athenian Amnesty and Scrutiny of 403.' *The Classical Quarterly,* 58(2), pp. 507–518.

Keith, A. (2011) 'Lycoris Galli/Volumnia Cytheris: a Greek courtesan in Rome.' *Eugesta,* vol 1.

Kelly, R. (2012) 'Wine, despair and women's clothing: gender anxieties in screen representations of Marcus Antonius.' PhD thesis, University of Ulster.

Kenyon, F. G. (1893) 'A Rescript of Marcus Antonius.' *The Classical Review,* 7, 10, pp. 476–78.

Madsen, D. W. (1981) *The Life and Political career of Marcus Caelius Rufus.* University of Washington ProQuest Dissertations Publishing.

Mann, E. M. (1926) 'Some Private Houses in Ancient Rome.' *The Classical Weekly,* 19(16), pp. 127–132.

Matyszak, P. (2009) *Legionary: The Roman Soldier's Manual.* London: Thames & Hudson.

Morgan L. (2000) 'The Autopsy of C. Asinius Pollio.' *Journal of Roman Studies,* 90, pp. 51–69.

Morstein-Marx, R. (2021) *Julius Caesar and the Roman People.* Cambridge: Cambridge University Press.

Nicolaus of Damascus 'Life of Augustus.' In *Fragmente der Griechischen Historiker,* translated by Hall, C. M.

North, J. (2008) 'Caesar at the Lupercalia.' *The Journal of Roman Studies,* 98, pp. 144–160.

Patterson, J. R. (2000) *Political Life in the City of Rome.* Bristol: Bristol Classical Press.

Pierce, E. D. (1922) *A Roman Man of Letters: Gaius Asinius Pollio.* New York: Columbia University.

Pollard, J., Reid, H. (2007) *The Rise and Fall of Alexandria*. London: Penguin.

Plutarch (1959) *Lives of the Noble Romans*. Fuller, E (ed.) New York: Dell.

Ramsey, J. T. (2004) 'Did Julius Caesar temporarily banish Mark Antony from his inner circle?' *Classical Quarterly*, 54.1, pp. 161–173.

Ramsey, J. (2008). 'At what hour did the murderers of Julius Caesar gather on the Ides of March 44 BC?', in Heilen, S., Calder, W. M. (eds.) *In Pursuit of Wissenschaft: Festschrift für William M. Calder* III zum, 75, pp. 351–363.

Rawson, E. (1985) *Intellectual Life in the Late Roman Republic*. London: Duckworth.

Reinhold, M. (1933). 'The Perusine War.' *The Classical Weekly*, 26(23), pp. 180–182.

Roberts, A. (1988) *Mark Antony: His life and times*. Upton-upon-Severn: Malvern Publishing.

Roller, D. W. (2010) *Cleopatra: A biography*. Oxford: Oxford University Press.

Rosenstein, N. & Morstein-Marx, R. (2007) *A Companion to the Roman Republic*. Chichester: Wiley-Blackwell.

Sampson, G. C. (2023) *The Battle of Pharsalus*. Barnsley: Pen & Sword.

Saunders C. (1923) 'The Political Sympathies of Servius Sulpicius Rufus.' *The Classical Review*, 37(5–6), pp. 110–113.

Schultz, C. E. (2021) *Fulvia: Playing for power at the end of the Roman republic*. Oxford: Oxford University Press.

Seagar, R. (2002) *Pompey the Great*, 2nd edn. Oxford: Blackwell.

Sewell, J., Smout, C. (eds.) (2020) *The Palgrave Handbook of the History of Women on Stage*. Oxford: Palgrave.

Sheppard, S. (2006) *Pharsalus 48 BC*. Oxford: Osprey.

Sheppard, S. (2008) *Philippi 42 BC*. Oxford: Osprey Publishing.

Southern, P. (1998) *Augustus*. London: Routledge.

Southern, P. (2012) *Mark Antony: A life*. Stroud: Amberly.

Stockton, D. (1971) *Cicero: A political biography*. Oxford: Oxford University Press.

Stothard, P. (2020) *The Last Assassin*. London: Weidenfeld & Nicolson.

Strauss, B, (2015) *The Death of Caesar*. New York: Simon & Schuster.
Suetonius, G. S. (1957) *The Twelve Caesars*. Translated by Graves, R. London: Penguin.
Summer, G. (2002) *Roman Military Clothing (1) 100 BC–AD 200*. Oxford: Osprey.
Syme, R. (1938) 'The Allegiance of Labienus.' *The Journal of Roman Studies*, 28, pp. 113–125.
Syme, R. (1939) *The Roman Revolution*. Oxford: Oxford University Press.
Tatum, W. J. (2024) *A Noble Ruin: Mark Antony, civil war and the collapse of the Roman republic*. New York: Oxford University Press.
Tempest, K. (2017) *Brutus, the Noble Conspirator*. London: Yale University Press.
Trafford (2021) *Sex and Sexuality in Ancient Rome*. Barnsley: Pen and Sword.
Treggiaria, S. (2007) *Terentia, Tullia and Publilia: The women of Cicero's family*. Abingdon: Routledge.
Trow, M. J. (2013) *A Brief History of Cleopatra, Last Pharaoh of Egypt*. London: Robinson.
Tyrrell. W. B. (1972) 'Labienus' Departure from Caesar in January 49 B.C.' *Historia: Zeitschrift Für Alte Geschichte*, 21(3), pp. 424–440.
Van der Blom, H. (2016) *Oratory and Political Career in the Late Roman Republic*. Cambridge: Cambridge University Press.
Watterson, B. (2017) *Cleopatra: Fact and Fiction*. Stroud: Amberley.
Welch, K. (1995) 'Antony, Fulvia, and the ghost of Clodius in 47 B.C.' *Greece and Rome*, 42(2), pp. 182–201.
Wylie G. J. (1993) 'P. Ventidius – from novus homo to "military hero".' *Acta Classica*, 36, pp. 129–141.
Yaple, Lauren E. (2022) 'The Impact of Women on the Life and Legacy of Mark Antony.' Honors Thesis, University of Nebraska-Lincoln. 392.

Acknowledgements

Thanks as always to everyone at Canelo, especially Craig Lye, my editor. Thanks to my agent Ed Wilson at Johnson & Alcock for advice and support. Thanks to family (Nome and Abbie) and friends. And most of all, to my readers, for sticking with this journey through the life of one of the most under-appreciated Romans of all!